MURDER ON MISTLETOE LANE

Books by Clara McKenna

MURDER AT MORRINGTON HALL

MURDER AT BLACKWATER BEND

MURDER AT KEYHAVEN CASTLE

MURDER AT THE MAJESTIC HOTEL

MURDER ON MISTLETOE LANE

Published by Kensington Publishing Corp.

MURDER ON MISTLETOE LANE

CLARA McKENNA

KENSINGTON
PUBLISHING CORP.

www.kensingtonbooks.com

KENSINGTON BOOKS are published by

Kensington Publishing Corp.
119 West 40th Street
New York, NY 10018

All Kensington titles, imprints and distributed lines are available at special quantity discounts for bulk purchases for sales promotion, premiums, fund-raising, educational or institutional use. Special book excerpts or customized printings can also be created to fit specific needs. For details, write or phone the office of the Kensington Special Sales Manager: Kensington Publishing Corp., 119 West 40th Street, New York, NY, 10018. Attn. Special Sales Department. Phone: 1-800-221-2647.

Kensington and the K logo Reg. U.S. Pat. & TM Off.

Library of Congress Control Number: 2023941504

ISBN: 978-1-4967-3820-2
First Kensington Hardcover Edition: November 2023

ISBN: 978-1-4967-3821-9 (e-book)

10 9 8 7 6 5 4 3 2 1

Printed in the United States of America

*To my beautiful, kind, creative, fun-loving,
generous daughter.
You are a gift.*

CHAPTER 1

Late December 1905
Hampshire, England

Grace Oakhill curled her fingers into Roger's little fist to hide the holes in her glove. Her eldest, barely six, bent over and snatched something from the ground.

"Look, Mummy!"

With elation gleaming from his wind-blown face, her boy triumphantly displayed a dirty, six-inch, broken tip of deer antler with deep gnaw marks.

"Jolly good, Rog!" Grace praised, putting on a brave face.

She despised having to bundle up the children, in their threadbare coats and too small, thin boots, and trudge them all this way in the cold. Not that Roger seemed to mind. But who was to mind them while she was gone? Little Malcolm, clutching her other hand, sneezed as if to emphasize the bleak picture they painted.

It was wretched being a beggar.

Mercifully, it was Christmas, when the pitiful were remembered with the annual tug at their betters' heartstrings or, more importantly, their purse strings. Grace was relying on it. She squeezed Malcolm's and Roger's mittened hands and kept walking.

She almost lost her nerve when she reached the drive and saw the manor house looming above them. She'd never dared to get so close before. Who was she to imagine these grand folk would care about her sick cow or her lame horse? What concern was it to them that Mr. Oakhill, having business in Basingstoke, had succumbed to fever during the city's recent typhoid epidemic?

Although left to fend for herself and her children, Grace wasn't without capabilities or resources. The cottage's hearth had come with certain commoning rights; the peat and the wood she and the boys were allowed to gather from the New Forest would keep them from freezing to death. She was an excellent embroiderer, and, it being Christmastime, her handkerchiefs, tablecloths, doilies, and napkins were selling well. But the rent was coming due, her cow had stopped producing milk, and her lame horse couldn't save itself from a barn on fire. How was she to deliver her linens to the more distant parts of the New Forest, let alone Hythe and Southampton? Grace was desperate, and her last hope resided here.

Smoke curled into the matching gray sky from chimneys, too many to count. Taking in the slightly acrid but pleasant savory scent, Grace tried to picture the multitudes of fireplaces, big enough to accommodate two people and with mantels made of marble, several roasting food, all roaring with hot, flickering flames. The biting wind cut through her daydream and her coat. She shivered, dismissing the wistful notion with a tug on the boys' loose grips.

Were the rumors she'd learned from Mrs. Conway, the haberdasher in Rosehurst, true, or was she wasting her time? Was she doing the right thing? Did she know what that was anymore? Grace pushed against the wind, and her doubts, up the gravel path, marking the route to the servants' entrance.

Grace gathered the boys into a reassuring hug, her back aching from doing what her husband was no longer around to do. She adjusted Roger's cap. Using her gloved thumb, she rubbed away whatever Malcolm managed to smear on the side of his neck. Steeling herself, she straightened, producing the brown paper packet from the inner pocket of her coat. Would this be enough? Grace could ill afford it otherwise. She told herself this wasn't a bribe but an investment in her boys' futures.

And they had to get through the winter first.

Grace faced the door and, bolstered by the cheery wreath of holly hanging on its plain, solid, wooden front, let go of Roger's hand, adjusted the blue felt toque she'd been married in, blown askew by the wind, and knocked.

Stella breathed in the sweet scent of cinnamon, cloves, and vanilla lacing the hot air enveloping her. She unwound the paisley, cashmere shawl from her shoulders, casting the colorful wedding present from Lyndy's Aunt Winnie onto the empty ladder-backed chair by the door. On this cold, dreary day, Morrington Hall's kitchen was a welcomed haven from the bone-chilling drafts that permeated the upstairs rooms. But where were the holly garlands Stella sent down?

Stella loved Christmas. At least, she used to. When she was a small child, it was a time for presents wrapped in red silk ribbons, glass ornaments shipped from Germany shimmering in the candlelight on Christmas Eve, and endless parties full of laughter. Mama would direct an army of servants, pulled from their duties elsewhere, to drape every door frame, windowsill, mantel, picture frame, and chandelier of their massive Kentucky home with evergreens. The scent of freshly cut boughs wafted through every room. And for days before, that scent would mingle with what Cook was preparing in the kitchen: pecan pie, chestnut stuffing, fruitcake laced with Bourbon, kettles and kettles of popcorn that Stella faithfully spent hours fashioning into balls or garland to hang on the Christmas tree.

When Mama left, the warmth, the frivolity of Christmas went with her. Daddy still entertained and lavished his guests with a decorated house aglow with glass trinkets and fine food, hoping to impress his neighbors, not cheer them. Her father would set Stella among the decorations, displayed in gowns of velvet and lace, to be admired and gawked at like the Christmas tree for as long as it suited him. Then she'd be banished from the festivities to a tray of food gone cold in her room. Left to her own devices in those shortening days before Christmas Day, she spent countless hours in empty horse stalls, threading endless popcorn kernels onto a string, knowing they'd never grace the Christmas tree. Her father disliked popcorn, a reminder of his past poverty, when he couldn't afford the machine-made ribbons that graced a wealthy man's tree, and of Mama. Stella's mother had started the tradition.

When it arrived, Christmas Day meant the obligatory trip to church and, afterward, Daddy compelling Stella to open her present in front of the envious servants. His gifts were always generous: a beautiful new dress, a porcelain doll, and a grand piano when she'd begun to learn to play. Unlike Mama, who gave handkerchiefs she embroidered herself or a wooden horse fashioned after Stella's favorite at the time, her father gave thoughtless gifts, all purchased to impress.

Now, with Daddy gone and Mama back in her life, everything would be different. This Christmas, Stella's first as a married woman, a viscountess, and a member of a new family, was going to be the best Christmas ever.

If only Stella could convince Mrs. Cole to do as she asked.

"I can't perform miracles, milady," the esteemed cook of Morrington Hall grumbled, vigorously wiping condensation from her spectacles with the corner of her apron. Behind her, kitchen maids bustled about their business: chopping fruit, whipping cream, cutting shapes out of dough. "These dishes you want aren't any I've made before."

"It's popcorn, Mrs. Cole," Stella said, trying to keep the exasperation from her voice. "Cooking it is as simple as pouring the kernels into a pan and turning on the heat." Not that Stella had popped the corn herself, but she'd witnessed their cook in Kentucky doing it countless times when she was a child.

The cook replaced her spectacles on the tip of her button nose. "Not so simple, what with the help I'm forced to work with. Such silly girls. They'd forget to put the kettle on if I didn't remind them." A sideways stare sent the new kitchen maid, her plump cheeks turned red, scurrying to fetch water at the long, copper sink. "And where am I to get popcorn, milady?"

"If they don't have any local, I'm sure we could order some from—" Mrs. Cole was shaking her head, her severely taut bun not loosening a wisp. "What about the fruitcake? I know you can make fruitcake."

"Indeed! I'll have you know I took Best Cake prize at the W.I. fete at Beaulieu last year."

"Then what's the problem?"

Mrs. Cole sifted through the papers strewn across the top of her desk, producing the recipe cards Stella had provided her over a week ago. Delighted by Stella's request, Mama had carefully copied and mailed the cards from her home in Montana.

"This calls for Bourbon. My recipe does not contain Bourbon." Mrs. Cole dropped the card as if the paper was on fire. She picked up another. This one spelled out Stella's mother's recipe for pecan pie. "And pecan pie? Whatever is that? Besides, did you take this up with the countess before she set all the menus? You do realize I have afternoon tea and dinner to prepare yet for a party of eight?"

"Are you saying you won't make anything I ask?"

Mrs. Cole flung her arms out in exasperation. "I've got an entire batch of mince pies gone missing, and I'll be at it all night making more. I most certainly won't have time to hunt down these exotic ingredients by Christmas." She tossed the second recipe onto the pile.

What was Stella to do? This was Mrs. Cole's kitchen. She barely tolerated Stella's presence, let alone her suggestions at the best of times. Stella could appeal to Lady Atherly but knew how well she'd succeed in that corner. Despite their fragile and unspoken understanding that Stella was now part of the family, Stella's mother-in-law never hesitated to warn her off corrupting the staff with her unconventional "American" ways.

Like asking for a kettle of popcorn.

"Not like that!" The cook snapped at the maid rolling out pastry dough. She marched across the kitchen to demonstrate. "It's like this. Like this."

Stella had no reason to complain. Lyndy was attentive, affectionate, and everything she'd hoped to find in a husband. Alice, Lyndy's sister, more shy than aloof, was easily excitable and open whenever Stella asked about the fashion and gossip found in Alice's American magazines. Lord Atherly's study, his inner sanctum, was open to her, assuming she had time to linger while he pontificated, in vast detail, on extinct horse fossils or the extreme weather at the archeological dig Lord Atherly had invested in on the Great Plains back home. And Lady Atherly, with the influx of cash Stella had brought to the marriage, busied herself with hiring more staff, renovating the gardens, and overseeing the extensive updates to the house Lyndy had proposed. She had no time to interfere in Stella's life.

And yet Stella struggled to find her place. All she had was time. Granted, during the first month after their honeymoon, she'd attended countless teas, dinner parties, and house calls from well-wishers who'd pop in at their leisure, longing to be free of her exhausting social obligations. Yet that's when the boredom set in. With little left on the calendar, Stella had anticipated returning to her favorite pastime—caring for and training the horses. But she was Lady Lyndhurst now and relegated to watching others do it for her. Unlike in Kentucky (or even before the wedding), she was now admonished from spending too much time in the stables. Anything beyond a daily ride was frowned upon.

Stella had been clever in establishing the Triple R Farm for Horses and Ponies charity. She could spend time caring for horses in the service of others; even Lady Atherly couldn't complain. Or so she thought. Despite the growing number to care for, her mother-in-law had insisted Stella leave the animals in the capable hands she'd hired. So, when Christmastime had arrived, seeing Lady Atherly apathetic about the holidays, Stella had decided to throw her energies into the festivities like her mother used to. And that included the menus.

"If that will be all, milady? I have to get back to it," Mrs. Cole said, not so subtly telling Stella to leave.

But Stella wasn't ready to give up. "Mrs. Cole. Could you at least . . ."

Stella let the words fade on her lips as Mrs. Nelson, Morrington's housekeeper, came haltingly into the kitchen, the rattle of her keys punctuating each unsteady step. The older woman's normally ruddy complexion was the shade of the flour Mrs. Cole sprinkled across the worktable. She held her palm tightly against the lace bodice inlay of her well-pressed black dress. Stella resisted the urge to guide the housekeeper to the nearest chair.

"Mrs. Nelson," Mrs. Cole said, brushing her hands on her apron, "whatever is the matter? You look like you've seen a ghost."

"It's nothing." Mrs. Nelson waved away the cook's concern, but her body betrayed her. A quiver took hold, visibly shaking her from shoulders to knees. The housekeeper's cheeks flushed at the sight of Stella. "Lady Lyndhurst! Is there something I can do for you?"

"I was about to ask you the same thing."

A slight catch in Mrs. Nelson's breath and an understanding passed between them—a request, an appeal for help as undeniable as any words uttered. Stella waited for Mrs. Nelson to elaborate. The housekeeper, poised to speak, cast a furtive sideways glance toward the preoccupied cook who'd returned to her task, unaware of the silent exchange. Then clamped her lips together.

"If I can help, I will," Stella offered encouragingly.

"That's kind, my lady, but—"

"Never mind her, Mrs. Nelson," Mrs. Cole said, slamming a dough onto the table and glancing up, challenging Stella to contradict her with a glare. "Her Ladyship was just leaving."

CHAPTER 2

"Lyndy, do you think I'll ever be accepted at Morrington?"

Lyndy brought Beau, his chestnut Irish Hunter, up alongside Stella and her beloved Thoroughbred, Tully, the dapple gray mare's upper lips stretched out, her ears pointed backward. If Lyndy didn't know better, the horse smiled as broadly as he'd seen her lovely owner do. Beau, on the other hand, swished his tail in annoyance.

"It will take time, my love."

The clouds never broke, and the cold cut through his thick tweed jacket, but Lyndy was never one to shy away from a brisk gallop across the heath. He'd been by the fire in the library reading the *Sporting Times* about a string of mishaps marring the Windsor Hurdle Race when Stella had tracked him down. She'd been rebuffed by the formidable Mrs. Cole and needed to, as she put it, "let off some steam." His poor wife had gotten into her head that she'd introduce his family to a few of her Christmas traditions but was having little luck. Lyndy had taken it up with Mother but to no avail. Theirs was a delicate peace, established when he and Stella had wed, with Mother acting far more civil than he'd expected. Yet Stella, rightfully so, still felt thwarted.

"It's not just your mother's disapproval or that Mrs. Cole wouldn't cook anything I asked, but Mrs. Nelson clearly wanted my help with something. And then didn't ask. I can't help wondering what it was and why she wouldn't say." Stella patted Tully's broad, thick neck.

"You must remember. Things are different now. You're Lady Lyndhurst."

"Ugh! If I hear that one more time!"

"Don't you fancy being my wife?"

The red blush on her cheeks, the loose tendrils of silky brown hair she tucked behind her ear, and the quickening rise and fall of her chest despite the constraining boning in her jacket signaled her answer. Lyndy fancied scooping her from her saddle into his arms, but Beau snorted at Lyndy's attempt to move closer. Foiled, Lyndy playfully ogled her legs instead as she adjusted her skirt, blown up by the wind. Stella caught him looking and rewarded him with a sly smile.

"That part I love."

I'm a lucky man.

The horses' hoofs clacked on the cobbles in the stable yard, already in part shadow. As the stableboy dashed out to take the reins, Lyndy spotted the silhouettes of three men pass the open stable door; their heads bent in conversation. Concern echoed from their slumped shoulders. Could something be wrong with one of the horses? Since the wedding, Lyndy had wanted nothing more than to bolster their number of Thoroughbreds, but Stella, with a keen eye for potential, was unwilling to compromise on inferior foals. She'd dissuaded him from every purchase he'd pursued to date. Currently, he pinned his hopes on Knockan Crag, a promising colt he'd spied during a visit to the Royal Stud at Sandringham on the way home from their honeymoon in York, but the royal racing manager was doubtful His Majesty was willing to sell.

Lyndy leaped from his saddle, automatically offering his assistance to Stella, who slid gracefully down without his help.

"What do you think that's all about?" He jutted his chin toward the stables as the men passed a window, slowly, as if none too concerned about the pace, too caught up in what they were discussing.

"Let's find out."

Inside the stone stables, all polished, mucked out, and ready for equine visitors, the warmth was more than welcome. They caught up with the trio: Gates, the stablemaster, the head groom (Lyndy could never remember the man's name), and Martin Green, the veterinarian they'd hired a few weeks back, conferring outside the box stall with the chewed, splinter wood doorframe, telltale evidence of its occupant.

"Lord Lyndhurst," Mr. Green said, dipping his well-oiled head ever so slightly.

The veterinarian, taken on to tend Morrington's horses and those on Stella's charity farm, was a youthful man in his midthirties with a long, open face and a slight build that disguised impressive upper body strength. Lyndy once witnessed the chap do all of Morrington's horse dentals in a row, holding up his instruments for three hours straight. He'd come highly recommended from connections Lyndy had in London. Lyndy could already see why. He was a likable fellow, competent, respectful but amiable, and quick with a laugh.

"And, my lady. You braved this weather, did you?" Green asked.

"We did," Stella said, vigorously rubbing her arms with gloved hands. "If it doesn't endanger the horses, we're always up for it. Aren't we?" She smiled at Lyndy.

"Indeed. Speaking of endangering horses, I couldn't help noticing the serious undertone to your conversation."

"It's Orson, my lord," Gates, the stocky, well-weathered stablemaster said. There wasn't a man Lyndy respected more than him when it came to horses. "He needs attending, but nothing for you to worry about."

"If you say so, Mr. Gates," Stella said, feeling the same about the stablemaster as Lyndy did. "And lucky for me, Mr. Green, your visit saves me having to track you down before Christmas."

"Oh?" The vet shoved the hand not holding his leather satchel into the deep pocket of his white, ankle-length work coat.

"I was hoping for an update on the horses on the farm. Anything worth mentioning before you take your days off?"

"Not that I'm aware of, my lady. After examining Orson, I'll be doing my rounds at the farm. I'll be certain to let you know if anything comes up."

If Mr. Green wasn't comfortable reporting to a woman, he had the grace not to show it. Since its inception, the Triple R was run exclusively by Stella. She'd insisted she needed something meaningful and productive to do. Why Lyndy couldn't fathom. Wasn't it enough to ride, read, and call on the neighbors? But if it made her happy, who was Lyndy to argue?

"Shall we?" Green said, indicating the stable hand should open Orson's stall door. Orson, ears swiveling rapidly, was waiting for them. "A leery one, are ya?" Green cajoled, taking a step forward.

Orson stomped the ground, kicking up hay and dust. Green swiftly backed out. The stallion rattled the door with a kick as the head groom slid it shut. The vet crouched and began rummaging through his medical bag.

"Shall Mr. Gates and I see you at the Knightwood Oak, my lord?" Green asked, choosing a tincture in a glass stopper bottle from his bag. "Tonight promises to be quite the event."

"Oh?"

"Didn't you know you have one of the finest dart players I've ever encountered in your employ?" Green regarded Gates with a practiced eye. "And Mr. Gates isn't half bad as well." Green, laughing, slapped Mr. Gates on the back.

"Lord Lyndhurst doesn't frequent the Knightwood Oak," Gates said, grudgingly amused.

"Yes, well." Lyndy never once considered patronizing the local pub. Drinking his quality whiskey in the comfort of his home was more to his liking. "But we'll be seeing you on Boxing Day, won't we?"

"You will, my lord."

"You're not participating in the Point-to-Point, are you, Mr. Green?" Stella said, referring to the annual New Forest Pony Race.

"No, my lady." Mr. Green laughed. "I've volunteered to be on hand if a pony requires medical attention. I'm far better at healing ponies than riding them."

Orson's hoof banged against the door again.

"Speaking of, we need to figure out what ails that poor chap."

"He's always like that," Lyndy chuckled.

Green cleared his throat. "I beg to differ, my lord. Orson's temperamental, but his rage is pain driven." Green produced a brownish tincture from his bag. The half-empty, glass-stoppered bottle caught the fading sunlight. "I didn't want to sedate him, but—"

"We'll leave you to it," Lyndy said, yanking his sleeve down, irritated and uncomfortable.

"But, Lyndy, wouldn't it be interesting to see—"

"The Kentfields will be here soon." He held out his arm for Stella to take.

"When did you become eager to greet the Kentfields?" she teased as he escorted her away. "I thought you were dreading their arrival?"

"I've no desire to see that fine, virile stallion unnaturally docile," he grumbled.

Stella coquettishly walked her fingers up his chest. "How about your desire to see how I'd make my fine, virile stallion unnaturally docile?"

Lyndy grabbed her hand, bringing her fingers to his lips. By God, he was a lucky man.

CHAPTER 3

The halls upstairs were as bustling as Mrs. Cole's kitchen. As she made her way through the house, Stella dodged chambermaids, footmen, assistant gardeners, and workmen installing the new steam heating system. Each paused to bob or nod, embarrassed to be caught hustling past. Stella had learned most servants were expected to do their tasks unobtrusively. Yet with chambermaids carrying extra linen, gardeners' arms filled with stacks of cut evergreen, and workmen lugging ornate wrought iron radiators around, Stella had no practical way to skirt them without acknowledging them. Which she was happy to do. Some were bringing glorious heat to the house, and others were transforming it into a magical place. Crisp leaves of holly and ivy draped from doorways and windowpanes. Ropes of yew or pine snaked through banisters and down the length of every hall. The festive color and heavenly scent, like a forest on a summer's evening brought inside, followed her from the front entrance all the way upstairs.

Stella approached her bedroom, wriggling her fingers from her gloves. Steps from her doorway, she was stripping the second one off when a workman in ill-fitting pants, held up with thick suspenders, bounded from the room. They nearly collided. Stella whirled back to avoid him. The man stood his ground, self-consciously brushing plaster from his faded, collarless shirt. Behind him, the hanging cluster of mistletoe swayed in the open doorway.

"Pardon me, milady. I didn't see you there."

"Obviously," she chuckled nervously, holding her hand to her chest, the gloves dangling from her clenched fist. "I'm just glad you didn't get me with that."

She pointed to the wrench propped on his broad shoulder. Longer than the length of her arm, the heavy iron tool appeared capable of doing as much damage as good. Gripping it tightly, the man lowered it to his side.

"I'd never, milady."

"Of course you wouldn't, Mr. . . . ?"

The workman rubbed his free hand against his pant leg. Stella half expected him to offer it to her. He smoothed away plaster dust clinging to his thick, brown mustache instead. "It's Stott, my lady. Ernie Stott."

Struck by a chill, Stella vigorously rubbed her arms, the damp still clinging to her riding jacket. Her bones could do with a good thawing.

"It is true Morrington Hall will be warm and toasty by Christmas, Mr. Stott?"

"That's right." He jerked his thumb over his shoulder at her bedroom. "Just finishing up."

"What a wonderful Christmas present."

The jangle of keys announced Mrs. Nelson's arrival before she rounded the corner. Indignantly wagging a finger, the housekeeper marched toward them. She'd undergone a complete transformation. The pale, rattled woman was gone.

"I've told you, men, time and time again, not to bother the family."

"He's not bothering me, Mrs. Nelson."

The housekeeper was adamant. "Get along with you now."

She shooed at Mr. Stott like a pesky fly threatening to land on a molded tomato aspic. Mr. Stott's nostrils flared.

"Merry Christmas, Mr. Stott," Stella said, getting a disapproving glare from the housekeeper.

"Milady." He swung his wrench to his shoulder, coming dangerously close to clipping the housekeeper's waving finger.

"Good Lord!" the housekeeper exclaimed, yanking her hand back.

Mr. Stott gave a curt nod to Stella before tramping away.

Mrs. Nelson refrained from saying her piece until the sound of the workman's heavy trod no longer reached them. "I know it's not my place to say, but you mustn't encourage them, my lady. It won't do for them to be so familiar."

"I appreciate your concern, Mrs. Nelson, but he was simply answering my questions."

Mrs. Nelson clucked her tongue. "I find it never does well to ask too many, my lady."

Stella couldn't disagree more.

"You seemed rattled earlier. Is everything okay? Was there something you wanted to ask of me?"

Peering over Stella's shoulder, the housekeeper settled her hands on her hips. "Wherever have you been, Ethel? Lady Lyndhurst has been waiting." She hadn't answered the question.

Why?

Stella turned to see her lady's maid scampering toward them out of breath. Stella smiled to see what Ethel carried in her hands.

"You don't want her to be late to receive Lady Atherly's guests, now do you?"

"No, Mrs. Nelson," Ethel managed between breaths.

"My lady." With that, the housekeeper took her abrupt leave as Ethel ushered Stella into the bedroom.

Satisfying her curiosity about Mrs. Nelson's caginess would have to wait.

"These came for you." Stella's lady's maid set the silver salver piled with envelopes on the dressing table. "I knew you'd want them straightaway."

"Thank you, Ethel," Stella said, unpinning her top hat and tossing it and her gloves on the chair.

The new radiator, installed against the far wall like a piece of shiny metal art, hissed. Grateful Mr. Stott had been as good as his word, Stella moved closer to the emanating heat, stepping out of her riding skirt and stripping off her riding jacket at the same time. She couldn't get changed fast enough. With Ethel's help, she wiggled into a mauve, embroidered, velvet tea gown, the silk underskirt slipping over her skin like water. How luxurious not to have to wear a corset. Feeling dry and warm again, Stella settled at the dressing table while Ethel tackled her windswept hair.

Opening her Christmas cards was one of Stella's favorite parts of her day. Separate from those addressed to Lord and Lady Atherly, these were holiday greetings sent to Stella from friends, family, and well-wishing locals. Each day brought more. She'd filled most of an album with the postcards. Those resembling paper sculptures, and designed to stand upright, covered the top of her chest of drawers. Unlike the wedding gifts her father had unwrapped, claimed, and coveted, these were all hers.

She reached for the first envelope in the stack. It came with no postmark, stamp, or return address and was addressed: *TO MY LADY*. It must've been hand delivered.

"I don't remember seeing that before," Ethel said through the hairpins clenched in her teeth.

Stella grabbed her silver letter opener and slit the envelope. The image was of a brown-haired angel in a flowing pink gown, closely matching the one Stella had on, floating on a pale background of clouds and stars. The inscription read: *HAPPY CHRISTMAS GREETINGS. AN ANGEL VISITS EARTH TODAY*. Handwritten in block letters, it was signed, *With love to my angel*. Lyndy was always surprising her, but he'd never sent her a love note before. To curb the emotion threatening to spill out, Stella clutched the card to her chest.

"If you look, my lady, I believe there's one from America."

Setting down Lyndy's card, Stella shifted through the others until she found a particularly familiar handwriting. She ripped it open with enthusiasm. It was from her mother. Colorfully illustrated with a family eating Christmas dinner, the card's intricate cuts created the illusion of peering through a window at the happy scene. On the back of the card, her mother had written, *Merry Christmas, Sugar. Next year, this will be us.*

Ethel bent to retrieve the silver and opal hair combs, and Stella seized the chance to slip from the stool. She padded in her stocking feet across the Persian carpet, a colorful, woven bed of stylized flowers.

"My lady. Your hair."

Opening the drawer of the mahogany nightstand beside her and Lyndy's four-poster bed, Stella expected to find the souvenir spoon her mother had given her for a wedding present. She wanted to display it beside her mother's greeting card. It wasn't there.

"Ethel, have you seen my souvenir spoon? You didn't move it, did you?"

"Of course not." Ethel joined her to examine the drawer. The maid shifted through its contents—a miniature of Lyndy, a stack of handkerchiefs, an unburned candle, a tin of Rountree's Licorice, and Stella's latest book, *The Maid of Bocasse*—as if expecting to find the spoon hiding beneath. "I know how precious it is to you. I can't imagine what's happened to it."

Stella bit her lip. "I didn't want to say anything, but this isn't the first thing that's gone missing."

"My lady! You should've told someone—me, Lady Atherly, or Mrs. Nelson."

"Until now, they were little things. Things I might've misplaced myself, things you wouldn't have noticed, like a bookmark or one of a dozen hat pins. But this"—Stella stared down at the space vacant of her spoon—"this I would never move."

Ethel rose onto her tiptoes to continue tending Stella's hair. "It's all these new maids. I worried something like this might happen. I'll talk to Mrs. Nelson, my lady. We'll find out who's moved your belongings."

Ethel, twisting up a length of hair, shoved in a comb, uncharacteristically scraping Stella's scalp. Stella winced. Ethel blanched.

"Forgive me, my lady."

"It's okay, Ethel. If I was sitting as I should . . . But you're right. If it wasn't one of the maids, maybe Lord Lyndhurst had Mrs. Nelson put my spoon into the silver safe."

The maid, gingerly pushing in the second comb, heartily agreed with Stella's reassuring suggestion. Yet even as she said it, Stella knew it wasn't true. Someone was stealing her things.

CHAPTER 4

Lyndy halted midstride and pivoted on his heel to make a hasty retreat.

"Ah, Lyndy, there you are." Mother looked up from her book, yet another biography of Queen Elizabeth I. "I've been meaning to speak to you."

"I don't have time, Mother. As you can see, I still need to change." Lyndy indicated his riding clothes.

He'd come into the library to retrieve his paper, wanting to show Stella the article on Tupper's competition in next spring's 2000 Guineas Stakes. He should've known his mother would waylay him. Didn't she have a bouquet to arrange somewhere?

Mother motioned for him to take a seat, setting her book down and smoothing her aubergine-colored skirt across her lap. Mother rarely wore anything short of drab.

She should wear brighter colors more often. It suited her.

"This won't take long."

Lyndy flopped himself onto the Chesterfield sofa and sighed, hoping she would get on with it. Whatever could she want to talk to him about? Had Mother learned of Stella's visit to the kitchens? Was she going to remind him, yet again, to rein in his wife's overly familiar behavior toward the staff? Or was it simply to complain about Stella's enthusiasm for celebrating the holiday with, as Mother called it, "her over-the-top, typically American" zeal?

Lyndy brushed at a clump of mud caked on his riding trousers. "You're not going to reiterate, yet again, how much of a waste of good money the Triple R Farm is, are you?"

To her credit, Mother had heartily approved of Stella's enthusiastic commitment to charitable works, at least the more conventional ones: the orphanage, the local cottage hospital, the usual "bread and blanket" schemes. But not Stella's newest venture—the Triple R Farm—a place dedicated to the care of old and injured horses in hopes of either returning them to their owners rested and recuperated or retiring them to a life of comfort. It was a lovely idea. In typical fashion, Mother had met the plan with skepticism and scorn. But with money no longer an object, Mother's objections were hollow.

Why must she waste his time?

"It is a ridiculous notion of a charity. But no, that's not what I want to talk to you about."

Maybe we should move to Pilley Manor.

The notion popped unbidden into his head. Stella's great-aunt, Miss Rachel Luckett, a kind, unobtrusive soul who accompanied Stella from America as her chaperone, was the only inhabitant of that large house on the edge of Rosehurst. And according to Stella, who lived there before their wedding, the housekeeper and cook at the dowager's house were competent and, more importantly, sympathetic to Stella's unbridled enthusiasm and charm. Yes, perhaps that was the answer. He'd rarely have to see his mother.

Pleased with his solution, Lyndy relaxed deeper into the leather sofa, willing to hear her out.

"Yes, well." Mother shifted in her seat and smoothed her skirt for the second time.

What was this all about? Why was Mother suddenly hesitant? Unnerved by such a rarity, Lyndy braced himself.

"This may be awkward," she began, "but I have a duty to ask." Lyndy suppressed his urge to bolt from the room a moment too long. Her words gushed off her tongue before he could act. "Is Stella performing her wifely obligations?"

Lyndy sprung from his seat, his arms outstretched. "How dare you ask such a thing?"

"You will not speak to me in that tone, Edwin Henry Searlwyn!" Mother's expression hardened like steel as the uncertainty from a moment ago evaporated in the heat of her indignation. "I am your mother, and I demand your respect."

Respect? She wanted respect? Then why ask a question whose very nature disrespected him and his wife?

Beset by well-bred compliance, Lyndy bit back his retort and strode past his mother. From one side of the library to the other, he paced the carpet, on each turn confronting the glassy stare of the ridiculous flamingo, its faded pink plumage striking among the other stuffed birds in the display case. It mocked him. He wasn't any freer than it was. His dream of moving to Pilley Manor melted as quickly as his anger.

"Calm yourself, Lyndy, and be still."

Lyndy gripped the labels of his riding jacket but kept moving. The grandfather clock in the grand saloon chimed three o'clock.

"Well?" Purposely, patiently, Mother laced her fingers together, resting her hands in her lap. She'd wait for his answer.

Lyndy grabbed the fire iron as he passed the hearth. Shouldn't the furnace be up and working now? He jabbed at the bed of coals in the grate, rewarded with a billow of smoke in the face.

"Well, what?" He coughed.

"If you are assuring me Stella is cooperating in the bedroom . . ."

"Enough, Mother." Lyndy would've laughed if he didn't feel so wretched. What did his mother want, a detailed description of their lovemaking? How he found Stella a loving, competent, willing partner in all things, including intimate acts in the bedchamber? Tempted as he was to see his mother blush, Lyndy bit his tongue again.

"I'm sorry, Lyndy, but I must know. Is she expecting?"

Lyndy, unseeing, tossed the fire iron toward its stand. His aim was off. It clattered against the metal coal scuttle and tumbled to the wooden floor, its hot tip barely missing the edge of the carpet.

"Is that what this is all about?" He snickered. "And here I thought . . ."

"Lyndy!" Mother sputtered as his meaning took root. "How could you think I meant . . . that?" She had the decency to look sheepish.

"I didn't know what to think, Mother." He emphasized the last word to denote how truly awkward this conversation was.

"I admit I went about this the wrong way." Mother crossed her ankles and tucked them under her chair. "But. Well . . . it has been several months, and we've had no word." She smoothed her skirt. Again. "And I thought . . ."

Mother was dithering, and she'd apologized. *What the devil is going on here?* Lyndy raked his fingers through his hair.

"I thought . . ." she repeated.

"That I was not acutely aware that producing an heir is my primary duty to this family?"

Mother cupped her knees with her palms, and weariness weighed heavily on her features for a moment. He'd never seen his mother so vulnerable. What had this conversation cost her?

Lyndy approached, his heart swelling with a tenderness toward her he'd never experienced before, and took her hand. It was soft and cold. She started at the unfamiliar gesture.

"Don't despair, Mother. We only just married in September. I promise you. You will be the first to know."

Mother nodded, appeased. She squeezed his hand before letting go. She rose, her Roman nose held high, and smoothed the hair at the side of her head as if ensuring her composure was in place.

"The Kentfields will be here soon. I suggest you change."

How had he never noticed the strength in her stance, the resilience in her proud countenance?

"Of course."

Grateful to be dismissed and released from the conflicting emotions plaguing him, Lyndy strode toward the door but paused before reaching it. Unwilling to test the delicate new rapport between them, Lyndy suppressed the question burning on his lips. Although an heir was essential, why was Mother this concerned so soon? Was there something he didn't know?

Instead, he said, "I've been meaning to ask. Why ever did you invite the Kentfields for Christmas? We haven't seen or been friendly with them for years."

Lord Edwin Kentfield was an old friend of his mother's family who supposedly used to visit Morrington Hall frequently when Lyndy was a child. But that was years ago. Lyndy had never even met Lord Edwin's son, Frederick, though they were of similar age. Why the sudden desire to rekindle the friendship at Christmas of all times? It was baffling.

As his mother formulated her answer, the formidable figure of the housekeeper appeared in the doorway. Mother stuck out her chin. "Because I am still mistress of Morrington Hall, and I may invite anyone I choose. What is it, Mrs. Nelson?" she snapped.

"If you'll pardon me, my lady. I was told you'd be in here," Mrs. Nelson said as Lyndy returned to the couch and snatched up his forgotten paper lying on the side table where he'd left it. "We need to discuss Sir Edwin's visit."

"I say."

Something in the housekeeper's tone didn't jar with Mrs. Nelson's characteristic deference to her mistress. If Lyndy didn't know better, there was a hint of insistence in her voice. Stoically keeping her attention pinned to the far book-covered wall, the housekeeper refused to meet Lyndy's challenging gaze.

"You may go now, Lyndy," Mother said, summarily dismissing him.

"But—?"

"Close the door behind him, Helena."

Helena? Lyndy hadn't known Mrs. Nelson's Christian name and never imagined he'd hear it first from his mother's lips.

When the door's latch clicked behind him, Lyndy lingered, hoping to hear more. He wouldn't stoop to putting his ear to the keyhole and accordingly couldn't make out a word. But the strained tone was unmistakable. Did Mother's concern over an heir run deeper than Lyndy supposed, leaving her so unsettled she allowed a servant to take that tone?

"As if I don't know!" Mother shouted, her words cleaving through the wooden barrier between them.

Is Mother now arguing with the housekeeper?

Lyndy, taking to asking questions as Stella did and, if need be, demanding them as only he could, had his hand on the knob, poised to enter when Fulton appeared in the hall. Like a child caught beside a broken vase, Lyndy stepped back and tucked his paper under his arm.

"My lord," the butler said. "I'm to inform Her Ladyship that her guests will arrive at any moment." The briefest of glances at Lyndy's attire was Fulton's only hint of disapproval; Lyndy had yet to change.

"Yes, thank you, Fulton. You'll find Mother inside."

Fulton nodded, knocked, and opened the door. Suppressing his desire to peek past the butler's shoulder as he crossed the threshold, Lyndy plunged briskly toward the stairwell, grateful to have something as straightforward to concentrate on as getting dressed for afternoon tea. How had a simple stroll in search of his *Sporting Times* led to a maelstrom of emotion and unanswered questions?

It's all Mother's fault. Perhaps moving to Pilley Manor, or somewhere even farther away, wasn't such a bad idea.

Lyndy glanced back at the library door left ajar, before taking the stairs two at a time.

CHAPTER 5

Stella waited in the drive with the family as the automobile kicked up dust and gravel on its approach. How weird and wonderful! Had it only been seven months since that fateful day when Lyndy, Alice, and their parents watched as Stella raced her daddy's Daimler up the drive toward a meeting that would change her life forever?

Stella snuck a side peek at the family beside her. Lyndy, impatient to get the formalities over and get on with his day, shifted his weight from one foot to the other, occasionally pulling on his sleeve or collar. In his favorite gray tweed jacket that complemented the silver streaks in his dark brown hair, Lord Atherly took a pause from explaining to Stella his desire to visit the latest paleontological expedition he was funding in Montana and lifted his lorgnette to see better. Outwardly, the father and son had changed little. Stella couldn't say the same for her mother-in-law and sister-in-law. Hair mounded like a crown on her head, Lady Atherly, who once radiated outright hostility, fiddled with the fringe of her shawl. Alice, the most withdrawn family member, bounced on the balls of her dainty booted feet.

What had they to be nervous about?

A brightly painted, impressively long, double-seated automobile pulled up and parked several yards away, drawing the interest of Mack, their energetic, scruffy mutt, who barked his greeting with enthusiasm. Without ceremony, a tall, trim man leaped out from the backseat, his duster coat swirling around him. He hoisted a brown leather golf bag from the backseat and onto his shoulder.

Who plays golf in December?

"If I didn't know better, I'd think Freddy has been too long in America," Lady Atherly said to no one in particular.

Everything Lady Atherly found a bit flamboyant, overly enthusiastic, or colorful, she attributed to an American "taint." How many times had Stella heard a similar comment? Too many to care anymore.

Frederick pushed the driving goggles onto his forehead, revealing himself to be boyishly handsome and about Stella's age. He smoothed his tidy blond mustache, lifted the eyebrow slashed through by a thin scar, and smiled lopsidedly at them. Alice stifled a nervous giggle. Had he heard Lady Atherly's comment? Remembering his manners, Frederick Kentfield opened the door for an older woman with the same long, lean face, draped from head to toe in a dust-covered sable. As she took her son's hand and alighted the car, she regarded Morrington Hall and those gathered with little interest, reminding Stella of an incurious cat deigning to disembark.

Mack, sniffing about the automobile, caught a whiff of something and, without warning, landed his wet front paws on the woman, muddying her sable coat.

"Down! Down!" she protested, her arms held ineffectually above her head.

Had Lady Atherly stifled a snicker? Lady Atherly wasn't fond of Mack, preferring cats, which were useful for catching rodent pests. Nor did she care for anything or anyone with unbridled enthusiasm. Stella waited for the reprimand that never came.

"Will someone call off this mongrel?"

Lyndy clapped, and the dog abandoned the newcomer to get petted by Lyndy.

"Met a new friend already, Isabella?" the driver of the auto quipped, chuckling at her expense.

He stripped off his driving cap and goggles and, despite the silver streaks in his beard, climbed out with the same vitality as his son. Despite the grime of the road on him, he led with his hand out and a lopsided grin on his face.

Lord Atherly stepped forward. "Sir Edwin, Lady Isabella, Freddy! Welcome to Morrington Hall. Edwin, you remember my son, Lyndy. He would've been in short trousers the last time you saw him."

Edwin? That was Lyndy's Christian name. What a coincidence. Or was it?

"It's good to see you all grown up, my boy." The men heartily shook hands.

"And our daughter," Lady Atherly said, presenting her youngest for inspection. "Lady Alice."

"Not much younger than my girls, are you, my dear?" Lady Isabella said, inspecting first Alice and then the damage to her coat. "How you do resemble your mother."

"And are just as beautiful," Frederick added, admiring Alice's sweet face.

Like the proper lady she'd been raised to be, Alice blushed at the compliment. She averted her gaze to the pebbles, glazed with frost at her feet.

With everyone but Stella's focus on Alice, Lady Isabella boldly sized up Lady Atherly, oblivious of any scrutiny. She rotated her gold and ruby bangle bracelet over and over. Was she making a mental comparison? Or was there a hint of something more?

"Indeed, Freddy, I heartily concur," Sir Edwin laughed. "You are quite lovely, my girl."

"Speaking of lovely, allow me to introduce my wife," Lyndy said, shooing Mack away. "Stella, Lady Lyndhurst."

Despite outranking her, Stella curtsied slightly to show respect to the elder Lady Isabella and heard a sniff of disapproval from Lady Atherly. Lady Isabella, still brushing at her coat, nodded in return.

"It's nice to meet you, Sir Edwin, Lady Isabella, Mr. Kentfield," Stella said. "Do you plan to play golf, Mr. Kentfield?"

At the sound of his name, Frederick Kentfield tore his eyes from Alice and distractedly touched the brim of his cap. "I beg your pardon?"

Stella indicated the bag slung over his shoulder.

"Oh, do call me Freddy." He laughed. "And no. Not in this weather. But I never leave home without my clubs, just in case. Call it a quirk of mine."

"Like my magazines," Alice said, her hands clenched to her chest. "I do love to cart them everywhere."

"I've heard so much about you, Lady Lyndhurst, from my daughters in London," Lady Isabella was saying with an undercurrent of disapproval, making it clear what she'd heard hadn't all been favorable.

"I'm not surprised. My wife's beauty, wit, and kindness precede her wherever we go," Lyndy said, challenging Lady Isabella to say more.

"It is indeed a pleasure, Lady Lyndhurst," Sir Edwin said, capturing her hand and bringing it to his lips.

Stella froze, heat flushing her neck. The gesture recalled a similar, more sinister incident on the day she arrived. Stella resisted tugging her hand from his grasp. Behind her, Lyndy cleared his throat. When Sir Edwin released it, she tucked her hand under her arm.

"I have to admit she's been quite good for us," Lord Atherly said conspiratorially behind a raised hand to Sir Edwin. But if Stella heard him, everyone else did too.

"No doubt," Lady Isabella said in all seriousness. "I heard she came with quite the dowry."

"You must be cold and weary from your journey," Lady Atherly said, changing the subject. Nothing mortified the countess more than an open discussion about the family's financial status.

Lady Isabella shivered on cue, her fingertips resting lightly on her chest. "Oh, yes. Coming down from London has been the most unpleasant undertaking. Why on earth my husband proposed we do it, brave the wilds at Christmas of all times, is beyond me." She cocked her head in expectation of her husband's response. Sir Edwin refused to take the bait. "My daughters would never ask me to leave London at this time of year."

"Our daughters never ask you to visit either," her husband joked callously. His wife's face drained of all color. "I'm sorry, my dear. Was that too close to the truth?" He bent to kiss his wife's cheek as if in contrition, but she stepped out of his reach, backing into the headlamp of the parked auto. It shifted under her weight.

"This bloody motor," she muttered.

"Stella has a 1905 Daimler, but I've never seen this model before," Lyndy said. "It's a Martini?"

"Right you are," Sir Edwin said, running his hand down the front bumper. "Got it a month ago."

"May I?" Lyndy asked, admiring the automobile's sleek curves with an eagerness he usually reserved for horses.

"Be my guest," Sir Edwin said.

"We'll leave you two to it," Lady Atherly said, suggesting the rest go inside.

Freddy offered to escort Alice in. Peering demurely at him through her lashes, Lyndy's sister didn't hesitate to wrap her hand around the crook of his arm.

"You can refresh yourselves in a hot bath if you'd like."

"That's too much to ask of you, Lady Atherly," Lady Isabella said, taking the earl's offered arm.

"Not at all," Lady Atherly said. "We have a new hot water system running to every bath."

"Really? I wouldn't have thought a provincial estate like yours would have any modern conveniences. If I had known, I mightn't have been quite so resistant to come." Lady Isabella chuckled mirthlessly.

The backhanded compliment visibly stung, but Lady Atherly recovered quickly, graciously taking Sir Edwin's arm, only to be rewarded by an over-the-shoulder scowl from Lady Isabella.

Why had Lady Atherly invited the Kentfields? And at Christmas? Having their company might put a damper on the holidays.

Lingering awkwardly in the drive, Freddy and Alice followed the older couples. Could they be the reason? Supposedly Freddy Kentfield was quite the catch. Could Lady Atherly be playing matchmaker?

Maybe Lyndy would know.

Lyndy was strutting around the Kentfields' auto like an interested buyer at Tattersall's.

"Do you know why your mother invited the Kentfields for Christmas? They don't seem to . . ." Lyndy paused, leaning forward to inspect something closer, then frowned. "What is it?"

"Nothing." His tone said otherwise.

Stella decided not to press it. If it was important, he'd let her know, eventually. He strolled to her.

"As to your question, I have no idea why the Kentfields are here. Mother was rather put out when I asked. Are you cold? Shall we go in?"

She snuggled against his arm and kissed him on the cheek.

"What was that for? Not that I'm complaining. It brings to mind a few ways I could warm you up." He leaned in, pulled down the extra scarf Stella had wrapped around her neck, and kissed her exposed skin. Shivers raced down her spine.

"It's for the sweet Christmas card you left in my room."

"What Christmas card?" he asked.

"Don't play coy with me."

His kisses traced the length of her neck, reaching her exposed collarbone. Tiny snowflakes began drifting around them, landing and melting in Lyndy's hair.

"I'm sorry, my love, but I don't know what you're talking about."

"Oh, Lyndy. Of course, you do." She playfully swatted his shoulder. "Who else would send me a card with *Love to my angel* inscribed on it?"

Lyndy abruptly stopped and lifted his head. "Someone wrote that to you?"

"Are you saying you didn't?"

Lyndy's muscles tensed under her touch. His jaw, moments ago nuzzled against her, strained under the sudden tension. Stella leaned back in his embrace, alarmed. She found confirmation in his eyes.

"I promise you I didn't, but I'll be damned if I don't find out who did."

CHAPTER 6

Could it be? A niggling sense of dread tickled annoyingly at the back of Mrs. Nelson's mind. *But how?* Priding herself on her fortitude, the housekeeper was confident that focusing on the day's tasks, all designed to test her patience, or so it seemed, would be enough to shake the shadow hanging over her until she had time to think it out properly. Or so she hoped.

She'd spent some time calming Mrs. Cole in the kitchen after discovering the mince pies gone, and then Lady Lyndhurst (*Bless her!*) had the pluck to make special requests. Mrs. Nelson respected the new viscountess. After all, Lady Lyndhurst was now a member of the family Mrs. Nelson had served since her days as chambermaid under the iron fist of Mrs. Birtwistle, the housekeeper for the seventh Earl of Atherly. But Lord Lyndhurst's new wife had some learning to do. She appreciated Lady Lyndhurst's enthusiasm; it was quite refreshing to have someone instill a bit of childlike wonder into the stodgy traditions, which seemed more drudgery than festivity. And given time, the American viscountess's suggestions might be more than doable. But now was not the time.

Neither was it appropriate for Sir Edwin Kentfield to be gracing them with his presence again. What was Her Ladyship thinking? And whose brilliant idea was it to install a new heating system at holiday time? Wasn't her job arduous enough not to add keeping an eye out for any growing familiarity between her maids and the workmen? Which is precisely what brought her to Louisa's door. The chambermaid had been spending far too much time swishing her feather duster in places she didn't belong.

The housekeeper rapped her knuckle twice before turning the doorknob and entering the room Louisa shared with Millie Jones. *Now there was a reliable girl.* Head in the clouds a bit too much for Mrs. Nelson's liking, but neat and polite, Millie got her work done. The room was appropriately empty. But not having located Louisa in any of the bedchambers or in the servants' hall, Mrs. Nelson half expected to find the chambermaid lounging in bed.

Where is that woman?

Disgruntled, Mrs. Nelson inspected the room, hoping to find something compromising that she could take up with the maid. As if making eyes at the workmen wasn't enough.

With the counterpanes on the twin wrought-iron beds smooth, the floor swept, and the fire grate sufficiently clean, she could find little fault in the small, tidy room until her gaze lit on a linen bundle on the dressing table. She crossed the room in rapid strides. Before she'd unknotted the cloth—one of the embroidered tea towels with tiny horseshoes in the color of new leaves Lady Lyndhurst supplied the kitchen—the unmistakable scent of nutmeg, candied citrus, and currants emanated from inside. The missing minced pies.

I knew it!

Louisa was one of the many new staff members populating the house. With the windfall of Lady Lyndhurst's inheritance, Lady Atherly hadn't spared a day in advertising for maids, footmen, and gardeners. Louisa and Bridget were the only additions to Mrs. Nelson's staff, but Louisa, with her unhealthy fascination with the workmen, had proved to be trouble enough for four maids. She was closing in on thirty. Shouldn't she know better? And now she'd been proven to be a thief!

The housekeeper shifted through dresser drawers, lifted every hat box lid, and rummaged through the trunk at the end of Louisa's bed, searching for anything else the maid might've pinched. This afternoon, Mrs. Nelson learned of several items missing from Lady Lyndhurst's bedchamber. After a scouring search, the housekeeper found Louisa had a penchant for red ribbons and had hoarded a stack of unused half-penny postcards of every scene imaginable. But nothing belonging to Lord Lyndhurst's new wife.

Determined to get this sorted, Mrs. Nelson, appreciating their heavenly scent, snatched up the bundle of stolen mince pies and made her way down the backstairs. She enquired after Louisa's whereabouts from a footman returning with a half-empty, three-tiered, silver cake tray, from the new under-parlor maid, broom in hand, and from Mr. Fulton, heading downstairs to change into his evening attire. Mr. Fulton, as efficient as always, had been the only useful one of the three, having seen Louisa and Millie hanging ropes of evergreen in the Music Room. The housekeeper, finding the maids in the hall outside where Mr. Fulton said she would find them, confronted the new maid with the linen bundle of mince pies dangling from her raised fist.

"And what do you have to say for yourself, Louisa?"

Louisa, the ruffles of her cap framing her freckled face, stepped away from the ladder she'd been holding for Millie, insolently crossed her arms, and blew a stray curl of her copper-colored hair from her forehead.

"Ah!" The ladder wobbled, clattering against the wall, and Millie, grabbing hold of the picture molding encircling the room, dropped the evergreen rope she'd been ready to drape along it. Louisa grabbed and secured the ladder again.

"Sorry, Millie."

Millie, perspiration dripping down her temple, nodded in gratitude.

"And where is your apology to me? To Mrs. Cole?" the housekeeper demanded. Without giving the maid a chance to respond, she continued, "What I can't fathom is why you would risk your position, a highly enviable one, I might add, for a few mince pies. It's beyond me."

To her credit, the maid didn't deny it. "Don't know, do I? Seemed so many Mrs. Cole wouldn't miss but a few." The woman shrugged.

The gesture, a dismissal of the seriousness of her situation, more than the misconduct itself, inflamed the housekeeper.

"I can therefore assume you didn't think Lady Lyndhurst would miss 'but a few' things either?" Knowing she had no grounds for the accusation, Mrs. Nelson took her frustration out on Millie. "Get down from there! How much garland does this house need?"

Millie dropped her chin to her chest and compliantly scrambled down.

"Oi, what you on about?" Louisa said, bracing the ladder with her ample weight to accommodate Millie's descent. "I admitted to the mince pies, didn't I? But that's it."

"Are you denying you stole from Lady Lyndhurst's room? A souvenir spoon, a handkerchief, a favorite silver bookmark?"

There went the folded arms again. "I never took anything from Lady Lyndhurst. Never."

"I won't be lied to. I won't have a thief under this roof. Pack your things. You are to leave this house immediately." The housekeeper pointed toward the green baize door at the end of the hall for emphasis.

"But—" Louisa sputtered and dropped her arms, the shock of dismissal cutting through her defiant pride. "But—"

"Forgive me, Mrs. Nelson," Millie said quietly. "I know it's not my place to say, but it's Christmastime. Where will Louisa go?"

"You're right, Millie. It isn't your place to say. But you're also right about it being Christmas, and I am not without charity." Mrs. Nelson admired Millie's loyalty but knew it to be misplaced. "And in the spirit of the holiday, Louisa, I will send you off with a week's wages." She held up a hand to forestall any complaints. "But I can't in all good conscience give you a reference."

Millie didn't stifle her gasp. Louisa, as stunned, gawked first at Millie and then at the housekeeper.

"No reference? It will be me ruination."

"You should've thought of that before you stole from a member of this household."

Her snub nose jutting up, Louisa shoved a long finger into Mrs. Nelson's face, so close she could smell the roast from the servants' dinner on the maid's breath. Taken unawares, Mrs. Nelson conceded a small step back.

"I never took anything from the likes of Lady Lyndhurst. She has been nothing but kind to me; she has. But I'll be taking my leave of this place, with me conscience clear. But you! Ruin me life for a few crummy mince pies, will you? Well! I'd watch your back; I would. And good luck sleeping tonight!"

Louisa bobbed her head once for emphasis before dropping her threatening finger. She whipped up a breeze as she swiveled around and stormed away.

"I have a mind to send you out on the street penniless, you ungrateful . . ." Mrs. Nelson, spotting Millie with her fingers partially covering her gaping mouth, didn't finish her sentence. "Don't you have somewhere you need to be, Millie?" she scolded, sending the younger chambermaid scampering away in the opposite direction.

Once alone, Mrs. Nelson's righteous anger cooled, replaced by that niggling apprehension again. Evergreen rope snaked around at her feet, filling the hall with their fresh fragrance. She kicked the nearest garland away. She, who never made it a habit to second-guess herself, didn't fancy the feeling that the insolent maid might be right.

Growing up in Kentucky, Stella couldn't have imagined such an evening: thatched cottages with tendrils of smoke curling from their chimneys, flakes of lacy snow dancing in the air, the occasional jingling of bells as sleighs pulled out for the first significant snowfall of the year, passing their small group of carolers, their cheeks ruddy from the cold and the occasional glass of mulled wine or sherry they'd been offered in reward for their song. It was "One Horse Open Sleigh" come to life.

She'd never gone caroling before. Not even before Mama left. Living on a horse farm in Kentucky, her father would've had to make an effort to escort them. Instead, he'd invited his guests to be serenaded by Stella in the comfort of their drawing room. Clustering around the well-lit doors of friends and neighbors while singing to them on a cold night was odd.

But not any more than Lord Atherly proposing the outing in the first place. Stella loved it.

Leaving Lady Atherly and Lady Isabella behind, the group had been congenial from the moment they set out into the snow after tea. They'd started at Pilley Manor, much to the delight of Aunt Rachel, who'd coughed intermittently throughout, and sang their way through the clusters of cottages on the outskirts of Rosehurst before reaching the village proper. With Lord Atherly and Sir Edwin in the lead, Stella, on Lyndy's arm, and Alice, interlocked arm and arm with Freddy Kentfield, strolled a few steps behind. Much to Alice's silent but evident delight, Freddy and Lyndy soon found common ground. Between houses, Freddy, a talkative man when released from his mother's watchful eye, peppered Lyndy with questions about the improvements they were making to the Morrington stables. Lyndy was only too happy to oblige.

Each house they visited offered a cheerful welcome; each was a moment of joy. Who could've guessed that not only did Lord Atherly have a rich baritone voice but that Lyndy, who she'd never heard sing once, matched his father note for note? The thrill of hearing the two men sing in harmony was all the warmth she needed. She'd teased Lyndy, reproaching him for keeping his talent hidden. Why did he never sing in church? Why hadn't he serenaded her? Didn't he realize how it melted her heart? A smile tugged at his lips as he brushed snow from the fur collar of her overcoat. But he didn't explain. Before she could probe further, their little group strolled up the short path to a gabled brick cottage, its front dominated by a curving bay window. The orange glow of the fire seemed to radiate warmth through the wavy glass panes. The door opened before they'd arrived, the firelight within casting long shadows onto the path and their faces. The man, assumed so by the long-stemmed pipe jutting from his lips, stood in silhouette in the doorway.

"Captain Stancliffe, we wish you good tidings this festive season," Lord Atherly bellowed like an actor on the stage.

Without any more of a preamble, he broke into "God Rest You Merry, Gentlemen," with the others quickly joining in. Lyndy's father had begun this way at every door, jolly, playful, and eager to sing. Except when he was speaking of his coveted horse fossils and the expeditions he funded to find them, Stella had never seen Lord Atherly so animated. In fact, the evening seemed to transform the Searlwyns. Lyndy was as quick to compliment as to tease the others, even patting his father's shoulder after a particularly well-performed harmony. Readily giggling at even the least amusing remarks, Alice sang lustily to compete with her brother and father and couldn't stop smiling. Was it the sherry? Was it the absence of Lady Atherly? Was it the spirit of the season that infected them all with joy? Stella didn't care. She'd never seen these three members of her new family enjoy each other's company so much.

When they'd sung all seven verses and ended with a flourish, Captain Stancliffe stepped back and invited them in. He wore a double-stitched, green hunting coat with a dark brown corduroy collar and, although not much taller than Stella, carried his muscular build with precision. Not ducking her head low enough, Stella banged the crown of her hat on the door frame as she stepped into a room of whitewashed plaster walls and thick, darkly stained beams overhead. A small, undecorated Christmas tree perched on a table in the corner.

With introductions concluded and a plate of mince pies shyly offered by Miss Stancliffe, whose stooped back contrasted with her brother's military posture, Sir Edwin said, "No chance of a hint as to where this race might start, is there, my good fellow?"

He winked at Stella. She smiled feebly at him in return.

"Seeing as you're a guest of His Lordship, I'll pretend you didn't ask," Captain Stancliffe chuckled, his teeth clenched on the tip of his pipe.

Freddy Kentfield bent his head to Alice's and whispered his confusion.

"The captain is in charge of this year's Point-to-Point," Lyndy explained.

"And is the only man who knows the route from start to finish," Lord Atherly added. "So no one can map out their route in advance."

"You're the one I need to speak to, then," Stella said.

Lyndy had explained the annual Boxing Day tradition—a race in which the riders go from one point to another, taking any route they want. The course differs every year, and only one person knows it beforehand. The endpoint is announced a

few days in advance, but the racers must wait until that morning to learn where it's to begin. Owning a New Forest Pony
was the one qualification.

The captain removed his pipe. "Indeed?"

"Why don't women race the Point-to-Point, Captain?"

"Because it's too dangerous, of course." Amusement flick-
ered across his face.

"But there aren't any rules to prohibit it?"

The lines on the captain's forehead deepened as he cocked
his head in concern. "Well . . . I don't—"

"Stella, my dear," Lord Atherly interrupted, growing somber
for the first time all night. "You aren't considering . . . ?"

Once relegated to the background, the crackling of the fire
was loud in Stella's ears as the silence fell, everyone anticipating
her answer. Lyndy's gentle squeeze on her arm, encouraging
her to back down, instead emboldened her.

"Why not?" She put all her enthusiasm and optimism into
her voice. "You know I'm as accomplished a rider as any of the
men who will race."

Lord Atherly's face brightened as he considered it. "That is
most certainly true."

"You are remarkable, my love, but there's something to
what the captain says. It could be dangerous."

Lyndy had good intentions, but Stella wasn't backing down.
She folded her arms across her chest. "Regretting gifting me
Morrington now, are you?"

As a wedding present, Lyndy had given her one of his ponies,
the magnificent filly that should've won the Cecil New Forest
Pony Challenge this past summer but was cheated out of it by
Lord Fairbrother's underhanded ways.

In response, Lyndy could only stubbornly stick out his chin
and tug at the lapels on his woolen overcoat. The captain chuckled and put his pipe back in his mouth.

"I think it would be splendid to have a lady represent the rest of us in the race," Miss Stancliffe said, speaking for the first time.

"Here! Here!" Sir Edwin agreed.

"Good Lord, no. I wouldn't chance it," Freddy said.

"It isn't really that hazardous, is it, Papa?" Alice piped up.

"Well, now, come to think of it, seldom has a fellow fallen except for that time John Market's pony encountered a snake nest. Harvey Milkham had to be called in." Stella's throat tightened at the mention of her dead friend, the snake catcher. "At best, it's cuts and bruises from the gorse, or at worst, it's smacking your kneecap against a tree."

"Which I've already encountered my share of," Stella said.

Lord Atherly nodded appreciatively. "What do say you, Captain? You know the route better than any of us. Do you think my daughter-in-law should be allowed to race?"

Captain Stancliffe removed his pipe and blew a string of smoke rings into the air. The pungent, sweet smell of tobacco competed with the scent of burning wood and the fragrant Christmas tree. "I do admire your mettle, Lady Lyndhurst, and admittedly am intrigued by your new charity. But I'm also certain I've taken up too much of your time. I must let you get on and let others enjoy your song. Thank you, Betsy." This he said as he shooed his sister back toward the kitchen with her tray. Miss Stancliffe grudgingly hobbled away as her brother escorted Stella and the others to his door. The pace of snowfall had increased. The footprints they'd made on the path were already gone.

The captain, his beard speckled with snowflakes as he waited on the doorstep, raised his pipe in farewell. "Happy Christmas to you all."

Responding in kind, the carolers trudged back into the night, the joy, the easiness, and the camaraderie dimmed. Why should that be? Because she'd asked a question? Or because she'd dared to ask the wrong one?

Lyndy put his arm around Stella's shoulders on the pretext of keeping her warm. "Sorry, my love. It seems there's an end to your plan to race," he whispered, a lilt of relief in his voice. "It's probably for the best."

"Shall we have a pint at your local when this is all done, Lord Atherly?" Sir Edwin was saying. How her father-in-law responded, Stella never heard.

Stella, her shoulders stiffened with resolve, wanted to shrug him off.

Lyndy might mean well, but whether he or the captain or any of the men liked it or not, she was going to race her pony against the best of them come Boxing Day.

CHAPTER 7

"Lady Lyndhurst."

The hiss cut through Stella's dream of riding Tully in the Point-to-Point Race, her dappled gray mare draped in red and green paper chains. She ignored it. It was the new radiators releasing heat. She shifted her weight on the bed, reached toward Lyndy to reassure herself he was still there, and rolled over again.

"Please, Lady Lyndhurst. I need your help."

The hiss became a whispered plea. The heat on her ear, tinted with the medicinal scent of tooth powder, tickled. Confused, she tried to roll away from the unpleasantness but felt resistance on her shoulder.

"Miss Stella!"

Stella's eyes fluttered open at the cry, and Millie's round face filled her entire view. Stella bolted upright, and the chambermaid leaped back, barely avoiding knocking heads with her.

"Oh, my goodness, Millie!" Stella held her hand to her chest. She squinted at the clock on the mantel, but it was too dark to see that far. Millie's candle was a tiny stub, and only a slight glow of embers marked what was once a roaring fire in the grate. "What time is it?"

"It's gone one," the maid whispered. "I'm so sorry, milady, but I didn't know what else to do." The maid wrung her hands, dotted red with tiny cuts from the evergreens, interlacing her fingers and twisting them repeatedly.

Stella cast a glance at the prone figure of her husband, his mouth gaping open, his arm flung above his head, before carefully shoving the bedclothes aside. The chilled air of the room whisked away any remaining drowsiness.

Why weren't the new radiators working?

"What is it, Millie?"

"It's Mrs. Nelson, milady. I'd finally finished cleaning the china and was getting off to bed when I heard moaning coming from Mrs. Nelson's room. She's ever so ill. Delirious even."

Stella padded across the carpet, competing with the chambermaid, who dashed to grab her quilted dressing gown first. After shrugging into it, Stella slid her bare feet into slippers.

"Have you alerted Fulton? Lady Atherly?"

The maid shook her head. "I couldn't do it, milady. I couldn't face Her Ladyship."

Stella didn't blame her. When Lady Atherly learned her housekeeper was sick with Christmas a day away, she'd be livid. "And Mr. Fulton doesn't fancy being bothered by maids."

Tears welled in the maid's eyes, and Stella laid a reassuring hand on the young woman's shoulder.

"It's okay, Millie. We'll check on Mrs. Nelson, and I'll tell whoever needs to know."

The chambermaid's body sagged with relief.

Millie led Stella upstairs to the female servants' corridor, a long, dark, unadorned hall, stopping in front of the only door with a small brass knocker. Millie stepped back to let Stella enter first. Mrs. Nelson's room was simple but comfortably furnished with a matching walnut headboard, washstand, and desk. A brown upholstered rocking chair sat in one corner. Despite the open curtains and the crisp new snow blanketing the ground, the clouds had moved in thickly as the night wore on, deepening the gloom. Stella could hardly make out the prone figure on the bed. Beside her, on the nightstand, a white porcelain chamber pot reflected the candlelight, appearing to hover like a ghost.

"I found her like this."

A memory of a body lying similarly in bed flashed in Stella's mind. But this wasn't a stranger in York; this was Mrs. Nelson. Mrs. Nelson, who'd yet to tell Stella what was worrying her.

Stella tentatively lifted the candleholder she carried. The room was no warmer than Stella's had been, yet Mrs. Nelson's forehead beaded with sweat, and strands of her hair were plastered to the sides of her face. She'd thrown off her bedsheet and lay shivering in her nightgown. Her cheeks were the color of tomatoes and blazing to the touch.

Stella peered into the chamber pot. It was empty.

The housekeeper's heavy eyelids cracked open at the contact, and she grasped Stella's wrist with a clammy hand.

"Why did I send the child away?" she demanded, without preamble. With no regard for etiquette, her unfocused eyes searched Stella's. Did she even know whom she was talking to? "I shouldn't have let the child leave."

"Get cool water and a cloth," Stella ordered, settling on the edge of the bed.

Millie disappeared like a shot. "What child, Mrs. Nelson?"

The housekeeper groaned incoherently, suddenly thrashing around in her bed. Stella, unsure what to do, hesitated to hold the woman down. Instead, she cooed to her soothingly, hoping the soft tones would ease the woman's distress. It didn't. Stella sat helpless, counting the minutes until Millie returned, witnessing the housekeeper's exhaustion force her body to settle and quiet.

When Millie finally returned with the pitcher, she filled the wash bowl with water. She dunked a square of cotton cloth and rang it out before handing it to Stella. Stella dabbed the sick woman's forehead.

"Millie, do you know what child Mrs. Nelson's talking about?"

"She must mean Louisa. Mrs. Nelson forced Louisa to leave tonight without a reference." A sudden gust of wind rattled the windowpane. "And in this weather."

Mrs. Nelson mumbled something.

Stella leaned in closer. "What's that, Mrs. Nelson?"

"How am I going to tell her?" the housekeeper muttered with jagged breath, rolling slowly onto her side. "How am I going to tell Maggie?"

"Who's Maggie?"

Stella waited for a response and, not getting one, turned to the maid for an answer. Millie shrugged. Stella handed the cloth back for more cool water. Without warning, Mrs. Nelson convulsed, doubled over, and retched, spewing the contents of her stomach across her pillow, down the side of her bed, and onto the floor inches from Stella's slippered feet. Specks of orange vomit riddled the smooth surface of the chamber pot.

Resisting the urge to gag at the putrid smell, Stella leaped up and backed away from the sickness, lumpy and puddling in a low spot on the bare floor under the housekeeper's bed. She collided with the chambermaid, frozen in place by the unexpected violence.

"This is Louisa's doing, innit?" Millie blurted heatedly.

"What is?" Millie, biting her lip, refused to say more. "Never mind, just go call Dr. Johnstone." He'd been the family's physician for over three decades. Stella met him when Lord Atherly collapsed the night of the engagement party.

When the chambermaid continued to dillydally, twisting her apron strings, Stella pushed her toward the door. Millie's skin turned green at the jarring, horrible, heartrending sound of Mrs. Nelson being sick again. Stella rushed to open a window as if answering the clattering of the wind to be let in.

"Now, Millie. Now!"

The man blew into his cupped hands. Despite the cold, he'd forgone gloves. Tonight's business was far too messy. He'd already ruined several pairs. Besides, working with his hands his whole life had toughened the skin like old leather. Still, the damp fought to numb his fingers, and he'd fumbled with his prize. He secured the thick twine rope by wrapping it around his wrist and letting it dangle at his side. Finding a winding animal track cut into the white, already partially drifted in, he followed it, crunching across wilted bracken, carefully side-stepping hidden clusters of dormant heather. With the snow falling fast, he'd have to rely on his memory and instincts as he hiked across the moor.

It was dodgy work, this, and not at all justified. But he thrilled at pitting his wits against the elements and, even more so, against the law. He'd followed orders his entire life. Now, living in this sleepy village known for its free-ranging livestock and ponies, he too felt like a domesticated bull left to its own devices, with few inhibitions left. What harm was there in what he did? No more than off-key bellows of "Here We Come A-Wassailing" emanating from the Knightwood Oak's drunken rabble as he'd passed the pub earlier. Weren't they all making merry in their own way?

A nightjar's chirr pierced the stillness directly above him, distracting him. The man's foot landed in a hidden swale. His ankle jerked to one side, unbalancing him and dropping him to one knee into the outreaching embrace of a prickly gorse bush. The sharp needles slashed at his thigh and arm, well-protected by his long overcoat. But his exposed cheek was vulnerable, and the gorse sliced through his skin, numbed by the cold, brisk wind.

He let loose the rope and hauled himself to his feet, brushing off snow, soil, and dried leaves he couldn't see in the dark. He snatched up the rope, securing it again in his fist, and continued on. Soon, he vowed, he'd halt these nights of solo adventure and settle back into a life of respectability.

But only if the woman says yes.

As he approached the cottages on the edge of town, a distant light accentuated the narrow road dividing the moor from the village. Towering, skeletal, leafless trees lined the lane, like soldiers at attention waiting for their commander to tell them what to do. As the light grew brighter, silhouettes of balled clumps emerged in the reflecting snow-filled air, clusters of mistletoe clinging to the upper reaches of the trees like baubles on a Christmas tree. Not fancying being caught out and having to explain himself, he crouched down to avoid the glaring headlights of the motorcar as it carelessly careened down the lane, swerving this way and that at breathtaking speed. Birds, roosting nearby, suddenly took flight, squawking and squabbling at the disturbance. Within a few seconds, the vehicle was gone, the thunder of its engine a fading rumble.

Rattled, he climbed to his feet, his hands unconsciously checking the fastenings of the rope, and stepped into the tracks the tires had left behind.

"For God's sake, slow down!" he shouted at the motorcar no longer visible beyond the darkened curtain of snow. "You're gonna get yourself killed."

With the candle in her hand flickering from the frequent drafts, Stella crept down the back stairs, hoping to avoid waking anyone. The morning was soon enough to announce the housekeeper was sick.

And not dead.

Though Lady Atherly may see it otherwise, it was good news, perhaps even a Christmas miracle. Mrs. Nelson was alive and expected to make a full recovery. At times, while waiting for the doctor, wiping the poor delirious woman's lips, bathing her forehead, Stella had had her doubts.

When he finally arrived, Dr. Johnstone, a thick-bodied man in his late fifties with a long, bushy, white mustache, had barged into the sickroom, grim and impatient, throwing his overcoat at Millie and depositing his leather satchel on the bed. He fired off a series of questions.

"Earlier in the day, had there been any sign Mrs. Nelson suffered from headaches? From weakness? From a dry cough? From fever?" Stella mentioned the paleness of Mrs. Nelson's face in the kitchen. He quickly discounted it and continued. "Was anyone else in the household ill? How fast was the onset of symptoms?"

Once ruling out typhoid fever, he declared her suffering from a less deadly ailment, most likely contaminated food. He'd unfastened his mismatched cuff links (one was onyx, the other dark blue enamel) and rolled up his shirtsleeves, announcing his intention of forcing Mrs. Nelson to empty her stomach, only to find she'd done it herself. After a brief examination, he'd retrieved his coat and bag, and ordered peppermint tea to settle her stomach as he strode out the room. He wished them a *"Happy Christmas"* from the hall and declared he'd see himself out. He'd been in the house less than fifteen minutes.

With Millie insisting on cleaning up the sickroom, the doctor had said to wake Mrs. Cole. Stella hadn't seen the need. She might be a viscountess now, but she could still make a cup of tea.

She slid her hand down the rail to keep from tripping in the semidark; a single wall lamp had been left on in the hall that spanned the length of the servants' domain. Straight ahead was the servants' hall, so she headed to the right toward the kitchen. Sudden low whispers by the open door at the end of the hall pinned her feet to the floor.

Who else is up at this late hour?

Stella blew out her candle and tiptoed toward them. She

paused more than halfway down, sure to stay in the shadow. The cold air reached her almost as soon as she stopped, the fresh, almost woody, scent of newly fallen snow a welcome respite from the smell of vomit still lingering in her nose.

A shadowy figure filled the doorway, their breath visible against the black night. A bulky, fringed shawl draped about their shoulders. Mrs. Cole spoke to someone, soft and secretive, their whispers too low for Stella to make out what they were saying. They hadn't noticed her approach. Stella crept closer.

The cook leaned against the door frame, revealing a glimpse of her visitor, a man silhouetted against the night. Stella trembled with that intangible sense of what the French call déjà vu. Where had she seen him before? She slid against the wall, inching further down the hall.

"You're a fool. What if you get caught?" Mrs. Cole was saying. "Don't think I'll thank you for going to jail on my account."

"Don't you worry about that. What do you say to my suggestion? Are you game?"

Considering the serious nature of whatever they were talking about, the man's voice was encouraging and patient. Stella couldn't place it, but she was positive she'd heard his voice before.

"What?" Mrs. Cole scoffed. "You want me to answer now?"

"What do you have to lose?"

"Are you daft? What do you think the family will do when they find out? Throw me a party?"

"Maybe?"

"You're not being serious."

"You know I am."

The silence stretched on. Stella's heartbeat echoed loudly in her ears. She had decided to retreat a few steps when Mrs. Cole sighed.

"I don't know."

The furtive glance Mrs. Nelson cast at the cook this morning when she'd decided not to tell Stella what she'd wanted to flashed into Stella's mind. She'd assumed Mrs. Nelson had been reticent to talk in front of the cook for privacy's sake. But was Mrs. Cole at the center of Mrs. Nelson's concern? The cook couldn't be contemplating doing something illegal, could she? It was inconceivable. But then again, Stella had learned the hard way people aren't always as they seem.

"You're right," the man said. "Don't think of it now. Perhaps it won't seem so frightful in the daylight."

"Better off with you then." The cook began to close the door. The man extended his arm toward Mrs. Cole, halting her ability to shut out the night.

"All I ask is you consider it."

"You know I will."

He placed his weathered hand on the cook's shoulder, and the weak hallway light illuminated the bright, white cuff of his shirtsleeve stretched out from beneath the heavy green jacket he wore. Slashed across the cuff and streaked down the side of the coat was a dark stain she'd seen too many times before— blood.

Stella couldn't retrace her steps fast enough.

CHAPTER 8

Stella's eyes fluttered open. A faint hint of sunlight crept through the crack in the curtains and lit on the irregular scraps of white, beaded wedding dress stitched into the crazy quilt covering the bed. It must still be early. The room was cold, but her bed was warm, her husband's body close. Not ready to face the day, she snuggled deeper under her blankets, hoping Aunt Rachel's wedding present, the hodgepodge patchwork quilt of mismatched fabrics and patterns of Stella's old dresses, would ward off the memories of her foray downstairs last night.

No such luck.

Rushing back the way she'd come, Stella had escaped detection but had forgotten poor Mrs. Nelson's tea. Instead, she'd headed straight for her bedroom. Stella had hauled out the heavy quilt, curled up beside Lyndy under its comforting weight, and relished his arm wrapping her in a sleepy embrace. As her breathing and racing heart slowed, she'd conjured up various sinister reasons why the man was covered in blood or why Mrs. Cole was secretly meeting with him. Sheer exhaustion had forced her to sleep.

But now, come morning, and in the safety of her bedroom, Stella was ashamed. She'd abandoned the ill housekeeper and Millie, and for what? An overactive sense of menace? Was it Mrs. Nelson's fault Stella's recent encounters with murder had her imagining the worst when confronted with inexplicable blood on a midnight visitor's clothes? Of course, there was an innocent explanation for Mrs. Cole's late-night assignation. Wasn't there?

"Good morning, love," Lyndy's breath, smelling slightly of last night's sherry, tickled her cheek.

Lyndy brushed hair from her forehead. Stella forced a smile. He leaned in for a kiss, slipping an arm beneath her and pulling her to him. In hopes of banishing lingering doubts, Stella greeted his lips with an intensity that surprised them both. As their need to be close grew, their kisses deepened. The door creaked open.

"Bloody hell!" Lyndy whispered against Stella's lips. "It's not time for your tray yet, is it?"

Since becoming a married woman, Stella had been served breakfast in bed. She'd balked at the practice when they'd first returned from their honeymoon in York. Spending so much of her childhood alone, Stella looked forward to the relaxed, social aspect of the morning meal. She also liked being able to choose her own food from the buffet. Despite Ethel's attempt to please, she never brought up enough. And why wouldn't Stella want to get on with her day instead of lazing around? It took a stern talking-to from Lady Atherly, demanding she accept the "luxury" of lounging in bed, for Stella to capitulate and stay put in the morning. Stella still didn't understand why.

Stella rolled in Lyndy's arms for a better view of the clock on the mantelpiece. But Bridget, one of the new maids, was already slipping silently inside. Discreetly averting her gaze, she plodded across the room to lie down and light the fire. Then she pulled the curtains open with a swift jerk. It made little difference. With thick, overcast skies, and despite last night's snow, the morning was gray to the ground. The maid left as quietly as she'd arrived. But the moment was lost. Stella pushed herself up onto her elbows.

"I wondered why the radiators aren't working."

"Indeed. I thought that was the point. No need for fires, no need to be intruded upon by skittering maids like unwelcome mice in the walls." Taking no notice of the added quilt, Lyndy flung back the bedcovers. "Which one was that, then?"

"Bridget."

"Another new one?" Lyndy shoved his feet into his slippers while reaching for the bell to summon Harry Finn, his valet. Unlike Stella, if he wanted breakfast, he'd have to dress first. "Mother certainly has taken advantage of your inheritance. Did you know she hired four new gardeners too?"

"That doesn't surprise me, but I am still shocked she agreed to update the heating system. What do you think changed her mind? Maybe she warmed to the idea of a bath that didn't require a maid lugging hot water up three flights of stairs?"

Lyndy chuckled at her pun. "Mother couldn't care less about the servants. She did it to impress Lady Isabella. Of course, if the heat and hot water don't work, it gives our unwilling guest more fuel for the fire."

Stella laughed at his wordplay. He bit his lip and smiled.

"By the way, what is the relationship between Lady Isabella and your parents?"

Lyndy threw on his dressing gown and clinched the belt around his waist. "Supposedly, Sir Edwin was once a fabulous family friend. Yet he hasn't been here in years."

"Why not?"

Lyndy shrugged and gestured toward the flames flickering in the grate. "Why'd Bridget tend to this? Where's the maid who normally starts our fires in the morning? Louisa, is it?"

Lyndy didn't have a knack for knowing the servants' names.

But with Louisa seeing them at the most vulnerable, Stella was pleased Lyndy at least knew hers even if she wasn't their maid anymore.

"Mrs. Nelson fired her."

"Why?"

"Millie seemed to think it had something to do with Mrs. Nelson getting sick."

"Mrs. Nelson's ill?"

Stella pulled the quilt up to her chin and told Lyndy everything that had happened, from Millie waking her up to Stella's narrow escape up the back stairs.

"And she'll be all right?"

"Dr. Johnstone said she would be."

"How did I sleep through all of this?" Before Stella could answer, he added, "Wait, does Mother know?"

"She will soon if she hasn't learned already."

"Maybe that's why the house is so chilly?" Lyndy laughed mirthlessly. "Houseguests at Christmas with no housekeeper at the helm? I wonder how Fulton is getting on."

"Especially with all the new maids skittering around," she said flippantly, teasing him with his own words.

He dashed to her side and tickled her in retaliation. She squealed as she slipped back into the lingering warmth of the covers and pulled the quilt over her head. Lyndy was trying to sneak his hands past the quilted barrier when someone pounded on the door.

"You'd think this was the Majestic Hotel," Lyndy grumbled, referring to the ill-timed interruptions they'd encountered on their honeymoon.

Stella flung the covers away, swiveled to the edge of the bed, and dangled her bare feet, as pale as the bedsheet from the cold. A draft cut through her nightgown.

"Let's hope not!" she said, pulling Aunt Rachel's quilt around her shoulders.

Those interruptions had entangled them in a man's mysterious death.

"My lord! Come quickly!" the valet urged Lyndy through the closed door.

Stella scrambled out of bed and into her dressing gown before Lyndy flung the door open.

"What's the meaning of this, Finn?" Lyndy scolded.

The valet, wearing a thick apron and half sleeves, indicating he'd been shining shoes, flinched but held firm. "Mr. Green is here, my lord, and Fulton said to fetch you, 'with a mind to make haste.'"

"Is it one of the horses?" Stella demanded, joining Lyndy at the door. Why else would the veterinarian be here at dawn on Christmas Eve? "Finn?"

"It's not . . . Please, just come." His voice came out like a choke, unable to say more. He didn't have to.

As they rushed past her door, Alice, her blond braid thrown over one shoulder, peeked out. She clutched her pink dressing gown to her neck. "What's going on?"

"Mr. Green is here, and something's wrong," Stella said as they raced past.

Something must be very wrong. The front door gaped open.

Framed in its narrow view was the veterinarian's horse, Honey, a mild-mannered mare the color of her name, still hitched to a black wooden sleigh with red leather seats parked in the drive. Behind Honey stretched her tracks and that of the sleigh, marking Mr. Green's approach through the pure white snow. On the periphery, people milled around. Servants, clustering together, shivered off to one side. The view captured unseeing stares of disbelief, eyes rimmed red with crying, handkerchiefs held in fists pressed against lips, hands not used to idleness twisting apron ties. Beyond them, Lord Atherly, normally distracted but stoic, paced as Stella had seen Lyndy do so often, in and out of view, treading a path in the snow.

"What the devil?" Lyndy called out to his mother.

"What is everyone doing out there?"

Lady Atherly, in her dressing gown with her fur cap thrown around her shoulders, turned her steely back toward them to respond.

Honey tossed her head, jingling the bells around her neck, obscuring what Lady Atherly said.

Sir Edwin, dressed in tweeds and boots for an early morning hike or ride, rushed up behind them. Bleary-eyed but concerned, Freddy, who'd thrown a dressing gown over his pajamas, was descending the stairs with Alice. Sir Edwin unceremoniously squeezed past them.

"What's happened?" Sir Edwin demanded.

"Perhaps Mr. Green would be kind enough to explain?" Lady Atherly said wearily, dark circles under her eyes.

Mr. Green, slipping the tan fedora from his head, stepped from beside the sleigh. His hair was disheveled. The chest and sleeves of his overcoat were drenched. He looked exhausted. Stella released Lyndy's hand, skipped down the stairs, and trudged through the snow toward him.

"What are you doing here, Mr. Green?" The unease around her grew with every step. Millie, whom Stella had last seen with a mop and bucket clenched in her fist, now appeared to be trying to eat her knuckles. No one breathed a word. "Finn said it wasn't the horses, but I want to hear it from you."

Stella's heart sank when the vet wouldn't meet her gaze. "Tully!"

She balled her dressing gown into each fist and took two running steps toward the stables before Lord Atherly, his pacing bringing him closest to her, stepped in to stall her.

"No, my dear," he said, holding up his palms like one might

soothe a skittish horse. "Rest easy. Tully and all the horses are well."

Stella could've slumped into his arms in relief. Pressing her hand to her fast-beating heart, she nodded in gratitude to her father-in-law.

"Then what's this all bloody about?" Lyndy demanded as he stomped through the snow, knees high, attempting to keep the shoes he'd hastily slipped on dry.

Honey whinnied, the bells' jiggles discordant with the horse's fear. The servants studied the snow-covered drive. Stella's in-laws glared at the vet, who turned his hat in hand. No one would answer him.

"Tell us why you're here, Mr. Green," Stella insisted.

"Yes, well . . ." The vet pinched his chin until it was red. "I woke well before dawn . . . and not having seen him since early evening, I set out to check on Orson this morning. As you re-call, I had to — "

"Yes, we recall, Mr. Green." Lyndy rubbed his hands up and down his arms. Neither he nor Stella had remembered to don overcoats. "And we've already established there's nothing wrong with the animals. So?"

"Well, I hitched up Honey, and on my way here, I came across . . ." He couldn't finish his sentence. He bit his lip, clip-ping a painful-looking fever blister, and he used his hat to mo-tion toward the sleigh. "I'm so sorry."

As Stella gravitated toward the sleigh, others stepped back. Everyone except Lyndy, who clasped her hand as they rounded the sleigh's side. Together they peered into it. Behind them, someone's breath caught in a stifled sob. Laying crumbled in the footwell of the backseat, among empty gunnysacks stamped in red with *RACEHORSE OATS*, was the body of a woman, her limbs limp and twisting in unnatural directions, her un-blinking gaze frozen on the gray clouds. Scratches, caked in dried blood, marked one side of her face. Bits of wool thread clung to her lace collar. Her dress was a patchwork of darkened splotches, reminiscent of a crazy quilt stitched out of mourning attire. Was it from the melted snow or spilt blood? Stella couldn't tell.

Mrs. Nelson was wearing her usual black dress.

CHAPTER 9

"Right! Explain to me again why we're here," Inspector Brown grumbled, pulling the collar against the back of his bare neck. His wife had recommended a muffler, but being called to Morrington Hall, Brown had expected a chat by a roaring fire, not an inspection of a stretch of snow-covered lane. He was getting too old for this. "Why is there reason to suspect this is anything but an accident?"

He'd performed a cursory examination of the housekeeper in Morrington Hall's drive. The woman had bloody scratches on the side of her head, and her left limbs bent at an unnatural angle. She appeared to be a woman who fell in the dark and broke her limbs, hitting her head in the process. Nothing more.

"Because, as I said before, Dr. Johnstone suspected she'd ingested something toxic and had no business being out in the middle of a wintery night," Lady Lyndhurst said. "The last time I saw her, Mrs. Nelson was too sick to even get out of bed. So why was she here?"

If it had been anyone but Lady Lyndhurst, Brown would've sluffed off any bit of concern and been back in front of his fire long ago. People get poisoned every day: from water, food, medicine, and cleaning solutions, to name but a few. Hadn't he heard the honeymooning couple had encountered a man in York who'd been asphyxiated by gas poisoning? Foul play was rarely suspected. The unexplained bit was the housekeeper's midnight trek in the snow. The weather certainly wasn't conducive for a pleasant stroll. As always, Lady Lyndhurst had made her point.

What had the housekeeper been doing out here?

Mistletoe Lane was a picturesque but isolated lane connecting Rosehurst with Burley, passing near Morrington Hall. Like a tunnel, thick, black poplar trees, known for having mistletoe thriving in their higher branches, lined the lane. Beyond the towering trees, dense forest darkened the road to one side, the open moor stretching on the other. Smoke, rising from the few cottages they'd passed on their way here, curled up into the gray sky in the distance, carrying the scent of burning peat on the breeze. No other sign of human habitation was in sight.

Beginning to lose feeling in his toes, Brown stomped his feet, leaving overlaying footprints in the snow. Surveying the lane, he realized if anything untoward had occurred here last night, all evidence of it would be under a blanket of snow. His and the other footprints marked their approach from where they'd left the sleighs a bit up the lane, but here only the tracks made by Mr. Green's horse, sleigh, and his subsequent lifting of the body into it remained.

Perhaps Dr. Lipscombe will prove more helpful.

After his cursory inspection of the body, Brown had led Mr. Green, with his grisly cargo, to the surgery of the medical examiner. Lord Lyndhurst's butler, Fulton, had agreed to telephone ahead, saving Brown the onus of rousing the elderly physician from his bed. After he, along with Mr. Green and Lord Lyndhurst, had assisted in bringing the body inside, Brown had left the dead housekeeper in Dr. Lipscombe's capable hands.

Brown kicked at the bracken and brush along the edge of the lane as the others did the same.

"Did you find or see anything near the body, Mr. Green?"

Brown had required Mr. Green's assistance to lead him to where he'd discovered the body, explain the pattern of footprints, and describe the state he'd found the body in. That explained his presence. Should it have surprised him that Lord and Lady Lyndhurst had also insisted on coming along? No, and yet it still did.

"I didn't notice anything," the veterinarian said, swallowing hard. "Should I have?"

"One can hope."

Brown had found little about the woman's person to indicate her intentions. She hadn't been wearing a shawl or overcoat and was missing her customary string of keys. When Brown inspected the housekeeper's bedchamber, those lay in a heap on the nightstand. And though her dress had lacked pockets, Brown had found a handbag and two small coin purses in a dresser drawer. Only the shoes on her feet suggested she meant to leave her room.

Spying something out of place, Brown lifted a branch and was rewarded by a shower of snow tumbling down from the leaves above, some slipping past his upturned collar and melting down his bare neck. Brown cringed at the snow's icy touch. He brushed the remainder off before inspecting what he'd found—a piece of clear, broken glass. He questioned why he pocketed it, assured it had nothing to do with Mrs. Nelson.

Because one never knows.

"What are we searching for, Brown?" Lord Lyndhurst demanded, seemingly as unpleased with searching the snowy brush in this cold as he was.

"Anything out of the ordinary, anything belonging to the housekeeper or anyone else for that matter."

"Something like this?"

Lady Lyndhurst, barely recognizable in all her furs and mufflers, was on her knees, reaching into a mound of snow. Sitting back on her heels, she lifted the corner of her prize—a gray woolen blanket. It was easy to see how Mr. Green or anyone could've missed seeing it. She pulled the bulk of it out from under the snow. A few small stains of blood dotted one of the heavily threaded edges. But did it belong to the victim?

"This was on her bed. I remember tucking it around her last night."

"Well done, Lady Lyndhurst." Not for the first time, Brown wished he could employ the American viscountess on the department's behalf. She was more observant than his station full of constables.

Brushing snow-crusted twigs and leaves from her overcoat, Lady Lyndhurst shrugged.

"She must've grabbed it in place of an overcoat or shawl. But was it because she was in a hurry? Or because she was feverish and not thinking straight?"

"From what you said, Stella, my bet's on a pinch of delirium," Lord Lyndhurst quipped.

"And the last time you saw Mrs. Nelson and this blanket, my lady?"

"It was after two when Dr. Johnstone left."

"Was Mrs. Nelson, like her blanket, covered in snow when you found her, Mr. Green?"

The veterinarian, blanching at the memory, nodded. He pulled a handkerchief from his breast pocket and wiped his red-tipped nose. "It was ghastly to see, I can assure you."

Brown had gotten up to relieve himself at half past four. The snow had abated by then. That gave him a window of little more than two and a half hours.

"Assuming she walked, it took her . . . how long, Lord Lyndhurst?"

"I'd say twenty, maybe twenty-five minutes."

"Or more, considering she was so sick," added his wife.

"Then, assuming it took Mrs. Nelson twenty to thirty minutes to reach this point, she would've had to have left Morrington Hall by four at the latest. But why choose this path? This lane is only one way to get to the village, assuming that was where she was going. There are others."

"And why assume she walked?" Lady Lyndhurst suggested. "Isn't it more likely she was driven, considering her condition? If her footprints can be covered by the snow, so can carriage wheel tracks."

Brown agreed. He couldn't rule either possibility out. "But by whom?"

Lady Lyndhurst shrugged.

Brown stomped his feet again. None of it made sense, and they weren't getting anywhere.

"Right! I say we leave it for now. Dr. Lipscombe will examine the body and determine whether Mrs. Nelson's death is a matter for the police. Without further evidence, I'm inclined to believe she died of her illness or a fall caused by it. And although it doesn't warrant further investigation at this point, if it suits you, my lord, I would like to speak to some of the Morrington Hall staff. To fill in the gaps."

Lady Lyndhurst's posture softened with relief. "I was hoping you'd say that."

Brown had come to learn through their many interactions on previous cases that Her Ladyship didn't like unexplained coincidences any more than he did.

"Though I doubt the countess will be pleased," she added.

"It will infuriate her," Lord Lyndhurst said with a hint of sardonic glee. "So, by all means, interrogate whomever you must."

Stella opened the next drawer and flipped through the tidy stacks of blank note paper and merchant receipts.

"I still don't think we should be doing this." Lyndy stood guard with his back against the door.

If there was a clue as to why Mrs. Nelson was found on Mistletoe Lane, Stella should find it here. Instead of complaining, Lyndy could be helping her search.

"I offered to do this by myself."

While Inspector Brown was busy interviewing the servants, Stella, unable to eat more than toast slathered with orange marmalade, had tried to preoccupy herself. She'd considered saddling up Tully but couldn't risk her mare stepping into a hole filled with snow. She'd offered to lend the maids a hand in finishing the decorating, but Millie was insistent it was all done. With few other choices at this hour, Stella had found a book and settled in to read in the library with Lady Atherly and Lyndy. The three had sat in companionable silence until Lady Isabella had arrived, a woven, two-sided wicker knitting basket draped over one arm.

"There you are, Frances," Lady Isabella had said. "I want you to know that, considering the circumstances, there will be no hard feelings if you wish us to leave."

"What circumstances?" Stella's mother-in-law had asked.

Lyndy glanced up from his sporting newspaper, his lips fixed in concern.

"Because your housekeeper's dead, of course. How can you possibly have a proper Christmas now with no housekeeper to keep things running smoothly?"

Lady Atherly stiffened her stance. "No need for you to leave, Isabella. We have it in hand."

"However will you manage? And at this time of year?" Lady Isabella settled into the leather armchair closest to the fire and procured an unfinished swath of forest-green yarn from her basket. Over the clicking of her needles, she added, "My daughter Emily once had a housekeeper give notice on Easter and . . ."

To avoid Lady Isabella's elaborate retelling of her daughter's difficulty finding a replacement, Stella had excused herself. She couldn't sit idle a minute longer, waiting for news from the inspector. She had to do something. Lyndy, seizing the opportunity to leave with her, had now become her unwitting accomplice.

"What are you looking for?" Lyndy asked.

"I don't know."

It wasn't a large room but brightly whitewashed. It held a mahogany desk covered in overlapping ledgers and pigeonholes stuffed with letters and receipts. A lace-covered side table, equipped with a red-glass shaded lamp and extra chair, sat beside it. A plush, overstuffed armchair and another side table held the corner between two bookshelves.

This was the study of a woman who'd been with the family for more than twenty-five years?

Besides some bric-a-brac from trips to the sea, a crystal bowl filled with freshly cut holly, and a single Christmas card from the local butcher's wife on the mantel, there was little to tell whose domain this was.

But Stella, wanting to be thorough, took time to delve into the housekeeper's things, however few there were. Too much time, in Lyndy's opinion, if the tugging on his sleeve and his tapping foot were any indication.

He selected a mince pie from a gold-rimmed plate left on top of the nearest bookshelf. "Would you like one?" Lyndy offered it to her. A perfect star had been cut out of the top of the pastry.

She loved the tradition of mince pies and "Stir-up Sunday," when Mrs. Cole tolerated visitors to her kitchen, allowing everyone to stir the Christmas pudding-to-be. Stella looked forward to embracing all of these new Christmas culinary traditions.

Just not now. With the scent of last night's sickness and the sight of Mrs. Nelson's body this morning still haunting her, even the cinnamon-laden aroma of the mince pie caused her stomach to churn.

"Maybe later." Stella waved it off and went back to her search.

Lyndy took a small taste of the spiced pastry. His face puckered in disgust as he gagged the bite down. He dropped it and the uneaten portion in the nearby wastepaper basket.

"I say, those are quite off Mrs. Cook's normal standards. Quite off, indeed."

Stella chuckled, experiencing the first lightness since learning Mrs. Nelson's fate. She picked a book from one of the bookshelves and read *Lett's Improved Housekeeper's Account Book and Diary*. She shook the book by its spine, hoping a telltale letter would flutter out. No such luck. She did the same to the others, each a practical guide relating to her role as housekeeper.

"There's nothing here."

"I did try to tell you," Lyndy said, brushing onto a pant leg the sugar from the mince pie still stuck to his fingers. It was a careless gesture Stella might do, but Lyndy? She wanted to kiss him. How far he'd come from that stuffy, arrogant man she'd first met. His mother would cringe. Lyndy gestured toward the door. "Shall we?"

As Stella passed, she glanced into the wastebasket to see the distasteful mince pie with Lyndy's one bite missing. It lay beside a piece of paper, tightly scrunched into a ball. Stella snatched it up, uncrumpled it, and smoothed it out on Mrs. Nelson's desk. On stationery embossed with a flamboyant *K*, a single sentence was written in a florid hand: *I hope our secret is safe with you.*

"*K* for Kentfield?" Stella wondered out loud.

"It has to be. But which one?" Lyndy said, peering over her shoulder. "And what secret did Mrs. Nelson know?"

"Assuming this was meant for her. It isn't addressed." Stella was inclined to tell the inspector, but Lyndy urged caution.

"Until we know the housekeeper died of anything but an accident, this might be better left between us. No need to air others' dirty laundry without justification."

Stella folded the paper and tucked it into Lyndy's breast pocket. "Just in case," she said, patting the spot.

Smoke dulled the austere edges of the hall as Stella and Lyndy emerged from Mrs. Nelson's study, and the smell of burned food was inescapable. Clattering and banging from the kitchen echoed toward them, with Inspector Brown's gruff voice audible but indistinguishable beyond.

Would Mrs. Cole know who *K* was? Stella would have to wait to ask.

One of the boiler workers appeared at the far end of the hall, coughing and waving his hat to dispel the smoke. He wasn't dressed in his work clothes but in a dark blue suit, what appeared to be his Sunday best. He carried the long, heavy wrench.

"Here to fix the boiler, Mr. Stott?" Stella called.

"Milady!" The workman, precariously balancing the wrench on his shoulder, used the tips of his fingers to straighten his tie.

"I thought you chaps finished up yesterday," Lyndy said.

"We did, milord," the workman grumbled.

"Then why was there no heat?"

"That's why I'm here, innit?" the workman muttered.

Lyndy raised an eyebrow at the man's tone. Mr. Stott's knuckles tightened on the handle of the massive wrench as he shifted it on his shoulder.

"Don't you worry. I'll fix it."

"Glad to hear it."

"Yes, we wouldn't want it to keep you from your Christmas festivities," Stella said, hoping to ease the tension. "And when you're finished, I'm sure Mrs. Cole wouldn't mind giving you refreshment before you go." A loud crash from the kitchen refuted Stella's assumption. "Though I'd skip whatever it was they burned in there."

The workman forced a chuckle.

"I'm certain Mr. Stott has better things to do than endure Mrs. Cole's incivility," Lyndy, impatient to distance himself from the disgruntled workman, said before bounding partway up the stairwell. "As do we." It was time to change for luncheon.

"Thank you kindly, milady, but I must be getting on."

"Merry Christmas again then, Mr. Stott," Stella said before tripping up the stairs after Lyndy.

As Lyndy pushed open the green baize door, a prickling on the back of her neck made Stella glance back.

Mr. Stott, his lip curled, stood at the bottom of the stairs, hat in hand, watching them ascend.

CHAPTER 10

Inspector Brown, fortified by the cup of tea he held in his lap, watched Mrs. Cole stomp about the kitchen as if it were a battlefield: readying the ammunition, bayoneting the advancing enemy, preparing for the inevitable casualties. The cook pounded dough. She checked boiling pots, dropping the copper lids down with a deafening clang. She chopped vegetables with knives that could slice off more than a man's finger. When a young scullery maid entered empty-handed, she pointed the girl back the way she came, demanding she be useful. Brown didn't know if this was grief manifesting itself or business as usual.

Noting the scent of cinnamon and baking bread, Brown didn't care. At least he wasn't sequestered in Lord Atherly's smoking room again. The third time was not the charm. Instead, Mr. Fulton had been kind enough to allow Brown to conduct his interviews from the comfort of the servants' hall, with the understanding he kept out of the kitchen. It was a wonder then that Brown now sat precisely in the corner of that bastion of productivity.

If only they hadn't burned the gingerbread. He'd fancied a piece with his tea.

Morrington Hall's housekeeper was dead. How? Why? Lady Lyndhurst thought the whole thing suspect; Brown had his own ideas. But if anyone knew, it would be her fellow servants: the butler, the cook, or the maids. Out of respect, Brown had started with Mr. Fulton. That capable fellow detailed Mrs. Nelson's efficiency, her strict but fair treatment of the staff, and, when prodded, her illness that consumed the final hours of her life. His description closely matched the account Lady Lyndhurst had volunteered. Next came a string of maids, from the two lady's maids to the scullery maid, who, much needed in the kitchen, was granted only a few moments and, like the others, seemed genuinely to know little of what occurred the night before. It was her inattention to her tasks that resulted in the ruined pudding.

So that left one maid, Millie Jones, who had yet to come downstairs from performing her duties in the bedchambers, and Mrs. Cole. The cook had grudgingly agreed to Brown's interview but only if she could continue working as necessary. Didn't he know it was Christmas Eve? Didn't he understand, without a housekeeper, what chaos could ensue if the preparation of the day's special menu was interrupted? Hadn't he seen what had happened to the gingerbread?

This last accusation she'd delivered as she smacked the pan against the table, hoping to dislodge the offending blackened mass.

Brown had taken all of the cook's abuse hoping she would know something, anything, that could shed light on Mrs. Nelson's late-night wanderings.

"And you can't think of any reason why Mrs. Nelson would've left her bed and gone out into the night?"

"Why should I?" Over her shoulder, Mrs. Cole barked an order at a kitchen maid, something about "the gooseberry sauce."

Prickles ran down the back of Brown's neck. He willed himself not to move to the edge of his seat and declare, *I know you're hiding something from me.* Instead, he sipped the last of his tea, grimacing; it had grown cold.

"Besides Mrs. Nelson taking ill, can you remember anything unusual about last night, or any time yesterday, perhaps?" It was the same question he'd posed to the others with no result.

"My mince pies went missing."

That wasn't what Brown was expecting. "And you think that's relevant to Mrs. Nelson's death?"

"What? No. Don't be daft. But you asked if anything unusual happened." She tested the thickness of the crust a maid was laying in a baking dish and nodded in approval. "Mrs. Nelson also had a visitor yesterday."

"Was that unusual?" Despite himself, Brown leaned forward.

"I'd say. Her parents are both gone, and she their only child."

"Who was it?"

"How should I know? They never came so far as the kitchen."

"Couldn't it simply have been a tradesman?"

"Why would a tradesman upset her?"

"She was upset after this visit?"

"Didn't I say she was? When she came in, her face was white as sugar." A faraway expression flitted across the cook's face. A crack in the crust as the older woman appeared on the brink of tears. Then she blinked, and the moment was gone. She removed her spectacles, wiping them on her apron. "That's all I know, so off with you. I have luncheon to prepare."

Bounding down the stairs, the round-faced maid nearly collided with Brown, fetching his hat and overcoat off the peg rack in the hall. "I have to tell you something, Inspector."

"Miss Millie Jones?" Brown had almost forgotten about her. With his interviews concluded, or so he thought, he'd been eager to get back for his wife's promised roast dinner. His son and family were expected to arrive any time now.

"I don't want to get anyone in trouble, but . . ." the maid said, breathing heavily from her sprint down the stairs.

"But?"

"But . . ." The maid crossed and uncrossed her arms. A strip of linen, tied off at the end, wound around her thumb.

"Cut yourself?" Brown pointed to her thumb.

"It's the evergreens. They can be ever so sharp."

"Right! What's this all about, then?"

"It's about Mrs. Nelson." As if it could be about anything else. "I thought you should know she dismissed Louisa, the newest chambermaid, yesterday. Without a reference."

"And you think this maid had something to do with Mrs. Nelson's death?" Had Lady Lyndhurst's penchant for seeing a fantastical murder in every unusual death been passed on?

The maid shook her head so passionately that her cap's ruffles fluttered.

"Do calm yourself, Millie. Mrs. Nelson's death was probably due to her illness, nothing more."

"You don't understand."

"It was an accident." Lady Lyndhurst had explained this particular maid had found the sickened housekeeper. Did she blame herself for leaving her unattended? "I understand you had to find your bed eventually, Millie. It was late. You were tired. No one blames you."

"But that's what I've been trying to tell you." The maid crossed her arms once again. "I think Louisa might be. To blame, that is. Before she left, I overheard her threaten to poison Mrs. Nelson's tea."

If someone had told Constable Waterman he'd be spending Christmas Eve on a train to Bournemouth, he would've called them daft. He'd expected to spend the day typing up this week's crime reports: an attempted burglary at Judge Peterson's tower in Sway, a domestic dispute between a farm laborer and his wife involving a spade, and three incidents of petty theft, two involving stolen turkeys. If he'd gotten done early, he wouldn't have minded spending a few extra hours at home with Meredith, especially now that she was expecting.

I'm going to be a father.

Waterman let the heady idea sink in as the scenery, a patchwork of grazing lawns, heath, and leafless woodland blanketed in fresh snow, sped past. Maybe he'd have to take his inspector's exam as Meredith had been urging him to do for years. The extra income would come in handy. But it would require a move away from the New Forest, the only place he'd ever known.

"Oi! Do you mind?" Waterman, packed in with the rest of them in the third-class carriage, leaned against the window to avoid being elbowed by the gent beside him as the man opened his broadsheet. The glass was welcomingly cool.

But would he fancy the extra responsibility? He stared at the domed helmet in his lap. It wasn't a question of choice, though, was it? He needed to provide for his growing family.

And I wouldn't have to go on pointless errands like this one.

Waterman wasn't one to question his boss, but how could anyone believe Mrs. Nelson's death was anything but the direct result of her illness? Yet on the word of a maid, Waterman was ordered to track down this Louisa Bright, the alleged poisoner. On Christmas Eve!

When the train arrived at Bournemouth Central station, Waterman disembarked, eager to tackle the task at hand as quickly as possible. If he located the maid or at least learned of her whereabouts, he could be heading back on the 6:40.

He retrieved his pocket notebook, flipped through to the right page, and found the information Inspector Brown had given him—the addresses Louisa Bright had supplied to Mrs. Nelson when she'd applied for the position at Morrington

Hall. The first on the list was Miss Bright's family home. After a bit of a hike through the seaside city, gathering the damp, salty air on his uniform overcoat, Waterman arrived at a newly built, three-story, gabled, brick house with a prominent curved bay window. It was far more posh than Waterman expected, the maid being in service and all. Perhaps Inspector Brown got it wrong. Perhaps this was the address of her past employer.

Waterman, uncertain whether to approach the front door or the tradesmen's entrance, opted for discretion and went around to the back. A harried-looking, middle-aged woman in a starched white apron answered the door.

"What can I do for you, young man?" She licked her palms and smoothed the loose frizz on the top of her head.

"Constable Waterman, ma'am." He showed his warrant card. "Is this the residence of Miss Louisa Bright?"

"Who? I don't know any Louisa Bright." She absentmindedly dried her hands on her apron. "Mind, there used to be a Bright family who attended the same church as the Kirklands, but they moved to India some years back."

"The Kirklands?"

"The family who owns this here house."

"Of course. Could Miss Bright have lived here before—?"

"Before what? Constable, I've worked in this house for this family for gone eighteen years." She leaned her ample hip against the doorsill. "What do you want her for? Maybe I can ask around?"

"That won't be necessary."

"How about a cup of tea then, for your trouble?" She peered out from the door to check the sky. "It'll be dark soon. I've got fresh mince pies straight out of the oven." The hall behind her did smell lovely.

"If it's all the same to you, I best be on my way." Waterman touched the brim of his hat.

"Pity. A strapping chap like you needs nourishing."

Waterman lifted his collar against the wind brewing at his back. "Good day, and Happy Christmas to you."

The second address brought him to a lane lined with white-washed Georgian terrace cottages, each door donning a similar leafy wreath of holly.

Like you'd see on a Christmas card.

Waterman lifted the wrought-iron knocker of number 22 and rapped three times. He whacked the side of his boot against the other to kick off the dirty snow he'd collected tramping through the slushy streets. No answer. He knocked again. When the door finally opened, it was by a frail, elderly man wrapped in a wool blanket, smelling of linseed and shoe polish. He squinted at Waterman's warrant card when he'd introduced himself. A flock of squawking seagulls flew overhead, and Waterman had to repeat himself three times.

"Louisa Bright, you say?" The old man held a hand to the back of his ear. "I don't know a Louisa Bright."

"Do you have a daughter or granddaughter, perchance, sir?"

"No, no. Only sons, you see. My eldest lives in London. He's a boot maker. Might've even made those." He pointed to Waterman's feet. "He has a daughter. Little Annie is starting to learn her letters. My middle son works for the London and South Western Railway at Weymouth but, like me, only has boys. My youngest, well, I don't see much of him." The old man offered a rueful smile, but then his expression brightened. "But they're all expected tomorrow night, you see, for Christmas."

"That's splendid."

Waterman ached suddenly to be in the bosom of his family. When had he last seen his father? Would he one day be this old man missing his sons? The constable hadn't intended a visit, but Meredith would understand his need to carve out a bit of time tomorrow to travel to Fritham. It was Christmas, after all.

"But no woman in her late twenties to speak of?"

What made Waterman think to ask, he didn't know. Was it the prospect of returning to Lyndhurst empty-handed? Or was he beginning to suspect that the maid Mrs. Nelson fired wasn't who she said she was? Louisa Bright, or whatever her name was, had provided two false addresses.

Maybe he was fit to be an inspector.

"Late twenties, you say? No, none. My wife was sixty-seven when she passed."

"A maid of that age, perhaps?"

"We did have a maid about that age before my wife died. She seemed a good girl, but I had no need of her once I was on my own. I let her go about three years gone now."

"Could you describe her?"

"I don't normally take much notice of maids, but who could ignore such a freckled face? She had a pleasant smile and lovely, copper-colored hair." The description matched the one Inspector Brown had given him. "I get a Christmas card from her every year." He turned as if to fetch it, but Waterman forestalled him.

"And what name did you know your maid by, Mr. . . . . ?"

"It's Allsup, Jacob Allsup, and my wife called her Liza. Don't think I ever knew her surname."

"You don't happen to recall where Liza's card was postmarked from this year, do you?"

"I do. Not much else to preoccupy me these days, young man. She mailed it from Rosehurst. In the New Forest."

Waterman allowed himself a satisfied smile as he touched the brim of his cap. "Much obliged, Mr. Allsup. You've been most helpful."

It was the same woman, and she'd been lying to everyone. Perhaps there was something to Inspector Brown's suspicions, after all.

CHAPTER 1 1

Lyndy emerged from his dressing room, flinging a tweed scarf around his neck. "Shall we?"

How handsome and relaxed he looked.

Stella, pinning a cameo brooch to her jacket, smiled at him. "Give me a few more minutes, and I'll be ready to go."

Lyndy laid his hands on Stella's shoulders, their eyes meeting in the reflection of the dressing table mirror.

"Have I told you how much I adore you today?"

"If you have, it bears repeating," she teased.

"I adore you," he whispered, kissing the crown of her head. "I adore you," he repeated, his breath warm on her cheek as he kissed it. "I adore you."

When his kisses traveled down the length of her neck, nudging down the lace of her high collar, she playfully shooed him away.

"The yule log, remember?"

Having found nothing to help Inspector Brown in Mrs. Nelson's study, Stella had reluctantly agreed to let her questions about Mrs. Nelson's death go, for now, and get on with the plans for the day. And that, despite Lyndy's sudden desire to do otherwise, meant "bringing in the yule log." It wasn't a Christmas tradition she'd ever observed, and she was more than willing to forage the nearby woodlands for a log large enough to burn from Christmas Day to Twelfth Night to distract her. Admittedly Lyndy's plan would've succeeded in doing that too, but the burning of the yule log was said to bring good luck.

And couldn't we all use more of that?

"Unlike any yule log that burns for a mere fortnight," Lyndy said, his lips still brushing her skin, "I'll burn for you forever."

His tone was lighthearted, but the shining in his eyes declared his sincerity. Stella's whole body tingled. One word, and they'd not leave the bedroom as promptly as they should.

As if on cue, the radiators clanged and abruptly hissed energetically.

"Go before I change my mind."

"Until later then." Lyndy nibbled on her ear before stepping back. Stella was still giggling when he retreated from the room.

With Stella bundled into one of her warmest walking costumes, a thick wool burgundy and cream plaid skirt with matching jacket, her chemise clung to her back as she waited for Ethel's return. Stella didn't mind. She'd been so cold after their trip to Mistletoe Lane she'd shivered through luncheon. Her first winter in England, and no matter what Stella did, the chill never seemed to leave her bones. Despite the room's now sweltering heat, or the warming cup of coffee she'd sent Ethel to fetch, once Stella stepped outside, she'd be freezing again. Which was why Stella went straight to the drawer where Ethel kept her new, brown leather, fur-lined gloves.

Finding them still in the box, Stella lifted the lid, pulled back the tissue paper, and frowned. There was only one glove. She hadn't even worn them yet. She'd ordered them on their last trip to Lymington.

How can one already be missing?

Stella's disappointment turned to concern when she considered how many other things had disappeared. A handkerchief, a hat pin, her souvenir spoon, a bookmark, and now a glove. Mrs. Nelson had suspected Louisa of stealing them. But what would a housemaid do with one glove?

It's got to be here. She couldn't face what it meant if it wasn't.

Stella yanked out drawer after drawer, rummaging through their contents before slamming them shut and starting on to the next. After tackling the dressing table, she checked both nightstands and then approached the mahogany dresser. On top of a stack of freshly laundered undergarments was a handwritten note on plain stationery addressed to "My dearest Stella." It was a poem, carefully written in block letters. It was unsigned and reeked of bay rum cologne.

> *I will be constant to thee as the rolling tide*
> *Or the lingering moonbeams where shadows deep abide.*
> *Never a harsh word speaking to thee, my only love.*
> *Only a low soft prayer for blessings from above.*

With the memory of Lyndy's touch still on her skin, Stella's stomach rolled, and she hurdled the note away like it had burned her fingers. It floated to the floor. At the click of the turning doorknob, Stella swirled around.

She crushed her hand to her chest in relief. "Oh, it's only you."

"My lady?" Holding the silver coffee tray before her, Ethel stepped into the room.

Of course it was Ethel. Who else, besides her lady's maid or Lyndy, could it be?

Ethel, setting the tray down, proceeded to pour her a cup. She offered it to Stella. "Lord Lyndhurst asked that I remind you that the men are waiting."

"Never mind the coffee." Stella pushed the cup away, spilling a bit of it.

"Is something wrong?" Ethel dabbed at the saucer to soak up the errant liquid with a napkin.

"Have you ever seen that before?" Stella pointed to the note.

Ethel retrieved it from the floor, and her cheeks grew red as her eyes swept over the words.

"Did you put that in my drawer?" Stella demanded, regretting her tone but desperate to know the truth.

At the sight of a stack of chemises poking out of the drawer, Ethel shook her head in vehement denial. "No, of course not. Why would I? My lord doesn't seem like one to need a go-between." She held it out toward Stella.

"I don't want it. Burn it."

"Burn it, my lady? It's rather a lovely sentiment. Wouldn't Lord Lyndhurst—?"

Frustrated by Ethel's hesitation, Stella ripped it from her grip with a vehemence that surprised them both and threw it onto the smoldering fire. The paper curled and browned before bursting into flame. Nothing remained of it but gray ashes.

So why did she still feel sick?

Stella swallowed down the bile rising in her throat. "I'm so sorry, Ethel, but I couldn't stand it a minute longer."

"But why? What's upset you so? I'm sure the viscount meant it"—she paused as she sought an appropriate word—"kindly."

"The viscount?" Stella dug her fingernails into her palms. How awful that Lyndy's affection should be tainted, in any way, by association with that monstrous poem. "You don't see, do you? You couldn't tell?"

With crinkled brows, the maid shook her head in confusion.

"The handwriting, Ethel. It wasn't the viscount's. He didn't put it there." She pointed to the drawer with her undergarments again. "And I have no idea who did."

The stark electric lights strung above Brown reflected off the whitewashed walls making him squint. The incessant dripping tap was enough to drive the dead to distraction. So why leave it? It wasn't so cold that the pipes would freeze. Brown shivered.

Or was it?

Brown hated attending these consultations with Dr. Lipscombe under ordinary circumstances, but on Christmas Eve, while his family impatiently awaited his return, it was almost as unbearable as the formaldehyde smell.

"My roast is getting cold. Can we get on with it?" Inspector Brown grumbled.

"I'm sure this woman would gladly swap places with you, Inspector."

Suitably chastened, Brown nodded for the medical examiner to continue. Dr. Lipscombe, his white hair and recently grown white beard lending an odd bit of St. Nicholas to the proceedings, pulled the sheet back from the dead body on the examination table. Her eyes were closed, and her graying hair lay loose about her bare shoulders, but there was nothing peaceful about Mrs. Nelson's face. Cleaned but jagged scrapes etched her blue-gray skin. Gashes on her cheeks and jawline resembled a pugilist's who'd lost a fight. Although no longer capable of words, Mrs. Nelson's lips shouted the violence she'd endured.

Brown had swept his gaze over Mrs. Nelson in the cart at Morrington Hall, too jaded from the countless bodies he'd encountered to notice more than a bit of blood and the awkward angles of her limbs. It had been an accident. Tragic, yes, but with no wrong for him to right, her death had warranted nothing more than his pity. Until Lady Lyndhurst's concern piqued his interest. Brown forced himself to study every inch, imagining the few times he'd interacted with the Earl of Atherly's housekeeper. She was efficient, tolerant, and cooperative. She'd even sent a maid to tidy up Lord Atherly's smoking room when Brown needed it to conduct interviews in previous investigations. Dr. Lipscombe was right. Christmas Eve festivities be damned.

"What can you tell me, Doctor?"

"The poor woman's stomach and intestines were swollen, and the contents of her stomach were putrid, I grant you, but I don't see signs of anything more toxic as you suggested might have been introduced into her tea. Dr. Johnstone's diagnosis of food poisoning is most likely the correct one." He held up a hand to deflect any premature objections from Brown. "I know what you're going to say, Inspector. The symptoms suffered by the deceased are similar to those caused by other poisons. But hear me out. We can easily rule out strychnine based on the deceased's lack of muscle spasms prior to death. And I've run a Reinsch test for arsenic, antimony, or mercury and detected nothing."

"If food poisoning was the cause of death, what made these scratches on her face—her fall?"

"Always in a rush, aren't you, Inspector?" Dr. Lipscombe tsked. "As I was saying, the deceased suffered from food poisoning. However"—he put his hand again up to stay Brown's tongue—"that was not what killed her."

"Right!" Brown suppressed the urge to tap his foot on the hard, tiled floor. "So, what did kill her?"

Uncharacteristically, Dr. Lipscombe hesitated, then expelled a long, drawn-out exhale. "In the end, blunt-force trauma resulting in a skull fracture that caused internal bleeding."

"She collapsed and died from hitting her head?" What rotten luck.

"You mistake me, Inspector. This woman didn't simply collapse and die from hitting her head. She could have died of any number of things, I'm afraid. Both femurs were fractured, several organs torn or bruised, and she suffered cervical spine distress. I would say this poor woman was struck by something much greater than a boulder on the side of the lane."

"Like what?" What could've caused such damage on a quiet lane early on Christmas Eve?

"From the extent of her injuries, my closest guess would be a moving train."

A train? Brown pinched the bridge of his nose.

"The nearest tracks are more than a mile away. Could the housekeeper have walked or even dragged herself from there to where she was found?"

"Not only could she not have moved that distance, but she also most likely didn't live longer than a few moments after impact."

"Someone moved the body?"

"I can't speak to that. However, from the livor mortis, I can tell you she lay crumpled in the same place for several hours. The rest is beyond my detection, I'm afraid."

Brown cursed the snow, the footprints, hoof prints, and carriage wheel tracks that crisscrossed the site. He couldn't blame the veterinarian for contaminating the scene, but now that Brown knew Mrs. Nelson's death might be far more sinister than a tragic slip in the road by an ill victim, it made his investigation that much more challenging.

"We can't rule out murder, can we?" Brown muttered, already regretting the inevitable disruption of his holiday festivities and those at Morrington Hall.

Dr. Lipscombe shook his head, his white beard wagging as he mercifully replaced the sheet over Mrs. Nelson's head.

"I'm guessing your roast will have to wait."

CHAPTER 1 2

Stella's boots crunched on the encrusted snow as she hopped from her father's Daimler. Long shadows stretched across the enormous swath of land before her, a patchwork of fallow crop fields, recently hayed meadows, stubby stands of heather, and a dense expanse of bare oak, ash, and elm, entirely encompassed by a newly built wooden fence. The not quite finished stone stable block loomed large near the end of the weedy drive. Grazing along the base of the nearest building, a swayback horse happily took advantage of the strip of grass poking through the melting snow.

Would she ever tire of the view?

She'd purchased the land using her inheritance. Although the money legally belonged to Lyndy, he'd needed little persuading to let her buy it. The previous owner's children had long since moved to London, and the eldest son had been actively attempting to sell the land since his father died in the last typhoid outbreak. Yet few in the area could afford it, and those who could had no desire to. As Lady Atherly diligently pointed out, "Who would be foolish enough to purchase such a large slice of inhabitable land (having only a humble cottage attached to it) when livestock can graze freely almost everywhere?"

But Stella knew better. She'd require plenty of good grazing land to rehabilitate injured ponies or retire run-down workhorses. Although the Searlwyns had the right to graze ponies freely elsewhere, the Verderers' Court, which ruled over such things, didn't allow horses, be they stallions, mares, or fillies of foal-bearing age, to intermingle with the New Forest Ponies and potentially taint the breed. So, she'd bought the land, built the stables, and hired a staff, grooms, stableboys, and a stablemaster who lived in the previous owner's cottage. She'd hired Mr. Martin Green. Was each as excited as she was to be a part of her endeavor? She'd liked to think so.

"Impressive, eh?" Lyndy gestured as the men climbed out of the car and joined Stella to admire the view.

A view that soothed the turbulence in her stomach, and mind, the anonymous note had exacerbated.

Wasn't Christmas a time for peace and tranquility, and charity? Were Stella's expectations of a happy Christmas too high? She wouldn't have thought so.

Until Mrs. Nelson died.

A pall of sadness hung over Morrington Hall despite Lady Atherly's attempts to prevent it. Stella's mother-in-law had insisted they hunt for the yule log, the gardeners bring the Christmas tree in as planned, and the kitchen prepare a proper Christmas Eve supper. She wouldn't object, she'd said, if the servants chose to cover their looking glasses with black crape or dress in mourning clothes if they wanted to, as long as it didn't interfere with their duties. Lady Atherly had insisted that it being Christmastime and there being guests, Mrs. Nelson would've understood if not heartily approved.

Stella wasn't so sure about Lady Atherly's plans for gaining Mrs. Nelson's approval. Still, she was silently, and guiltily, relieved that the boughs of holly and garlands of evergreen weren't replaced with swaths of black crape, that the Christmas tree would be trimmed with gaudy baubles and not left outside in the cold. Someday, Stella would honor Mrs. Nelson's memory. She'd learn what the housekeeper had wanted to tell her and act on the news however necessary. She'd prod Inspector Brown to investigate her death further. But for now, Stella was grateful to escape to the Triple R Farm to hunt for a yule log.

But how am I going to tell Lyndy about the love poem? He'll be furious.

"This is all Stella's doing," Lyndy said, a half smirk plastered to his prideful face.

"My, my, young lady. That's quite the accomplishment," Sir Edwin said, saddling up beside her. A bit too close. Stella resisted the urge to step back. "It extends as far as the eye can see and is solely to rehabilitate the animals?"

"It is," Lyndy said. "Of course, Mr. Martin Green, our veterinarian, also sees to the horses at Morrington too. Speaking of which."

The veterinarian emerged from the far stable, his shirtsleeves rolled to his elbows, and his work coat draped in the crook of his arm. As always, he toted his worn leather bag.

Stella called to him. He waved and soon joined the group.

"Aren't you cold, Mr. Green?" Stella said, a shiver running down her spine just looking at him.

"The old mare went into labor this afternoon." He wiped the sweat from his forehead with his bare, muscular forearm.

Ten days ago, a heavily pregnant mare, believed to be well over twenty years old, was found tied to the farm's gate with no note or indication of her owner. They took the mare in without question. What desperation could've led someone to abandon the horse, Stella couldn't imagine. But it was that hopelessness that she hoped to alleviate.

"Attending a difficult birth has its way of keeping you

warm." The vet chuckled mirthlessly. To answer the question on Stella's face, he added, "Mare and filly are miraculously both doing well. Thank goodness."

"How are you holding up?" Lyndy said. "After this morning, that is."

A few months ago, Lyndy wouldn't have given a second thought as to how someone in his employ fared. Stella wanted to kiss him for his thoughtfulness but would save her sign of approval for later.

"As much as can be expected," the vet admitted, his free arm reaching across his chest and clutching the one holding the leather bag. "It was such a shock. Have you heard anything more from the police?"

"No," Stella said. "Inspector Brown is still trying to figure out if the maid poisoned Mrs. Nelson and why the housekeeper was out of her sickbed in the middle of the night."

"It's passing strange," Freddy said.

"I forget my manners," Lyndy said. "Mr. Green, may I introduce Sir Edwin Kentfield and his son, Mr. Frederick Kentfield. They are our guests for the holidays. Mr. Green is our new veterinarian."

"Freddy," Frederick Kentfield said, offering a hearty handshake.

"Martin."

"Of course, we saw Mr. Green this morning," Sir Edwin said, acknowledging the vet with a light touch to the brim of his tweed cap. "Ghastly business."

"Indeed." Lyndy tamped snow down with his feet.

With the memory hovering among them, no one else spoke. Mr. Green donned his work coat, the heat of his exertion having worn off. Freddy regarded a buzzard lazily circling above them. Sir Edwin stared into the middle distance. Stella deeply breathed in the crisp air keeping the image of Mrs. Nelson's mangled body at bay.

A horse's nicker, carried across the still, snowy expanse, broke the silence.

"You seem so familiar," Mr. Green said, producing a handkerchief from his work coat and wiping his dripping nose. "Have we met before today?"

"I can't say as I recall," Freddy said. "Can you, Father?"

Sir Edwin stiffened. "No, no, I think it's highly improbable. We always used Brumby to tend our horses."

"Oh, right," Mr. Green conceded. "I must be mistaken." Yet his chewed lip said otherwise. Then his eyes lit up. "Were you at the Knightwood Oak last night? It was quite the crowd, and after a few, it all got a bit fuzzy, but I seem to recall—"

"You must be mistaken, Mr. Green," Sir Edwin said, cutting the vet off.

"Actually—" Freddy began.

"Mr. Green is mistaken."

Freddy, whom Stella had only seen jovial and warm, cast a cold, reproachful glance at his father.

What was that all about?

Right!" Sir Edwin clapped once, a forced smile on his face. The nearby swayback gelding skittered sideways in surprise. He laid a hand on Stella's shoulder and leaned closer, his breath smelling of the oysters she'd avoided eating at lunch.

"Shall we have a bit of a look around and see if we can't find ourselves a yule log?"

He winked and then strode across the field toward the woodland's edge, leaving his son to dash to catch up.

Stella was glad to see him go.

"That's me off then," Mr. Green said, drawing Stella's attention back. She'd been following the Kentfields' march across the paddock, their heads bent in conversation. With the breeze picking up, she hadn't made out a single word.

"After the day you've had, you deserve to put your feet up," she said.

"With a whiskey or two," Lyndy added.

"Now, that does sound lovely, my lord," Mr. Green chuckled. "I wonder how late Mr. Heppenstall stays open on Christmas Eve?" The vet, the anticipation of visiting the pub on his face, moved to pass by them.

Stella, waylaying him a moment longer, said, "I hope you know you did all you could for Mrs. Nelson."

The vet responded with a humble shrug. "I wonder. But it's kind of you to say, my lady."

"Merry Christmas, Mr. Green. We'll both see you at the race on Boxing Day." Her emphasis on *both* made him smile.

"Indeed, you will, my lady. And I'll make sure both ponies are in racing condition. May I wish you and Your Lordship a very Happy Christmas as well." With a deferential nod, he took his leave.

As the vet hitched Honey to his carriage, a picture of Mrs. Nelson's broken body in the footwell flashed in her mind. I *should get Mr. Green a new carriage.* If she pictured the dead housekeeper, she imagined he did too. As Mr. Green's carriage rumbled away, she sought the bucolic vista of the Triple R Farm to erase the unhappy mental scene and fortify her for her next unpleasant task. It worked its charm again.

"Lyndy, today, among my chemises, I found—"

"Are you coming, Lyndy, Lady Lyndhurst?" Sir Edwin called from the shadowy edge of the woods. "There's bound to be a good log in here."

"What was it you were saying?" Lyndy said, offering his arm.

Stella lost her nerve. She held up the red ribbon they'd brought to tie to the log. "We have the perfect yule log to find. It can wait."

CHAPTER 13

"Inspector Brown to see Lady Lyndhurst," Fulton announced.

Stella wiped the ladyfinger crumbles and Bavarian cream clinging to her lip from her last bite of Charlotte Russe, tossed aside her napkin, and rose. With a sudden clattering of teacups and saucers to the table, so too did Sir Edwin, Lyndy, and her father-in-law. Still not used to the courtesy—her father wouldn't have stood in respect unless a Kentucky Derby winner was at stake—Stella promptly motioned to the gentlemen to sit down.

Despite the tragedy that had struck the house, Mrs. Cole had outdone herself. Spread on the table, embellished with a ring of glossy ivy garland, were two- and three-tiered cake stands laden with a variety of sandwiches, mini lobster vol-au-vent, cheese bouchées, cream scones, rhubarb and custard scones, mince pies, Bakewell tarts, Scottish shortbread, and raspberry meringues, along with the crowning Charlotte Russe that sat on a pedestal plate. Stella couldn't have envisioned a more festive meal, with its accents of red berries and lobster, green cucumber slices, and watercress sprigs.

And this is only Christmas Eve tea! What could Mrs. Cole be preparing for dinner?

Had this been planned to impress the Kentfields, were they enjoying an annual tradition, or had Mrs. Cole poured her grief into her cooking? Whichever it was, despite her curiosity about what the inspector had come to tell her, Stella was reluctant to leave.

"I can't imagine any policeman in London being so impertinent as to interrupt our afternoon tea," Lady Isabella scoffed, the gold rim of her teacup touching her lip. "Neither Emily nor Maud would abide it either."

Lady Atherly's breath was audible as she smoothed her skirt over her lap, but she remained surprisingly mum on the subject. Stella couldn't let the comment pass.

"It may seem like an imposition, Lady Isabella, but we're lucky the inspector is considerate enough to keep us informed. Especially with the unusual circumstances of Mrs. Nelson's death and the time of year. I'm sure he could think of more pleasant things to do this afternoon than interrupting us."

Lady Atherly's lips rose in approval as she added, "Indeed. I'm sure you'll agree, Isabella, that we do what we must to keep this a private matter. We wouldn't want your daughters to read about our housekeeper in the papers, would we?"

"Yes, well, may it not come to that." Lady Isabella shifted in her seat. Yet she couldn't let the topic rest. "Though I can't imagine what the housekeeper could've been up to, wandering far from where she ought to be."

"Now, my dear," Sir Edwin chided, "it isn't right to speak ill of the dead."

"You would say that, wouldn't you, darling?" Lady Isabella shot back before deliberately turning to Lord Atherly. "Mrs. Nelson was in your employ for many years, I take it?"

Lord Atherly, stopping midbite of his minced pie, which Stella hoped tasted better than the one Lyndy had sampled, regarded Lady Isabella and then his wife. "I can't say I know how long Mrs. Nelson had been with us. Around the time we were married, wasn't it?"

"Yes," Lady Atherly said, gently halving a cream scone horizontally with her fingers. "All the more reason we shall miss her."

Stella studied her mother-in-law. A hint of uncharacteristic blush colored her high cheekbones. Contrasting against Lady Atherly's light gray silk tea gown, the pink hue flattered her features. But what was the cause of it? Was she being sincere, or was she trying to put an end to the discussion? Again, Stella suspected it was a little of both.

"Ah-hem." Fulton, forgotten by the door, cleared his throat. "My lady. The inspector awaits you in the hall."

"Shall I accompany you?" Lyndy asked, setting down his plate.

Was this a good time to tell him about the poem? She hadn't gotten a chance on the trip home from the horse farm, with Sir Edwin and Freddy in the backseat listening in. Maybe if she told him before they met with the inspector, Lyndy would have to curb his anger.

And maybe Santa Claus is real.

"Sure." She had to tell him sometime.

"Isn't he in the hall?" Lyndy said when she'd taken his hand and led him toward the adjoining library.

"He is, but I need to tell you something first."

Inspector Brown, his hat clutched in his grip, his hands behind his back, was admiring the harvesttime landscape painting of Oxford, home to Lord Atherly's alma mater, that hung in the hall when Stella and Lyndy approached. Though he still clutched his fists, Lyndy had taken the news better than she'd hoped.

He'd been furious, of course, but had held back the brunt of his anger for her sake. Would he let her out of his sight until they discovered the culprit? Probably not.

I can live with that. Stella snuggled closer into Lyndy's arm.

"William Turner of Oxford, I see. Nice one, that," the inspector said. Facing the couple, he hesitated. "Is there something the matter, my lord?"

"Nothing that concerns the police yet," Lyndy said through clenched teeth.

The inspector hesitated, squinting at Lyndy and allowing him a chance to change his mind. Lyndy stayed silent, stubbornly jutting out his chin.

"Right!" Brown smoothed his tidy mustache. Had it gotten grayer since the wedding? Stella hadn't noticed it earlier. "I do apologize for the intrusion, but I have an official request to ask of you, Lady Lyndhurst."

A shiver of dread (or was it excitement?) shot down Stella's spine. "You've discovered something, haven't you?"

"I've spoken with our medical examiner. Your housekeeper was suffering from a type of poisoning, from spoiled food, as Dr. Johnstone suspected, but that's not what killed her. Nor was it from a fall, as I suspected. She died from internal injuries sustained after being hit by a tremendous force."

Stella's mind raced. Mrs. Nelson had been out on a lane in the middle of the night. What could have hit her that hard? "She was hit by an automobile." It wasn't a question.

Inspector Brown threw back his head and laughed. "Your talents are being wasted, my lady. Do you know how long it took me to work that out?"

Stella glowed with pride. "So, I'm right?"

"As far as we can tell. Dr. Lipscombe thought perhaps she'd been hit by a train, but that's improbable, seeing the nearest tracks are over a mile away."

"She could've been moved," Lyndy suggested, his anger momentarily abated.

"My first thought as well, but why? Why remove a body from train tracks only to leave it on the road? Wouldn't you move it to hide it?"

He was right. That didn't make sense.

"You'll want to examine Daddy's car." Although Stella had inherited his entire estate, including his automobile, the Daimler her father bought when they arrived in England last May would always be his. "So you can eliminate us from your inquiries."

Brown nodded apologetically. "Thank you for understanding, my lady."

"Do whatever you need to," Lyndy agreed. "The Kentfields, our guests visiting for the holidays, have one too. A Martini. Both are parked in the carriage house."

Except they weren't. Only the Daimler was there.

"I forgot," Stella said, breathing in the comforting scent of fresh straw, baled and piled up outside the carriage house, one last time before a stableboy closed the doors behind them. "Frederick Kentfield took Lady Alice and Aunt Rachel for a drive."

Stella could still picture Aunt Rachel's resigned expression at Lady Isabella's request for a chaperone. She'd arrived from Pilley Manor for tea. Stella's great-aunt, brought to England as Stella's chaperone, wasn't a fan of taking drives but was expected to oblige as the only maiden woman in the family. Stella had offered to take her place, but neither Lady Atherly nor Lady Isabella would hear of it.

"Viscountesses are chauffeured in motorcars. They don't ride in the back as chaperones," Stella's mother-in-law had said. Or, as Lady Isabella had bluntly put it, "How else is darling Miss Luckett to earn her keep?"

For once, the two women had agreed on something.

"They should be back soon, though. Aunt Rachel won't let Alice and Freddy miss Christmas Eve tea." Stella's great-aunt had been looking forward to the lobster vol-au-vent from the moment she'd learned it was on the menu.

"Never looked a lobster in the eye I didn't eat," she'd chuckled, elbowing Lyndy in the side before she'd left.

"If they're not back by . . ." Inspector Brown pulled his pocket watch out by its silver chain. He grimaced at the time. "Oh, my wife will have my head for how late I am."

Despite his grumbling, Inspector Brown, living up to his title, searched every inch of the Daimler from grill to bumper. Once, he ran his thumb across what he believed was a scratch in the paint. His thumb came away smudged with dried mud.

"As I suspected, it's in perfect condition. You wouldn't happen to have noticed any damage to the Kentfields' motorcar?"

Lyndy cleared his throat but said nothing.

"Not that I noticed," Stella said.

"Tell him about last night," Lyndy suggested.

"My lady?" Inspector Brown pulled out a small brown notebook and flipped it open. It reminded her of Constable Waterman and his ubiquitous note-taking.

"It's thoughtful of you to let Constable Waterman stay home with his family today." Inspector Brown fumbled with his pencil. It clattered to the stone floor. He snatched it up as if it had offended him.

"I sent him to Bournemouth to check up on the dismissed maid," he muttered sheepishly. "Now, you were saying?"

The dismissed maid? What had she to do with this?

"Oh, no. I'm not letting you off that easily. Why are you following up on Louisa Bright?"

He told her about Millie's revelation. "But seeing as the poisoning, whether intentional or not, wasn't the cause of Mrs. Nelson's death, I've a mind to leave the maid be."

"As you should. The poor woman was dismissed without a reference. Do you know how devastating that can be?" Stella was convinced the maid hadn't stolen anything from her. But who else could it be? The author of the anonymous notes? "Besides, I have someone else for you to consider."

"Truly?" Inspector Brown said. He licked the end of the pencil, poised to write what she said.

Stella relayed the incident between Mrs. Cole and the man the night before.

"A late-night rendezvous is odd in itself," she concluded, "but the man had blood on him."

"Could our housekeeper have bled on him from somewhere other than the cuts and scratches we could see?"

"She did have some significant cuts, but it depends on how much blood."

"It was hard to tell."

"And you have no idea who this man was?"

"His voice was vaguely familiar, but no one I know well. An acquaintance maybe?"

"Right!" Inspector Brown stuffed his hat back on his head. "As usual, you have been most accommodating, my lord, my lady. If you think of or learn anything else, you'll be sure to let me know." He touched the brim of his cap to take his leave.

"You are treating her death as suspicious now, Inspector?" Lyndy asked.

A lump formed in the pit of Stella's stomach. She so wanted to be wrong. "It couldn't have been an accident?"

"If you accidentally hit someone, Lady Lyndhurst, would you leave them on the side of the road?"

She had her answer.

CHAPTER 14

Mrs. Cole lifted her stark white apron, the third she'd put on today, and wiped her brow. The kitchen, resembling a railway station with troops departing, was hot. Mrs. Cole was used to it. She thrived on the clatter and chaos, on the aromas and baking heat. But even the soothing sound of a whistling kettle couldn't settle her nerves today.

How could this have happened?

In one day, her whole world had been turned upside down. Her visitor last night hadn't been wholly unexpected, but what he'd come to say had kept her up all night. And now Helena Nelson was dead. If the cook had been anyone else, she'd fancy going back to bed.

The overwhelming sweetness of citrus jolted her from her momentary inattention.

"I said to chop the orange peel, not mince it into mush."

Mrs. Cole had a mind to yank the blade from the girl's hand but couldn't rely on her hand being too steady. She couldn't possibly allow any of her staff to see how unsettled she was. Especially this new kitchen maid who came with ideas beyond her station; on her first day, she'd expected to make pie crust. The chit had some hard lessons to learn.

"Is the fish course ready yet?"

"Yes, Mrs. Cole," Alva, her senior kitchen maid, said.

The cook inspected the crumbled fried fillets of sole stuffed with highly aromatic tarragon butter. She showed her approval by not insulting Alva, by reminding her to sprinkle the fried parsley garnish when it was time to plate it up.

Preparing Christmas Eve dinner, with its multitude of specialty dishes, was well underway. Lady Atherly had all but insisted it be perfect. Christmas Eve had never been celebrated with such fanfare before. Was the addition of outside guests to impress or the influence of the young American viscountess? Either way, Mrs. Cole had been up to the challenge.

And now? She wasn't so confident.

From all accounts, afternoon tea had been a consummate success. However, most of those dishes had been prepared or were in the oven when she'd learned of Mrs. Nelson's death.

Helena's dead. Mrs. Cole still couldn't quite believe it.

Then came the accusations, whispered from one person to the next when her back was turned, as if she didn't hear every tap, twist, and scrape on the cutting board. Was there any truth to it? Did a chambermaid poison Morrington's housekeeper? Typically, the cook paid little heed to inconsequential rumors among servants, but this was different. She'd known Mrs. Nelson since they both came into service—she as a scullery maid, Mrs. Nelson as an under-house parlor maid. In those days, Morrington Hall housed twice the staff it did now.

If one of Mrs. Nelson's maids caused her death, or if anyone was directly responsible . . . Mrs. Cole shuddered at what she might do if she learned the truth.

"Mind that the sauce for the pheasant gets finished."

She swept through the room, trying to banish the dark thoughts, barking orders to the footmen, tasting dishes, hounding the new maid to finish this or that and move on. By the time the roast was in the oven, she'd garnered some level of calm. How was she to know everything would go topsy-turvy? At least, no one would fault her for dinner. It would be as spectacular as Lady Atherly demanded, from the consommé to the roast to the jellied custards and elaborate blancmange.

"You weren't completely forthcoming with me earlier, Mrs. Cole." Like a bad penny, Inspector Brown had turned up on her threshold again.

"Go away, Inspector."

"If only I could, Mrs. Cole," the inspector sighed.

"Can't you see we're preparing dinner for the family?"

"As is my wife for mine. I do realize I've come at an inconvenient time, but seeing as I'm now investigating a suspicious death—"

The clanking of a copper pan smacking the stone-tiled floor stilled the inspector's tongue. Mrs. Cole whirled about to see the new maid standing aghast over the jellied custards lying in a puddle of orange-flavored cream on the floor. If no one had been there to witness, Mrs. Cole would've boxed the girl's ears or chased her with a rolling pin, threatening to toss her out into the cold.

Mrs. Nelson had done that. She'd dismissed a chambermaid. *Now she is dead.* Murdered.

A surge of anger made her chest hurt. Yet, tingling with the added unfamiliar pinch of fear, Mrs. Cole held back the tongue-lashing she would've released on anyone within hearing distance, allowing her stern glare of disapproval to be enough.

"Clean that up," she barked. "Get out the extra custards. We're going to need to make the sauce again."

"Right!" the inspector said, barely containing his exasperation. "I need to ask you a few more questions, Mrs. Cole. Would you prefer to do it here or in private?"

"As you can see, I don't have the liberty to indulge you at the moment."

"Very well. I'll ask you now, in front of your staff."

His wording gave her pause until she spied the new maid mincing the orange peel again. *Will the girl never learn?* She wrangled the knife from the surprised maid's grip and pushed her aside with her hip.

"You chop, not mince." She set the blade's tip on the cutting board and demonstrated with quick, even strokes.

"Mrs. Cole. When I questioned you earlier, you were remiss in telling me about your late-night visitor."

"I don't know what you're talking about."

"I have a witness. Who was he, Mrs. Cole? And why did he have blood on his shirtsleeve?"

Mrs. Cole let his words take hold, twisting in her belly until she could no longer control the fear and anger she'd been stifling. Before she knew what she was doing, she'd raised the knife and pointed it at the policeman.

"Get out of my kitchen!" she shrieked.

A singular hush descended. Never had the kitchen been so quiet at mealtime. Maids and footmen alike froze, like a tableau in midaction, backs bent to fetch trays, hands in midswipe with a towel, feet glued by the oven door. A distant bell tinkled in the servants' hall.

"Gladly," the inspector said, stepping gingerly backward before retreating. "But rest assured, I'll be back. You have questions to answer."

How could he know? They'd been so careful. What would she say when the inspector came back? *Because he will be back.*

"Make haste, everyone," Mrs. Cole shouted, desperate not to show her distress. "We still have a dinner to prepare."

When no one moved, she slammed the knife sideways on the table. The thwack animated the staff like the release from a magic spell, and the kitchen was abuzz again.

"And dinner will be perfect!" she declared to anyone still listening. *For it may be my last.*

*   *   *

Stella stood before the dense, dark-green fir tree, inhaling its aromatic fragrance, her cheeks straining to accommodate the wide smile she couldn't keep off her face. Earlier, doubts were raised about the appropriateness of such a grand celebratory gesture, considering the tragedy that loomed over Morrington Hall. Lady Atherly had ignored the grumbling, insisting they forge ahead with their original plans. Whatever her motives were, it was one of the rare occasions where Stella and her mother-in-law agreed. If any house needed a bit of Christmas joy, it was this one.

And the Christmas tree, stretching up toward the ceiling, was everything it promised to be.

Stella had gleefully watched as Fulton directed an army of gardeners, recently hired by Lady Atherly, to haul in and install the giant tree in the grand saloon. It must be fifteen feet tall. The Christmas trees of her childhood could fit on a tabletop. This mammoth fir practically filled the far end of the vast room. With the tree in place, the footmen soon began to bring in box after box of what Stella assumed were decorations.

"It's lovely, Mother!" Alice clasped her hands as she shared her unabashed glee with Freddy Kentfield. He enthusiastically agreed.

"It's a lovely specimen, Countess," Lady Isabella said, the rare compliment attesting to the tree's perfection.

"I agree, Mother," Lyndy said. "I can't remember another quite like it." To Stella, he added, whispering in her ear, "Previous years weren't half the size."

"It's quite remarkable, Frances," Lord Atherly said, craning his neck to take in the tree's lofty height.

"Bravo, Lady Atherly," Sir Edwin said. "Such a tree rivals that which I've seen in photographs of His Majesty's at Sandringham."

At this, Lady Atherly beamed with pride, her genuine smile

spreading crow's-feet around her eyes. Stella had never seen her so pleased.

"My daughters would never have a tree so big," Lady Isabella quipped, watching Lady Atherly's reaction. To her credit, Stella's mother-in-law didn't give her one. "It will be a bother to decorate, I dare say."

"As if you ever bothered," Sir Edwin muttered.

Freddy, admiring Alice as much as the tree, frowned. "Father," he admonished in an undertone. Sir Edwin shrugged.

"I can't think of a better way to spend a dark wintry evening," Stella said, peering into the nearest box as James, the first footman, lifted the lid.

Nestled inside were colorful, hand-blown glass ornaments coated in a metallic finish. They varied in shape and color, two to six inches big, from simple globes of gold to green grapes and silver artichokes. Each a tiny, colorful spectacle in itself, they glistened in the light of the chandelier above. Stella reached in and pulled out a cobalt-blue globe, letting it twirl at the end of its ribbon.

Following the footman, like a dog on a scent, she admired the contents of each box as he opened it: yards and yards of silver ribbon, delicate, intricate paper moons, stars, and butterflies, red, gold, and green glass figurines of bells, birds, and Santa Claus. Stella recognized a few similar ornaments from her childhood tree, but even Daddy would've been impressed by the volume of such opulence. Stella couldn't wait to see how all this would transform the tree.

Not sure whom to address—Fulton, who seemed to be in charge of the proceedings, or Lady Atherly, who was mistress of the house—Stella held up the blue globe, addressing no one in particular. "May I?"

"Please do, my dear," Lord Atherly answered. "They won't hang themselves."

Stella climbed the ladder, Lyndy promptly replacing the second footman in holding it secure. She chose a sturdy branch and threaded the loop of ribbon onto it. She descended, pecking Lyndy on the cheek as she passed, and stepped back to admire her handiwork. The globe caught the glow of the light as it twisted on its axis and sparkled. It was beautiful but alone in the vast green needles of the fir tree.

"Come on, Lyndy. Help me."

"Yes, please. Everyone, join in," Lady Atherly said. "As Lady Isabella reminded me, there's much to be done."

Freddy and Alice approached the same box, and after giggling when they'd reached for the same ornament and their fingers touched, they selected gilt paper cornucopia cones to hang. Stella had made several as a small child, which someone, her mother, she suspected, secretly would always fill with red and white peppermints. These Stella would offer to her favorite horses on Christmas morning. Peppermint was still one of Tully's preferred treats.

Soon everyone, even Lady Isabella, who seemed reluctant to participate, was hanging ornaments, draping ribbon, or securing the unlit candles in place. When, after an hour, they were still at it, Stella suggested they invite the staff to hang something, much to the chagrin of Lady Isabella, who took up her knitting needles to avoid mingling with the servants. Although Lady Atherly would have scoffed too, a few months ago, she came to Stella's defense.

"What a charitable and practical idea, Stella. This is their home as well as ours. They should feel they've had a hand in decorating Morrington's Christmas tree."

Lyndy's mouth gaped, Stella's astonishment reflected on his face. His mother, too intent on directing the footman in placing the candles, took no notice. Lyndy snatched Stella's empty hand and tugged her to the back side of the tree. With the long, dense branches giving them a modicum of privacy, Lyndy encircled her with his arms, cradling her head against his chest. If fir needles weren't poking through the silk of her dress, the moment would've been perfect.

"Who is this woman that resembles my mother in appearance only?" he jested.

Stella caught a glimpse of his reflection in a nearby ornament. A half grin tugged at his lips. Stella eased back so she could study him. He casually brushed back a lock of hair from his forehead, his eyes twinkling like the shining decorations around them. He leaned forward to kiss her. She couldn't imagine ever loving him more.

"It's Christmas, Lyndy. Miracles are known to happen."

Lyndy's laugh erupted for all to hear.

"What are you two doing back there?" Lady Isabella snapped over the *click, click, click* of her knitting needles.

Lyndy stole a quick kiss and was still shaking his head when they rounded the tree to find a wide-eyed Alice, her lips bright and rosy, skirting the empty tower of boxes with a sheepish Freddy in tow. She and Lyndy weren't the only couple inspired to seek a private moment.

Had it been the other couple Lady Isabella had scolded? Probably. It was Stella's turn to laugh.

With every ornament hung and the empty boxes removed, the party, including the few servants who had the leisure to linger, stood back to admire their handiwork. It was as if fairies had offered up their finest creations: spun glass, glittering gems, flowing swaths of undulating ribbon in honor of the perfect tree.

"When I first saw the unadorned tree, I didn't think it could be prettier," Alice said. "But what a beauty it is now to behold."

"I couldn't agree more," Freddy said, brushing his scarred eyebrow. Still captivated by the sight before her, Alice didn't notice he wasn't looking at the tree.

"I'd go as far as to say it's the most beautiful tree I've ever seen," Stella said. And she meant it. She'd been with Daddy on a visit to the Governor's Mansion in Frankfort at Christmastime once. Governor Bradley had a magnificent tree, which seemed humble compared to this. "Thank you, Lady Atherly."

"For what?"

"This day has been difficult for everyone. Thank you for allowing us this." Stella cast her hand out toward the magnificence of the room: the tree, the brightly burning yule log, almost an entire tree trunk dominating the large, deep fireplace on the other side of the room, the glass punch bowl filled with steaming wassail arriving as she spoke. "For making my first Christmas at Morrington special."

Lady Atherly stiffened. Then she tilted her head as if listening to a voice only she could hear. After careful consideration, she said, "My pleasure, Stella."

"You call having your housekeeper killed special, Lady Lyndhurst?" Lady Isabella scoffed, speeding up the pace of her knitting. "It's tragic, if not almost scandalous. I can't imagine my Emily or Maud having the audacity to go on as if something so horrendous like that never happened."

She'd delivered her disapproval with such nonchalance, Stella dug her fingernails into her palms, fighting the anger that threatened to overshadow her calm and joy.

What does she know?

This had been the most tumultuous year of Stella's life. She'd lost her home, country, and father. She'd reunited with her mother and found Lyndy and a place in this new family. Because of this, the holiday probably had taken on more importance than it should have. She accepted that. But who was Lady Isabella to accuse Stella, or any of them, of not grieving correctly? Of course, she mourned Mrs. Nelson's death and planned to help Inspector Brown in every way she could to find her killer, but she'd be damned if she was going to let an ignorant stranger spoil this magical moment.

Standing close to the punch bowl, Stella hastily snatched a warmed glass and ladled herself a cup of wassail, spilling a few drops onto the linen tablecloth. The spicy, calming aromas she'd stirred up while avoiding the floating slices of roasted apple and shards of cinnamon bark filled her senses. Her frustration dripped away like the liquid from the raised ladle back into the bowl.

"It's scandalous if we forget Mrs. Nelson and all she did in the service of this family."

Stella raised the glass, steam still rising from the mulled punch. Fulton took her cue and motioned for James to ladle out the others' drinks. With everyone served, Stella hoisted her glass higher, catching the sparkling color of the Christmas tree like a prism.

"To Mrs. Nelson."

"To Mrs. Nelson," a chorus of voices solemnly answered over the continued clicking of Lady Isabella's knitting needles.

CHAPTER 15

"That was handsomely done," Lyndy said, stripping off his waistcoat. "Toasting good ole reliable Mrs. Nelson."

He deftly unfastened the button of his collar before briskly tackling the buttons of his shirt. They'd dismissed Ethel and Finn early, allowing the valet and lady's maid to visit nearby relatives for the evening, and so were undressing themselves. The moment Lyndy reached the last button, he yanked off his shirt, letting it lie where it fell, and rounded the bed to aid Stella in unfastening the hooks of her corset.

"You certainly took Lady Isabella down a peg or two. Perhaps that's why she was overzealous at charades?" Lyndy rolled his eyes.

After Stella's toast, someone had proposed playing charades. It had been a heated contest, the men against the women, lasting well into the evening hours. Every time Mother or Papa suggested putting an end to it, Sir Edwin or Lady Isabella, taking a loss for their side as a personal affront, would insist on one more round. Finally, after reading a phrase he'd been selected to act out, Sir Edwin crumpled the note card and agreed it was time to retire to bed.

Lyndy had retrieved the wad of paper discarded on the floor. It had read, "Snake in the grass."

"By the way, Lady Isabella didn't write the note we found in Mrs. Nelson's study," he said, recalling the charade card. Lyndy knew the other women's handwriting. It hadn't belonged to any of them nor matched that on the *K* stationery.

"Why can Lady Isabella be so . . . ?" she said, searching for the best word.

"Annoying? Pathetic? Absurd?" Lyndy offered as Stella pulled free of her corset.

"Tactless. She didn't even know Mrs. Nelson, yet had to try to spoil the evening by invoking the poor housekeeper."

Lyndy had studied his wife all night, watching childlike giddiness and joy war with melancholy as memories of the all too current loss flitted across her lovely face. Stella, empathetic and kind, mourned Mrs. Nelson's death more than most.

Mrs. Nelson had been a fixture at Morrington Hall Lyndy's whole life, yet he knew less about her than he did Beau, his Irish Hunter. He lamented the woman's unfortunate fate and pitied what family she might have, had she any. But, like all unpleasantries, he quickly put the incident out of his mind. Stella wasn't like him, thank goodness. Another reason he loved her so much. But he did regret that Mrs. Nelson's death would weigh on her until she'd uncovered the truth.

"Let's forget all about that ugly business and do our utmost to enjoy ourselves now, shall we?"

He pulled the sleeve of her chemise from her shoulder and kissed her bare skin. He swept aside her long, unbraided tresses and kissed the exposed nape of her neck. She drew him into an embrace, lowering his head to hers as her mouth sought his.

A distant thud outside startled their lips apart.

"What was that?" Stella asked.

Lyndy shrugged in response. "It's nothing, my love. Now, where were we?" He tried to recapture the mood of a moment ago, caressing her cheek, still turned toward the window, but it wouldn't do.

The wind that had dissipated the clouds earlier, revealing a strikingly starry sky, had grown calm. As someone mentioned earlier, it was the proverbial "silent night." With the window cracked open for a bit of fresh air, he could hear the horses snort in the stables over a hundred yards away, bats on the wing as they hunted for their Christmas dinner, and now the grating, inexplicable crunching of gravel in the drive.

"That's not nothing," Stella whispered as if the night prowler on the drive outside might hear.

There was no reason for anyone to be out there, not on Christmas Eve, not at this time of night. And yet...the sound continued.

"You're right. Somebody is out there"

Bloody hell! Is someone spying on us?

As one, they moved to the window. The stars were bright, but the moon cast little light. No one loitered below them as Lyndy had feared, but movement near the stables caught his eye. Despite the darkness, a motorcar inched its way down the drive, its headlights off. The driver was indiscernible. Lyndy couldn't even say what make the vehicle was. Was someone stealing the Daimler or the Kentfields' Martini? Or had someone arrived, unbeknown to them, and was now leaving?

"And that someone," Stella said, "doesn't want anyone to know what they're up to."

"What are you doing?"

Lyndy was suddenly quite put out. Not only with whoever was out there but with Stella. He knew what this all meant, her snatching up her quilted dressing gown and shoving her feet into her slippers—he wasn't getting her into bed anytime soon.

"I'm going out to the carriage house," she said. "To check on the horses and see if someone's taken one of the autos."

Not wanting to be left behind, Lyndy cinched the tie around his waist tighter than he should in frustration and followed Stella into the hall. As they descended the stairs, Stella glanced into the room below. Lyndy followed her gaze to the Christmas tree, a silhouette towering in the shadows of the grand saloon, its fresh, rich scent wafting up from below. But determined as she was, Stella didn't stop. Reaching the front door ahead of him, she fumbled with the lock, which Fulton had dutifully secured before going to bed, before yanking open the door. A crisp cold flooded into the hall.

"At least let me fetch our overcoats," Lyndy insisted.

Rubbing her hands up and down her arms, she agreed. Lyndy felt his way to the cloak closet, grabbed the warmest overcoats he could find, and returned to help Stella into the smaller of the two, the one with a thick, fluffy fur collar. Still, it was ridiculously big on her.

"Isn't this Freddy's?" Stella laughed, holding up her arms, the too-long sleeves flopping down. "At least I won't need a muff." She tucked her hands into the opposite sleeves and stepped outside.

With no wind, the overcoats were enough to ward off the chill, but the path was damp, and Lyndy wished he'd remembered to get boots as well. Their slippers, though allowing for a clandestine approach, were soaked by the time they entered the stable yard, still and peaceful but for a persistent snore from the rooms above. Stella shoved the stable door aside. Perceiving Stella's scent, Tully nickered in greeting from inside. Stella sighed in relief. While she checked on the horses, Lyndy sought a lantern and a box of matches.

Together, they approached the carriage house, its door ajar. Stella put her finger to her lips and disappeared inside before Lyndy could stop her. Slipping in behind his wife, he held the lantern aloft. Stella was crouching over a figure slumped against the family's dogcart. Parked beside it was the Daimler. The Kentfields' Martini was gone.

"Mr. Gates!" Stella fell to her knees at the stablemaster's side.

How dangerously fragile this proud, forceful man appeared, slack jawed, his head drooping crookedly against his chest, his taut, weathered skin so pale. As she reached out tentatively to take his pulse, he stirred, moaning. Stella sat back on her heels in relief.

When she'd discovered Mr. Gates collapsed and unconscious, she'd feared the worst. How many crumpled, dead bodies had she and Lyndy come across? Too many. Thank heaven Mr. Gates wasn't one of them. But he wasn't out of danger yet. Wearing only a sleeveless undershirt beneath his suspenders, the stocky stablemaster shivered in the cold. Stella bounded to her feet, forcing a confused Lyndy to make way.

"Be mindful of the glass, my love."

Glass?

Lyndy held the lantern high, casting a wide circle of dim light that reflected off the Daimler's shiny metal fenders and the scattered bits of broken glass clustered near where Sir Edwin's auto should be. Immobilized, Stella was momentarily back in the Guildhall in York after the blast during the late Queen Victoria's statue unveiling. But a groan from Mr. Gates spurred her back into action. She fetched the red plaid, woolen blanket from the backseat of her father's Daimler and gingerly tiptoed back.

"Can you hear me, Mr. Gates?"

On her knees again, with only a passing thought to the grime she was rubbing into Freddy's overcoat, she tucked the blanket around the stablemaster. He'd tilted his head back against the side of the dogcart but had uttered nothing comprehensible. It frightened her. He would've objected to her ministrations if he were even a little bit well.

"Don't you dare die on me!"

Of all the staff at Morrington Hall, Stella admired the man who managed the stables the most, and not because her beloved Tully was in his care. Mr. Silas Gates had been the first person, man or woman, to be kind to her when she'd arrived at Morrington Hall last spring. Without question or reservation, he'd not only defended her right to be in the stables, a place most thought inappropriate, but had welcomed her presence. And, of course, he knew and loved the horses.

Like Mr. Green. Stella hoped she'd found a similar spirit in their new veterinarian.

Mr. Gates's heavy eyelids slowly raised, and Stella shot a grateful smile up at Lyndy. "My lord. Miss."

Lyndy frowned, stiffening at the address.

Mr. Gates had forgotten to address Stella properly. Or she should say, in his state, he'd failed to address her by her title in front of Lyndy. Between them, the stablemaster always called her *miss*. Although she adored being Lyndy's wife and wasn't tired yet of being called Lady Lyndhurst, she was treated like everyone else in the stables.

Well, almost like everyone else.

When she was with Mr. Gates, there were no pretensions between them. By calling her *miss*, he behaved as though she was still Miss Kendrick, the naïve woman who'd come to England with her Thoroughbred racehorse, unaware of the fate her overbearing father had contrived, who'd envisioned her new family willing to accept her, who'd had no idea what being a wife or viscountess meant. She cherished that. Both knew she wasn't the same person, but it was a respite from the duties, the expectations, and the memories to pretend she was. Once Lyndy had overheard. It had been the cause of one of their first arguments.

"He shouldn't call you that," Lyndy had complained. "It's disrespectful."

"I don't mind."

"But you should."

"Why?"

"Because you are my wife, you are a viscountess, and no one, especially not a member of the staff, should ever address you as *miss*."

"What's the harm in it? I like it."

"As I said, it's disrespectful."

"If it's about respect, it doesn't matter what he calls me, for who, besides you, respects me more than Mr. Gates?"

Stella had won that argument. But she'd hoped Mr. Gates's saying it now didn't bring it up again.

"Are you okay, Mr. Gates?" Stella repeated.

"The horses," the stablemaster mumbled, struggling to stand. "I must check on the horses." He fumbled with the blanket, attempting to hoist himself up only to slump back again. It was difficult to watch.

"Don't get up," Lyndy commanded. The servant in Mr. Gates obeyed, resting his head back again. Though he was shivering, locks of his fair hair clung to the perspiration on his face.

"It's okay," Stella said, replacing the blanket around his shoulders. "The horses are fine. I checked. But you aren't. Did you fall? Are you sick? Should we telephone Dr. Johnstone?"

Was the stablemaster suffering from the same sickness that Mrs. Nelson had? Had he been poisoned too? Stella glanced up and saw the same concern on Lyndy's face.

Mr. Gates began to shake his head but regretted it. Groaning, he put his palm to his brow. "There's no need, my lady. As long as Fulton can spare a bit of aspirin powder."

Lyndy nodded, either in approval of Mr. Gates's proper address, to affirm an ample painkiller supply, or to show his relief. Stella couldn't tell which. But his tone was sympathetic when he asked, "What happened here, Gates?"

"I heard someone entering the carriage house."

His thick, shaking finger pointed at the large open door. The winged silhouette of a bat whooshed across their view of exposed sky. Stella flinched and crouched closer to the injured man.

"Charlie had done too much celebrating with the lads. He's still a boy, that one. Can't hold his drink. But it being Christmas Eve, who was I to tell him no? I'd been up nursing him when I heard someone come into the yard and then in here. Can't complain anymore about Leonard not oiling the hinges enough, now, can I? I never would've known otherwise."

"Perhaps that would've been for the better," Lyndy said. "At least you'd be tucked up in a warm room. How did you come to be on the floor?"

"I left Charlie, came down to investigate, and *whack*!" He closed his eyes as if the recollection was exhausting.

"Someone hit you?" Stella said.

"On the back of the head." He rubbed the sore spot. "But I'll live. Could've been worse."

"Hit you with this, perchance?" Lyndy had bent down and, reaching under the Daimler, retrieved a bent brass headlamp with a few shards of glass still wedged inside. Stella had seen one like it on the Kentfields' Martini. "Could this dent be in the shape of your head?"

"Right you are, my lord." Mr. Gates managed a pathetic chuckle but winced in pain for his efforts.

"You could've been all cut up."

"As I said, my lady, it could've been worse."

"I'm glad it wasn't." Stella paused, a thought popping into her head. "Supposing this was what hit you, Mr. Gates; I have to wonder why?"

"I assume Gates surprised his attacker, who then grabbed what was on hand," Lyndy said.

"That's reasonable, except how did the attacker manage to unfasten it? Headlamps don't just come off."

Silence. Neither man had an answer.

"Speaking of attackers."

Mr. Gates, with a glimpse of his usual self, warded off the obvious next question with a raised hand, his palm dirty from the stone floor. "Before you go asking, my lord . . . it was dark, and they came up behind me. I'm afraid I never caught a glimpse of the scoundrel."

"Pity," Lyndy said. "For, besides clobbering you, they also made off with Sir Edwin's motorcar."

CHAPTER 16

Mrs. Robertson held the giant jumble of keys in her palm, the significance of its weight not lost on her, before securing the keys to the empty chatelaine attached to her belt.

"Merry Christmas," she whispered to herself, not at all as pleased as she had reason to be.

Aye, 'tis an honor to be chosen, but she'd have to forgo her visit to see Robbie, her sister's lad, who'd taken up a position in London after returning from America. Not to mention, the housekeeper was stepping into a dead woman's shoes with no guarantee of a permanent placement. Nonetheless, until the situation was sorted, Mrs. Robertson would see to it that this house ran smoothly, despite the holiday, despite the tragedy that saw her carting a trunk over from Pilley Manor in the wee hours of the morning.

With the symbols of her station securely dangling on her hip, she disregarded the desire to size up the situation by examining Mrs. Nelson's ledgers and files on her desk. It was Christmas morning, so first things first. She smoothed down any wisps in her taut, graying blond bun, which might've escaped on the way from town, took a deep breath, and set off for the kitchen. She passed no one in the hall. Odd, aye, but it was Christmas morning, after all. The servants' schedules were bound to be a wee bit off. But what of the fragrant scent of baking bread that should be emanating from the kitchen? Why did she not hear the hiss of a boiling kettle or the clanking of pots and pans? Instead, her footsteps reverberated loudly on the wooden plank flooring in the awkward hush.

Was no one about? Had the others been given the day off?

At last, she heard voices, troubled whispers. She halted at the threshold, aghast at what she saw. Two kitchen maids worked at the nearly empty, long wooden table, one peeling potatoes with a recklessness that sent half the peelings onto the floor while the other halfheartedly kneaded a dough, her apron coated in flour. A third maid, huddled over the sink with a tall, sandy-headed footman, filled a kettle. *Was she just now putting the kettle on?*

This would not do, not one wee bit.

"Where is Mrs. Cole?" Mrs. Robertson demanded, hands on hips.

The footman snapped to attention, staring at the rows of service bells hung above the door. The maids froze, the youngest allowing the kettle to overflow.

Mrs. Robertson had hoped to start with introductions. She believed first impressions were important. And from the sudden cowering of the kitchen maids, she hadn't failed to make a strong one. They regarded one another as if hoping the other would speak first.

"Out with it, lassies."

"We don't know," the oldest of the three said, leaving her dough on the table to turn the running water off. "We've started, but Mrs. Cole hasn't arrived yet."

"Has no one gone to her room to fetch her?"

The maids exchanged glances of disbelief. "We would never presume to do that, ma'am," the only maid with a tongue said.

"It's Mrs. Robertson, not ma'am, if you don't mind. I'm housekeeper of Pilley Manor, the dowager house in Rosehurst. I'm here to serve in Mrs. Nelson's place."

"Yes, Mrs. Robertson. Sorry, Mrs. Robertson," the girl bobbed as if the countess had suddenly appeared below stairs.

"As you were." She pointed to the meagerly supplied table. "Mrs. Cole or no Mrs. Cole, breakfast isn't going to make itself. And you!" she said, singling out the young one, snickering something to the footman, making the girl jump. "Put the kettle on and then lead me to Mrs. Cole's room."

Satisfied with the reinvigorated activity in the kitchen, Mrs. Robertson followed the maid to Mrs. Cole's room, composing a few choice words to chasten Morrington Hall's cook. She rapped on the closed door with her knuckle. No answer. She knocked harder. No answer.

"Mrs. Cole. You are required in the kitchen." No response.

Before fumbling with a set of keys whose locks she hadn't tried yet, she tested the door. It was unlocked and creaked as the housekeeper pushed it open a crack. The dim hue of a winter's dawn provided little light.

"I don't know if you should go in there," the maid said, taking a step back as if she'd seen a kelpie rear its head from inside Mrs. Cole's room.

"What's this?"

"She might be dead." The maid jutted her chin toward the door. "Mrs. Cole, I mean. Like Mrs. Nelson? Do you think Louisa could've done that too?"

So that's it, is it? The lass would've heard the same rumor Mrs. Downie, cook at Pilley Manor, was spreading about Mrs. Nelson being poisoned by one of her chambermaids.

"Wheesht, lass, and stop yer havering. Go back and help get breakfast ready."

The maid bolted, glancing over her shoulder once, lightly knocking into the narrow hall's wall. If need be, Mrs. Robertson could find her own way back. Eventually. She'd never been inside Morrington Hall and was impressed at its enormity. Pilley Manor was respectable, but nothing like this. She knocked again while peeking in her head.

"Mrs. Cole, it's Mrs. Robertson, the new housekeeper. I'm coming in."

She shivered from the cold. The fire had long gone out. Was managing this large a household so different from the dowager house? Shouldn't the maid have lit it by now?

The maid. The maid. Not knowing the lassies' names, she didn't know what else to call them. Neither had she bothered to wish them a Happy Christmas.

This wasn't going the way she'd planned. Better to start again, with the cook.

"Happy Christmas, Mrs. Cole. I don't mean to disturb you, but I'm afraid you've overslept."

The housekeeper felt along the wall for the sconce and, finding it, turned the knob to start the gas. The light flared into being, and the simple, tidy, whitewashed room came into full view.

The bed was made, the blue and tan floor rug perfectly centered, the nightstand and dressing table tops devoid of any clutter. Devoid of anything at all, in fact. Not a comb, hand mirror, book, or bottle of crushed rose toilet water. It was also devoid of a person.

Mrs. Cole wasn't there.

"I truly apologize for this intrusion, my lord, but it seems we have a situation."

"What's that you say, Fulton?" Lord Atherly mumbled, still half asleep.

"It seems Mrs. Cole, along with Sir Edwin's Martini, are no longer on the premises."

"I don't understand you. Why are you waking me at this ungodly hour?"

"The cook and a motorcar have gone missing, my lord."

Mrs. Robertson, remaining behind Fulton in the hall, heard everything, but not even on her tiptoes could she see past the butler's back. Coughing into his fist, Fulton momentarily revealed a gap between his large statuesque figure and the door jam, and Mrs. Robertson stooped to peek through it.

From what she could glean, they stood outside the earl's dressing room, where a vast mahogany wardrobe spanned the length of the far wall. The earl and Her Ladyship must sleep separately as the gentry were wont to do. Not that Mrs. Robertson would know. Having served solely widowed or spinster ladies at Pilley Manor (She tried to forget her brief employment under Lady Lyndhurst's father—a right proper eejit. *May He Rest in Peace*), Mrs. Robertson had never been required to provide sleeping arrangements for a married couple.

However, according to Mrs. Downie, if Mrs. Robertson put any credence into anything her cook said, the newly wed Lord and Lady Lyndhurst did indeed share a bed.

As it should be.

Mrs. Robertson silently chuckled. As if she, a woman who'd devoted her whole life to service and who'd never enjoyed but one wee kiss from a laddie, and that long ago, should have an opinion on the matter.

"Something happened to Sir Edwin's motorcar, you say?" Was that a hint of glee in His Lordship's voice?

"And the cook," Fulton dutifully repeated. "Neither are anywhere to be found."

"Does Lady Atherly know?"

"I thought it best to speak to you first, my lord."

"Rightly so. The countess will be most unsettled."

The bed creaked, followed by a rustling of heavy bedclothes. His Lordship was getting up. Fulton sprung to retrieve His Lordship's dressing gown, and Mrs. Robertson's view widened.

Paneled in mahogany wainscot with a built-in wardrobe and a matching mahogany chest of drawers, it was a dark room, even with the drapery open. His Lordship sat on the edge of a wee bed pushed against the side wall, his bare feet resting on the thickest Persian carpet Mrs. Robertson had ever seen. As he stood, allowing Fulton to cover him, he reached for something on the nearby round table. Was that a sun-bleached bone in his hand? The freestanding mirror in the corner caught Mrs. Robertson's reflection, craning her neck around the door jam, brazen curiosity painted on her face. She promptly stepped out of view.

"Leave it to me, Fulton. I'll break the news to Her Ladyship. And to Sir Edwin." A faint smugness hovered on his lips. If Mrs. Robertson didn't know better, she'd think Lord Atherly was pleased with the prospect. "We'll keep it between ourselves for now. Nothing else has gone missing, I take it?"

He held up what looked to be a jawbone in his hand. The butler seemed to understand a hidden meaning in the gesture. Mrs. Robertson's stomach clenched, and she resisted the urge to genuflect. Whatever were they going on about? Skeletons?

"No, my lord. I personally checked to see all your horse fossils were accounted for."

Horse fossils? So, Mrs. Downie wasn't talking rubbish. Of all her tall tales, who would've guessed the one about His Lordship funding far-flung expeditions in search of horse fossils was true? The woman was still a wee bit daft for suggesting that's how Lord Atherly lost his fortune, though. Wasn't she?

"And you searched everywhere?" Lord Atherly was saying, combing his fingers through his hair. He was grayer about the temples than Mrs. Robertson remembered seeing him at the young couple's wedding a few months back.

"Yes, my lord. I dare to say we've left no stone unturned."

Mrs. Robertson revisited the flummoxed expression on Fulton's face when she, without, yet again, a proper introduction, disturbed him in his study with the news of the missing cook. Upon finding Mrs. Cole's bedroom empty, she'd taken the liberty of opening the wardrobe and dresser drawers. They'd been emptied with no note, no explanation for the cook's sudden departure, to be found. Armed with this knowledge, and in light of the circumstances surrounding the unfortunate Mrs. Nelson's death, Fulton had efficiently rallied everyone, dread replacing the usual Christmas cheer as the entire staff searched the house and grounds. Would they find the missing lass in the garden, cold and stiff, clutching a suitcase, having faced a similarly strange end as Mrs. Nelson? But, not so much as a loosened button had been found. Instead, Mr. Gates, recovering from a thump on his head, had announced to the footmen come to search the stables that the Kentfields' motorcar, too, was gone.

Had Mrs. Cole, of her own volition, absconded in the night?

"And she's left no word?"

"No, my lord. We believe she might've taken the motorcar."

"Don't be ridiculous. Mrs. Cole can't drive." Before either servant could question how the lord of the manor could know this, he added, as if it were an afterthought, "Good Lord, Fulton. What are we going to do? It's Christmas Day! Lady Lyndhurst will be bitterly disappointed if we don't give it our best."

"If I may, my lord?" Mrs. Robertson said.

She rose to her tiptoes to be seen, and when that didn't work, she unsuccessfully attempted to squeeze past Fulton, blocking her way. Pushing against him with her shoulder had no effect. He had a full foot and a good five stone on her.

"Who is that?"

"Mrs. Robertson, the replacement housekeeper," the butler explained without yielding her an inch.

"By all means, come in, Mrs. Robertson."

The butler stepped aside (as reluctantly as he had accepted her right to accompany him upstairs), and Mrs. Robertson, hands folded in front of her, stepped across the threshold.

"I don't mean to be presumptuous, my lord, but these are drastic times, are they not?"

He nodded. "Say what you wish to say, Mrs. Robertson."

"Mightn't Mrs. Downie from Pilley Manor be brought up to serve in Mrs. Cole's stead? Lady Lyndhurst's great-aunt, our sole resident, is expected to join the family at Morrington until New Year's. And she takes but a wee coffee for breakfast anyway."

"That is an excellent idea, Mrs. Robertson. You arrange it, Fulton. I don't mind mentioning the motorcar, but will I have to tell Lady Atherly about the situation with the cook, I wonder?"

"The menus for today, and I suspect, for the duration of your guests' visit, will already be in place, my lord. I can assure you; Mrs. Downie is up to the task. If it pleases, Your Lordship, Lady Atherly won't even have to be told until then."

Mrs. Robertson took a risk, suggesting such a thing, but if Mrs. Downie's gossip was right, it wouldn't be the first secret this house would be keeping.

"Yes, yes," he said, punctuating the air with the tip of the jawbone. "That's just the solution necessary. Happy Christmas, Fulton, Mrs. Robertson."

"And to you, my lord," was the echoed reply.

Mrs. Robertson backed into the hall, her keys jingling at her side, and stifled the urge to let how pleased she was show on her face. The first day as housekeeper at Morrington Hall, Christmas morning, at that, and she'd been sorely tested. *And not found wanting.*

After promising to send His Lordship's valet up, Fulton closed the dressing room door and peered down at her, his expression unreadable. Having worked with Tims, the butler at Pilley Manor, Mrs. Robertson expected an unkind remark made out of jealousy. But this imposing man offered her a slight nod of approval.

"Well done, Mrs. Robertson. I do believe you saved Christmas."

CHAPTER 17

Why had Stella spent a fitful night tossing in her bed, twisting the bedclothes around her, stealing Lyndy's covers? It was Christmas morning. She should've been jubilant about the prospects for the day, but the attack on Mr. Gates had dampened her holiday spirit. Yet again, violence had touched their lives—first Mrs. Nelson and now the stablemaster.

Who would do such a thing?

They'd learned so little about Mrs. Nelson's attacker, and now this. Stella's mind reeled. Why take the Martini and not the Daimler? Was it that much more valuable? Were the two crimes related? Could Sir Edwin's automobile have been used to kill Mrs. Nelson, and the perpetrator wanted it hidden before Inspector Brown came back? But that would implicate Sir Edwin. He didn't even know Mrs. Nelson. Or did he? Had he sent the note they'd found in Mrs. Nelson's study? Had he sent Stella the love poem?

She winced at the notion, but it had to be someone living or staying at the house. Stella couldn't bear to contemplate the ominous implications.

Groggy and dispirited, Stella had forced a cheery "Merry Christmas" when Ethel arrived with the breakfast tray. Despite the tempting aromas steaming off her plate, she'd left it untouched. Instead, she'd peppered Ethel for news, disappointed the maid had nothing new to add.

Once dressed, Stella had stolen off to the stables to get answers on the valid pretext of seeing Tully, who eagerly accepted an extra brushing and a peppermint stick. Finding the stable staff at breakfast, she'd wished them a "Merry Christmas," relieved to see Mr. Gates, as "right as rain" as he claimed he'd be, wolfing down a hearty plate of eggs, breaded chops, roasted potatoes, and toast. A sore bruise and a slight remnant headache were his only complaints. But he couldn't tell her any more than she already knew either.

"Do you think the auto was the one that killed Mrs. Nelson?" she'd asked.

Not one to speculate, Mr. Gates, peeling a mandarin sent down from the manor house as a Christmas treat, had merely shrugged.

Stella couldn't shrug it off. Even now, strolling arm and arm with Lyndy as Lord and Lady Atherly led their party down the snow-dusted lane toward St. Peter's for church service. Too much had happened with too few answers.

Who will be next to be attacked, the new gardener?

A few paces ahead of the Kentfields, Stella couldn't help stealing glances over her shoulder at Sir Edwin and his son, despite getting fluffs of fur in her face each time. Freddy stared unabashedly at Alice's back as she strolled beside her parents. Sir Edwin, his wife unusually quiet on his arm, admired his surroundings—a tiny blue-capped, yellow-breasted bird flitting through the hedges, the bleak overcast sky, unshod pony tracks in the snow—all with a pleased smile on his lips. Mr. Gates had confirmed that Sir Edwin had been told of his missing auto. So why wasn't Sir Edwin more upset? Was he that rich that it didn't matter? Stella was burning to ask but knew now wasn't the time.

The church, with its ancient walls that appeared as extensions of the earth and its thousand-year-old guardian, a yew tree towering beside the entrance, loomed above the hedgerows. The bells, pealing their joyous welcome as if breaking the spell, momentarily banished all her concerns and questions. This was where she and Lyndy were married. It evoked nothing but love and safety, and trust. How could she not bask in it?

Sir Edwin's sharp laugh broke through Stella's reverie as he greeted an old acquaintance. The churchyard was bustling with more villagers than she'd ever seen in one place, all dressed in their Christmas finery. Martin Green was chatting with Mr. Heppenstall, the owner of the Knightwood Oak pub, and Captain Stancliffe and his sister mingled with the banker and his wife. Servants, merchants, and even several men who worked on the boiler were there. Many "Happy Christmas" wishes were exchanged, as most well-wishers hadn't seen the newlywed couple since their return from Yorkshire. Stella, feeling her spirit rise again, bestowed a smile on everyone.

With its profusion of carnations, chrysanthemums, and feathery ferns, the inside of the church smelled like a greenhouse anointed with incense. Near the altar, banked by bouquets of snow-white roses, sat a humble Christmas crèche, its small painted figures huddling beneath a hand-hewn manger covered in moss—a tiny island of wood in the church's sea of stone. Stella loved the nativity scene for its simplicity. Like one built with love by a gifted child.

Finding their seats, Stella inched next to Lyndy until their shoulders and thighs touched. With her hands stuffed into her muff, she still shivered. The ancient walls were filled to capacity and more, but it wasn't enough to keep the chill at bay. Only after she sang the four rousing verses of "Joy to the World" did Stella's muscles warm and relax.

Reverend Paine presided. While reading the Gospel, the first few verses from St. John, he peered down from his perch, his spectacles reflecting the flickering light cast from the candelabra below. Stella stifled a yawn. As the vicar launched into his sermon, Stella tried to focus on his message of God's love and Jesus's joyous birth, but his patronizing voice droned on, and she regretfully lost interest. This was the one part of Christmas that reminded her most of her father.

Despite his lack of faith and good deeds, Elijah Kendrick always insisted the family attend Christmas morning service at Christ Church Episcopal, dressed in their most expensive attire. She'd enjoyed it as a young child, before her mother's "so-called" death, the holy hush of the crowd, the incense, the singing, but as the years progressed, she'd come to see the mandatory attendance for what it was—a show of wealth, of hypocritical grandstanding. Daddy hadn't attended out of any desire to improve his soul and become closer to God but because that's "what all people of good breeding and high society do."

When she'd suggested they go to Christmas Eve service for a change, her father had scoffed. "Who will see the quality of your dress in the dark?"

As Stella let her eyes wander over the flowers and the engraved memorial plaques on the wall she abruptly tensed, suddenly having the feeling of being watched. Not the subtle glances of admiration or curiosity she'd become used to being the new, and American, Lady Lyndhurst, but of a penetrating stare. Stella glanced on either side of her and saw only forward-looking faces. She swiveled in the pew to see the masses behind her. A head instantly bent down.

There! She hadn't imagined it. But who was that? Her last impression was of a ubiquitous golden brown derby hat. She stared at the spot where the man had disappeared from view behind a sea of churchgoers, the men's top hats as tall as the ladies' brims were wide, hoping his head would eventually pop back up.

"Stella, my love? What is it?"

"Ever had the feeling you're being watched?" She righted herself in her seat, fidgeting with the pearl button on her glove.

"All the time." Lyndy chuckled, indicating someone with a sideways tilt of his head. His mother was frowning at them.

"No, this felt different."

A second glance over her shoulder was rewarded with crinkled brows, forced smiles, and flashes of annoyance from those in the pews closest behind her. She leaned in closer to Lyndy and clutched his arm. Despite being surrounded by a mass of worshippers, she felt vulnerable.

The anonymous poem, filled with unwarranted and unwanted affection, appeared in her mind's eye. Why had it made her feel violated? She was friendly to so many. Could it have been a field hand, a farmer, a merchant she'd smiled at, misinterpreting her genuine friendliness?

Or was it from someone who knew her or at least assumed they did? A footman or one of the stable hands she spoke to every day? Without thinking, she glanced over at the Kentfields. The unsigned Christmas card and the love note had both arrived around the time they had. When Sir Edwin caught her looking, he winked. With her ears burning, she promptly stared straight ahead.

"Lyndy, do think it's possible that—?"

Before she could finish, musical chords from the organ burst forth, and voices lifted in "O Come All Ye Faithful," with Lord Atherly's rich baritone rising above the rest. As the last note reverberated against the stone walls, Reverend Paine raised his arms in benediction.

"Tell me outside," Lyndy whispered in her ear.

"God sent his angels from glory to bring shepherds the good news of Jesus's birth. You have heard his story, the story of

God's own Son. May he fill you with joy to bring this good news to others today. Amen." With that final blessing, Reverend Paine dismissed the congregation.

Being the church's patron family, Stella, Lyndy, and her in-laws were the first down the aisle. The sense of being studied like a prayer book returned. Stella scrutinized the pews for the brown Derby hat but saw no one she recognized. After wishing the vicar the happiest of holidays, Stella dragged Lyndy by the hand away from possible eavesdroppers. Lyndy, mistaking her intention, drew her behind the giant yew and, ducking beneath the wide brim of her hat, kissed her. She returned his embrace but quickly pulled back.

"We need to find out if Sir Edwin wrote that note to Mrs. Nelson. Compare his handwriting with it."

"You think he was involved in her death?"

"I don't know, but . . . do you think Sir Edwin could've written that love poem?"

The words tumbled out of her in a rush, too quick to take back. Lyndy went rigid, his fists clenched.

"Happy Christmas!" Miss Stancliffe's call interrupted Lyndy's response. She and her brother waved as their carriage rumbled past. Stella forced a smile.

"And to you!"

"The sheer audacity," Lyndy was muttering, having been reminded of the offensive note, "and to *my* wife." He tugged on the lapels of his overcoat, his jaw so tight the tension was visible in his neck. Stella reached for him, laying her hand on his arm, and so engrossed with his obsessing, he flinched. He hurriedly laid his over hers in reassurance, enfolding her hand in his hot and sweaty fingers.

"Rest assured, my love, we will get a sample of his handwriting, and if it proves to be him . . ."

Stella didn't let him finish his sentence, placing her finger against his lips. "We'll face him together."

* * *

The Christmas crackers popped in staggered mini explosions as the family and their guests paired up and yanked the shiny paper-covered tubes. Surprises spilled out onto the dining room table: pieces of paper with love verses or rhymed mottos, colored paper bonnets or masks, and tiny trinkets in the shapes of animals, jewelry, or toys. Laughter, and the slight scent of gunpowder, filled the room. Stella eagerly donned her purple, three-pointed, paper hat. She'd never done this before.

She loved it.

Despite the unexpected silliness, to Stella's surprise and delight, no one had refused to participate, not Lady Atherly, Lady Isabella, or even Lyndy. How cheerful everyone was, nestled along a table decked with fragrant bouquets of red and white roses beneath twists of red ribbon and holly draping down from the chandelier, merrily enjoying Mrs. Cole's delicious dinner.

The Christmas pudding was brought in and set aflame at the end of the meal, highlighted by a roast turkey served with braised chestnuts. Applause and gasps of delight erupted from around the table as if, like Stella, no one had ever seen such a marvel before. Was it the anticipation? Stir-up Sunday had been weeks ago. Each person had been offered the spoon for a turn at stirring the batter while making a wish. Lyndy had refused to tell her what he'd wished for, but Lady Atherly had no such reluctance, boldly voicing her desire for an heir.

Was that what it would take for Lady Atherly to accept Stella as one of the family? Maybe.

"This fruitcake has bourbon in it!" Lyndy exclaimed after sampling one of the other desserts, his half grin aimed at Stella.

"You're right," Lord Atherly said, taking another bite.

"That's not Mrs. Cole's usual recipe," Lady Atherly said.

Had Mrs. Cole made something for Stella after all? Stella

took a slice and confirmed it was laced with Daddy's favorite bourbon.

"What dish is this?" Lady Isabella asked when a footman offered her a piece of a third dessert, a nutty, caramelized creation Stella could smell from across the table.

"It's called pecan pie," Fulton answered from his position near the buffet table. "I believe it's a specialty of the region of America from which Lady Lyndhurst hails."

"It's popular in many parts of the States," Stella said, giddy with happiness. She still couldn't believe Mrs. Cole had made it. "Anywhere the pecans grow."

"And it's a Christmas dish?" Lady Isabella asked, still considering the dubious offering.

"Back in Kentucky, we'd eat it any time, including at Christmas. It's one of my mama's favorites."

"I can't wait to tell my daughters what exotic offerings you provided, Lady Atherly," Lady Isabella said, refusing the pie with a scrunched face and a shake of her head.

But several others, including Sir Edwin, Freddy, Alice, and Lyndy, tried a piece. Stella couldn't resist one either. With the sweet caramel melting on her tongue, the pie was better than she remembered.

"It is indeed rich, my girl," Sir Edwin exclaimed, but added, "and quite delicious," when an expression of triumph crossed his wife's face. Lady Isabella pouted in denied annoyance.

"I say, yum!" Freddy declared to Alice's delight.

"Very well. You all seem to be enjoying it. I might as well try a small bite." Lady Atherly's declaration sent the footman scurrying to the other end of the table. "You are right, Sir Edwin," she said, having tasted it. "It is different but delightful. I do prefer Mrs. Cole's fruitcake, with or without the liquor, but brava, Stella, for introducing us to it. We shall have to include pecan pie on next year's menu."

Stella met Lyndy's bewildered gaze with her own. Had Lady

Atherly complimented Stella in front of the guests? Had that ever happened? Lyndy shrugged, perplexed, but Stella smiled, seeing it as another sign that her mother-in-law was warming to her.

Another Christmas miracle.

Stella sat back, dabbing her napkin at the crumb of pie in the corner of her lip, satisfied and full. This evening had been almost perfect. Almost.

If only she could get some answers: about Mrs. Nelson's death, the thefts, the attack on Mr. Gates, and the anonymous love poem. The last was the easiest one. Having missed their opportunity during charades to see Sir Edwin's handwriting on the phrase slips, how could they convince him to write something down?

With dinner finished, they skipped the usual routine of the men staying behind to drink port and instead gathered together in the grand saloon, warmed comfortably by the burning yule log, to witness the Christmas tree being lit. Happy gasps and little claps of applause burst forth as the soft glow of the candles reflected from every shiny surface, every glass bauble, from every inch of the tree. It was magical.

Beneath the tree's flickering candlelight, Stella snuggled into one of the gilded, plush settees with Lyndy while presents that had been piled on a table nearby were passed around: a considerably thoughtful signed volume set of *The Development of the Skeleton of the Limbs of the Horse* from Lady Atherly to her husband, a delicate diamond bangle for Lady Isabella from Sir Edwin. Even Freddy had come prepared, handing out boxes of Wingrove's chocolates to everyone. Stella and Lyndy winced as they received theirs, having had a tragic encounter with Horace Wingrove on their honeymoon. Alice's had an envelope slipped under the gold bow. Imagining what it said brought the anonymous love poem to Stella's mind again.

"What a beautiful bracelet, Lady Isabella," Stella said, eying the tag still hanging from a ribbon on the box in that lady's lap. It had something written on it. Stella arose to admire it closer. "May I?"

"If you'd like."

As Lady Isabella held up her wrist for inspection, Stella glanced at the handwriting on the tag. In a distinct florid hand, it read, "To Isabella. From Edwin."

Stella retook her seat, relief filling her lungs, concern twisting in her stomach. Sir Edwin, thank heavens, wasn't the author of the anonymous love poem (though now she was no closer in determining who was), but he had written the note they'd found in Mrs. Nelson's study. What did that mean? Did he kill Mrs. Nelson? Over a secret she didn't keep?

Before Stella could mull over her discovery anymore, Lyndy placed a small black velvet box in her hands.

"I hoped to give you something else today, but it hasn't yet arrived. In the meantime, you can open this."

She pried the lid off. "Oh, Lyndy!"

Stella rocketed into Lyndy's arms, tipping the settee backward and nearly toppling it. In her fist, she clutched a brass, tea caddy souvenir spoon with the famous cross keys on the tip and the word *York* etched into its handle.

Stella had collected souvenir spoons her whole life, but when she'd left Kentucky, she'd been forced to leave her collection home to collect dust. Since then, she'd started afresh, with one she'd bought in Southampton the day she arrived in England and another her mother had given her as a wedding present. And now this. It was the most thoughtful gift Lyndy could've given her.

"It's wonderful."

"You can place it in that." He pointed to a mysterious white lump under the tree.

She eased away from him, stepped over to the tree, and lifted the sheet covering her present.

Beneath was a custom-built oak cabinet with intricate scrollwork and a glass front. The back wall, fitted with silver clasps to hold spoon handles, was filled with spoons. Her spoons from Kentucky. She clasped her hands to her chest, struck mute by the affection, the elation, the gratitude that surged through her. She stammered to find the right word.

"How?"

"I contacted the caretaker of your house in Kentucky and had them shipped over."

"When?"

Lyndy laughed at her monosyllabic efforts. "The day you told me of your mother's wedding gift. I thought it only right it be with the others."

"You must've been planning this for months," Lady Atherly said, an odd mix of disbelief and admiration on her face. "And you never told her?"

"I knew it would take that long to guarantee they'd arrive on time," Lyndy said, tugging irritably on his sleeve. "And I wanted it to be a surprise, of course."

"You mistake me, Lyndy," his mother said, her voice soft and a bit hurt at his defensive tone. "It's an exceptionally considerate gesture."

"Oh." It was Lyndy's turn to be stunned by unexpected kindness.

While watching Freddy, who was helping his mother open her chocolate box, Alice swooned. "It's incredibly romantic, is what it is." She was clutching her newest stack of American magazines Stella had specially shipped.

Lady Atherly and Alice were both right. And the souvenir spoon from York wasn't the kindest gift Lyndy could've given her. Reuniting her with her long-lost spoon collection was.

When had he become so thoughtful?

"Thank you," Stella said, kissing Lyndy's cheek. "I love it. Now, to see my gift to you." She bounded up, grabbed Lyndy's hands, and yanked him to his feet.

"Where are you two going?" Lady Atherly called as Stella led Lyndy from the room.

"Lyndy's present is outside." Once in the hall, she whispered, "Sir Edwin didn't write the love poem."

"Saves me having to knock seven bells out of him."

"I thought you'd be happy to know. I'm hoping you'll like this too."

She nodded to the footman to open the front door. Lyndy, slack-jawed, gaped at the beautiful chestnut Thoroughbred colt, framed like a picture, standing in the drive. Mr. Gates, who had also been waiting for his cue, the lit Christmas tree, held the racehorse's reins, a satisfied smile on his lips.

"Is that . . . ?" Lyndy sputtered.

"The very one."

Almost from the moment he'd seen the horse a few months ago, Lyndy had spouted his desire to acquire Knockan Crag, the undefeated two-year-old whose sire had won the Eclipse Stakes at Sandown.

"Merry Christmas," she said. "I hope you like your present."

Lyndy, a second shy of bounding out the door, hesitated long enough to wrap his arms around her and lift her off her feet.

"Oh, my love, you are the gift."

And then, with her firmly planted back on the floor, he was unabashedly running bareheaded into the cold to meet his new champion.

CHAPTER 18

"And then, do you know what she told me?"

Stella peeked through the open doorway as the cook from Pilley Manor paused for dramatic effect, pinning each maid around the table with her kind but piercing green eyes.

"That the supposed 'nephew' visiting for the holidays was actually Mr. Jones's 'natural' son. Who the mother is, Nelly didn't know."

"Mrs. Downie?" Stella exclaimed, stepping into the blissfully warm kitchen and interrupting the conversation.

Chairs scraped back as the kitchen maids scrambled to their feet, bobbing in unsyncopated curtsies. Mrs. Downie, never one to rush anything, pushed herself up slowly with a great show of bending elbows, hunching shoulders, and a few well-timed grunts.

"My lady," the cook said, dusting off her enormous backside as if she'd sat in something. "You're looking well."

"As are you."

Stella knew Mrs. Downie from the time she'd lived at the dowager house in the months preceding her wedding. She had a talent for gossip as much as for cooking, both of which Stella had thoroughly enjoyed. Whether or not that's why the cook tolerated Stella's atypical habit of coming to the kitchen, requesting special meals, and even taking tea or coffee with her and Mrs. Robertson, the housekeeper, Stella couldn't care less. All that mattered was that they got along well.

"I didn't mean to interrupt your dinner."

She'd forgotten that having prepared Christmas dinner for everyone upstairs as well as for all the other servants, these women would only now be sitting down to their celebratory meal. It smelled as good as hers had.

The cook waved off any concern. "How might we help, my lady?"

"I . . . ah . . . I'm so happy to see you." She reached out toward the cook, beaming, barely able to stifle the desire to hug her. "But what are you doing here? Where's Mrs. Cole? I came down to thank her."

"You, girls, finish your food," the cook said, wiping the corner of her mouth. She dropped her napkin to the table and stepped away. When the youngest maid's gaze darted nervously up at Stella, Mrs. Downie added, "Lady Lyndhurst won't begrudge you that, will you, my lady?"

"No, please, enjoy your dinner. And Merry Christmas."

With a jumble of muttered, "Merry Christmas, my lady," following her, Stella took Mrs. Downie's cue and stepped back into the hall. Based on the number of furtive glances over her shoulder, the cook had something more she wanted to say.

Like that day with Mrs. Nelson.

But when had Mrs. Downie ever not openly shared news? What was she hoping to shield the maids from? A queasy feeling seeped down Stella's throat into her stomach.

"What is it, Mrs. Downie? Has something happened to Mrs. Cole?"

Before the cook could answer, Stella's mind jumped from

one conclusion to the next. Had Mrs. Cole been attacked or poisoned like Mrs. Nelson? Did the strange man have anything to do with it? Was Mrs. Cole dead?

"You asked why I'm here," Mrs. Downie said. "Well, it's not my place to say, my lady, but Mrs. Cole is gone. Up and left in the night, and, from what I heard, without so much as a by-your-leave."

How could Stella not have known? They ate her food, sang her praises, and not a hint from anyone that Mrs. Cole had left hours ago.

"Who else knows?"

"Mr. Fulton, Mrs. Robertson, who discovered her missing when she arrived from Pilley Manor this morning. And Lord Atherly, of course."

There it was. A conspiracy to hide the cook's abrupt departure from Lady Atherly and her guests. But why had no one confided in her? The exclusion hurt. Maybe she'd been too quick to assume the servants trusted her.

Or maybe becoming Lady Lyndhurst had changed everything.

"Has anyone searched for her?"

"Is she dead like Mrs. Nelson, you mean?"

Stella had forgotten how blunt Mrs. Downie could be. She could almost pass as an American. The comparison would've made her smile if the news wasn't so bleak.

"That is what I was thinking."

"You can rest assured," Mrs. Downie said, wiping her hands on the apron she still wore. "Mrs. Robertson told me that Mrs. Cole took all her belongings with her. Dead women don't do that. But she also left no note as to why or where she went."

As if she didn't want anyone to follow her. Like the thief who clobbered Mr. Gates and snuck off in Sir Edwin's automobile in the middle of the night.

Could that have been Mrs. Cole? Did she even know how to

drive? Was she also capable of running poor Mrs. Nelson down if she did? Stella couldn't deny the former cook was volatile and sometimes outright hostile, but murder? It was inconceivable. Then why else disappear in the night? Unless the someone who stole Sir Edwin's Martini drove away with her. The mysterious man with the blood on his sleeve, maybe?

Stella put her hands over her ears as if to shut out the atrocious conjecture setting her mind racing. Couldn't it all have a simple explanation? Mrs. Cole was a cantankerous woman who, in a burst of temper, decided she'd had enough. Or perhaps the death of Mrs. Nelson had driven her to leave? But where would she go? How would she live with no reference? And why on Christmas Eve?

Could this have anything to do with the firing of Louisa Bright?

"Did you enjoy the puddings, my lady?" Mrs. Downie said, pulling Stella out of herself.

"It was you who made the pecan pie and put bourbon in the fruitcake, wasn't it?"

Stella had been touched and more than a little surprised that Mrs. Cole had deviated from the menu and accommodated not one but two of her requests. Knowing it was Mrs. Downie in charge of the kitchen, it made more sense. Stella couldn't help but be a little disappointed.

"I saw the recipe requests in Mrs. Cole's waste bin. I recognized your handwriting from all the times you wrote them out for me. Your father left plenty of bourbon at Pilley Manor when he died, so I thought it would be a nice surprise. I'm only sorry I couldn't get me hands on popcorn. That sounds a treat."

"Thank you, Mrs. Downie. Everything was wonderful and delicious. Even Lady Atherly enjoyed a bite." Stella couldn't resist putting her hand on the woman's arm. "I'm so happy you're to be our cook. With Mrs. Robertson here, I feel like I have allies downstairs again."

The cook laughed, congenially patting Stella's hand like a child. "We're happy to oblige, my lady. But it may not be permanent once the countess finds out. So, put in a good word, won't you?"

"You bet I will."

As the cook turned to return to her dinner and Stella turned to tell Lyndy what she'd learned, a question popped into Stella's head.

Stopping on the third stair, she turned to ask, "Have you ever heard anything about Mrs. Cole in connection with a man, Mrs. Downie?"

If anyone knew, it would be the cook.

"Like a suitor, my lady?"

Stella hadn't considered that. She'd been so caught up in thinking the worst. "Any association she'd want to keep quiet."

It might've been easier to explain the details, but the news of Mrs. Cole's midnight rendezvous would be village gossip within hours.

Mrs. Downie, staring at the ceiling, tapped her chin with her knuckle for a moment or two and then frowned. "I can't say as I have. She didn't seem to have any family or suitors or the like. Why?"

"Just wondering. Merry Christmas, Mrs. Downie."

The cook looked askew at her, suspecting Stella wasn't telling her everything. "And to you, my lady."

It had been an evening of merriment, singing carols with Alice's accompaniment, and playing games: snapdragon, charades, and sardines, the only one Lyndy truly enjoyed. When it was Stella's turn to hide, knowing his wife, he quickly found her in the wardrobe of the bedchamber she'd been assigned that first night she'd spent at Morrington Hall.

How long ago that seemed now.

Being the first, he'd happily squeezed in beside her, hoping the others never discovered their hiding place. He should've known the first topic on Stella's mind was the disappearance of Mrs. Cole. Lyndy had argued the improbability of the cook having stolen Sir Edwin's motorcar before persuading his wife there were more rewarding ways of spending their time. Now, stretched out with his sporting paper on his lap, he could still taste the cinnamon from Stella's lips.

The article before him expounded on the virtues of next year's crop of three-year-olds, including Knockan Crag. During his visit to the stables, Lyndy had found the colt every bit the Thoroughbred racehorse the writer of the article described him as—spirited, strong-willed, and magnificent.

The writer could be describing my wife. Lyndy chuckled.

What had he done to deserve such a lovely present, or for that matter, such a remarkable wife? Was it an American tradition to give such extravagant gifts? His usual presents from his parents and sister were cuff links or a box of cigars that sat in the smoking room for Papa to enjoy, not a promising Derby winner.

And he'd thought his spoon cabinet a grand gesture. Happily, he'd arranged for something more.

"Seems we chose well," Sir Edwin said, swirling a glass of whiskey while staring into the yule log's crackling fire. "Should burn through New Year's without a doubt."

After the long day (or two) of excitement, the others who had joined Lyndy in the library were equally subdued; Papa had already retired to his study. Mother had picked up his Christmas present to her, the latest biography of Sir Robert Peel. With her feet curled beneath her, Stella cuddled beside him on the Chesterfield sofa, reading Dickens's third Christmas novel, *The Cricket on the Hearth*. Their library contained all five. Lyndy hadn't bothered to read any but *The Haunted Man*, whose title had fascinated his nine-year-old self. Lady Isabella, sipping a sherry, produced needlework from a wicker basket at her feet.

Knowing Sir Edwin wasn't secretly in love with Lyndy's

wife had made for a much more congenial evening. At least where Lyndy was concerned.

"I doubt it," Lady Isabella argued, arranging the wooden hoop in her lap. "That is oak, Edwin. You know as well as I do that Maud insists cherry should be used as the French do."

Mother's eyes flicked up from the page she'd been reading and paused. Lyndy anticipated her reply but was sorely disappointed when she returned to her book. Sir Edwin gulped back his whiskey but said nothing.

Alice's giggle breached the strained silence.

Lyndy regarded his sister. She and Freddy sat heads bent together over a quiet game of the Prince's Quest, her stack of American magazines gathering dust on the shelf behind them. Lyndy didn't know much about Freddy Kentfield beyond his proficiency at the game of golf (from what Lyndy had heard, the fellow was quite good) and his attentiveness to his sister. Lyndy resolved to wire a few friends in London to learn more about the chap before Alice got too attached. He'd been remiss with Cecil Barrow. He wouldn't be accused of it again.

Lyndy returned to his paper, an advertisement for motorcar repair catching his eye. How many times had he seen it and never noticed? But now, knowing what he did about Sir Edwin's motorcar and how little Sir Edwin had acknowledged its theft, the advertisement seemed to leap off the page.

"Sir Edwin, I wonder if you could tell me why—?"

Mother slammed her book shut. Startled, Lady Isabella knocked her embroidery hoop into her empty glass of sherry. It toppled over with a soft clank. Fulton, lingering silently in the corner, whisked it away and replaced it without comment.

"Will you not stop, Lyndy? Enough with the interrogation."

Lyndy's jaw slackened. "Interrogation? Whatever are you on about, Mother? I simply wanted to ask Sir Edwin—"

"Exactly. You want to ask him more questions. When did you become so interested in things that are not your concern?"

"It's all right, Frances," Sir Edwin said, winking at Lyndy. "If the boy wants to ask me something, who am I to say no?"

Frances? Who but Papa and Aunt Winnie called his mother that? Suddenly there were questions far beyond the state of his motorcar Lyndy wanted to ask Sir Edwin.

"Well, I'm going to bed," Lady Isabella abruptly interjected, cutting off anything Lyndy might want to say. She cast aside her needlework, finished her new glass of sherry, and popped to her feet. "Are you coming, Edwin?"

Sir Edwin shrugged at Lyndy lightheartedly, as if the women had conspired against them, said his good nights, and obediently followed his wife out of the room.

"It was a full day, a lovely day, but I believe I will retire as well." Mother smoothed the dark burgundy silk of her dress across her lap. This was the second time she'd worn a flattering color in so many days. When had Mother started wearing anything but drab brown or gray? "Good night, children."

With his mother gone, Stella, who'd been peering over her book silently witnessing the heated exchange, lay her head on Lyndy's shoulder. Silky strands of her hair brushed against his cheek, smelling of rosewater and rosemary.

"What do you think that was all about?" she whispered.

Lyndy kissed the top of her head. "That's a good question, my love. A very good question indeed."

CHAPTER 19

With nothing but a patchwork of raggedy gorse bushes to stop it, the biting wind blew across the open moor, its uneven ground puddled with melted snow.

"Are you certain you want to go through with this?" Lyndy asked.

"Of course. I c-c-c-can't wait," Stella stammered, her back muscles tensing from the cold.

Stella wasn't going to let the cold stop her. Once she and her pony, Moorington, found their stride, only her face would feel the chill. At least, she hoped so. Stella rubbed her gloved hands together, envying the men in their heavy-knit sweaters, woolen caps, and weatherproof coats. They didn't need to "keep up appearances." But if Stella wanted to join them in the Point-to-Point Race, Lady Atherly had insisted she do so attired as the lady she was. Which meant nothing warmer than her usual riding costume: black top hat, white shirtwaist blouse, black jacket, and riding skirt. Thank goodness that also included her gloves.

"At least there's no sign of rain," was Lyndy's jovial retort to her obvious discomfort.

Stella studied the darkening, overcast sky. How any sunlight seeped through was beyond her. "I think you're being overly optimistic."

Lyndy laughed. He was in his element, sitting comfortably astride Rufus, a chestnut gelding, his cheeks flush with the cold. How Stella loved to see him relaxed, happy, and invigorated.

He leaned over, closing the gap between their ponies, and whispered, "I think you're going to show these men a thing or two."

Moorington snorted at the other pony's proximity, her breath like a misty fog projecting outward. She sidestepped and then backed up, impatient to put distance between them. Stella stroked the pony's neck as Lyndy and Rufus trotted away.

Stella was definitely going to try her best!

They'd learned of the race's starting point by hand-delivered card this morning, and from the size of the gathered crowd, the messenger had been busy. Hundreds of spectators had braved the weather to gather in a clustered line to one side. Among those were Lord and Lady Atherly, Alice, Lady Isabella, Captain Stancliffe's sister, Miss Elizabeth, and many other familiar faces from the village. Those ladies, unlike Stella, were comfortably attired in their heaviest overcoats and hats, with their hands stuffed into fur-lined muffs. But what did Stella care? She wouldn't've switched places with any one of them for the cost of a full-length sable coat. She was going to race with the men. The excitement of it all would keep her warm.

That, and the anger burning in her breast at the snide comments from those who disapproved of her decision.

As they passed through the crowd to join the other racers at the starting line, murmurs followed them, confirming that she was, in part, the reason so many had braved the elements. No woman had participated in the Point-to-Point before.

How many were cheering for her? How many hoped to see her fail?

"I thought the only Americans who knew how to ride rough were cowboys."

"I'll wager she's tossed into a puddle when the gun goes off."

"If any woman can do it, it's Lady Lyndhurst."

"She'll be lucky to finish." That last unknown speaker sounded uncannily like Stella's father. Her ears burned beneath her top hat.

"Finish?" She shouted down to the sea of heads nearby. She was hoping the doubting man was among them. "I'm going to win."

Laughter (Lyndy's being the loudest), cheers, and disagreeing grumbles followed as she encouraged Moorington to trot to the starting line.

As Stella tried to position her nervous pony toward Lyndy's, Martin Green, his medicine bag clutched in his fist, made his way toward them from the opposite direction. Inspecting one pony after another as he went, he studied each animal's gait, rubbed his hands down their legs, examined their mouths for cuts from the bit, and checked their coats for scratches or whip marks. After each assessment, he rewarded the pony with a sugar cube. It wasn't routine, Lyndy had explained, but after last year when George Parley disregarded his pony's painful bucked shins and raced him anyway, Captain Stancliffe insisted on it. After his arrest this past summer for additional crimes, Mr. Parley wasn't among this year's competitors.

"Good morning, Mr. Green," Stella said as the vet approached.

"A bit chilly for me, my lady."

Stella shot Lyndy a smug look, and he laughed.

"I agree, Mr. Green. It's freezing. But the ponies don't mind, do they?" She patted Moorington's neck again as the vet inspected her filly as he'd done the others.

"No, these lovelies free-range all year. They're used to it. I can imagine they'll enjoy the run." He offered Moorington a sugar cube and then patted her shoulder. "She's good to go, my lady. I wish you luck."

"Thank you, Mr. Green."

The vet stepped aside as Sir Edwin and Captain Stancliffe urged their mounts to join them. Sir Edwin, wanting to participate, had persuaded Lord Atherly to sell him a New Forest Pony, allowing him to become an official commoner. It was a blatant disregard for the spirit of the race, if not a complete disregard for the rules, but Stella heard no one complain about Sir Edwin racing.

Because, of course, he is a man.

Mr. Green examined Sir Edwin's pony as Captain Stancliffe urged his mount closer, causing Moorington to sidestep again. Seeing this, the captain frowned but said nothing.

The captain acknowledged Mr. Green with a nod as the vet approached the captain's large, well-muscled gray gelding. With such strong hindquarters, he was a powerhouse in equine form. This was the horse to beat.

"Good morning to you, Captain," Lyndy said.

"A lovely morning for a race, is it not, Lord Lyndhurst?" he replied. "And such a gathering as we haven't seen in years. I wondered if we don't have Lady Lyndhurst to thank for that. Good morning, my lady."

"Captain," Stella said. "A confident pony you've got there."

"Yes, Major knows who's in charge here. I am his subordinate, after all." He chuckled. "By the way, my lady, I'd like to speak to you, in private if I may."

"Don't try to talk her out of it, Stancliffe," Lyndy said. "She is determined."

"Yes, well, that is evident, if not well-advised. The rules don't prohibit it, so if she's game, who am I to argue? No, this is about something else entirely."

"Say that again, Captain." Something triggered Stella's memory. A memory of the night Mrs. Nelson died. What was it?

"I said I'd like to—"

"Ladies and gentlemen!" a man in a stovepipe hat, his hands cupped around his mouth, shouted over the wind and the din of the crowd's conversations. "Welcome to the annual New Forest Boxing Day Point-to-Point Race, which allows each racer to determine his . . ." The announcer's gaze fell on Stella. "Eh, his . . . I mean . . ."

"I mean to speak to you about your—" Captain Stancliffe continued during the announcer's stammering pause.

". . . his or her own course to the finish line!" the announcer finished. "If the racers will prepare their ponies and approach the starting point."

"We'll speak later," the captain said. "The best of luck to you, my lady."

"To you too," Stella said as the captain found a place further down the line. Moorington snorted. Stella turned to Lyndy. "He doesn't think I'll keep my seat either, does he?"

"Don't worry, my girl," Sir Edwin interjected. "Win or lose, it's all in good fun."

Lyndy shook his head. "Ah, but, Sir Edwin, he who underestimates my wife will soon see the error of his ways."

That's it! Win, lose, game. Stella remembered what Captain Stancliffe had said, which made her think of the night Mrs. Nelson died. "If she's game." The stranger had said something similar to the missing cook that night. Hearing it again, Stella recognized the voice.

It belonged to Captain Stancliffe.

"I, on the other hand, know better than to count you out," Lyndy said.

"I appreciate that but, Lyndy, I—"

Gunshot blasted overhead.

"See you at the finish line, my love," Lyndy exclaimed as his pony bolted ahead of the field.

*   *   *

The other ponies spurred into action. Moorington lurched forward into a canter before lengthening her stride into a gallop without Stella's urging as if the filly, too, had something to prove. The wind stung her face, the pony's hoofs pounded the ground, and within moments all of Stella's bravado disappeared. Riding Moorington sidesaddle across the moor, down muddy, water-filled carriage ruts, through low, uneven clumps of purple heather, and between copses of prickly gorse that snagged at her jacket and skirt when the pony got too close, was nothing like riding Tully. Stella often rode the moors, but Tully was a pure Thoroughbred with a champion pedigree who galloped like a bird on the wing. Stella barely noticed her move beneath her. Moorington, on the other hand, jostled and jolted Stella with every raise of her hoof, rattling her teeth and any thoughts about the captain's connection to the missing cook or the dead housekeeper momentarily from her brain. All her concentration was bent on keeping her seat.

A free-ranging pony, Moorington was scarcely more used to a saddle and rider than a wild mustang. It didn't help that the filly was determined to follow the others, albeit at a distance, no matter the roughness of the terrain, no matter how hard Stella tried to redirect her. Moorington had a mind of her own, crashing recklessly across the mire through the bushes and puddles alike. Ahead of her, the other ponies jockeyed for the most accessible passes, kicking up mud while Moorington, avoiding the pack, instinctually kept at least a few paces back.

Stella wiped away a dab of mud from her cheekbone. *So much for playing the part of a lady.* She was completely splattered with it.

Why had she not at least taken a practice run with the pony? An accomplished rider but spoiled by her father's Thoroughbreds, Stella had been overconfident. And her reputation and pride would pay the cost. Not only was she not winning, but she was last in the field, and the distance widened between them with every stride.

The naysayers had been right. She would be lucky to finish.

As the first minute turned into two and then three, she surrendered the control of the pony and trusted the filly to know what she was doing. Stella held on for the ride, keeping as low as possible, ducking or leaning away from branches that sought to unseat her, clenching the pommel heads tightly with her thighs. But when they reached a stretch of grazing lawn, with only sodden grass to contend with, and seeing a few men in her sights, she encouraged the filly to pick up the pace. Finishing last would be okay, but finishing in the top tier would be better.

"Come on, Moorington. Let's show the boys what we can do."

With that bit of encouragement, Moorington dug into her reservoir of speed, and the pair slowly gained on the men. As they were nearing the next outcrop of heath, Stella used all her experience to prevent Moorington from following the others straight into the thick stand of golden bracken but bank to the left, keeping to the cropped grass along the edge. Despite the extra length and no uneven ground cover to impede her, Moorington gained and eventually passed two riders.

"Atta girl, Moorington," Stella cheered as she passed.

The wind whipped the words from her lips. If she could barely hear herself, neither the men nor her pony could either. It didn't matter. She'd passed some of the other racers and was intent on catching more. From the sudden lengthening in her stride, Moorington was too.

With a stretch of woodland fast approaching and no way around it without losing much-needed ground, Stella relaxed the reins and let the filly take the lead again. The stand of mixed shrubs and trees was spaced close enough to block out the overcast sky. The pair rode in deep shadow for a few moments, dodging the outstretched limbs on the particularly narrow path.

When they burst into the open again, another grazing lawn stretched before them.

With a large cluster of riders in sight, Stella's focus was on them when the pony abruptly drifted sideways to avoid something. She twisted in her saddle. Growing smaller by the second was a figure in the shadow of the tree line, crumpled on the wet ground. If it weren't for Moorington, Stella would've raced by unknowingly.

Stella urged Moorington to circle back, but the filly, confused by the mixed signals, balked, jerking her head in protest.

"Whoa, girl! Whoa!"

The two riders they had passed closed in on her. Despite her shouts and her frantic gestures, they continued past. With scorn etched on their weather-burned faces, one came close to clipping Moorington as they raced by. The filly reared to her tallest height, her forelegs pawing the air before her. Stella leaned against the pony's neck, one arm hanging on with all her might, her muscles quivering from the effort. Sweat foamed on the pony's coat, making it slick. The force and momentum pulled her backward, and Stella's grip slipped. With a hard thud, Moorington dropped her hoofs to the ground. The saddle slid beneath her. Cold, tense, and jerked off balance, Stella lurched to the left and was hurtled off. She landed with a splash on all fours in a boggy puddle.

Cold, muddy water dripped down her cheeks, tasting of gritty moss. Mud squished between her gloved fingers and seeped through the thin fabric of the riding pants; having caught on the pommel heads, her apron skirt had unsnapped and opened, leaving the pants exposed. Drenched, her teeth already beginning to chatter from the cold, she was grateful the soft ground had broken her fall.

It could've been worse.

Moorington, subdued by the sudden turn in events, grazed warily a few steps away. With the boning in her corset making it hard to breathe, Stella stayed on her knees for a moment before hoisting her skirt, heavy and laden with water and mud, over her arm. She lugged herself to her feet and limped back to the body she'd seen on the ground.

Dreading what she might find, Stella didn't hasten her advance. Had it been two days since Mrs. Nelson had been discovered like this? Was it to be Mrs. Cole's fate too? As she drew closer, the body grew in definition. It wasn't a woman lying there but a man in riding clothes.

"Lyndy?"

Oh, dear God, please don't let it be him.

Stella ripped at the last of the fasteners of her riding skirt as she ran, abandoning the heavy burden on the ground. She skidded on her knees as she threw herself beside him, then scuttled backward as fast as possible.

"Oh, my God!" she cried. To stop from gagging, her hands flew to cover her mouth.

He lay buckled on his back, his left arm draped across him, and his right flailed out to the side. His eyes were closed, and his forehead, speckled with bits of mud, lay in a depression in the ground. His hat dangled from a branch on a nearby shrub. Stella didn't have to feel the vein in his neck to know she wouldn't find a pulse. With a shard of splintered thighbone jutting through his pant leg, Captain Stancliffe lay in a pool of blood.

CHAPTER 20

Lyndy didn't wait for Stella to finish before riding to meet her. He'd been proud to see her appear in the distance, the crowd cheering her on. But as she drew closer, the cheering fell to a hush. Something was wrong. Her posture was off, overly stiff. That wasn't like the horsewoman he knew. With her skirt missing, her white, though mud-splattered, riding trousers beaconed like a flag of surrender. He'd expected her to be worse for wear, but even at this distance, she looked a fright. Tresses of hair dangled from beneath her top hat, the knees of her riding trousers were caked in mud, and her cheeks blazed bright red. But when he urged Rufus to Moorington's side, it was Stella's dull expression that concerned Lyndy the most. He'd seen it too many times before. She was in shock.

Lyndy slid from his saddle, grabbed the filly's bridle, and led her toward the waiting crowd.

"Stella, what happened?"

"I had to leave him there. He was too heavy for me to move. Lyndy. He's the man who—"

A pony's sharp whinny cut across the open ground as Sir Edwin, Freddy, and Mr. Green strode out to meet them. In the distance, a group of New Forest Ponies had gathered, equine spectators of the race. That couldn't be the captain's gelding among them, could it?

Now that he thought of it, Captain Stancliffe had yet to finish. That wasn't like him either. Something terrible must've happened.

"Lady Alice sent me to check on you, my lady," Freddy said in a concerned rush. "I'm to report back. Are you well?"

"Me? I'm fine."

"Has your filly had a problem, my lady?" Mr. Green asked, already visually inspecting Morrington for complications.

"No, it's Captain Stancliffe." Stella twisted in her saddle. "I found him back near the last woodland stretch. I don't know where his gelding is. I think he was thrown."

Heads turned in the direction she pointed, all expecting to see the retired military man limping toward them. Not seeing a figure in the distance, Lyndy's heart sank.

"Was he so injured, he couldn't ride or walk back?" Sir Edwin asked.

"Don't you understand?" Stella snapped in frustration.

The cold, the fatigue of the race, and the shock of whatever happened were setting in. He could tell she was doing her best, but her patience was gone. Lyndy needed to get her home. Now.

"Captain Stancliffe is dead."

Despite expecting them, her words made Lyndy clench the bridle so tight the leather dug into his palm. He'd so wanted to win that he'd abandoned his wife to the elements, the rough terrain, and ultimately the dismal discovery of yet another dead body. Why had he left Stella to fend for herself? *Because I know my wife.* She wouldn't have wanted it any other way.

He handed the bridle to Mr. Green, shrugged off his jacket, and motioned for Stella to dismount. She collapsed into his arms. He draped the coat around her shoulders and hugged her close for warmth.

News of Captain Stancliffe's death rapidly spread once they

informed the race's officials and Inspector Brown, who happened to be on hand as a spectator in the crowd. In a borrowed wagon, several of the men hastened back to where Stella said the captain lay.

"That can't be," Papa said when he heard, breathing on his lorgnette and wiping the fogged lenses with a handkerchief. He peered through them, hoping to spy the fallen man. "The captain fought on horseback his whole life. He's renowned for being one of the best horsemen the Forest has ever produced."

"Accidents happen, William," Mother said, taking in Stella's disheveled appearance. "Even to the best of horsemen."

Lyndy bristled at his mother's way of reprimanding Stella for her supposed foolishness without being blatant about it in front of Lady Isabella. But that lady had no such compunction.

"Didn't I say, Lady Atherly, that this was bound to end badly? I can't imagine allowing one of my daughters to partake in such a dangerous endeavor. Could've easily been Lady Lyndhurst laying out there."

Lyndy, his jaw tightening, took a breath to say something in Stella's defense. Stella stayed his tongue with a hand on his arm.

"And it almost was," she whispered, her shaky breathing visible in the air.

"Did you . . . ?" Alarmed, Lyndy took another, more scrutinizing inspection of her. Those caked knees, the unkempt hair, the wet clothes. Had she fallen? Had she injured herself? "Are you . . . ?"

"As I told Freddy, I'm fine."

He knew what that meant. She wasn't, but Stella didn't want to make a fuss. She squeezed his arm. Lyndy put his hand on hers protectively but said nothing more about it.

"Green!" he shouted instead, spotting the vet nearby. "I believe I spotted Captain Stancliffe's pony out on the moor with a few others. Look him over, would you? See if you can detect anything that might've caused that gentleman to lose his seat."

"Of course, Lord Lyndhurst."

After bundling Stella into the warmth of a carriage, her lack of protest indicating the extent of her upset and fatigue, Lyndy marched across the field to where the vet had tied Major to a gorse bush. A single buzzard circled lazily above him.

"Nothing seems out of the ordinary," Mr. Green said when Lyndy approached. The vet ran his hands over Major's barrel. The pony seemed docile enough, almost sluggish.

"Yes, but doesn't his head carriage appear a bit heavy? And what of the foam lathered on his neck and flank?"

"Must be exhausted, that's all. He has just run a race."

As the vet pointed out, Major was nearly asleep on his feet. But if nothing was wrong with the pony, then what caused the captain to fall?

As Mr. Green looked on, shifting his weight from one foot to the other, Lyndy inspected Major's tack for a loosened strap or an irritating metal edge.

"Anything amiss, my lord?" the vet asked.

"Not that I can tell."

But something has gone wrong. A good man was dead.

Inspector Brown took mental note of the position of the body. Where was Waterman (and his pencil) when you needed him?

Probably sitting feet up before the fire with his missus., his belly full of kippers and sausage.

Of course, the constable had earned it. What with finding out about Louisa Bright's false names. Even if they were still trying to track that one down. The maid may not have poisoned the housekeeper, but she still might know something to help in his investigation.

What had compelled Brown to leave his loving family and warm hearth to stand out in the cold, getting his feet wet? Brown was loath to admit it was to see Lady Lyndhurst attempt the Point-to-Point. He'd attended one other when Waterman competed a few years back. That year it had snowed. He'd vowed never again. And yet, here he was, crouched beside a dead man while the mud squished around his boots.

And to his utter disappointment, the lady hadn't even properly finished the race.

Brown had done all the preliminary checks of the body when the sound of carriage wheels rumbled toward him. He ignored it, unbuttoning the dead man's overcoat, waistcoat, and shirt. He'd removed the odd, dirty black fabric covering him and cut away a swath of trouser leg where the bone protruded. *Nasty that.* Even to his untrained eye, there was no doubt what caused the poor beggar to bleed out. His thighbone had shattered, cutting a large vein in his leg. But Brown had to be thorough. He still didn't know why.

The ground was cold but soft enough to absorb his fall if he had been thrown from his horse. Scrapes on the back of his head said he'd fallen on his back. But a thighbone was bloody strong. What could've caused such an injury? Brown's first thought was a motorcar. Like the housekeeper. But any such vehicle would've been heard if not also witnessed by the racers. A continued search of the man's body, his pockets, and even the soles of his shoes revealed nothing more.

A horse whinnied, and Brown glanced up. The carriage continued through a cluster of curious onlookers gathered at a respectful distance. He wasn't sure whether he was glad or exasperated to see who it was. He certainly wasn't surprised. He valued their help, but hadn't the lady been through enough?

Brown stood and brushed what he could from the bottom hem of his trousers. "Ah, now, Lady Lyndhurst, Lord Lyndhurst," he said as the couple joined him. "You shouldn't have come out here." Lady Lyndhurst, her hair haphazardly stuffed into her top hat, looked comical wearing a man's jacket.

"If it had been up to me . . ." Lord Lyndhurst said with resignation.

"I thought you might need to speak to me, Inspector," Lady Lyndhurst said in her self-defense, cradling her elbows in her hands. "I'm the one who found him."

"Right!" Brown hadn't been told who, simply that a body had been found. He should've known. "And this was during the race?" She confirmed it with a nod. "He was exactly as he is now?"

"Yes. I didn't touch or move him. I didn't even take his pulse. I only covered him up with my riding skirt."

So that's what that was. It was kindly done, but it had confused the situation needlessly.

Brown blew warmth into his cupped fists. This job required thicker gloves.

"No need for you to check for signs of life upon seeing the blood, I'm sure."

"I didn't see it at first," she admitted. "I thought it was a puddle darkened by the shade of the shrubs."

Brown could imagine her fright at discovering the captain didn't lay in rainwater. *She may still be in shock—another reason for her not to be here.* But who was the one to say but the detective in charge?

"We're assuming he was thrown from his pony," Lord Lyndhurst said, surveying the area.

With the shrubby woodland at their backs, the windswept moor stretched before them. In the distance, a few stragglers remained near the race's finish line. Darkened clouds on the horizon threatened rain or worse.

"Yet there were no necessary jumps or branches to avoid. And from what my father tells us, Captain Stancliffe was an excellent horseman."

"Perhaps something startled the horse?" Brown suggested.

While the two men spoke, Lady Lyndhurst had inched closer to the body and was now leaning over it. "He's been crushed by his pony, hasn't he?"

Why hadn't Brown thought of that? "What makes you say so, my lady?"

"I'm sure, as a retired cavalry officer, Captain Stancliffe has fallen off dozens of times. He'd know how to do it safely. But this. The only reason I can think of is that the pony fell, too, and rolled over him. Even then, with the soft ground, it might not have been fatal. But if the leg took the brunt of the impact . . ." She turned her face away, catching sight of a buzzard circling above. "It happened once to a training jockey when I was little. He bled to death on the track before anyone could save him."

Brown crouched down again and ran his eyes over the dead man. "A tragic accident, then?"

Lady Lyndhurst was shaking her head. "Another alleged 'accident'?"

"I was wrong to make quick assumptions about Mrs. Nelson's death," Brown conceded. "Though we have yet to officially rule that a murder. Suspicious, yes, but nothing beyond that. What makes you think this is the same?"

"Christmas Eve, I overheard a conversation between Mrs. Cole and a man whose face I couldn't see. The light shined on his sleeve when he reached out to touch Mrs. Cole. There was blood on it. I'd recognized the man's voice but couldn't place it. Now I know. It was Captain Stancliffe."

"What is so unusual about that, Lady Lyndhurst?" Brown knew the young lady was more observant than most, but that didn't preclude him from challenging her suspicions. "Perhaps the man cut himself shaving?"

"The conversation took place well after midnight, Inspector. The same night Mrs. Nelson was killed."

Lord Lyndhurst put his arm around his wife's shoulders. "And you think Captain Stancliffe had something to do with it?"

"It can't be a coincidence, can it? Mrs. Nelson died that night. Mrs. Cole has since disappeared. Now he's dead."

"I agree they'd be extraordinary coincidences, and I appreciate the information, Lady Lyndhurst, but I believe the captain's death is nothing more than an unfortunate accident."

"How can you be so certain?" the lady challenged.

"Mrs. Nelson was struck by a motorcar. Hence Captain Stancliffe couldn't have been the culprit."

"Why not?" Lord Lyndhurst asked. "Automobiles are becoming increasingly common these days. Besides the Kentfields' Martini, I saw two others last week."

Brown straightened, his knee joint cracking as he rose. "As a cavalry officer, he made it a point never to ride in or own a motorcar. You can ask anyone. The man thought the machines an abomination."

Seeing what a horse can do, Brown wondered if they were any less dangerous.

Lady Lyndhurst hugged herself tighter. "There are now two people dead in three days, and we have more questions than answers."

Feeling a headache coming on, Brown pinched the bridge of his nose. "I'm afraid so, my lady. I'm afraid so."

Stella drifted through the riders and spectators still milling about at the finish line, ignoring the occasional "What happened?" being honed in as she was on Captain Stancliffe's sister. The older woman, silent and stunned with a blue and gray carriage blanket draping from her stooped shoulders, was encircled by a few others of her age, all unable to meet her questioning gaze.

Inspector Brown had shooed Stella and Lyndy away from the captain's side, eager to get the body to the medical examiner, arguing there was nothing more she could do. But what had she done? To uncover Mrs. Nelson's killer, to find the missing cook, to prevent the military man's demise? Very little. She'd let her desire to celebrate the perfect Christmas as part of her new family cloud her judgment. But what of the spirit of Christmas? What of the need for justice?

At least Inspector Brown had agreed to let Stella do this.

"My lady," Miss Stancliffe said, slightly bobbing when Stella approached.

"We've come from speaking to the police."

"They say Humphrey's been injured, my lady. Is he all right?"

"I am so sorry, Miss Stancliffe." Stella instinctually placed a comforting hand on the older woman's arm. She was trembling.

"He isn't all right, is he?" she whispered, choking back tears.

"It looks like your brother was thrown and then crushed by his pony. He's dead, Miss Stancliffe."

"But—"

Stella anticipated what the captain's sister was going to say. "Even the most experienced riders can be caught off guard. I'm so sorry. Do you have someone to take you home?"

Miss Stancliffe shyly pointed toward her carriage and driver, then her knees buckled. Stella, a heartbeat ahead of another nearby woman, dashed to support her.

"Now, now, Betsy." The stout woman, with springy gray eyebrows beneath a dark blue, wide-brimmed felt hat, helped Stella stabilize Miss Stancliffe on her feet. She shoved a linen handkerchief into Miss Stancliffe's hand and added, "Chin up. Humphrey wouldn't want you to make a scene. How's about a nice cup of tea?"

Miss Stancliffe, dabbing her eyes with a shaky hand, managed a weak smile. "You're right, as always, Margaret."

"Mrs. Margaret Heppenstall, at your service, my lady," she said brusquely, easing her arm around Miss Stancliffe's shoulder, transferring her weight from Stella. Heppenstall? Wasn't that the name of the owner of the Knightwood Oak? Could this be the publican's mother? "No need to bother yourself anymore. I'll see to Betsy."

After a deferential bob of her head, Mrs. Heppenstall led her friend away, the two women trudging toward the carriage. While fighting against a growing weariness, Stella found Lyndy discussing the accident with a few other riders and Mr. Green. The buzzard she'd seen earlier soared past and landed in a nearby oak, a dead rabbit dangling from its talons.

"And you didn't see anything untoward?" Lyndy was asking.

A round of nos dashed Stella's hopes of finding a witness.

"At least not at first," Sir Edwin said. Sir Edwin was the only other one of their party to stay behind. Everyone else had returned to the warmth and comfort of Morrington Hall. "I think I saw his pony struggling to keep up."

"That was me, Sir Edwin," Stella said grudgingly, stomping her feet. She couldn't feel them anymore.

"No, no, my girl, you were too far behind us for me to see you." Stella winced at his blunt assessment. "The captain and I were neck and neck. Until suddenly, we weren't. I glanced back once, and Major seemed a bit heavy in his carriage, almost struggling to keep pace. I thought nothing of it at the time."

"Come to think of it, I noticed something too," a man, with the scent of cows on him, said. Pushing back his wool cap, he rubbed his forehead as if physically conjuring up his memory. "But it was out of the corner of me eye. A stumble, maybe? With me pony getting on so well, I didn't want to risk turning to see."

"And this was before the woodland?" Lyndy asked.

Sir Edwin and the other rider agreed.

"So, Major wasn't simply startled by something when the captain cleared the trees. He was already sluggish and maybe even stumbling," Stella said.

"But look at him now," Sir Edwin said, pointing to the gelding now tied to the back of Mr. Green's wagon. "He appears quite normal."

Did he, though? She couldn't tell from this distance.

"He is," the vet confirmed. "I can assure you that is one hale and healthy animal."

"But, if he's right as rain, what happened to leave a man dead?" The other rider, whose name Stella never learned, scratched his forehead, a line of mud stuck to his skin where his cap had been.

"We're assuming," Sir Edwin said, "that the pony stumbled on something, or into a depression, perhaps, threw the captain, and then rolled on top of his legs, crushing him?"

"That's what we suspect," Lyndy answered. "Yes."

"Good Lord, what a bad break," Sir Edwin said, seemingly unaware of his poor choice of words.

"Yes," Stella began, her muscles strained from the damp cold, her mood tense with frustration, "but what made Major fall behind in the first place?"

Despite the impressive accumulative knowledge between them, no one had an answer.

CHAPTER 2 1

Stella disembarked from the carriage and joined the other ladies before the imposing gray stone structure looming over them. Within minutes after returning from the windswept site of the Point-to-Point finishing line, she'd changed into something warm and dry and was rumbling back across the Forest to this lonely spot. But she was already feeling better. What nicer distraction from the recent deaths and disappearances (and all the unanswered questions surrounding them) could there be than to give gifts to children?

Having burned through the clouds, the sun glistened off the damp web of dormant ivy vines creeping across the building's front walls, reflecting the partially cleared sky at them from dozens of undersized windows. It didn't improve the cold aspect of the institution.

As Lady Atherly led the way toward the broad arched front entrance, Stella studied the well-groomed grounds, including the fenced-in vegetable garden, tilled and ready for spring, for any sign that hundreds of children lived inside the building's walls. She found none.

But that was why they were there, wasn't it? To brighten the lives of these little ones, even if only for the day?

Boxing Day, and its customs of helping the less fortunate, was a tradition she'd never heard of before (Daddy not being known for his charitable disposition) but one Stella had fully embraced. Armed with her inheritance and a husband sympathetic to any cause that made her happy, Stella planned to do more than bring cake and clothes to the workhouse once a year. She wanted to be a positive force all year long. She'd set her sights on the Triple R Farm to help the animals and the people who relied on them. Improving Mrs. Young's Home for Orphaned Girls was next.

Waiting to greet the women in the cavernous but thickly carpeted front hall was a statuesque woman whose port-wine stain covering her left cheek could be seen from the doorway. Above her hung an excessive riot of colorful paper chains. Though Stella expected a stern mistress, like so many of her governesses, the matron offered them a broad smile and a slight curtsy.

"Welcome, welcome, ladies. How kind of you to take time to visit us, Lady Atherly and Lady Alice. And I see you've brought others."

"Mrs. Young," Lady Atherly said, gracious and condescending, "may I introduce Lady Isabella Kentfield. Her family are guests at Morrington Hall for Christmas. And this is my daughter-in-law, Lady Lyndhurst."

"How do you do, Lady Isabella? We are honored." Mrs. Young squinted at Stella, her mouth crinkled in amusement. "I am pleased we finally meet, Lady Lyndhurst. I have heard much about you."

"Not all bad, I hope," Stella quipped, ignoring her mother-in-law's pinched, disapproving expression.

The matron's shoulders quivered with suppressed laughter as she wagged her finger teasingly. "Not all."

Stella liked her immediately. "I've heard such good things about your work here."

"That's kind of you to say, my lady. Shall we?"

As Mrs. Young indicated a side room, Lady Atherly motioned to James, the footman, waiting patiently by the door, to begin bringing in the baskets they'd brought. As the stacks of baskets grew, Mrs. Young watched in mute shock.

"My word!" she said haltingly, her hand laid against her chest. "How very generous of you, Lady Atherly."

Stella's mother-in-law acknowledged the gratitude with a silent nod. Yet it was Stella's doing—the buns, the books, the pork pies, the dolls, the evergreens for decoration; Lady Atherly had argued against it, implying an ugliness to excessive generosity.

"It would give the wrong impression," she'd said. "It would set a precedent of expectation that one couldn't possibly live up to year after year."

What did Stella care? It was Christmas. What was the point of giving to charity if it didn't bring lasting joy and relief?

"A cracker with a toy in it for every child?" Mrs. Young shook her head in disbelief after lifting the lid on the nearest basket.

"And an orange," Alice added enthusiastically. She gladly endorsed the idea when she'd learned of Stella's plan.

"I thought it too much," Lady Isabella said. "My daughters patronize their local orphanage, of course, but they—"

"What's Christmas without loud noises and a few fun surprises?" Stella interrupted.

"How right you are, Lady Lyndhurst," Mrs. Young said. "The children will be quite overjoyed. Please, I've had tea set out in the parlor."

Again, the matron indicated the room off the hall. Warmed by a roaring fire, furnished with overstuffed wing-backed chairs, and wallpapered in a pattern of oversized sunflowers of yellow, green, and gold, the room had a cheerier aspect than Stella expected. But she was a little put off that such a spread had been laid out for them. On the tea table, beside the blue and white floral cups and saucers, were plates overflowing with iced gingerbread cake, mince pies, and currant scones. Stella assumed the abundance was to humor Lady Atherly and her like.

But shouldn't this go to feed the children?

Taking the proffered teacup from Mrs. Young, Stella said, "I'd love to meet the girls. Where are they? I haven't even heard a peep."

The building was immense, but sounds such as childish laughter would travel easily along the long, high-ceilinged corridors. Stella should know. How often had her father complained, when Stella was upstairs in the nursery or her bedroom, that he could hear her noise?

"Isn't that the way of all properly raised girls?" Lady Isabella said, selecting a large slice of gingerbread. The rich scented cake made Stella's mouth water. "Wouldn't you agree, Lady Atherly?"

Lady Atherly, dressed in drab green, offered no response as she took a dainty sip of her tea. Had a single unladylike giggle or screech ever escaped those lips? Or from those of Lady Isabella? Stella doubted it.

"Frederick, of course, was the most boisterous of boys, but my girls, on the other hand, were quite demure and peaceful in their childish pursuits."

Mrs. Young, politely ensuring the lady had finished, waited a moment or two before responding to Stella's request.

"I'd be delighted to introduce you to the children, Lady Lyndhurst. But to answer your question, it's the reading hour. Our girls can be quite the gaggle of geese in silliness and volume, but they do love their books. Even the most restless among them will settle for a story."

"When you're blessed with children, you'll understand what I mean." Having finished her gingerbread, Lady Isabella set down her fork and continued as if the matron hadn't spoken.

This last comment was directed at Stella but, with a sweep of the lady's gaze, oddly included Alice.

Without the armor usually provided by her ever-present stack of magazines, Alice became consumed with the contents of her plate, averting Lady Isabella's persistent stare. Stella faced her challenger, silently daring the woman to ask what Lady Atherly had done so once a week since she and Lyndy returned from their honeymoon.

Lady Isabella pinched a piece of crust from a mince pie and popped it into her mouth.

"Are you pregnant yet, Lady Lyndhurst?"

And there it is.

Lady Atherly nearly spit out her tea in horror. Her mother-in-law hated having the family's business discussed in front of strangers. (Even if it was her heart's desire.) Lady Atherly's hands shook, sending her cup and saucer clattering back to the table. Alice popped her head up, hoping to read Stella's reaction. Stella, her ears burning, dug her fingernails into her palms to stay calm. Again, she and Lady Atherly agreed; this was none of anyone else's business. Besides, it had only been a few months. Couldn't she be allowed to enjoy being a newlywed for a bit longer?

As Stella formulated her response, Mrs. Young cleared her throat. "Forgive me for not mentioning it sooner, Lady Atherly. But may I offer you my condolences on the death of Mrs. Nelson."

"Thank you, Mrs. Young," Lady Atherly sighed, her hands folded tightly in her lap. Stella suspected she meant it more than just for the woman's condolences. "That is most kind of you."

"Did you know our housekeeper?" Alice asked.

"What curiosity you have, Lady Alice," Lady Isabella said. "I can't imagine my daughters ever dreaming of asking such a thing from a new acquaintance."

Was it Stella's imagination, or did Lady Atherly roll her eyes?

"Sadly," Mrs. Young said, politely answering Alice's question, "I met her for the first time . . . four days ago."

The day before Mrs. Nelson died. Stella's curiosity instantly trumped her growing frustration with Lady Isabella and her legendary perfect daughters.

"Really? Where was that?"

Her voice betrayed the sudden thumping of her heart. This was the first mention of Mrs. Nelson leaving Morrington Hall that day. Did Mrs. Young know something that could help the police? Or that might help Stella learn the truth behind Mrs. Nelson's unspoken request?

The clock in the hall chimed twice.

"Why, here, of course. I rarely make it into the village."

"Whatever was she doing here?" Lady Isabella tsked, inadvertently, in trying to voice her disapproval, asking the question on the tip of Stella's tongue.

"She'd come inquiring after a particular child placed in our care years ago."

"What child?" Lady Atherly demanded, none too happy to have the conversation circle back to the topic of children in connection with Morrington Hall.

"Not her child, surely?" Lady Isabella said as if it were a foregone conclusion that Morrington Hall's housekeeper was of dubious morals.

"Goodness, no," Mrs. Young said, chuckling. "Mrs. Nelson was checking on someone's background. I assumed she meant one of her maids."

"Were you able to help her?" Stella asked.

"I could confirm that we had several girls of that age when I arrived to take over the post, but not much more than that, I'm afraid. Any specific information is quite confidential. Even if I wanted to oblige her, many records from that time burned in a fire."

"And when did you take over the post?" Stella asked.

"It was in 1878."

Twenty-six years ago. Louisa was in her late twenties. Could that have been whom Mrs. Nelson was asking about?

Stella took her first sip of unsweetened tea, scrunching her nose. It was too bitter for her taste.

"Then to learn the poor woman was dead," Mrs. Young said. "I regretted not being of more help, but whatever Mrs. Nelson was hoping to learn doesn't much matter now, does it?"

The other three women agreed with reassuring utterances of variations of "No, no, I suppose not."

Stella, keeping her opinion to herself, wasn't so sure.

CHAPTER 22

Dressed in a garish, flouncy dress of alternating strips of cadmium yellow, sea green, and magenta, the actor bounded on stage; his wig, a towering heap of blond curls, bobbed with every step. The audience, particularly the children below, enthusiastically booed and hissed at his entrance. Comfortably settled into the second row of the best box seat in the theater, Stella had a perfect view of the entire stage.

She leaned into Lyndy and whispered, "Why is that man dressed like a woman?"

Lyndy smiled indulgently at yet another one of her questions. "He's the evil auntie." That didn't tell her anything.

"I'd guessed that. But why—?"

"Shhh," Lady Isabella hissed, not for the first time.

When Stella had been told they and the Kentfields were going to the theater for a traditional Christmas pantomime, she had no idea what to expect. But she'd assumed since Lady Atherly was attending that it would be a well-known, respectable play. She never could've guessed it was a topsy-turvy musical with women playing men's roles, men playing women's roles, clowns, villains, fairies, and more. It was a production for children, who packed the theater, giggling, wiggling in their seats, and occasionally shouting commentary at the players on stage without reprimand. According to Lyndy, it was part of the fun.

And it was fun. Ablaze with light, the stage was ornamented with a painted background that artfully resembled the Forest beyond the village, and was populated not only with colorful characters but expertly constructed false trees looming on both sides of the stage. It didn't matter that Stella was unfamiliar with the play; she could laugh and boo by taking her cues from the others. Loosely based on an old English children's story, *Robin Hood and the Babes in the Wood* recounted the tale of two orphaned children who, with the aid of Robin Hood, Maid Marian, and their band of Merry Men, must escape the clutches of their evil aunt. This evil aunt was the actor Stella had questioned Lyndy about, his costume stuffed with pillows to give him a rotund but comical shape. Jaunty musical numbers, ballet interludes, and humorous routines between two robbers paid by the evil aunt to kill the children rounded it all out. It was the most fantastical production Stella had ever seen.

Another joyful tradition she'd missed out on as a child.

Laughter, song, and children's enthusiastic voices swirled around her, with Lyndy, Lord Atherly, his lorgnette pressed to his eyes, and the others joining in. Despite being tight-lipped, even Lady Atherly seemed entranced by it all, trying, maybe, to capture a childhood joy long forgotten. Stella delighted almost as much in the levity it brought out in her new family as the panto itself. She was smiling so much it almost hurt.

Then one of the clownish robbers delivered a death blow, a playful bop on the head to the other clown. The victim flopped to the stage, all arms and legs, jerking and wiggling in a comic display, eliciting a roar of applause from the crowd. Amidst the clamor, Stella froze, her hands clasped tightly in her lap. First, Mrs. Nelson's broken body and then Captain Stancliffe's crumpled figure flashed behind her eyes, blotting out the spectacle on the stage. She shivered as if she still raced across the cold moor.

As everyone around her picked up the chorus of the next song, Lord Atherly singing the loudest, Stella sifted through her thoughts, questions brewing with every stanza of the song. Why had Mrs. Nelson been out that night? Why had she gone to the orphanage? Had it something to do with Louisa, the chambermaid? Or with what she was going to ask Stella and never got the chance? Could Mrs. Nelson's death be related to the captain's? Was it a coincidence that he died of another supposed accident two days later? Could the captain have killed her, despite what Inspector Brown said? If not, what explained the blood on him that night? Was Stella seeing evil lurking—as Robin Hood did now from behind a tree, in his long black beard—where there was none? But then, where was Mrs. Cole?

While the players bounded about the stage, boisterously and unabashedly declaring themselves to be something they weren't, Stella couldn't shake the feeling she was missing something.

Without warning, Stella's senses tingled, pulling her from her reverie. She was being watched again. She scoured the audience below but didn't see a single upturned face. As she settled back into her seat, trying to recapture her earlier enchantment, motion nearby caught her eye. Sir Edwin had abruptly ducked his head.

Had he been staring at her?

Lyndy, following her gaze and seeing Sir Edwin absorbed in the contents of his program, whispered, "Aren't you enjoying yourself, my love?" He must've noticed her clouded expression. He stroked his knuckle gently against her cheek. "Still thinking of this morning?"

"Shhhh!" Lady Isabella hissed.

On stage, a villainous laugh was followed by a firecracker

explosion. Stella flinched. Children in the audience shrieked in delight as a cloud of smoke engulfed the evil auntie. Lord Atherly coughed into his fist.

"I still don't understand why—" Stella began as the smell of flash powder reached their seats.

"It's supposed to be comical," Sir Edwin offered, cutting Stella off. "The very idea of women dressing as men is completely ridiculous." He was answering her earlier question, not the one she was going to ask. "And being outlandishly obvious about it makes it all the more absurd." He winked at her.

She offered him a lackluster smile. She was tired of his condescending familiarity. "I'm sorry, Sir Edwin, but nothing about murder is amusing."

Alone in the library for once, Lyndy laid his sporting paper in his lap. Peppering the columns of upcoming events were mentions of this or that annual motorcar race.

"Bloody hell," he said to no one but the glassy-eyed stuffed birds. *I can't escape it.*

Stella hadn't been the only one distracted at the pantomime last night. Lyndy had enjoyed the inane antics and silly songs, but Stella was right. He'd always considered the killing of the "baddies" all in good fun—good triumphing over evil and all that. But having experienced murder close at hand, it all seemed to be in bad taste now.

If only it had ended there.

Upon the evil sheriff's introduction into the storyline, Lyndy had been reminded of the theft of the Kentfields' motorcar. When he'd brought it up to Sir Edwin, inquiring why Inspector Brown hadn't been called in, Sir Edwin had eluded the conversation with his insistence Lyndy "not spoil the mood with such talk." Sir Edwin's dismissal had had the opposite effect. Lyndy, who would've demanded the police investigate without delay, could think of little else.

Why would Sir Edwin not pursue it? It was a question Lyndy had tried to ask, twice, and been rebuffed. Had it something to do with the housekeeper? The notion, as abhorrent as it may have been, had resided, latent, in the back of his mind all night. Hadn't Lyndy noticed damage to the Martini the day the Kentfields arrived? Granted, that was before Mrs. Nelson's death, but it spoke to a driver with a recklessness about him. In all the months Stella had driven her father's Daimler about the Forest, never once had she banged, dented, or scratched the motorcar. Contrary to Lyndy's protestations to the opposite, she was a conscientious driver. But Sir Edwin had damaged his, loosening the headlamp and denting the bumper, perhaps on the trip down from London.

And how could Lyndy forget the contentious conversation between the housekeeper and his mother? There was a secret there, one that concerned Sir Edwin, confirmed by the cryptic note they'd found in Sir Edwin's hand. Could that secret be at the root of the servant's death? Could Sir Edwin have run over Mrs. Nelson to keep her from revealing it?

Lyndy popped out of his comfortable chair and smacked his thigh with the folded racing news. Striding out of the library, he crossed through the empty grand saloon where the yule log still burned bright and the glorious Christmas tree held court, its fragrance reaching him before he'd stepped foot in the room. In the hall, he aimed for the telephone stand. Lyndy picked up the telephone receiver, cringing at the crank's loud scraping sound. After a visual sweep to ensure he was still alone, he instructed the operator who answered to connect him with the motorcar repair garage he'd seen advertised in his sporting paper.

"I say. Have any motors arrived in the last few days with heavy damage to the body's frame?"

"Oi, what's the meaning of this?" the disembodied voice demanded. "As if I have nothing better to do than to chat on this contraption all day."

"I beg your pardon?"

"I only got this installed a month ago, and now two telephone calls in one morning! First the police and now you. I'm starting to regret it, I am. Who are you, by the way? What's this all about, eh?"

Lyndy bristled at being so addressed. He'd have slammed the receiver down if he didn't need the information.

"Viscount Lyndhurst, if you must know, and I'd curb your tongue. A woman has been killed by a motorcar. My housekeeper, in fact."

"Deepest apologies and condolences, Your Lordship," the man on the other side of the line said, sounding rightly abashed. "Them police never said. I wish I could help, but I've only got the one motor, and it's got a broken crank. Frame's fine. You might try ringing the other shops about."

"And where might they be?"

"If you'll hold a minute, I'll get their names."

True to his word, the man returned with a list of garages that were scattered throughout southern England, including a few with telephone numbers. Lyndy thanked the man, rang off, and began contacting them. He discovered that Inspector Brown, whether similarly supplied with a list or not, had beaten Lyndy to it every time. Each repairman had the same answer. No motor in need of extensive frame repair had been brought in.

He called the last one with a working telephone and was surprised to discover Inspector Brown had not been in contact yet.

"Indeed, my lord, we do," the garage owner said. "Seeing as we specialize in body repair."

"Then you must have Sir Edwin Kentfield's motor." It was a long shot, seeing as several garages were left on his list. "He's staying at Morrington Hall over the holidays and had completely forgotten which garage he'd brought it to."

Lyndy's pulse quickened. He glanced about the hall again. A footman, carrying a tray filled with the dishes of a half-eaten breakfast, passed from the dining room but paid Lyndy little notice.

"Indeed, it's here, my lord," the voice on the line said, "and you can reassure Sir Edwin that his motor will be ready as promised."

Lyndy placed his hand over the receiver and choked back an incredulous laugh. He'd found Sir Edwin's motorcar!

But who'd brought it in for repair? Would the repairman even know? Anyone could claim to be Sir Edwin. Or had it been Sir Edwin? And why? Was it to fix the damage previous to Mrs. Nelson's death, or was it the murder weapon, as they say? Yet, if it were the latter, why drive it to Bournemouth in the middle of the night?

"That's splendid. Sir Edwin will be delighted to hear it."

Lyndy tapped the metal switch hook to disconnect. Upon hearing the click, he replaced the receiver and returned the telephone to its stand, considering what he should do next. Telephone Brown? Go to Bournemouth and interrogate the repairman further? Confront Sir Edwin? Making up his mind, he bounded up the stairs to his bedchamber, where Stella was taking breakfast.

First and foremost, he needed to tell his wife.

CHAPTER 23

Inspector Brown stared at the decapitated deer head on the wall. He never understood the appeal of killing an animal for sport and then mounting its head for posterity to admire. What he also couldn't abide was Lord and Lady Lyndhurst withholding information that could be relevant to his investigation. *Which was going nowhere.* With the maid and the cook still missing and the inquiries of the motorcar garages coming to nothing, Brown had found himself at a loss. Until now. At least the couple had come to their senses and made a clean breast of things.

He'd been cautiously optimistic when the telephone call came in from Morrington Hall. It always meant news. Had the cook returned? Had Sir Edwin finally agreed to allow Brown to inspect his motorcar? But when he'd heard what Lord Lyndhurst had to tell him—that His Lordship had noticed damage on Sir Edwin Kentfield's car days ago, how that same car had been driven off Christmas Eve, the stablemaster left for dead, that a threatening note from Sir Edwin had been found in the housekeeper's study, and that no one had thought to tell him before now—Brown had been better at controlling his anger than his disappointment.

Hadn't they a long history of helping him with his inquiries? Hadn't he been more than accommodating in the past? Why the reluctance now?

Brown had calmly assured His Lordship he'd be there as fast as he could while insisting, in the utmost polite manner, that Sir Edwin be prevented from leaving the manor before he got there. But the moment Lord Lyndhurst rang off, Brown slammed the receiver down, sending the telephone clattering to the floor, the ever-present *click-clack-click* of the desk sergeant's typewriter pausing momentarily in response. As he snatched his hat from the rack and stormed out of the station, Brown had ignored the lad's questioning gaze.

Brown, rubbing the back of his neck, let his gaze linger a moment longer on the deer's head. He hadn't stewed in his anger for long, finally having a good lead, but why must they insist he use this room again?

"Thank you for obliging me, Sir Edwin."

Sir Edwin leaned back into the leather captain's chair, his interlocked fingers supporting his head, his legs casually crossed before him.

"I'm happy to help, Inspector, but as I hardly knew the housekeeper, I don't know how much use I can be."

How many countless witnesses and suspects had Brown questioned in this exact manner? Lord Atherly's smoking room was becoming a secondary police interrogation room. On every occasion that Brown entered this place, investigating yet another suspicious death, he'd hoped it would be his last. Today hadn't been any different.

"Do you know how I spent my morning, Sir Edwin?"

"I have no idea."

"Well, I will tell you. I've been on the telephone, speaking to motorcar repair garages all over Hampshire and beyond, while my constable is somewhere between here and Winchester in pursuit of tracking down those without such modern equipment."

Brown studied Sir Edwin for a reaction. His quarry reached for a box of cigars from the side table, shielding his face from Brown's scrutiny. "Oh, yes?"

"It has been a tedious process, mind you, but not without its reward. Do you know what we discovered?"

"I don't." Sir Edwin chose a cigar before clipping off the tip. He lit his match against the round, ribbed, glass match-striker and raised the flame to his cigar. "But I do believe you are about to tell me."

"We discovered that the one in Bournemouth is servicing your motorcar, Sir Edwin."

When Lord Lyndhurst had told Brown, he'd immediately connected it with the maid. Hadn't the last known address for Louisa Bright, or whatever her real name was, been in Bournemouth? But what connection there was between Sir Edwin and the chambermaid, if there was one, Brown had yet to find out.

"It's a motorcar, Inspector. It requires periodic servicing."

"This is a specialty shop. One that does only frame repair. Such as in the case where a motorist has hit something and needs the dents seen to."

After a few quick draws of breath, Sir Edwin blew a large plume of smoke into the air, adding to the rich, sweet, woody aroma that already permeated the room. "Now, now, Inspector. You aren't suggesting that I hit Mrs. Nelson?"

"Did you?"

"Why would I?"

"That's not an answer, Sir Edwin."

He took a few more puffs before answering. "Very well." He pointed the fingers holding his cigar at Brown. His nails had been recently manicured. "I admit to damaging the Martini, yes. I hit a blasted hedge planted too close along a curve driving down from London. That is all. Dented the fender and as good as knocked my headlamp clean off." He went to take another puff.

"Right! Tell me then, Sir Edwin, if you would. Why the need to duck out in the middle of the night and bash poor Mr. Gates in the head for good measure if you merely met with a jutting hedge?"

Sir Edwin coughed, sputtering as he sat upright, waving away the smoke.

I have him!

By all accounts, any number of people at Morrington Hall, servants and residents alike, let alone ne'er-do-well villagers, could've stolen the vehicle and taken it to Bournemouth. All it took was a rudimentary aptitude to drive—the keys, it seems, were kept in the ignition. But Brown had trusted Lord and Lady Lyndhurst's instincts that Sir Edwin was involved. And it paid off. Yet again.

"How did you . . . ?"

"Lucky for you, Mr. Gates has a thick skull." Of course, the stablemaster had seen nothing, but if Sir Edwin concluded otherwise from Brown's statement, that was on him. "Now, I think you should tell me everything, don't you?"

Sir Edwin snuffed out his cigar, crushing the stub in the silver ashtray. His hand was shaking. Rising to his feet, he strolled to a small wooden cabinet and flung open its doors. Deep inside, as if hidden from view on purpose, lay a decanter and whiskey glass. Sir Edwin tilted his head, asking over his shoulder, "Do you mind?"

It was but a few hours past luncheon, but who was Brown to judge? Without waiting for a response, Sir Edwin poured himself more than a mere dram and knocked it back in one swig. He poured himself a second before settling back into his chair.

"I didn't give the spar with the hedge a second thought until I overheard you spell out your suspicions to Lord and Lady

Lyndhurst about Mrs. Nelson being killed by a motorcar. I panicked; I admit it. But can you blame me? It's Christmas. My family and I are guests of the countess. I didn't want us to be caught up in anything so salacious as a murder inquiry."

"So you slipped out with your motorcar in the middle of the night because you were afraid you'd be a suspect in the house-keeper's murder?"

"That's not at all what I said. Besides, how could I be a suspect? I was in bed with my wife the night Mrs. Nelson was wandering about, getting herself killed."

"And hitting Gates?"

He took a sip of his whiskey. "I do regret that. Again, I panicked. I didn't expect anyone to be about at that hour. I'm genuinely relieved to hear the man isn't worse for wear."

"And that he isn't pressing charges?"

"Yes, that too," Sir Edwin said as if the idea had never crossed his mind.

"Right!" Did Brown believe him? He wasn't certain. But he was convinced Sir Edwin was still holding something back. "What did you and Captain Stancliffe speak about yesterday before the Point-to-Point Race?"

The switch in topic did what Brown intended; staring into his glass, Sir Edwin was caught off guard. He stopped swirling his whiskey and abruptly looked up.

"Captain Stancliffe? That was an accident." He put his feet flat on the floor and leaned forward defensively, pointing a finger at Brown. "Bloody hell, man. I'd just met him. Now you think I had something to do with his death?"

"I simply wish to know what you two spoke about." Brown had seen the two together before the race. He'd thought nothing of it at the time.

Sir Edwin, taking a breath, leaned back again. "Lady Lyndhurst's Triple R Farm for Horses and Ponies, if you must know. Through a mutual acquaintance, the captain discovered that I was considering donating to it. That I'd come down from London to see it for myself."

"And?"

"And he asked my impression. I believe he also intended to contribute to the viscountess's venture. He even tried to speak to Lady Lyndhurst about it before the race began. You can ask her."

Brown assured him he had every intention of doing so and then stood. After drinking the last of his whiskey, Sir Edwin set the empty glass on the table and rose as well, carefully concealed relief (to anyone but a seasoned detective) etched on his features.

"By the way, Sir Edwin. Do you know the name Louisa Bright?"

The man furrowed his brows. "Should I?"

"Know any Elizas?"

Sir Edwin shook his head, genuine confusion on his face. "I have a third cousin named Eliza. Why?"

"This would be a maid, sir."

"I have as little to do with maids as possible, my dear fellow." Sir Edwin chuckled, reverting a bit to his condescending levity. "Have you met my wife? She'd have my head."

Despite the flippant bravado, Brown believed him. *At least about the maid.*

"You've been most helpful, Sir Edwin. Do not hesitate to contact me if anything comes to mind that might aid us in our inquiries."

"I'm certain that won't be necessary. I've told you all I know." Sir Edwin flashed Brown a self-satisfied smile. "Good day, Inspector." He sauntered unhurriedly across the room while Brown bore a hole in the man's back.

Regardless of what the blighter said, this was not the last Brown would see of Sir Edwin Kentfield.

CHAPTER 24

The holly wreath had been replaced by ribbons of black crape flapping on the Stancliffes' door. How sad. With Mrs. Nelson's death, Stella's mother-in-law had resisted plunging the entire household into mourning. She'd allowed the servants to don bands of black crape around their arms but stopped at that. Using her guests as an excuse, Lady Atherly had insisted the housekeeper would've preferred everyone to enjoy the festivities she'd worked so hard to prepare. Wouldn't all semblance of a typical Christmas be dashed if black had replaced the green that dominated the décor? she'd argued. The poor Stancliffe household didn't have a choice. Stella's mother-in-law had been able to justify her decision because, despite living at Morrington Hall and serving its occupants faithfully for decades, Mrs. Nelson had been a servant, not a family member. Mrs. Nelson deserved better.

She deserved justice.

Stella shivered as a cool breeze ruffled her fur collar, tickling her neck. Lyndy rapped on the door again with his knuckle. A slow shuffle inside signaled that someone had heard them but was taking their time to answer the door. Eventually, it cracked open, and Miss Stancliffe peered out, the lace edging her bonnet encircling her head like a black halo. She cupped her cheeks with her hands.

"Lord and Lady Lyndhurst?" she said, in a startled, booming voice, as if she'd caught a deer on her doorstep nibbling at her roses. "What are you doing here?"

"We've come to check on you, Miss Stancliffe, and to tell you what we've learned," Stella answered. "May we come in?"

"You'd like to come in?" Miss Stancliffe repeated, glancing over her shoulder. "One moment, please." She closed the door, leaving the couple out in the cold.

"I say!" Lyndy pulled up the collar of his overcoat, stomping his feet, and rubbed his gloved hands together. "I pray she doesn't keep us waiting too long. It's bloody cold out here."

Lyndy would've preferred to spend the day in the stables with Knockan Crag and pouring over the horse's pedigree with Mr. Gates. Stella didn't blame him. She'd managed an early ride with Tully, cold or no cold, hoping to make sense of the world again. Although any time with her beloved mare was soothing, Stella's restlessness hadn't abated. Two people were dead, and both had been prevented from telling her something before they died.

The curtains in the nearest window moved. A small patch of fogged windowpane persisted in the corner. Was Miss Stancliffe spying on them from inside, hoping they'd go away?

"Explain to me again why we're here," Lyndy complained.

"It's only right. I found the captain's body, and you took the pony." Lyndy directed Major to be stabled at the Triple R Farm under the watchful eye of Mr. Green until Miss Stancliffe decided what to do with him. "She needs to know what we know."

After relaying everything they'd learned and suspected to Inspector Brown earlier, Stella was drawn to call on the captain's sister as well.

"Besides," Stella added, "I have a few things I want to ask her."

Growing impatient, Lyndy knocked again. In immediate response, the door flew open, fluttering the black crape ribbons with the sudden, swift motion. Looming large before them wasn't Miss Stancliffe as they'd expected but Mrs. Cole, Morrington Hall's missing cook.

"Mrs. Cole?" Lyndy blurted in surprise. "What's the meaning of this?"

Like the mourning sister huddling behind her, the cook was dressed in black. She wasn't wearing a cap or apron. Had Stella ever seen her without them?

With her arms on her hips in defiance, Mrs. Cole wordlessly stepped aside, allowing Stella to precede Lyndy into the modest hall.

As she passed, Stella couldn't help but notice what the cook's spectacles couldn't mask, the dark shadows beneath her eyes, the puffy redness of their rims. Once the door and the cold were shut out, Mrs. Cole led them into the same small but comfortable drawing room they'd visited before. Again, Stella had to duck her head. Miss Stancliffe shuffled ahead to the chintz-covered armchair closest to the blazing fire. Abandoned on the floor beside it was a basket of undarned stockings. Clutching a handkerchief to her breast, the captain's sister gazed at the Christmas tree on the table, decorated with simple colored glass balls. Each one reflected her weary face.

Mrs. Cole, left to perform the civilities, offered them a seat as if she, and not Miss Stancliffe, was mistress of the house. Stella and Lyndy took the settee opposite. Mrs. Cole sat when they did.

Another first. What was going on?

"Is this where you've been all this time? Lady Atherly has been most put out," Lyndy said, brushing at his sleeve, his voice warming to his lecture. "Here it is Christmas, and we have a house full of guests. You've quite let us all down, Mrs.

Cole. Did you not consider anyone but yourself?" His condescension was never attractive.

"Lyndy." Stella laid a hand on his arm. "As you say, it's Christmas. A time of peace and charity? Shouldn't you let Mrs. Cole have her say before you draw any conclusions?"

Stella so wanted a simple explanation. The cook hadn't taken Sir Edwin's automobile. She hadn't been anywhere near the Point-to-Point Race when the captain died. Maybe her disappearance had nothing to do with Mrs. Nelson's murder.

"Very well. Mrs. Cole?" Lyndy leaped to his feet and began wearing a path in the carpet. "What were you thinking absconding in the middle of the night without a word?"

Instead of the typical disgruntled retort, the cook bowed her head, clenching her hands in her lap, and stifled a sob. Lyndy, alarmed by the turn of events, gestured to Stella to do something.

Stella shrugged and then leaned forward, asking softly, "Would you like to tell us what happened?"

"He's dead, isn't he?" the cook snapped. "That's what happened."

There was the old Mrs. Cole! Stella sat back, reassured. Being on the receiving end of the cook's caustic retorts was far better than watching her trying not to cry.

"Do you mean Captain Stancliffe?"

"Of course!" The cook's head shot up, tears making her angry eyes sparkle. "Who else would I be talking about?"

"Now, now, Mrs. Cole, you've caused quite a stir." That one phrase encompassed the whole staff searching for her, the need to recruit Mrs. Downie to take over on Christmas Day, the suspicion she'd stolen Sir Edwin's automobile, or the fear that she'd gone the same way as Mrs. Nelson. Leave it to Lyndy to resort to such an understatement. "I do believe you at least owe us an explanation."

"Mrs. Stancliffe," a middle-aged woman in a plain black

dress and starched apron interrupted as she entered the room. Keys jangled at her waist. "Shall I make tea?"

Miss Stancliffe didn't stir from her musings to correct the maid's mistake. Instead, Mrs. Cole answered. "Yes, do."

That's why she's wearing widow's weeds!

"When was the wedding, Mrs. Stancliffe?" Stella asked.

Lyndy, his brows pinched, stopped his pacing. "What the devil—?"

"Humphrey and I married on Christmas Day." The cook held up her hand. On her finger rested a gold band glittering in the fire's glow.

"I'm so sorry." Stella had been married a few months and relished every minute. This poor woman had only had her husband for a day.

"My deepest condolences, Mrs. Cole, but you still haven't explained your abrupt departure from Morrington Hall," Lyndy pressed. "Marriage is not an automatic excuse for abandoning your commitments to my family."

"If you'll forgive me saying so, my lord, your mother would never have allowed me to continue on if she knew of my desire to marry. Besides, it was a bit of a rash decision."

"I'd say." Lyndy chuckled under his breath at yet another obvious understatement.

A bowl of various nuts sat on the end table. Stella could smell them from where she sat. Lyndy selected one and popped it into his mouth.

"Please, Mrs. Stancliffe," Stella said. "You were telling us why you left."

"Yes, well, Humphrey and I had been quietly courting for years. Only Helena, Mrs. Nelson, knew. A week back, the captain proposed. I was hesitant to accept. Marriage would cost me my position, my home, and the only life I've ever known. It was Mrs. Nelson who encouraged me. I accepted Humphrey's proposal the day she died."

She held up a hand, forestalling Lyndy's reply. "And before you reproach me on your mother's behalf, my lord, I'd always planned to give notice. I'd planned to marry in a few months. Then Mrs. Nelson fell ill, and the rumors began. The veiled accusations. The quiet murmurings that they didn't think I could hear."

"What accusations?" Stella asked.

"That I'd poisoned her. Me!" She slapped at her skirt as if she'd found flour soiling it. "It all became quite untenable. And that was before that new veterinarian found Mrs. Nelson's crushed body. Why should I face another day in that house when I had the promise of a new, happy start here? To think of it, at my age!"

"Didn't my mother deserve the courtesy of an explanation?" Lyndy said. "Blasted, Mrs. Cole, we thought you too were dead!"

The widow blanched. Had the idea never occurred to her? And then red blotches, like burn marks, blossomed up her neck.

"I did leave a letter explaining all of this. If that silly girl who starts my fire every morning tossed it on the grate for kindling, I can't be held responsible. I didn't hire her." She crossed her arms, challenging anyone to find further fault.

What is taking the maid so long with the tea?

"Either way, we've found you now and are thrilled you're safe," Stella said, hoping to change the subject. "And speaking of being safe, we brought Major to the horse farm where he'll be looked after for however long it takes for you to decide what to do with him."

"We did that, in part, because during the race, the pony appeared uncharacteristically sluggish after a time," Lyndy added. "I've spoken with Mr. Green about it, and he agrees that Major might've taken or eaten something that caused him to . . ." Lyndy paused.

"No need to mince words, my lord," the widow said. "Just tell me what happened."

"The pony collapsed, throwing the captain off and then crushing him."

Mrs. Stancliffe regarded her sister-in-law with a softened expression Stella had never seen on the cook's face. "The police never told Elizabeth the details. Only that it was an accident." Doubt colored her last word.

"But you think otherwise," Stella said.

"Why would I? It sounds perfectly, tragically straightforward, doesn't it?"

"But?"

The widow locked her ankles and shoved them further under the chair. "But for that night, the night Humphrey brought me the rabbit he'd caught."

That explains the blood on his sleeve.

"The captain, poaching?" Lyndy said, dropping down beside Stella on the settee. "That upstanding military man? I can't believe it."

"Believe it, my lord. He's been poaching for these past two years, always bringing me a portion of his bounty. It's why he told none of this to the police."

"Are you saying my favorite meat pie is made with poached rabbits?" Lyndy said, aghast.

"What didn't your husband tell the police?" Stella prodded.

"That night, he'd been to a large warren out near Mistletoe Lane when he saw a motorcar speed past. He'd been afraid he'd been spotted. When the news about Mrs. Nelson reached him, he realized he might've seen whoever ran her over. I think both were true."

"You think the driver killed your husband to keep him from revealing who was behind the wheel?" Stella asked, lurching forward.

Is that what the captain wanted to tell me that day? That he'd seen Mrs. Nelson's killer?

"Didn't he tell you who it was?" Lyndy asked before Stella got the chance.

"No. He didn't want to burden me unnecessarily if he was mistaken. It was my wedding day, after all."

Lyndy let out an audible sigh of frustration and began picking through the bowl of nuts again.

"What did your husband do with that information?" Stella asked.

"I haven't the foggiest."

"He told me," Miss Elizabeth Stancliffe, her voice dreamy and far away, said. "Humphrey planned to confront the driver, offering a chance to confirm or deny his suspicions. After all, like his death, the housekeeper's too might've been an accident." A sob burst from her. The former cook rose, a weary but patient bent to her lips, and took Miss Stancliffe's fragile, outstretched hand. The gold band suddenly lost its luster. "Whatever am I going to do without him, Maggie?"

Maggie? Hadn't Mrs. Nelson, in her delirium, said something about a Maggie?

"You have me now, Betsy."

The maid carrying a porcelain tea service on a tray finally arrived, but it was too late. Lyndy bounded to his feet.

"Our sympathies, again. We'll see ourselves out."

As they ducked back into the hall, Miss Stancliffe called, "My lady, please give Major to some deserving soul. Humphrey admired your work at your rehabilitation farm."

A lump formed in Stella's throat. "I will, Miss Stancliffe. Your brother's generosity won't be forgotten."

CHAPTER 25

"I knew this was a mistake." Isabella stared at her reflection, pinching her cheeks for the desired effect. The color that rose to the surface of her skin complemented her blue tea gown. "We should've gone to Manchester to spend Christmas with Emily."

What could go wrong had gone wrong. First, that horrid drive down from London. Why had Edwin insisted? Isabella wanted to take the train. And then the countess's housekeeper's suspicious death. Whatever would Emily's John say when he heard of it? And finally, the fatal accident during the race. Of course, she'd objected to Edwin's participation. She knew how dangerous it could be. Had he listened to her? Had he acknowledged her keen foresight afterward? Of course not.

Edwin rested his hands on her shoulders, and Isabella tried not to flinch. He met her eyes in the looking glass. "Might I remind you that neither Emily nor Maud invited you?"

Isabella winced.

She didn't need reminding how uncharitable her daughters were. Both successfully married, and neither appreciated how tirelessly Isabella had worked these past two Seasons on their behalf. Nor had they the consideration to invite her for Christmas. Whatever had she done to deserve such apathy?

"You could've stayed in London for the holidays," Edwin added.

Perhaps that would've been better. And yet, if she'd refused Lady Atherly's invitation, Edwin and Freddy would've gone without her. Even Christmas at Morrington Hall was better than spending it alone.

"And leave Freddy to throw away his affection on that shy, awkward girl?"

"Alice is delightful," Edwin said, removing himself to the corner armchair. "Reminds me of you at that age."

Isabella scoffed. "Hardly!"

Isabella was never so pale or so thin or so painfully silent. From what she'd heard, Lady Alice Searlywn's attention was more often than not buried in American magazines instead of spent in diverting conversation. *Who does that?* Lady Alice was rumored to be as unaccomplished with watercolors and needlework as her American sister-in-law. Granted, she was socially superior to Freddy, and her piano playing was satisfactory, but it took more than a pleasant tune and a title to make her son a good wife.

Isabella raised her eyes toward heaven. *However did this happen?*

Isabella had witnessed Lady Alice firsthand two Seasons ago, confirming her suspicions that the girl was unfit for Freddy. She'd dismissed her out of hand. With her daughters married, Isabella had not attended the Season this year. That was her mistake. Where else could Freddy have met the Earl of Atherly's youngest? How else could he have become enamored with the girl? Isabella knew her son. She loved him deeply, but he was a romantic, anything but practical. Consider how he spent his days—playing golf! Freddy, she had no doubt, had been at least partially responsible for securing the invitation to Morrington Hall.

But her son instigated nothing on his own.

Isabella squinted at Edwin, bouncing his foot over his knee as he skimmed the sporting pages. Was Edwin completely innocent in encouraging the attachment? Wasn't it he who suggested a Christmas in the country for a change, manipulating her impressable son? Until this moment, she'd blamed Lady Atherly, assuming it was her suggestion, hoping to catch Freddy for her Alice. But as plain as the creases that snaked across Edwin's forehead as he read, Isabella had little doubt he had a hand in this. Although he'd acknowledged a former acquaintance with the family, he'd refused to elaborate. Isabella was no fool. Something deceptive was afoot.

"What did the police want?" she said, breezily enough, picking up and weighing the glass perfume bottle in her hand, its floral fragrance escaping through a crack in the stopper. Would it hurt him if she threw it hard enough? But Edwin was no fool either and sat well out of range.

"It was nothing." He couldn't be bothered to look up.

"Having the police speak to you is never nothing, and you know it. Thank goodness it happened out here in the wilds. If an inspector appeared on our doorstep in London, I'd never live it down." When he continued to read, infuriatingly reticent on the matter, she swiveled in her seat and glared at him threateningly. "What did they want, Edwin?"

"They asked about the Martini. It's been missing from the carriage house since Christmas Eve."

So that was why they'd been bouncing about the moors in a borrowed carriage.

"What happened to it?"

"How should I know?" He slapped his paper against the

armrest, fussing like a child who won't be held responsible for anything. Not even the disappearance of his toys.

"Explain to me then where you were these past few nights?"

Although they hadn't slept in the same bed for years, Isabella was keenly aware of Edwin's snoring, whether in the bedchamber next door or down the hall. On their first night at Morrington Hall, she'd woken several times, startled to find herself in a strange place, and although she would rather die than admit it, she'd sought the comforting sound of Edwin's snore in the room next door. On the first occasion, Isabella had heard nothing but the creak of the wind against the windowpanes. On the second, she'd crept to his bedchamber to see if something more terrible than being married to him had happened. But alas, she didn't find her husband's body cold and stiff, just an empty bed, unslept in. Suspicious, Isabella had stayed up the following night, reading long after he'd said good night, listening for his snores. Only in the earliest morning hours did she finally hear him.

"Where do you think I was? I was in bed asleep."

"No, you weren't."

"However do you know that? Unless you were checking up on me."

When Isabella allowed a triumphant smirk to touch her lips, Edwin gasped. It was subtle and quiet but more satisfying than his boisterous snores.

"I'll ask again, Edwin. Where were you?"

"I was in bed. As I told the police."

"You're lying, and unless you tell me where you were, I will tell them so."

"And bring scandal upon our family?"

He was right. She'd threatened him before she'd thought it through. She'd fancied getting back at him for mentioning her estrangement from her daughters. He was so unkind. But if he had anything to do with the housekeeper's death, he wouldn't be the only one to suffer. It would be the ruination of the Kent-field name. Isabella had to think of Freddy and the girls.

"We both know you're not capable," he said. He winked.

What a moment ago seemed the proper path blurred as Edwin's knowing smugness provoked Isabella to abandon common sense. She rose to her feet with defiant deliberation.

"You aren't going to tell me where you were, are you?" she said.

Lowering his eyes back to the bits about cricket matches in India or whatever he was reading, he said, "There's nothing to tell." As she strolled purposefully toward the door, he cajoled, "Where are you going? Pray. You aren't cross with me, are you, my darling? You know, I never meant anything by it. Emily and Maud adore you. But you remember what it was like to be a newlywed."

By now, he'd risen and was reaching for her, encouraging her to stop and submit to his embrace. But like everything he did, the attempt at reconciliation was futile, and he knew it.

"I do remember. Pity. Now I think I'll go down to tea."

Pacified she'd do nothing more dramatic than arrive too early for tea, Edwin pecked her cheek with his dry lips and returned to his chair. Isabella waited until she was alone in the hall to wipe the kiss away.

"Lyndhurst police station," the disembodied voice announced.

"This is Lady Isabella Kentfield." Pleased by the muffling effect of the overcoats crowded around her in the cloakroom, she raised her voice slightly as she spoke into the telephone receiver. "I must speak with the inspector in charge of the investigation into Lord Atherly's housekeeper."

"Inspector!" someone called on the other end.

She peered through the opening she'd left in the cloakroom, hoping to catch anyone passing by. The telephone cord, stretched across the hall, was hard to miss. She had an excuse for her odd behavior at the ready but hoped to avoid having to use it. But all she could see was the oak wainscoting on the wall opposite and a scattering of evergreen needles on the Belgian carpet at her feet. In her haste, she must've disturbed the garland draped over the cloakroom door.

"Inspector Brown here," a voice in her ear said a few moments later. "What can I do for you, Lady Isabella?" His tone was measured, but there was a quality to it that Isabella would describe as eagerness masked by annoyance.

"I've learned that my husband, Sir Edwin, claimed to be in bed when the poor housekeeper was killed."

"Yes, that's right. And he said that you'd be willing to confirm that. Are you saying that you are not?"

"I most certainly am not! My husband was not where he said he was that night or the next."

There. It was done. She couldn't take it back now.

"Right! I am much obliged to you, Lady Isabella, for being so forthcoming." Though no doubt satisfied to learn of such deception, the policeman oddly sounded confused.

"Will you come and arrest him now? Isn't that what you policemen do?"

"I will certainly speak to Sir Edwin on the matter. But until I have more conclusive evidence or a motive that links him to the crime, I won't be able to arrest him."

"Oh, very well!" Isabella slammed the receiver down.

She pushed her way back through the overcoats, noting a line of grime on the hem of the coat she'd recently purchased for Freddy. She sighed at the boy's recklessness and shoved the door wide. Evergreen needles, dried from hanging for days without moisture, rained down on her head. Sputtering and swatting the prickly bits from her dress and hair, she tripped on the telephone cord.

"Tea is served in the drawing room, my lady," Fulton, Lord Atherly's butler, said, peering at her from a safe distance as if she didn't resemble a discarded Christmas tree.

She handed out the telephone, hoping he'd take charge of it.

"My lady." Fulton barely raised an eyebrow. "Would you care to make a call?"

"Some help you men are!" she scoffed, pressing it into his hands as she stormed past, still brushing needles off.

She'd known Edwin was a blackguard, but how frustrating to learn that all men seemed as incompetent and obtuse!

CHAPTER 26

"Eakins, you may leave us," Lady Atherly said, stepping aside of the open door.

Without hesitation, Ethel let Stella's mangled tresses fall, dropped a handful of hairpins onto the dressing table, and scurried away.

Lyndy had been itching all day to test out his new colt. Stella, never needing an excuse to spend time in the saddle with Tully, had joined him. The clouds had lain heavy and low over the Forest, but the air was still and almost warm compared to the bitter chill of yesterday's race. With all the questions the newly widowed Mrs. Stancliffe had churned up, Stella had hoped the bracing ride would clear her head. It hadn't, and Lady Atherly arriving unannounced as Stella changed for tea didn't help.

What did she want? She'd never stepped foot in Stella and Lyndy's bedroom before.

Stella swiveled around to face her mother-in-law, but Lady Atherly gave nothing away. As usual, her posture was steel-rod straight, her nose slightly raised. Only her hands clasped so tightly her knuckles were white signified anything was wrong.

"What is it?" When the lady said nothing, Stella leaped up, shoving back the cushioned bench. It scraped along the wooden floor and banged against the dressing table's leg, rattling the glass scent bottles and hat pin holder. "What's happened? Is Lyndy okay?"

Stella had left Lyndy in the stables to discuss Knockan Crag's exercise routine with Mr. Gates. She envisioned him unconscious in a horse stall. Could he have gotten kicked or trampled, or crushed? If it happened to Captain Stancliffe, it could happen to Lyndy. Why else would Lady Atherly be here?

"As far as I'm aware, my son is perfectly well," Lady Atherly said, closing the door behind Stella's lady's maid. "As his wife, I suspect you know better than I the condition of his health."

Stella blew out a long breath, aiming for the strands of hair Ethel left dangling in her face. They fluttered away briefly before falling in her eyes again. Stella brushed them aside. "Then what is it, Lady Atherly?"

The countess, drawn to the vase of red and white carnations on the chest of drawers, fiddled with the bouquet, rearranging the stems to a nicer effect and toppling Stella's upright Christmas cards. As Stella righted the cards, Lady Atherly left her to it and settled on the edge of the bed.

"I need your help."

Stella froze like the icicles decorating the card in her hand. How should she respond? Lady Atherly wasn't one to ask for help, ever. Stella didn't want to frighten her off. Not only because of the unique situation but because it reminded her of Mrs. Nelson's request. Would Stella ever learn what Mrs. Nelson had needed? And here, Lady Atherly was giving Stella a second chance to be helpful.

And to possibly get into her good graces.

Stella resolved that the simplest action was best. Setting the last card upright, she faced her mother-in-law. "What can I do?"

Lady Atherly averted her gaze to stare at the flames flickering in the grate. "I'm aware of the assistance you've provided the police on several previous occasions." If by occasions she meant murders, she was right. "I was hoping you might lend your talents to investigate Mrs. Nelson's death."

"Oh!" How did she tell Lady Atherly that she'd already been helping the police and that they suspected one of her guests? Wasn't it Lady Atherly who'd invited Sir Edwin and his family down for Christmas?

Stella, buying herself time, lowered back down onto the bench, catching a glimpse of herself in the dressing table mirror. The metallic stitching on her tea gown shimmered, its pink silk clashing with the bright red flush on her cheeks. Her hair was a tangled mess, flopping this way and that from the partial bun Ethel hadn't finished pinning. Stella blew at an errant strand again.

"You'll be happy to know that Lyndy and I have already been doing everything we can to find out what happened."

"Hence my request." Lady Atherly smoothed the cranberry-colored silk of her tea gown across her lap.

"What exactly do you want me to do, Lady Atherly?"

The Countess of Atherly raised her chin and pinned Stella to her seat with her challenging stare. "I want you to clear Sir Edwin of Mrs. Nelson's murder."

Stella caught the gasp before it escaped her lips. *Lady Atherly suspects Sir Edwin too?*

Questions sputtered on the tip of her tongue. The first she gave voice to was, "What makes you suspect Sir Edwin is involved?"

Lady Atherly rolled her eyes and scoffed. "That wife of his, or so he's told me, has informed Inspector Brown that Sir Edwin was not in bed when he said he was. And his owning a motorcar, which is now missing, makes him suspect."

"Yes, it does." Stella hadn't heard what Sir Edwin claimed to the police, but if she believed Lady Isabella, he didn't have an alibi. "Could he be guilty?" Stella asked gently.

"Absolutely not!" Lady Atherly's outburst brought a rush of color to her face. But Stella wasn't going to be deterred by her mother-in-law's indignation. She was the one who wanted Stella's help, after all.

"How can you be so certain?" Again, an awkward pause as Lady Atherly broke eye contact and cleared her throat. "What aren't you telling me, Lady Atherly?"

Lady Atherly intertwined her fingers in her lap. "You can be assured of Sir Edwin's innocence because I know he wasn't anywhere near Mistletoe Lane when Mrs. Nelson was meandering about in her poisoned stupor."

"Because he was with you?" Stella said. She was guessing, but by the way this otherwise stoic woman flew from her seat, Stella assumed she was right.

Lady Atherly jabbed a finger at Stella. On it was an emerald and diamond ring Stella had never seen before. "Before you get any ideas, we were in my morning room, talking."

There was more to what she was admitting. Why else the abrupt change from worry to defensiveness? Lady Atherly began pacing the carpet, so like her son.

"Sir Edwin and I once knew each other well, but haven't spoken in quite some time. We spent the night reminiscing and lost track of time."

"Then why not tell that to the police?"

As if in defeat, Lady Atherly collapsed back onto the edge of the bed. "Because we don't want Isabella or William to know we were alone, together, all evening."

"But you were just talking."

"Yes. That night we were." The implication of other nights spent doing more sent Stella's mind reeling.

"You're saying you once knew each other very well," Stella clarified, emphasizing her last two words. Lady Atherly, her shoulders sagging, turned the emerald ring over and over on her finger. Stella had never seen her like this.

"Edwin and I were in love, Stella. But our parents persisted in making more advantageous marriages for both of us. Edwin to that insipid woman who brought with her a sizable dowry. Me to the next Earl of Atherly. I was quite unhappy at first. William, though not unkind, was as preoccupied with his fossils then as he is now. And Edwin, well, he was hard to give up."

Stella reached out and touched her mother-in-law on the arm. It was hot, even through her sleeve. Here was a woman who'd married as Stella had, because her family had told her to. But unlike Stella, she'd had to give up, not her homeland but the man she loved. If Stella had been kept from Lyndy, she'd be miserable too.

Lady Atherly laid her hand over Stella's.

"But you did? You gave him up?"

"Eventually. But only after Isabella suspected and we were forced, for the good of our families, to never see each other again. Until now."

"I'm so sorry, Lady Atherly."

Lady Atherly withdrew her hand, pinching her face into her characteristically disapproving expression. She shifted beyond Stella's reach. "I don't want your sympathy!"

As if stung, Stella sat back stiffly. "I meant no offense."

Lady Atherly expelled a loud sigh. "What I meant was that I'm not seeking comfort or compassion. I'm revealing this to you because, for an unfathomable reason, I trust you. You've made something of my son, more than I could've ever hoped. He loves you, and I believe you are doing your best, despite your circumstances and upbringing, to make him proud. What I need is not your sympathy but your help."

Had Lady Atherly ever spoken to her with such candor before? Or expressed anything more positive or supportive than a subtle begrudging acceptance? Stella fumbled with a response, stunned and giddy with joy, resisting the urge to leap up and wrap her mother-in-law in a crushing embrace.

"Thank you, Lady Atherly. I do try."

"Sir Edwin could hang if he's found guilty," Lady Atherly said impatiently. "We'll need you to do more than just try."

The moment was gone. The wall between them rose again. But Stella had seen it crumble and fall. That was good enough for now.

"I'll do whatever I can to clear Sir Edwin's name."

"Thank you. Remember, no one else is to know. No one, not even my son."

"I promise not to tell anyone else, but I won't keep secrets from Lyndy."

"But that's why I approached you and not him. Lyndy must never know."

As the reasons why swirled in her head, Stella steeled her resolve. Her parents kept secrets from each other. *And look where that got them.*

"If you don't tell him, I will."

"Very well. It does you credit." Lady Atherly rose to leave. "I trust you will be discreet when you tell him?"

"Of course. And I will make him promise not to let it leave this room."

Lady Atherly crossed the room but hesitated before the closed door. She tilted her head, the mount of curled hair on her crown barely moving.

"There was a time," she mused, "that I wouldn't have put any faith in such a promise." She glanced over her shoulder at Stella. "But I think Lyndy can be trusted now." She stopped shy of saying, "Thanks to you," but the words hung invisibly between them.

As Lady Atherly reached for the doorknob, Stella blurted, "What does Mrs. Nelson have to do with yours and Sir Edwin's past?"

She'd suppressed the question as she allowed the connection and emotion between her and her mother-in-law to blossom. Now that the moment was gone, she had to know.

"Very well," Lady Atherly chuckled mirthlessly. "You are nothing if not unrelenting. If you must know—"

"It's vital if we're to clear his name."

"Yes, well, Mrs. Nelson was a chambermaid during . . . that time. Long before Lyndy was born. *Helena* was what I called her. William was meeting with a famed archeologist in London when Edwin last came for a visit. Mrs. Nelson caught Edwin and I"—she cleared her throat—"embracing. She, alone, knew."

"And?"

Lady Atherly scowled. "And she was most unhappy to learn of the Kentfields' Christmas visit. She had the audacity to question my motives. As if I haven't moved on."

"But has Sir Edwin? Moved on? Did he have a reason to harm Mrs. Nelson? Did she threaten to reveal your secret?"

"That, my dear Stella, is the problem," Lady Atherly said. "She'd threatened to and died before she got the chance."

Bored with the pretense of enjoying himself, Lyndy threw down his cards. He slumped against the back of his chair and took a sip of his port. It was too sweet; he should've opted for something more balanced, like whiskey.

Must I keep this up?

He wasn't the only one out of sorts. Papa had removed himself to his study hours ago, and Mother had said little all night beyond what was necessary to perpetuate the game. Sir Edwin and his wife conversed as if the other wasn't in the room, and even Stella's smile, when she finally took her first trick of the night, was fleeting. How he missed Stella's excitement. Her joyous anticipation at spending Christmas at Morrington had been infectious. With the holiday tarnished now, as it was, she'd put up a brave face, but Lyndy sensed the strain.

Only Alice and Freddy, sequestered in the corner combing through Alice's latest magazines—how Fred found it amusing, Lyndy couldn't imagine—uttered anything resembling an enthusiastic word. Was it that everyone was exhausted after the sustained merriment of the season? Or had the deaths of Mrs. Nelson and Captain Stancliffe put a strain on even the most jubilant of the company? Or could the others, as Stella and he did, suspect one among them was involved? Any one was reason enough to dampen the evening's mood.

"That's one for me," Lady Isabella said, laying out her next card.

Lyndy rubbed his forehead; the pink swirls on the back of each card seemed to be giving him a headache. He'd had enough.

"Well, this has been fun. Shall we retire, Stella?" Lyndy jostled the table as he pushed off it to his feet. Sherry in Lady Isabella's glass sloshed dangerously close to the rim.

"Lyndy!" his mother chided.

"Good idea," his wife said simultaneously.

Stella rose to a concurrence of various lackluster wishes for a restful night that followed them out the door. When they reached the top of the stairs, she put her head on his shoulder. He kissed her hair.

"What's wrong, my love?"

"I'm dreading telling you something. It's been weighing on me since teatime."

Lyndy halted in the middle of the hall, his chest tightening. He found it suddenly difficult to breathe. "What is it?"

He'd never been one to speculate, let alone fret, but what could she possibly mean? She'd never hesitated to trust him with her innermost musings and concerns before. What could be so heinous she feared mentioning it?

"Not in the hall." She tugged on his arm, hoping to propel him toward their bedchamber, but Lyndy, making no attempt to hide his alarm, wouldn't acquiesce. "Oh, Lyndy," she cooed, "it's got nothing to do with you and me." Lyndy breathed easier until his wife added, "It's about your mother."

The moment he closed the door behind them, he began to pace, preparing himself for the worst. What could Stella know that he didn't about his mother? But then again, how well did he know her? He'd spent his childhood craving her attention and affection and his adulthood seeking to avoid her. Was Mother ill? Had she killed Mrs. Nelson? The very notion surprised him. How could he possibly consider the idea? Yet hadn't Mrs. Nelson confronted her in a tone Mother wouldn't tolerate from anyone? Or has Mother been plaguing Stella with demands for an heir? Mercifully, Stella ended his agonizing speculation before he'd crossed the room.

"Your mother admitted to me today that she was with Sir Edwin when Mrs. Nelson was killed."

Is that all?

He wanted to scold Stella for aggrandizing the situation. (Yes, it meant they'd been wrong to suspect Sir Edwin, but what did Lyndy care, he scarcely knew the man.) And then it hit him. Mrs. Nelson was killed late in the night. But that would mean . . .

"Are you saying Mother and Sir Edwin are having an affair?" Lyndy shouted, aiming his anger and shock at the woman he loved instead of the woman who deserved it.

"Shhh!" Stella went to the door and peeked into the hall. "I promised her I would keep her secret. She doesn't want anyone to know." When she closed the door again, she leaned against it. A few pine needles had fallen into her hair.

Blast it! When is someone going to see that the dried garland is taken down?

"They spent the night talking, that's it. They aren't having an affair." She hesitated, and despite the reassuring facts she'd re-layed, a lump formed in Lyndy's throat.

"But?"

"But they did have one, once. A long time ago."

Lyndy balled his hands into fists, resisting the urge to slam them into the smooth counterpane on the bed. Instead, he wrestled with the buttons on his jacket, waistcoat, and shirt, pulling each layer off as if the touch of the fabric on his back offended him. Finally bare-chested, his suspenders dangling at his hips, Lyndy allowed the cool air on his skin to soothe his anger. He dropped to the edge of the bed and wrenched his shoes off.

Why was he so angry? For his father's sake? For his own? Why did it feel like a betrayal to discover his mother was once as passionate, impulsive, and reckless as he once was? To learn that despite her past, she'd still made countless attempts to thwart his marriage? Or was it the hint of something lingering at the edges of his mind that he couldn't bring himself to voice?

"Does Papa know?"

"Your mother doesn't think so. She thinks Lady Isabella suspected at the time but wasn't sure if she ever learned the truth." Stella hadn't moved from her position against the door. Was she giving him the room he needed to vent? Or was there more, and she needed the distance between them for the courage to say it? "They haven't seen each other since. Until now."

"Why now?"

"She didn't say."

"Why confide in you?" Lyndy inwardly flinched. It sounded like an accusation.

Because it was.

How could his mother tell Stella and not him? It stung more than he was willing to admit. But it wasn't Stella's fault. Stella was the most sympathetic of listeners. If Mother was to confide in anyone, why wouldn't it be Stella?

With the patience he adored and didn't deserve, Stella responded as if she hadn't heard the edge in his tone. "She wants me to help clear Sir Edwin of any suspicion in Mrs. Nelson's death. To use my 'influence' with the police."

She divulged everything Mother had told her: how Mrs. Nelson was the only other person who'd known of the affair and had threatened to tell, how Lady Isabella had telephoned the police refuting her husband's alibi, how Mother had sworn Stella to secrecy. What other secrets was Mother holding? Did he even want to know?

"I agreed to help any way I could, but I refused to keep anything from you. We promised to love and honor each other the day we married. And that means never keeping secrets. I never have, and I'm not going to start now. Not even for your mother."

"How I adore you!"

Lyndy, reassured by her honesty and overwhelmed with love, sprung from the edge of the bed and bounded across the room, nearly tripping over the shoes he'd tossed carelessly on the floor.

"Be careful," Stella admonished laughingly.

He pulled Stella into his embrace, her hands cool on his bare back as he smothered her with urgent kisses. There was something more she'd wanted to say. Something, from the way she'd bitten her lip, she was holding back. Not a secret then, but one of her perceptive observations or perhaps a question for him. It could wait.

He spun her around, her relieved giggle fueling his ardor as he guided her toward the bed. Without pause, she kicked his shoes out of the way.

Mother be damned. Stella was his, all his, and he didn't deserve her. But he intended to try.

CHAPTER 27

When Mrs. Robertson had sent word that someone was down-stairs wanting to speak to Mrs. Nelson, Stella, knowing her mother-in-law was preoccupied in the conservatory, had the visitor brought up to the library. Now, that someone, a waif of a woman with neat blond curls peeking from under her black felt hat, assessed, in apparent awe, the bookshelves encir-cling the room. When her eyes rested on the glass cabinet filled with stuffed birds, the woman squinted as if she wasn't seeing things right. Stella urged her to join her by the case.

Stella had doggedly spent as much time as she could in the li-brary; this morning, she'd come down to read straight after breakfast. It was such a cozy room, especially now with a crackling fire, the fragrance of drying evergreen boughs, and the thick leather Chesterfield couch to curl up on. But it was still haunted by the specter of Vicar Bullmore. He'd been the first dead body she'd ever seen. With her frequent visits, Stella had hoped to exorcise his ghost. But he wouldn't leave. Instead of ending the haunting, as the number of dead bodies she'd seen mounted, Stella had become habituated to it. The same went for the large mahogany display case of birds killed and collected by the current and former Earl of Atherly: honey buzzard, sparrowhawk, purple heron, magpie, curlew, hawfinch, stonechat, purple heron, lapwing, and Dartford warbler. Their glazed glass eyes were always staring at her. But once she'd given each a name (she called the buzzard Wyatt after a neighbor's boy from Kentucky), they'd lost their haunted appearance and grew friendlier.

If only that had worked for the vicar. He'd already had a name.

"Have you ever seen anything like it?"

"Never." The woman leaned so close to the case her breath fogged the glass. She stepped back, embarrassed.

"Would you like to take a seat, Miss Oakhill?" Stella gestured toward the Chesterfield couch and eased into the well-worn leather club chair.

"It's Mrs., milady. And if it's all the same to you, I'd like to stand."

Of course she would.

Time and time again, since she'd become the viscountess, servants, merchants, dressmakers, and more, most of whom would've gladly taken Stella up on her invitation before, now insisted they were more "comfortable" on their feet. Stella didn't insult them by insisting, but it was something she regretted. At least she could try to keep the conversation short. From what Mrs. Robertson had said, Mrs. Oakhill had walked to Morrington Hall from who knows where.

"Mrs. Robertson said you were asking for Mrs. Nelson?" Before she told Mrs. Oakhill what she surprisingly didn't already know (news like the housekeeper's death is usual fodder for the village gossips), Stella hoped to get some answers.

"Yes, milady. I visited before Christmas hoping to speak to Your Ladyship and to give you this." Mrs. Oakhill produced a package of brown paper tied with twine from inside her black woolen overcoat and offered it to Stella. "A Christmas gift for you. If you'll have them."

Inside were a dozen beautiful handkerchiefs embroidered with holly. Stella admired the handiwork.

"That's nice of you, Mrs. Oakhill. I'll use them proudly. They're nicer than the ones I commissioned for Lord Lyndhurst."

A shy but satisfied grin crept across Mrs. Oakhill's lips. "Much obliged, milady."

"But why not give them to me when you came last time?"

"Mrs. Nelson said she would speak to you on my behalf and promised to visit with news on Boxing Day. She never came."

Mrs. Nelson had never said a word. Or had she? Was this what the housekeeper wanted Stella's help with?

"What did you wish to speak to me about?"

"I'd heard Your Ladyship offered to help commoners with their veterinary bills. I have two ponies out on the Forest, but my horse has gone lame. I embroider all sorts, and it's near impossible to deliver my linens on foot. And without my horse, I can't find my ponies. I'm doing my best, milady, but one can only go so far on foot. Soon, I'll be struggling to feed my children."

"Are you trying to do this on your own?" The woman's black crape dress hadn't escaped Stella's notice.

"My husband died of typhoid just gone September."

Stella had heard of the heart-wrenching outbreak in Basingstoke but didn't know anyone directly affected. Until now.

Two widows in two days. And at Christmastime too. At least here was a chance to do something. Stella stood and took the woman's hands in hers. They were hot and clammy.

"I am so sorry to hear about your husband. Of course I will help you."

The woman tensed at the unsolicited touch but didn't pull away. Stella released her grasp (it was so hard to remember not to be too familiar) and took a step back. The visible relief on the woman's face stung.

"I'll send our veterinarian, Mr. Green, to your home today to examine your horse. And if he finds it necessary, your horse, what's its name?"

"Sally."

"Sally can recuperate from her injury at the Triple R Farm for Horses and Ponies, my farm set up for that purpose, free of charge, while she heals. In the meantime, I can loan you another horse to ride and deliver your linens."

Mrs. Oakhill, whether from her long walk and her choosing to stand or from overwhelming relief, buckled at the knees. Stella lunged forward, hoping to catch her, but she wasn't fast enough. The widow collapsed to the carpet with a reverberating thud. Stella dashed to the bellpull and rang for help. Thankfully, by the time Fulton appeared, Mrs. Oakhill had revived and was sitting up, her back pressed against the legs of the couch.

"Can you please bring Mrs. Oakhill some tea and something to eat?" In Kentucky, Stella would've ordered a big pot of coffee or maybe something even stronger, but she'd learned that most English preferred tea for every occasion.

"Very good, my lady," was Fulton's properly indifferent response before disappearing again. He'd barely given the woman on the floor a questioning glance.

"I must apologize to Your Ladyship," Mrs. Oakhill said, plucking off a strand of hair stuck to her damp, blazing, red cheek. As Mrs. Oakhill struggled to her feet, Stella reached toward her, without touching, in case she collapsed again. "I've been ill, and it seems I'm not quite myself yet."

Stella insisted Mrs. Oakhill sit down, grateful that, this time, the woman heartily accepted. Fulton promptly arrived with the tea, toast, marmalade, and a mince pie. Mrs. Oakhill scrunched her nose in disgust but politely took the offered plate. After a few bites of the buttered toast, she took one sip of the tea and set it back on the table.

"Forgive me, milady. I've been poorly after eating something that had gone off. My stomach still isn't what it should be."

"That's why you didn't come back sooner?"

Mrs. Oakhill nodded weakly. "I would've, even if I didn't feel up to it myself, but my children weren't well either. You see, I have a neighbor who could mind them for me today. So, I came. Although she's been very kind, I couldn't wait for Mrs. Nelson any longer. I'm not one to ask for charity, but I'm growing desperate."

"Well, it's good that you didn't wait, or else you'd be waiting until your children had children."

"I don't understand."

"I'm sorry to be the one to tell you, but Mrs. Nelson died on Christmas Eve. Hit by an automobile on Mistletoe Lane."

"Oh, dear God, no!" Mrs. Oakhill went pale despite the feverish glint to her skin and abruptly hung her head between her knees.

Why would she take it this hard? Mrs. Oakhill hardly knew Mrs. Nelson. Or so Stella assumed.

Stella knelt by her side, laying a comforting hand on her back. "You're still ill, Mrs. Oakhill. Let me call the doctor."

"No, I'm so sorry, my stomach is a bit queasy, but it isn't that," she whimpered, her voice muffled by her skirt.

She slowly lifted her head, and Stella sat back on her heels. A fevered surge of alarm blazed across the poor woman's face.

"If it's not your stomach, Mrs. Oakhill, what is it?"

The woman grasped blindly for the chair's armrest and leaned as close to Stella as she dared. She lowered her voice to a shaky whisper.

"What could it mean, milady? I live on Mistletoe Lane."

"I've never ridden in a motorcar before," Mrs. Oakhill said, grasping the brim of her hat. The fresh air had done the woman good; she had color back in her face. "I'd no idea it could be so thrilling."

Thrilling? Stella had inched along like a marsh slug, trying not to unsettle the poor woman's stomach again. Her usual speed was several times as fast.

"Or so loud," Mrs. Oakhill added over the rumble of the motor.

Stella's laugh died in her throat as they puttered beneath the leafy globes of mistletoe clinging to the bare trees lining the road. Without the brilliance of the snow cover, the lane took on a dingy, grim appearance. Stella watched the stretch of road where Mrs. Nelson died fade into the distance in her rearview mirror.

What was Mrs. Nelson doing there that night?

"That's us," Mrs. Oakhill pointed.

Stella parked the auto in front of a tidy redbrick cottage with a chocolate-brown colored thatch roof and a wrought-iron gate. Thick dormant vines snaked up the trellis by the front door. A small fenced-in paddock abutted the house with a white-washed wooden stable on the far end, large enough to shelter a horse or two. It was a prosperous, well-kept property by all outward appearances. Until Stella looked closer. Chunks of the moss-covered stone wall that delineated the yard from the road had crumbled onto the lawn. Broken cross boards marked weak spots in the picket fence. Despite the time of year, no smoke curled from the cottage's chimney.

Instead of jolly evergreen, a wreath of black flowers decorated the door.

"Would you like to come in, my lady? I'll put the kettle on. It's the least I can do to repay your kindness in driving me home."

Stella followed Mrs. Oakhill up the path to her door. Inside, the rooms were small, cozy, and well-kept, but unrepaired chips marred the entryway plastered wall, and Stella could still see her breath. There was no sign of a Christmas tree.

"I do apologize, Lady Lyndhurst. The fire must've gone out while I was away." Mrs. Oakhill hastily set to lighting a fire from the meager supply of kindling and peat in the wood box beside the grate.

"No need. I'm used to it. Before we had the boiler system installed, Morrington Hall was always a little chilly."

The woman smiled appreciatively at Stella's attempt to overlook her troubles. "It's hard to find time to harvest the peat. My husband always did that."

As he'd always repaired the picket fence and maintained the stone wall?

"You must miss him."

"To be honest, I don't have time."

How sad! And obviously true.

From the moment she'd finished with the fire, the widow busied herself with fixing the tea, toasting bread over the fire for her sons, due from the neighbor's any minute, and then excusing herself to milk the cow. She had yet to slow down. Stella, who'd taken her offer to sit, soon regretted it, shifting uncomfortably in the best chair in the room. Riddled by guilt and restlessness, Stella stood and strolled around the room, admiring the fine needlework on the couch cushions, the side table doilies, and a framed sampler on the wall.

"Did you make all of these?" Stella asked when Mrs. Oakhill returned with a tray. The widow's handkerchiefs were well made, but some of these pieces were exquisite.

"I did. As I said, that's why I need my horse. I can only sell at the markets I can walk to. That means Rosehurst, Lyndhurst, and Minstead. I usually sell them as far as Ringwood and Lymington, but by the time I got there, the market would be over."

No wonder. Ringwood was almost twelve miles away. It would take hours to walk that far.

Stella continued moving around the room, stopping to study

the framed photograph prominent on the mantel. It was Mrs. Oakhill's wedding photograph. In her white gown and veil, she stood shoulder to shoulder in a sterile studio beside a tall man with a strong jaw and thick mustache. Each wore a somber expression.

"Would you like sugar or milk, my lady?"

"Both, please."

As she stepped away to join the widow on the couch, her foot nudged a basket on the floor. It was filled with colorful ribbons, loose bobbins of thread, and swaths of varied fabric. Stella had seen baskets identical to this one on countless picnics.

"Mr. Jenvey makes the best baskets, doesn't he?" Stella remarked as the widow handed her a cup of steaming tea. "I know Lady Atherly and Mrs. Nelson agreed that Morrington Hall would only buy from him." Stella's throat tightened on the housekeeper's name.

"Oh, I can't afford Mr. Jenvey. For you're right, my lady. They are fine indeed."

At that moment, the door flew open and two bareheaded little boys, their cheeks red from the cold, the hems of their pants caked in mud, raced into the room. Shouting and fighting over something gripped tightly in the older one's fist, their arms remained intertangled as they advanced into the parlor. They skidded to a halt on seeing Stella, their mouths each forming a small little O. Their argument momentarily forgotten, they hid behind their mother's skirts when introduced.

"Now, be good boys, and don't bother the fine lady." With black scarves wrapped around their necks, the boys settled on the carpet by the fire to eat their toast. "The basket was a gift from Mrs. Nelson," Mrs. Oakhill added, referring to their interrupted conversation. "She sent over a Christmas basket filled with all sorts of treats for the boys. She was most kind."

The widow smiled fondly at her sons, the youngest, Malcolm, licking the butter from his fingers. Stella sipped her tea in silence until curiosity got the better of her.

"There didn't happen to be mince pies in the basket?"

"Indeed, there were. I was quite pleased. I hadn't had time, what with everything, to make them. And what is Christmas without mince pies?" She forced a smile that didn't reach her eyes.

"But they weren't as tasty as you'd expect, were they?"

Mrs. Oakhill's face flushed again. "I didn't want to sound unappreciative, but I must admit they were slightly off."

Stella's heart skipped a beat. *I knew it!* Louisa hadn't poisoned Mrs. Nelson after all. Mrs. Cole's mince pies had been the culprit.

"We ate them anyway, didn't we?" the widow said.

The boys scrunched their faces. The youngest stuck out his tongue, still coated with toasted bread crumbs. "Blah."

"Malcolm! That's not how we speak to a lady guest."

"But they were yucky, Mummy."

"They were, weren't they?" Stella offered. Both boys heartily agreed.

"How did you know?" Mrs. Oakhill asked.

"We found mince pies in Mrs. Nelson's study that had spoiled. Since Mrs. Nelson got sick, too, they're probably what made you all sick. I'm sorry, Mrs. Oakhill, though I'm certain Mrs. Nelson had no idea they were spoiled when she sent them to you."

Stella had no such certainty but said so anyway.

"There's no need to apologize, milady. It was meant well."

"And I mean to do everything I can to get you and Sally back on your feet." Stella set down her teacup, slapped her thighs, and stood, energized to help this little family more. "What do you say we all say hello to the old girl? And then maybe a short spin in the automobile for the boys?"

"You are too kind," Mrs. Oakhill said, hesitant but smiling.

"Yay!" The boys leaped from the floor and raced, shouting and shoving to be the first one out the door.

The crisp, clean breeze stung Stella's cheeks as she zipped down the lane, sending her motor veil flapping around her. Mud splattered up from the road, and carrion crows, cawing in protest, scattered as Stella raced toward home. She relished the speed as much as the Oakhill boys had enjoyed the short spin she'd taken them on. They'd bounced enthusiastically on the padded leather backseat the entire trip, boisterous and happy, despite recently losing their father.

Like me.

Memories of Stella's murdered father threatened to creep in. She pressed harder on the gas pedal, mentally outgunning the hovering melancholy. When she reached the spot where Mr. Green had found Mrs. Nelson's body, she hit the long shadows stretching across this tract of Mistletoe Lane like a wall and slammed on the brakes. The automobile skidded in the mud, its back end swerving back and forth twice until coming to a stop. A rabbit bolted down the lane away from her.

Stella hopped up to the back of her seat for a better view. Beneath the towering trees, Mistletoe Lane ran unimpeded and uninhabited as far as she could see. In both directions. Which direction had the automobile that hit the housekeeper come from, that of Rosehurst or Mrs. Oakhill's cottage?

Did the young widow kill Mrs. Nelson?

The question leaped into Stella's head like an Irish Hunter over a two-foot fence—unhindered and forceful. But Mrs. Oakhill didn't have an auto, said she'd never even been in one. Stella believed her. Besides, why would she come to Morrington Hall seeking Mrs. Nelson, knowing she'd killed her? She hadn't even known she was dead. Did that mean the person driving the auto hadn't come from her direction? No, but it was unlikely. Beyond the Oakhills' home was a vast track of mixed heathland and grazing lawn with only a few other cottages scattered around. No major thoroughfares or direct routes from nearby towns or villages. Stella slumped back into her seat, staring straight ahead. Most likely, the driver was coming from the direction of Rosehurst, as they knew Mrs. Nelson was. But where was Mrs. Nelson going?

Stella spotted a second rabbit watching warily from further down the lane. A nagging memory propelled her to quit the Daimler and trek toward it, carelessly dragging her coat hem along the soggy verge and kicking up the sweet-musky scent of decaying leaves. Upon her approach, the rabbit dashed toward a tangle of aboveground roots, disappearing down a hole in a bank built up underneath. Surveying the landscape, she spotted several similar burrowing mounds. How had she not noticed them before? From her vantage point, the Daimler was clearly visible. Could this be the rabbit warren Captain Stancliffe had been poaching that night? Was it possible he saw the automobile that killed Mrs. Nelson? Or was it a coincidence that the captain, a man renowned for his horsemanship, was thrown from his own pony to his death two days later?

Stella didn't trust coincidences. That one, or the one that placed Mrs. Nelson inexplicably on the road to Mrs. Oakhill's cottage the same night the young widow visited Morrington Hall for the first time.

Her feet growing numb from the damp and cold, Stella trudged back to the auto, inadvertently following in Mrs. Nelson's footsteps.

Mrs. Nelson had to be going to or returning from a visit to Mrs. Oakhill. Stella was sure of it. But why?

CHAPTER 28

Stella sped around the corner, preoccupied and not paying particular attention to her driving. Rehashing over and over the questions churned up by her visit to Mrs. Oakhill, she didn't see the grizzled old gray donkey rooted to a swath of dull sunshine in the middle of the road until it was too late.

"Watch out!"

The donkey blinked at the oncoming automobile but didn't budge.

Stella wrenched the steering wheel hard to the left, swerving around the stubborn animal. Slamming on the brakes, she skidded across an ice-filled rut. The momentum plunged her through the brushy thicket that filled the gap between the lane and the towering trees. Jostled and jolted like a dancing marionette, Stella clung to the wheel. She tried to avoid crashing into a tree, but her gloves slipped on the wheel's polished wood, and the left corner of the automobile collided with the trunk. Propelled sideways, Stella rammed her elbow into the speed lever.

Then it was over.

The Daimler had stopped, steam hissing from its engine.

Stella scrambled out and stumbled away, her neck sore, sharp pain shooting through her elbow. Her whole body ached from the tension. But she was on her feet. Letting the stillness settle around her, she contemplated the damage. Besides crushing the radiator, the impact had crumpled the auto's metal hood, dented the front bumper and left fender, and broken a headlight. One of the tires on that side was going flat. The Daimler wasn't going anywhere.

It could've been a lot worse.

Cradling her elbow to ease the pain, Stella waded through the brush, her already muddy duster coat snagging on branches as she went. Back on the road, she approached the donkey, squinting as she stepped from the shade to the more brightly lit spot. Despite the accident, the donkey hadn't moved.

Stella had come across this free-ranging old animal before, minus the gorse tangled in its wet fur. According to Lyndy, his sister had named it, pretending it was her pet.

"I know you," she said. "Are you okay, Headley?"

Headley took no heed, his calm demeanor suggesting Stella was far more shaken than he was.

Stella surveyed her situation but couldn't see much. Beyond the wreck of the Daimler, the road continued to curve. What was she thinking driving that fast? She could've killed Headley if she hadn't reacted in time. And then it hit her.

Had the driver of the car that killed Mrs. Nelson done the same? Come across the housekeeper stumbling down the middle of the road and been taken by surprise? But this curve was a half mile from where Mrs. Nelson was found. That stretch was a straightaway. Anyone would've seen her, wouldn't they? Even in the dark? That's what headlights were for.

She must've been killed on purpose.

As if in agreement, Headley brayed, the loud, shriek-like call jarring in the winter quiet.

*   *   *

Behind her, a horse snorted. Stella turned as a cart, pulled by a Cleveland Bay, came around the bend. The cart's driver pulled beside her, taking in the state of her auto. It was Mr. Stott, the boiler repairman.

"Are you all right, Lady Lyndhurst?" His gaze swept slowly over her. Stella shifted her weight from one foot to the other, uncomfortable under the scrutiny.

"I'm fine, Mr. Stott. Thank you."

"Can't say the same for your motor, though, can you?"

"No, I can't." Stella forced a chuckle. She wasn't in a particularly chipper mood.

"Let me offer you a lift back to Morrington Hall, my lady." Before she could object, he climbed down to offer his assistance. His overcoat smelled of stale wood smoke.

"Thank you, but it's not that far of a walk."

"Nonsense. It's on my way." He reached toward her elbow, as Lyndy might've done, to guide her toward the cart. She flinched at his touch.

"See. You're hurt. I insist." He gestured toward his cart again.

"No. I'm fine."

She set off in the direction of her home, hoping that would be the end of it. But Mr. Stott wouldn't leave her alone.

"Then I'll walk with you. To be sure you make it home safely."

"That's nice of you, Mr. Stott, but as I said, I'm fine and wouldn't want to keep you."

"It's no bother. Besides, I know a shortcut." He grasped the horse's bridle, leading it back the way it had come, and walked beside her. The empty cart rumbled behind them. "It's just up here." A farmer's track cut across the grazing lawn.

She'd begun to shake from the cold. Her head was pounding now, every muscle in her back and neck ached, and her heart was racing. She was more injured than she was willing to admit. She was desperate to get home. A shortcut was the thing she needed. But Stella hesitated as the workman led his horse away from the road and onto the open landscape. Having Mr. Stott on hand to escort her home should've seemed like a lucky break. So why did she want to get rid of him?

"This way, my lady."

In following him, Stella slipped on a slick rock and stumbled. She vehemently waved off Mr. Stott's attempt to help her.

"Are you still sure you want to walk?"

"I'm fine." She trudged forward, stubbornly putting one foot in front of the other instead of accepting the workman's offer of a ride.

"So, what happened back there?"

Stella said nothing. Resigning herself to his company didn't mean she had to explain herself. And maybe he'd get the idea she didn't want to talk anymore. No such luck.

"Well, as you found out, one can't be too careful in the New Forest. I know you didn't grow up here, but if you're going to drive your motorcar about, you need to remember there's live-stock everywhere. Even in the middle of the road."

He sounded like Lady Atherly, or worse, her father. Miserable and losing her patience, she wanted to shout at him, to tell him to go away, but suspected it would be in vain. With no other recourse than to put up with him, she picked up her pace, focusing on the line of hedge in the distance, signaling they were finally approaching the edge of the village. Unless she was more rattled than she realized, Mr. Stott's "shortcut" had added to the trip.

Would we ever get there?

"Perhaps you could even find someone to drive you about?" he continued, oblivious to her rising frustration. "I, myself, have taken a fancy to motoring. I don't have one yet, but I've borrowed one a time or two to learn how to drive."

Stella stiffened—if it were possible to tense her muscles more than they already were. Could he have killed Mrs. Nelson? Could Mr. Stott, by *borrow*, mean take someone's auto without permission? He certainly had access to her Daimler and Sir Edwin's Martini. What about the other houses where he worked? Stella's wasn't the only auto in the area.

They strode in silence as Stella considered what best to do. As they joined the road again and the safety of familiar surroundings, her curiosity won out.

"Whom do you know that has an automobile?"

"Come now," he admonished. "Not only nobs have motorcars."

"That's not what I meant." Stella caught her first glimpse of Morrington's chimneys poking above the trees. She was almost home. "I just wondered whose auto you borrowed."

"Ah. I see. I have a friend who owns an auto repair garage in Reading."

Stella silently sighed in relief. Reading was a long way from here. The likelihood that Mr. Stott was driving in a borrowed car on Mistletoe Lane was slim.

But why was he traveling on Mistletoe Lane today?

"See now. We're almost here," Mr. Stott cheerily said as they crossed under the shadow of the archway, heralding the start of the Atherly estate. The warm smile on his face transformed him.

Had Stella judged him too hastily? Maybe the accident had clouded her judgment. Wasn't he being neighborly and helpful? Why had she been so annoyed?

"Now, aren't you glad you had company to distract you?"

"Yes, thank you, Mr. Stott." She rewarded him with as bright a smile as she could muster. She stopped to pluck burrs from her duster coat. "I think I can manage from here."

"No. I'll see you to the door."

"When we get to the house then, if you have time, be sure to call at the kitchens. Besides the new housekeeper, we also have a new cook. She's much more welcoming than Mrs. Cole. I'm sure she'd reward you for your kindness with tea and cake."

Mr. Stott scowled. "If it's all the same to you, Lady Lyndhurst, I'll be on my way."

What had changed his mind? His horse shifted her weight and whinnied as if wondering the same thing. With her head hanging low, her eyes partially closed, the mare appeared as ready to go home as Stella was.

But as Stella continued, Mr. Stott didn't stop or ride off. He accompanied her down the drive in silence but for the crunch of the gravel beneath his heavy tread, stealing angry glances and tugging the slow-moving mare behind him.

She hadn't misjudged him. This fellow unnerved her. Stella imperceptibly inched sidewise, putting as much space between them as possible. She would've run for the front door if she could still feel her feet.

"Stella!" Lyndy flung open the door and raced down the few front steps. "By God, you had us worried. Are you hurt? Where have you been?"

Lyndy hovered between wanting to chastise her for the fear clutching his heart this past half hour and needing to feel her safe in his embrace. As usual, Stella decided for him, rushing into his outstretched arms. Oddly, she smelled distinctly of burned peat. Shaking, she clung to him.

"Who is this fellow?" Lyndy sized up the chap with the cart. *Where had he seen him before?*

"As you well know, the name's Stott, my lord. You bathe in comfort, thanks to me." *What is the fellow going on about?* "I was passing by when I saw—"

"How did you know I could've been hurt?" Stella interrupted, giving no heed to Stott kicking the gravel in displeasure. It wasn't like her.

"Green came across your crashed motorcar. You weren't with it. Alice and Freddy are out searching for you. Mother insisted I stay here. I was about to saddle Beau when I spied you from the window. Are you hurt?"

Stella flinched when Lyndy held her out at arm's length to see for himself.

"I'm fine."

How many times had he heard that? He didn't believe a word of it.

"You are hurt. I'm going to cancel tonight's concert."

"No, Lyndy. It's too important. Miss Dare can only come tonight."

A month ago, word of Stella's Triple R Farm for Horses and Ponies had reached the ears of Miss Zena Dare, one of the stars of the pantomime they'd seen. She'd offered to perform at Morrington Hall to raise funds for the charity. But with her tight schedule, tonight was her sole opening.

"As I was saying, I came across Her Ladyship," Mr. Stott interjected, "and offered her a ride home. She refused, but I wouldn't let her walk back alone, injured as she was."

Still, Stella said nothing. If Lyndy didn't know better, he'd think Stella refused to acknowledge him. It was left to Lyndy to do so. He shoved out his hand.

"Much obliged, Mr. Stott, for your assistance bringing Lady Lyndhurst home safely."

"I didn't do it for you," Stott said, refusing to shake Lyndy's hand.

Lyndy pulled it back and tugged sharply on the sleeve of his jacket. "Good day to you then."

Ignoring Lyndy, Stott touched the brim of his wool cap and nodded at Stella. "Good day, Lady Lyndhurst."

"Mr. Stott."

The workman stepped up into his cart and circled his horse to leave. Watching him go, Lyndy wrapped his arm around

Stella's shoulder. She relaxed against him, burrowing her face into his chest. The motor veil encircling her hat tickled his chin.

"You are injured, aren't you?"

The stubborn woman would only say, "Let's go in."

As they turned toward the house, the steady creak of the cart stopped. Lyndy glanced down the drive. Glaring over his shoulder with his lip curled, Mr. Stott sat stiffly only a few dozen yards from where he started.

"Forget something, Mr. Stott?" Lyndy called curtly. *Like your manners, perhaps?*

Mr. Stott grunted something incomprehensible before urging his horse forward.

"Is he gone?" Stella asked, purposefully not looking.

"He is."

"Thank goodness. I never thought he'd leave." Again, her uncharitable response was not like her. Guiding Stella gently to the steps, he insisted, "You must tell me what happened. Who is this Stott?"

Stella laughed, patting him on the cheek.

"He's one of the workmen who installed the boiler system. I've seen him around the manor dozens of times." Granted, Lyndy might've seen him once, not dozens of times. "We saw him when we came out of Mrs. Nelson's study that day. How can you not remember?"

"But what happened?"

"He was just passing, like he said, and walked me home." Her tone was light but with an uneasy edge to it.

"That's all right and well, but what happened with the motorcar?"

Fulton opened the front entrance, and Lyndy ushered Stella into the warmth of the hall.

"It was Headley. I came on him stubbornly standing in the middle of the road. Daddy's auto is a wreck." She grew more animated as she stripped the veil, hat, and duster coat off, placing them in the butler's care. It was a delight, and a relief, to see.

"Don't concern yourself over it, my love. As long as you're all right. I've got the names of several repair shops."

Stella brushed away his words like a horse's tail would swat at flies.

"But, Lyndy, I need to tell you about Mrs. Oakhill, this widow who came to Morrington while you were out working with Knockan Crag. I drove her home since the poor woman had walked from her cottage on Mistletoe Lane. And yes, I crashed the Daimler, but it was worth it. You won't believe what I found out."

CHAPTER 29

The music room, or the Blue Room, as Lyndy called it for the dominating color of the décor, was filled to capacity. Chairs had been salvaged from every corner of the manor to accommodate all the guests. Stella couldn't be more thrilled. Almost every person invited, from the Bishop of Winchester to Baron Branson-Hill and his wife, had attended the musical event, generously donating to the cause. Stella had had no idea it would be such a success.

When she'd suggested it, Lady Atherly had opposed the idea, asserting, "It is beyond vulgar to ask anyone to pay to be entertained at Morrington Hall." But when Princess Beatrice, whom Stella had met in York, in sending her regrets, had declared it a charming idea, the countess had changed her mind. Now, with a room filled with music, laughter, and countless glasses of champagne, Lady Atherly smiled charmingly at her guests. As if it had been all her idea.

Stella didn't care. Let her mother-in-law bask in the role of hostess. Stella might've learned to chat and smile and flatter, but she dreaded these society events, and after the fright of the accident and the unnerving trip home with the boiler man, she wasn't sure how much socializing she could take. Yet she couldn't leave. They were all here to support her charity. She'd been gracious in bidding Miss Dare good night, but afterward, when Lyndy had suggested they sneak out for a few minutes of "fresh air," he didn't have to ask twice.

With her face tingling from the cold and her elbow still throbbing, Stella relished the cheery warmth of the room when they stepped back through the French doors. The chandeliers, adorned with red velvet ribbons, sparkled from above and off every champagne flute. Earlier fresh evergreens had replaced the dried garland over the doors and mantelpiece. She hadn't noticed. Now, their rich fragrance permeated the room.

Alice was sitting down at the highly polished grand piano. Earlier, Miss Dare, the captivating seventeen-year-old whose constant smile lit the room, had performed several numbers from popular musical comedies, including two from her role in *The Catch of the Season*. Entertaining and delightful, she'd been well-received with a standing ovation. Unfortunately, she'd had to catch the last train back to London before the evening was out. After she'd left, it fell to Alice, an accomplished and obliging pianist, to entertain the guests.

As Alice settled in, Freddy stood beside her to turn pages. He finished his drink in one gulp and set down his glass on the piano. Stella and Lyndy retook their seats. Lady Atherly, too distracted by something Reverend Paine was saying, didn't notice their late return. However, Lady Isabella's glower clearly showed where her attention was.

What do I care?

Stella grinned over her shoulder as if unaware of the lady's disapproval. Lady Isabella plastered a prim, false, toothless grin on her lips. Sir Edwin, seated beside his wife, didn't take note; his attention was on the attractive Baroness Forster on his left. The baroness laughed at something Sir Edwin said, and Lady

Isabell smacked Sir Edwin on the thigh with her fan. Sir Edwin muttered an objection.

Stella faced forward, preparing to listen to Alice's playing, but her mind was too caught up in thought. The man arguing with his wife behind her was once Lady Atherly's lover. Sir Edwin was not Stella's ideal, but who's to say what he was like in his youth before he'd been forced to marry a woman he didn't love? When they'd first met, Lyndy wouldn't have been Stella's choice either. But they were lucky. From their continued squabbling, Sir Edwin and Lady Isabella hadn't been.

And Lady Atherly?

Stella stole a glimpse of her mother-in-law two rows away, patiently listening to Baron Branson-Hill, a family friend, boast, no doubt, about his latest equine acquisition. What was Lady Atherly thinking? Did she still regret her decision to do her duty and give up the man she loved? Or had she grown to embrace it? Stella had seen the undeniable concern and affection Lady Atherly had revealed when Lord Atherly collapsed the night of her and Lyndy's engagement party. But then why invite Sir Edwin and his family here for the holidays? Could Lady Atherly be encouraging the obvious attachment between Alice and Freddy? Or was there something more? Stella regretted not asking when she had the chance.

Alice began to play, and Stella's mind emptied, the bickering behind her silenced. The notes of a Chopin nocturne floated from the piano like a tonic. For a little over four minutes, the world was at peace. The last note hovered over the hushed audience until it faded into silence.

Bishop, barons, and ladies alike launched from their seats as the room erupted with applause. Alice blushed, even more so when Freddy took her hands and kissed them.

Stella was still clapping when a male voice cut through, saying, "Are we not to hear from Lady Lyndhurst as well?"

Stella's hands ceased in midclap. She searched the audience, hoping to spot the culprit. Sir Edwin winked at her. Could she ignore him?

"Show 'em how it's done back home, Stella!" Great-aunt Rachel called.

"How about it, my love?" Lyndy, seated beside her, forgetfully put his hand under her elbow and urged her to stand. She winced in pain. "Oh, Stella, I forgot." He took his hand away. "But please, do sing your Kentucky song for them. They'll adore you for it."

Stella had had no intention of singing. She had a passable voice, the one thing her father had complimented her on, but nothing compared to Miss Dare. Stella would sound like a crow after that songbird. But with enthusiastic encouragement, even Lady Atherly signaling her approval, Stella found herself facing a room full of anticipating faces.

"Do you still remember 'My Old Kentucky Home'?" she asked her sister-in-law, still at the piano. Alice had played it countless times at Stella's father's request.

"Of course." Alice whispered something to Freddy. Not needed to turn pages, Freddy took his seat beside his mother.

Hesitant, Stella began to sing, her voice scarcely carrying over the strains emanating from the piano. She'd found her footing by the time she'd reached the second stanza. It was a simple tune that evoked a tumult of emotion. Roiled up in the memories of singing it for her father were reminders of the life she'd left behind and promises for the new one she'd begun here. She finished with the chorus, singing boldly, ignoring the admonishment of the words. Tears rimmed her eyes.

> *"Weep no more, my lady.*
> *No, weep no more today.*
> *We will sing one song.*
> *For the old Kentucky home.*
> *For the old Kentucky home, far away."*

Embarrassed, she wiped the corners of her eyes with the back of her hand. The audience didn't seem to mind, rewarding her effort with enthusiastic applause.

"Atta girl!" Aunt Rachel called. Holding a handkerchief to her eyes, she leaned toward Lord Atherly beside her. In a voice that always carried over a crowd, she added, "Our Stella sings as pretty as a Carolina wren."

Lord Atherly, despite having no experience with the American songbird, agreed.

"How about we sing Christmas carols now?" Stella said.

Alice struck up a rollicking version of "Deck the Halls." Lord Atherly joined her at the piano, leading the audience through the first verse. Everyone, whether moved by the music or less inhibited by the flowing champagne, joined in. Everyone except Lady Isabella, who pursed her lips as if they might betray her and let a joyful note slip out.

Stella felt sorry for her. Did she know she hadn't been Sir Edwin's first choice? She must. Why else contradict her husband's alibi to the police? But then why spend Christmas at Morrington Hall where Lady Atherly was mistress? Was the marriage between Freddy and Alice so advantageous she'd subject herself to the opening of old wounds?

Lyndy's jolly "Falalalala" cut through Stella's musings and stirred her heart.

Poor Lady Isabella. Had she ever been as happy as Stella was right now?

Downstairs was blissfully empty but for Mrs. Downie enjoying her own baking. The lingering aroma of the kitchen beckoned as much as Mrs. Downie did, waving Mrs. Robertson to the table with a fork in hand. The housekeeper rubbed the back of her neck and crossed the threshold, grateful for a wee bit of sympathetic company. She and Mrs. Downie had worked together for years, and although Mrs. Robertson had to rebuke the cook on occasion, they were, in truth, each other's oldest friends.

As Mrs. Nelson and Mrs. Cole were purported to be.

With the influx of guests for the evening's entertainment, it had been a busy day, and her staff had worked hard. On her way from the bedrooms to the kitchen, Mrs. Robertson had passed a cluster of maids bending their ear to the crack in the green baize door closest to the music room. A jolly song filtered through. She'd nodded her approval when Millie, one of the youngest, took on the appearance of a frightened rabbit. Mrs. Robertson wasn't one to stifle her staff's enjoyment if there was no need. Granted, she'd had to be more forceful than usual in her management of her new household lest the lower servants think her soft, but keeping it up was exhausting. Hence the relief in finding only Mrs. Downie in the kitchen.

Mrs. Robertson dropped into the nearest chair and slumped forward to rub her ankle. Had she ever walked so much in her life? To acquaint herself with every room and assess which tasks were being done sufficiently and what needed better doing took more than the housekeeper had imagined; she'd never overseen such a great muckle house. But once she was satisfied, knew the manor inside and out, she'd be content to let the others traipse about without her.

"Not wanting to hear the music yourself, then?" Mrs. Downie said. Without asking, she set a steaming cup of tea and a slice of caramelized nut pie before the housekeeper.

"It's grand, but I think it best to let the others enjoy it without me peering over their wee shoulders."

Mrs. Downie nodded in agreement. "And it gives us a bit of peace and quiet. I never suspected how loud and busy this great house could get. I'm not complaining about moving up, mind, but I do miss the simplicity of Pilley Manor now and again."

"Aye," was all Mrs. Robertson got out before taking a much-welcome sip of her tea. Mrs. Downie had added lemon, honey, and a wee dram of something stronger. It slid down easily, warming her insides. "Though Mr. Fulton assures me it isn't always like this, what with the holidays and the guests . . ."

"I should hope not, or I'll be finding myself a nice man to marry to escape."

"Whatever are you on about?"

"Mrs. Cole, the former cook. I've heard more than a bit about that one. I'm glad I never had to share her kitchen." Mrs. Downie produced a folded piece of plain stationery from her starched white apron and tossed it on the table between them. It was addressed to Lady Atherly.

"Seems the cook left of her own accord, after all."

"Thank goodness for that. But where's it been, might I ask?"

"Scullery maid found it when cleaning the grate in Mrs. Cole's room. It had fallen behind the coal hod. She didn't know what to do with it, so the girl gave it to me. I forgot about it until just now."

Mrs. Robertson dragged the paper across the table toward her, running her fingertips hard along the crease to keep it closed.

"Did you read this?"

"It fell onto the floor, writing side up," Mrs. Downie said, drying her hands in her apron.

"Can I help that I saw a bit of what was written when I picked it up?"

"I can imagine how many times you had to drop it for it to land in such a way."

Mrs. Downie shrugged in mock innocence. "If you want to keep your business private, put it in a sealed envelope, I say."

"Aye. I'm sure you do."

Mrs. Robertson shook her head before taking another long sip of her tea, debating whether she should immediately bring the note to Lady Atherly's attention or wait. She left it on the table.

"If you're not going to read it, I can tell you what it said," Mrs. Downie offered.

Mrs. Robertson pinched the bridge of her nose, nodding almost imperceptibly as if that would relieve her of any culpability.

Mrs. Downie pulled back a chair and settled into it. Cupping her hands around her teacup, the cook leaned in to impart the contents of the letter: Mrs. Cole's anger at the insinuations that her food had poisoned Mrs. Nelson, her unwillingness to stay on under such untenable conditions after Mrs. Nelson's untimely death, her accepting Captain Stancliffe's proposal of marriage.

"At least Lady Atherly will have closure on the subject." Mrs. Robertson slipped the paper onto her lap, vowing to bring it to Her Ladyship's attention in the morning. No need to bother the countess now.

The two women each took another sip of their tea. The hiss of the radiators filled the momentary silence.

Is it ever quiet here?

"How was your visit to your sister's?" Mrs. Robertson asked, lamenting having to cancel her trip to visit her sister's lad. Mrs. Nelson's death had changed everything. For Mrs. Robertson, it was mostly for the good, but how she missed that bonny nephew of hers.

"Smashing, though I have to say she couldn't bake a pie if I brought her one already made. But enough of that." She glanced about her before leaning in closer. "Do you know what I learned from Willie, the greengrocer's boy, when he brought the veg for tomorrow night's dinner?"

According to Mrs. Downie, Willie was a veritable fount of information. The worst of the village gossips, more like. Patiently waiting for the cook to continue, Mrs. Robertson sampled the pie. It was too sweet for her liking. She pushed the plate away.

"It's one of the most shocking things I've ever heard. I'm not even sure I should repeat it."

Mrs. Robertson had heard Mrs. Downie declare this before and knew from experience the cook always repeated it.

"And Willie got it from Mrs. Smith over at Exbury House, so it's not just something he'd heard. By now, the whole village knows."

"What did they hear that was so terrible, Mrs. Downie?" Mrs. Robertson rubbed her neck again.

The cook glanced around again, dropping her voice to a compelling whisper. Despite herself, Mrs. Robertson leaned forward.

"That one of the workmen who was here installing the boiler system—Short or Stott or Smith, doesn't matter what his name is, well . . ." Mrs. Downie pushed back her chair, rounded the table, and sat beside the housekeeper. Although they were alone, she cupped her hand to whisper in Mrs. Robertson's ear. "Willie said that this Smith said that he and our lady mistress are . . ."

She paused. Mrs. Robertson suspected it was for dramatic effect, but in fact, Mrs. Downie was struggling for the word.

"Are . . . how do I say this? He's been at the Knightwood Oak, claiming to be close to Her Ladyship. If you get my meaning."

"What?" Mrs. Robertson couldn't stifle the laugh. "This Smith, or whatever his name is, claims to be in a personal relationship with Lady Atherly? I can't imagine the countess even knows he exists." Mrs. Robertson had heard it all. This was the most preposterous rumor Mrs. Downie had ever repeated.

Scowling, Mrs. Downie shook her head as she sat back, crossing her arms against her ample bosom. "Not the Countess of Atherly, Mrs. Robertson. This man is suggesting he knows our Lady Lyndhurst."

The laughter died on Mrs. Robertson's tongue, replaced by a lump in her throat.

Lady Lyndhurst, or Miss Kendrick, as they'd known her, had lived at Pilley Manor for several months before her wedding. With her unusual but upfront and friendly way, she charmed her way into both women's hearts. Mrs. Robertson wouldn't hear a word against her. And said so.

"It's not me saying this!" Mrs. Downie rose abruptly, scraping her chair's legs on the floor, and began whisking the plates and cups from the table. Mrs. Robertson hadn't even finished the tea. "But that's why I'm telling you. I fancied you should know."

"You're right, Mrs. Downie. This heinous rumor is not of your doing. But it has to stop. Don't tell another soul."

"Are you going to tell Her Ladyship?"

Again, Mrs. Robertson wasn't sure which "lady" the cook referred to. She also didn't know which one she would approach with the news. If she was going to repeat the rumor at all.

"All in good time."

She stared at the envelope in her lap. It resembled the one that had arrived earlier by post. The one asking for a reference for Louisa Bright, the chambermaid Mrs. Nelson fired. The one Mrs. Downie said was suspected of wrongdoing. Mrs. Robertson hadn't known what to do with that either. Perhaps she could relate all three tidings to Lady Lyndhurst in the morning and let her decide what was best.

Mrs. Robertson tapped the table lightly, satisfied she'd arrived at a solution, never once admitting the prospect of facing the countess with such disagreeable news made her tremble. She'd been here but a few days, and despite her aching legs and pounding head, she couldn't imagine wanting to do anything else. *Let Mrs. Cole marry.* Mrs. Robertson loved what she did. But if Lady Atherly didn't fancy the message, the messenger would be out on the street as swiftly as Louisa Bright.

"You took away my tea, Mrs. Downie. I could do with a wee dram more. And a wee bit stronger this time?"

Mrs. Downie winked knowingly and shuffled off toward the stove to oblige.

CHAPTER 30

Stella needed fresh air. She'd sung carol after carol ending with the round of "Ding Dong Merrily on High" that left everyone happy and breathless. With the champagne flowing, the night grew into a more boisterous affair than it started, with small clusters of people laughing and exchanging stories. It was satisfying to see everyone at such ease. Lyndy was across the room, deep in conversation with Baron Branson-Hill, Sir Edwin, and Baron Forster. Knowing her husband, he was bragging about his new Thoroughbred colt. And rightly so. Knockan Crag was a beautiful horse with excellent prospects. Stella was elated that she'd been able to gift him to Lyndy.

Stella opened one of the French windows and slipped unobtrusively out into the moonlit garden. The night was clear and calm, stars flickering between whisps of passing clouds. The cool air quickly licked the heat off Stella's skin, but she relished the refreshing chill. The din of voices faded behind her as she strolled across the lawn to the formal gardens, the heels of her silk evening slippers, not meant for the outdoors, sinking into the damp ground with every step. She settled on the edge of the dormant fountain, a porcelain cherub clutching a bushel of fruit in the middle of an empty pool coated in a sheen of ice. The stone's cold seeped through the fabric of her dress. She ignored it, closing her eyes and relishing the moment of solitude.

In all the years she'd spent entertaining herself in the stables, the gardens, or the seldom-used rooms of her father's mansions, wishing she had siblings or playmates, she'd never dreamt that she'd ever want to be alone. But once in a while, the craving arose. That's when she'd saddle up Tully and go for a ride. But even then, she wasn't by herself. She had Tully. She adored Lyndy and was learning to fit into her new family, but she was seldom alone. Rarely did Lyndy make plans or have duties that didn't include her accompanying him. And if she found he'd gone off without her, Ethel, Lady Atherly, Alice, a chambermaid, or Mrs. Nelson was there to fill the void.

Mrs. Nelson.

Stella flinched at the sudden, high-pitched scream of a distant red fox. It was so humanlike.

Had Mrs. Nelson screamed when the oncoming automobile careened toward her? Had the driver heard her and ignored it? Stella shuddered at such possible callousness. She still didn't know why the housekeeper had been out on Mistletoe Lane that night. Was she going or coming from Mrs. Oakhill's house? If so, why? And who would want to kill her? Only Sir Edwin seemed to have anything resembling a motive.

He and Lady Atherly.

Stella gasped. How could she think such a thing? Yes, Lady Atherly was often haughty and condescending and had employed all sorts of underhanded tricks to keep Stella and Lyndy apart before the wedding. But kill Mrs. Nelson? The countess wouldn't stoop that low. Would she?

Hating this train of thought, Stella rose, eager to return to the lights and warmth of the music room. A branch broke behind her. She increased her pace. Yards from the house, a shadowed figure emerged from the hedgerow that shielded the path to the servants' entrance from sight.

Lyndy?

The question died on her tongue. As he approached, his silhouette emerged; the curve of his shoulder, the tilt of his head, the stance of his legs was all wrong. Stella pretended not to have seen him and tried to walk past.

"Going in so soon?"

The man blocked her way. The light streaming from the windows revealed half the man's face.

"Mr. Stott? Is there something wrong with the boiler again?" She forced a light laugh but inwardly shied from the expression on his face, a mixture of menace and longing. Instead, she concentrated on the people inside, clearly seen over the workman's shoulder. Sir Edwin and the Bishop of Winchester were sharing a laugh.

"There never was. I don't do shoddy work. But I did turn it off."

"Why would you do that?"

"Needed an excuse to come back, didn't I?"

"You did?"

"Don't be daft, Lady Lyndhurst. Or should I say Stella? You know I came to see you again. So we could be together." He took a step toward her. She instinctually backed up.

Chills having nothing to do with the evening air crawled down her back.

"Don't you want to be together? Answer me," he insisted, without giving her a moment to respond. "You've never been tongue-tied before."

Stella wanted to scream at him to leave her alone, that she had been friendly to him as she was with everyone, but knew it was better to placate him long enough to get back into the house.

"I'm very flattered by your attention, Mr. Stott, but—"

"Ernie. You must call me Ernie."

Digging her fingernails into her palms to stay calm, Stella swallowed against the bile in her throat.

"Ernie. As I was saying—"

"I'm not sure I liked what you were saying, Stella." He closed the distance between them. Stella pivoted to run but her heel caught in the soft grass. He seized her wrist and clamped onto it like a vise.

"Let me go!" She tried yanking free, but he was too strong.

"Not before I get what I came for."

He grasped her sore elbow and reeled her in like a fish. She kicked at him.

"Let go of me!" she screeched.

At that moment, someone, probably Alice, struck up something loud and energetic on the piano. Filtered through the manor's wall and windows, it sounded discordant and disjointed. Between the music and the voices rising to join in, the party's enthusiastic cacophony drowned out her scream.

"You know you don't want me to."

The workman plunged his face at her, his breath reeking of ale, his lips pursed as he tried to force a kiss. She twisted and squirmed in protest, ineffectually trying to punch him with her fists. Twice his lips missed, brushing her cheeks. On his next attempt, she slammed the top of her forehead into his face with all the force she could muster.

"You bloody bitch!" Growling in protest and pain, he released his grip and clutched his nose and cheekbone.

Pain flared through Stella's head. The earth tilted, and her stomach flipped, but free of her attacker, she lunged away from him knowing it would be a matter of seconds before he was after her again. But miscalculating, she threw her weight too much and landed on her knees.

She started to crawl toward the house, her knees tangling in the fabric of her dress. The French door opened, and two figures emerged from inside. They were giggling and clutching each other closely.

"Help!" she called, her voice feeble and shaky.

"Stella?"

A mumbled curse erupted from the shadows at the sound of Alice's sweet, concerned voice. Alice and her companion dashed across the lawn. Stella slumped in relief.

"Oh, my God! What happened?" Alice asked.

Stella, her heart pounding, her breath ragged, merely shook her head. She couldn't voice what had happened. Not yet. Freddy Kentfield was helping Stella to her feet before she dared to look over her shoulder.

Ernie Stott was gone.

"All right! All right! I'm coming!" The incessant pounding didn't stop. Inspector Brown trudged to his front door and cracked it open. A draft of biting air slipped past. "Lord Lynd-hurst?"

Standing on his threshold were His Lordship and Lady Lynd-hurst. A carriage, with a driver rubbing the sleep from his eyes, was parked in the empty street, the horses' breath visible in the cold. Above them glittered a brilliancy of stars.

"I beg your pardon, my lord, my lady, but what couldn't possibly wait until morning?"

"My wife has been attacked." Lord Lyndhurst, his jaw tight, clenched his fists at his side. "I demand you do something." From the scent on his breath, His Lordship had been drinking champagne. A bit too much, perhaps?

"My lady?" Brown ran a practiced eye over the viscountess. She was wrapped from head to toe in fur, yet hugged herself as if still cold. "Are you well?"

"I'm fine." She forced a fleeting half smile for his benefit. Brown wasn't fooled.

"The blighter must be found," Lord Lyndhurst said, pounding the stone step with his foot. "He must be held accountable."

"He does. I agree," Lady Lyndhurst said. "But we didn't have to do this now. Inspector Brown had obviously already gone to bed."

Brown swallowed hard, self-conscious to be standing before them in his nightshirt and bare feet.

"Involving the inspector was your idea. I fancied finding the scoundrel myself." Lord Lyndhurst raised a fist as if seeing this attacker before him.

"And do what, my lord? Take the law into your own hands?" Thank heaven Lady Lyndhurst's levelheadedness had prevailed. No telling what the enraged husband might do. Or what would happen (to either of them) if Brown had to arrest Lord Lyndhurst for assault or worse. Brown opened the door wide and stepped aside. "Now, come in from the cold, will you?"

When they hesitated, he impatiently motioned them in, admonishing them for remaining on his doorstep. "Do you want to wake the neighbors too?"

After insisting they go through to his parlor while he dressed, Brown donned something more suitable and reassured his wife, who'd been awoken by the commotion.

He rejoined the young couple as Lord Lyndhurst was saying, "I don't care. The man took liberties. I don't know what American customs dictate, but here, that was beyond the pale. He must be found tonight."

Lady Lyndhurst, who'd taken off a glove and been running the red velvet ribbon draped on the Christmas tree through her thumb and forefinger, sighed. "I'm not saying—"

"Please," Brown interrupted, indicating for them to sit. He rekindled the fire and, once satisfied it would burn on its own, settled into his well-worn leather armchair across from them, keen to the irony of turning his parlor into an interrogation room. "Right! Now, start from the beginning."

Lord Lyndhurst opened his mouth to oblige, but a look

from his wife silenced him. Instead, she told Brown the tale of Mr. Ernie Stott, a workman who had been a frequent visitor to Morrington Hall as he installed the new boiler system. Lady Lyndhurst recounted the numerous times she'd greeted him in the hall.

"As you know, Lady Lyndhurst is most charming and friendly to all," the viscount couldn't help but add. "But this chap got the wrong idea."

To this, Lady Lyndhurst agreed. "I thought nothing of his attentiveness. But then, when I crashed the Daimler yesterday, it so happened that Mr. Stott was passing. Despite my objections, he insisted on escorting me home. I wonder now if it wasn't a coincidence."

"The blighter was following you?" The viscount's fury was in danger of being unleashed again.

"Maybe. I don't know."

"My God, I'll kill him!"

Lord Lyndhurst leaped to his feet, his jarring weight causing the floor to bounce. The glass baubles on the tree jiggled and jingled against each other. One of Mrs. Brown's favorite curios, a painted mallard duck, tumbled off the far side table. In one swift motion, Lord Lyndhurst snatched the porcelain figurine from imminent ruin and placed it roughly back in place. He began pacing the short distance between the settee and the western windows as if he hadn't paused to save the statue.

"I'm sorry, Inspector," Lady Lyndhurst said. "I didn't mean for you to be dragged into this at this hour."

"Who knows where the bloody scoundrel will be by morning," her husband argued.

"He's right, my lady," Brown said, eyeing her volatile husband. "Pray continue."

Lady Lyndhurst stared into the fire, the flickering light softening her features. And yet the effort of continuing was evident in the lines in the corners of her mouth.

"Tonight, we had a fund-raiser for my horse farm charity.

When I went outside during the party, Mr. Stott, who'd been hiding in the bushes, accosted me."

"He restrained you, trying to force you to kiss him," Lord Lyndhurst clarified.

"Luckily, Lady Alice and Mr. Kentfield scared him away."

"I insist you find him, Brown." Lord Lyndhurst stopped his motion to tug at the collar of his overcoat. "If you don't, I will."

In his sternest tone, Brown said, "My lord. It's best to let me handle this."

Lord Lyndhurst nodded curtly and continued his pacing. Lady Lyndhurst ran her fingers over the smooth glaze on Mrs. Brown's duck. Brown had interviewed enough witnesses, enough suspects that he knew when someone was holding something back.

Gentling his voice, Brown added, "But, my lady, I need to know everything. What is it you're not telling us?"

Lord Lyndhurst halted. "Stella?"

"Remember how I told you things have been coming up missing from our bedroom?"

"I do. But what . . . ?" Understanding dawned on the viscount's face, his fists balling again at his sides. "You think that bloody . . . ?"

"Lady Lyndhurst?" Brown said, cutting off His Lordship's tirade to curb his growing frustration. "Care to enlighten me?"

"Mrs. Nelson accused the maid, but I believe Mr. Stott might've stolen them from our bedroom. He had ready access. And thinking back, he always had an excuse to be outside our bedroom door."

"He's most likely the one behind the anonymous Christmas card and a love poem, isn't he?" His Lordship added.

Brown had no idea what that meant but didn't want to interrupt to find out.

"He must be." Lady Lyndhurst suddenly paled, her mouth

growing slack, words already forming on her tongue. Brown sat up, knowing a revelation was to come. "What's more, when we returned to the house this morning, Mr. Stott mentioned 'borrowing' an automobile and learning to drive. He didn't say from whom or when, but . . ."

"My lady? Do you suspect Mr. Stott of killing Mrs. Nelson?" Brown had learned, the hard way, not to discount Lady Lyndhurst's intuition.

"I saw Mrs. Nelson belittle him, berating him like a child. Could he have taken such offense that he killed her?" She shook her head. "That sounds far-fetched, doesn't it?"

"Not necessarily," Lord Lyndhurst said, finding his seat beside his wife again. He removed his hat and ran his gloved fingers through his hair. "The housekeeper had done it in front of you. With his delusions of an attachment, he might've found the humiliation intolerable. If he resorted to attacking you, whom he purported to adore, then what might he be capable of toward the housekeeper who emasculated him?"

"Right!" Brown slapped his knees and stood. The young couple sprung to their feet to meet him. "We need to discover where Mr. Stott lives. I agree with Lord Lyndhurst. No time should be wasted in tracking this fella down."

Without hesitation, the trio headed for the door.

Shrugging on his overcoat and grabbing his hat from the rack by the door, Brown called to his wife, "It might be a late night, my dear."

But what was a little sleep loss if he caught Mrs. Nelson's killer?

CHAPTER 31

The two-story, three-gabled, brick cottage sat back from the road. Lyndy pushed open the wrought-iron gate in the brick wall that enclosed a garden of well-edged but bare borders and closely clipped lawn waiting patiently for warmer weather. Yet the pruned holly bushes, set close to the house against the red brick, made the cottage appear dressed for the holidays.

"Seems nice enough," he said, following Stella up the brick path to the front door.

What a contrast to that bloody bastard's tiny, ill-kept cottage they'd visited last night. Over Inspector Brown's objections, they'd accompanied the policeman to the wretch's home, which they discovered upon consulting the Hampshire Directory to be but a few minutes' carriage ride from the inspector's home. The straw roof needed repair, tangled weeds obscured the cobblestone walk, and blinds concealed the interior from view.

The boiler man had the infuriating gall not to be there. But they discovered after Lyndy forced the door that all of Stella's missing items were. There was an exquisitely inlaid writing desk, clear of clutter or dust among the piles of pipe fittings and discarded food tins. How a man of his class could afford such a piece, Lyndy could not imagine. Upon closer inspection, each tiny drawer contained an item: a glove, the souvenir spoon, a pair of stockings, and more that had belonged to Stella. Revolted, his outrage coursing through his veins and pounding in his ears, Lyndy smashed the desk with his fists.

Better to have pummeled the boiler man!

The outburst had a tempering effect, softening Lyndy's hostility long enough for Stella and the inspector to hustle him outside. They'd parted soon after, with Stella's belongings and promises from the inspector to locate and arrest the workman in hand.

The morning had come too quickly. Lyndy woke with a parched mouth, the memory of champagne still on his tongue. Stella's lady's maid had roused them, chattering on excitedly, aggravating his headache, and shoving envelopes into Stella's hand. Upon reading and sharing their contents, his dear wife hadn't hesitated to drag Lyndy out of bed. Although not understanding the urgency (*Hadn't the maid been cleared of suspicion, after all?*), Lyndy had reluctantly accompanied Stella to this address in New Milton, a ten-minute train ride from Rosehurst. After last night's revelations, he couldn't fathom letting her go alone.

But why must the sun burn so bright? Where was the usual winter gloom?

Lyndy raised and lowered the brass knocker several times as Stella peeked into the nearest window. The sunlight on the window made it impossible for Lyndy to see anything but reflections of her and the bare garden behind them.

"Do you see anyone?"

She shook her head. He knocked again. The maid who had once tended their bedchamber opened the door. She clutched a sleek, black and gray tabby cat to her chest.

"Lord Lyndhurst!" she yelped. "What are you doing here?"

"I suggest you invite us in, Louisa," Lyndy said. "Now."

"But Mrs. Allston isn't at home," the maid protested. The cat meowed in concert.

"All the better, don't you think?" Stella said, navigating the holly bushes to join them.

"Milady," the maid said, her chin dropping to the top of the cat's head, stepped back, and the couple entered a long hall draped in intertwining garlands of holly and ivy. "How did you find me?"

"That's not the question you should be asking," Lyndy advised, none too pleased that he'd been forced from his warm bed to spar with an insolent chambermaid.

"Mrs. Allston contacted Morrington Hall, checking on your reference," Stella said. "You know, the one Mrs. Nelson never provided."

Her shoulders slumped, Louisa pointed toward a room off to the right. "We can talk in there if you prefer."

"No, we won't be long," Stella said, stomping her feet on the colorful Belgian carpet running the length of the hall. "I have one question to ask you, and then we'll go. Were you ever a resident of Mrs. Young's Home for Orphaned Girls?"

The maid scrunched up her face. "Beg your pardon? No. I grew up in Winchester and know full well who me mum and dad are. I'm the spitting image of me mum, so I know I'm hers."

"Is your mother's name Maggie?"

"No, Laura. Why?" The cat squirmed in the maid's arms, demanding to be released. The maid lowered it to the floor. "What's this all about?"

"Mrs. Nelson visited Mrs. Young's the day she died, asking after a child there from years ago. I thought it might have to do with you."

"I might've been better off if I had grown up there."

"Why do you say that?"

By Lyndy's count, that was four questions. When had Stella ever asked just one?

"Dad used to smack me sisters and me with a wooden spoon. When I was twelve, he found a position for me as a scullery maid to bring in extra income. And he'd arranged for me employers to send every penny I made home. I wanted something better, I did. So, I worked long enough to get a good reference and moved as far away as I could afford. I've been making me way in service ever since."

"And making up new names as you go?"

The maid sucked in her breath. "But how—?"

"Inspector Brown found you out. It doesn't look good for you, Louisa."

"I swear on me little sister's soul, milady, I never did anything to Mrs. Nelson. And I never took anything . . . of yours." The slight hesitation suggested she wasn't telling the whole truth.

"We know," Stella said. "Mrs. Nelson was unjust to accuse you. I don't know why she would've, do you?"

Stella must've heard the maid's hesitancy as well. The maid fussed with the lacy cloth covering the side table, straightening a wrinkle. On it was a tray filled with unopened Christmas cards and a bowl filled with peppermint candy. The aroma made Lyndy think of the horses.

Which is where I'd rather be right now.

"Louisa," Lyndy encouraged gruffly, the tabby rubbing against his trouser leg. He crouched to pet it and was rewarded with a soft, soothing purr.

Catching Lyndy's admonishing glare, the maid began to wring her hands. "Actually, milady, I do. I took some of Mrs. Cole's mince pies. They looked ever so nice, and I took only a few when I knew Mrs. Cole was to make plenty more."

"And Mrs. Nelson found out?" Stella asked.

"She found them in me room and confiscated them. I hadn't even eaten one yet."

Mrs. Nelson hadn't taken them back to the kitchen, though, had she? He and Stella had found the pies in the housekeeper's study. She'd kept them for herself.

"Lucky for you that you didn't," Lyndy said. "We suspect they'd gone off and were what caused Mrs. Nelson to become deliriously ill."

The cat abandoned Lyndy and trotted off down the hall.

"Do you like it here?" Stella said, changing the subject as abruptly as the cat had changed its mind.

The maid blinked. "Um, I suppose so, milady, though I've only just taken the position. I was lucky to find anything on such short notice."

"Did you like working at Morrington Hall?"

The maid's hand wringing stopped as she clasped them to her chest. "I did. Ever so much."

"What would you say to a second chance?"

The maid momentarily covered her gaping mouth. "To work at Morrington Hall again?"

Stella nodded.

"Stella, I don't think Mother—"

"Even knows about the maid's dismissal yet," Stella provided, interrupting Lyndy's objection.

She was right. Mother had been kept ignorant of all of the household changes, except for the replacement of Mrs. Nelson. *How easily it had been done too.*

"We'll have to wait until Mrs. Allston can find a new maid," Stella said. "How long you stay, of course, would be contingent on you minding Mrs. Robertson—whom I know to be firm but fair—and never taking anything that isn't yours again."

"Oh, yes, milady. I'll do anything to go back to Morrington Hall."

"Good, then it's settled. You let us know when Mrs. Allston has found your replacement, and I'll send you the train fare and tell Mrs. Robertson when to expect you."

Leaving the maid bouncing on the front step, calling out her gratitude, Lyndy followed Stella down the brick walk toward the street.

"Do you think that wise? Allowing a known thief back into the house?"

"She's learned her lesson. Besides, they were only a few spoiled mince pies. It is Christmas, after all."

"I am forever in awe of the depth of your compassion, my love."

Stella flashed him an impish smile and tapped him playfully on the dimple on his chin. "How do you think I put up with you?"

Lyndy grabbed her finger and kissed it, laughing, his headache forgotten. Without warning, the bright smile slipped from her lovely face, replaced by a sober, thoughtful frown.

"What is it, Stella?"

"I was just wondering. If Louisa isn't the child Mrs. Nelson asked about, who is?"

CHAPTER 32

"Do you think she'll like him?" Stella dropped from the saddle and gave the gentle, dun-colored gelding a firm pat.

After returning from New Milton, she and Lyndy had headed straight for the Triple R Farm. Experiencing Louisa's elation and gratitude at getting a second chance spurred Stella to want to do more. Wasn't that the meaning of Christmas? Finding joy by helping those less fortunate? And Louisa wasn't the only one in need.

"How can she not? It's a fine animal," Lyndy said, wrapping Beau's reins around the Oakhill cottage fence. "A fitting tribute to the captain."

Stella had thought so too.

Before Stella could tie Major up, the front door flew open and out dashed the Oakhill boys, bareheaded and lacking overcoats. Little Malcolm stumbled, his worn, hand-me-down boots too big for him, tripping his older brother as the two raced toward the pony. Offered something from their fists, Major nickered encouragingly for more.

"Boys, boys! Wherever are your manners?" As she stepped

from her hall, Mrs. Oakhill wiped her hands on her apron, embroidered with tiny green wreaths at the waist. "Say good morning to Lady Lyndhurst before you accost her pony. It's an honor to see you again, milady."

The boys dropped their gazes, Roger scuffing his feet impatiently on the grass, and the pair obediently said in unison, "Good morning, Lady Lyndhurst."

"Good morning to you too, boys." Stella ruffled Malcolm's hair before introducing Lyndy to the Oakhill family.

The widow blanched, not having seen him until he'd stepped out from behind the captain's pony. She tucked a loose strand of hair behind her ear and then bobbed a quick curtsy. "Your Lordship."

"Pleasure, Mrs. Oakhill."

"Have you seen Mr. Green?" Stella asked.

"I did, milady. He's not certain about the cow yet but assures me my horse will recover, though it'll take months. I'm truly grateful to you and Your Lordship for sending the veterinarian."

"Think nothing of it," Lyndy said.

"But—"

"We didn't call to receive your gratitude, Mrs. Oakhill, though I am happy to hear Mr. Green could help. We came to give you something. Call it a late Christmas present." Stella held out the reins to Roger. "Can you take charge of him? His name's Major."

With an erect posture and solemn nod, the boy reached for the reins and clutched them tightly. Not to be left out, Malcolm grabbed the back of his older brother's shirt. Stella handed each boy a small stick of peppermint before offering the pony a piece of the sweet-smelling treat. Major sniffed it for a moment before taking it from Stella's palm.

"Is Major ours then?" the littlest asked after taking a few licks of the candy.

Stella bent to be at the boy's level. "He is. He needs a new home. He recently lost his owner. Like you lost your dad."

Together, the two boys gazed up at their new companion. Major swished his tail and nickered again.

"Oh, my," Mrs. Oakhill said, struggling to speak. "You are too kind, both of you."

"I take no credit," Lyndy said, holding his palms up. "This was all Lady Lyndhurst's doing."

"Boys, why don't you show Major his new home." When her sons had led the willing pony toward the small stable, Mrs. Oakhill added, "Mrs. Nelson said you were kind, milady, but . . ." Pressing her fingers to her chest, she paused to compose herself. "I had no idea how right she was."

At the mention of Mrs. Nelson, Stella recalled her conversation with the chambermaid earlier. Why hadn't she noticed before that Mrs. Oakhill was Louisa's peer?

"I know this is going to sound strange, Mrs. Oakhill, and I don't mean to be intrusive, but did you ever happen to be a resident of Mrs. Young's Home for Orphaned Girls?"

Lyndy shot Stella a questioning glance.

"I was. I lived there until my seventeenth birthday. How did you know? Did Mrs. Nelson get a chance to tell you? She said she might."

Stella's breathing quickened. *This is what Mrs. Nelson wanted to talk to me about.*

Was she finally going to get some answers?

"No, only that she was inquiring about a child, about your age, at the orphanage the day she died. Are you saying Mrs. Nelson was your mother?"

"No, but Mrs. Nelson suspected she knew who was. She asked me not to mention it to anyone until she'd confirmed the truth."

"What exactly did she tell you?" Lyndy beat Stella in asking.

Mrs. Oakhill dropped her gaze, fidgeting with the tie of her apron. "Not much, except she insinuated that my mother worked at Morrington Hall."

"I say!" Lyndy chuckled incredulously. "That's absurd. If not Mrs. Nelson, who could that possibly be?"

"I don't know, milord, but if she was right, Mrs. Nelson said my mother's name is Maggie."

The name Mrs. Nelson muttered in her delirium. The name Miss Stancliffe called her new sister-in-law.

"It's Mrs. Cole," Stella said. "I mean, the widowed Mrs. Stancliffe."

"Truly?" Lyndy said. "Mrs. Cole had a baby?"

"Who?" Mrs. Oakhill held her hand to her throat, shaking her head, flustered and confused. "Are you saying you do know her?"

"Yes, Mrs. Oakhill," Stella said gently. "We know her very well. Your mother is Morrington Hall's former cook."

"Where are we going?" said Grace, as Mrs. Oakhill insisted they call her.

She and her boys, bundled up in overcoats and blankets, huddled in the back of the Oakhills' cart as Stella guided Major toward a particular gabled, brick cottage in Rosehurst. Lyndy on Beau followed behind.

"As I said, there's someone I want you to meet."

Stella urged the pony to a halt before the cottage, and Roger, the oldest of the two boys, squirmed from his mother's arms and leaped down. He snatched a bare branch from who knows where and began to run it along the picket fence that edged the property. Before the rest could climb out, the door flung open.

"What's this? Can't a body have a bit of peace and quiet?"

The littlest boy grasped for his mother's skirts and began to cry.

"Oh, my, Col. What is it, love?"

The boy pointed and wailed, "It's Jacob Marley!" referring to a character in Dickens's popular Christmas ghost story.

Captain Stancliffe's widow, hands on her hips and scowling, did resemble a joyless specter. Standing in the doorway, dressed in black, she blended into the hall's darkness, her spectacles glowing in the slanted rays of the late morning sun.

"Lord and Lady Lyndhurst? What's the meaning of this?" She wagged her finger at Roger's continued raucous activity along the fence and Malcolm's frightened cry.

"Oi, Rog," Grace called. The boy dropped his stick and began kicking the tree Lyndy was tying Beau's reins to. "Enough now!"

Grace raised her head from comforting her youngest son to snap at her oldest, and the former Mrs. Cole grew paler still.

"Who? How?" she sputtered, rendered nearly speechless.

"Mrs. Stancliffe," Stella said, "this is Mrs. Oakhill and her sons, Roger and Malcolm. Mrs. Oakhill, this is Mrs. Stancliffe, the former cook at Morrington Hall."

Grace cupped her hands over her nose and mouth. "Is she . . . ?"

"Mrs. Stancliffe. Your Christian name is Margaret or Maggie, isn't it?" Stella asked.

"How the devil did you know that?"

Despite the cook's harsh demand, Stella beamed with excitement.

I was right!

"Mrs. Nelson told me," Grace said. "I came to Morrington Hall seeking help from Lady Lyndhurst a few days ago. Mrs. Nelson was more than obliging, promising to speak to Her Ladyship on my behalf. She sent me a basket of food fit for a Christmas feast. Attached was a note indicating that Maggie had prepared it. She suggested Maggie may be my mother."

A sharp sob escaped the former cook's lips. She raised a hand to her cheek and then, trembling, reached out toward Grace. She abruptly snatched her hand back.

"Mum?" Grace whispered tentatively.

"Gracie?"

The two women awkwardly faced one another in awe.

Stella could empathize. Hadn't that been her a few months ago when she was unexpectedly reunited with her mother?

To break the growing silence and release the ever-increasing knot in her stomach, Stella asked, "How did Mrs. Nelson know?"

Mrs. Stancliffe blinked rapidly, scanned the street for potential eavesdroppers, and waved them inside. "Please, please, come in."

Leaving the boys to play in the yard, Grace, Stella, and Lyndy crossed into the warm hall and stepped into the drawing room. A tea service lay on the table with two empty cups and crumbs of something seasoned with cloves and nutmeg, all that remained on the plates. Miss Stancliffe, with a heavy woolen blanket on her lap, dozed by the fire, her chin resting on her chest.

How much she reminded Stella of Aunt Rachel. *Maybe the two women should meet?*

"Mrs. Nelson would've seen the resemblance immediately," the former cook said softly, mindful not to wake her sister-in-law. She motioned for them to sit. "You, my dear, are the spitting image of me at your age."

Grace blushed, her hands cupped tightly in her lap. Mrs. Stancliffe, forever the curmudgeon, was a woman transformed, struggling to keep the smile, the joy from her face, or the questions from spilling off her lips. Stella couldn't understand the restraint.

These English! Why not just throw your arms around each other and be done with it?

"Have you truly known Mrs. Nelson since your youth?" Grace asked.

"We've been in service together almost our whole lives. We've served His Lordship's family long before he was born."

Mrs. Stancliffe sat for a moment, then thinking better of it, called to the maid to bring more tea. She began to roam around the room, pausing to straighten a stack of books on a square side table.

She was poking at the fire when Lyndy asked, "But Mrs. Nelson knew of Grace, didn't she?"

"Helena was the keeper of secrets. No one was better at it. Part of what made her such a valuable housekeeper. When I'd found myself in a delicate condition while still a kitchen maid, she was the only one I could trust." With a sharp jab at the fire, reminiscent of the former cook's typical irritation, she sent sparks flying. "Your grandmother, Lord Lyndhurst, would've had me out on my ear if she'd found out."

Setting aside the iron poker, she eased down into the chair closest to Grace. She tentatively reached for the young woman's hand. Grace grasped it warmly.

"I had to give you up, you see. Helena found a midwife who'd deliver you in secret. The midwife took you away. I never learned what'd become of you, neither of us had, let alone that you lived so close."

"They never told you when you came of age, Grace?" Stella said.

Mrs. Oakhill shook her head. "I assumed my mother had died." The same lie Stella had lived with for years. Her father's doing. "They believed it for the best not to tell me."

For the best? How could that be? Stella's ears burned at the pointlessness, the precious time wasted.

How often did she resent the time she'd lost with her mother? Was still losing. Yes, they'd enjoyed a day together in York (though they could've skipped the confrontation with a killer) and wrote to each other almost daily. But it wasn't the same. Mama lived in Montana. Would Stella ever see her again?

Lyndy reached for Stella's hand, linking his fingers through hers. He was an outsider in this conversation. He'd lived with his mother's overbearing presence for every minute of his life. That was his regret. But he understood what the loss meant to

Stella. She squeezed his hand back, the heaviness in her chest easing, and smiled.

"I hope you'll forgive me, Grace," Mrs. Stancliffe said. "With your father unwilling to marry me . . ." A frosty edge had crept into her voice.

Could this be the source of the cook's temper? Had she been stewing in bitterness all these years?

"You had no choice, Mum," Grace said. "I'm trying to raise my boys without their father. And I've had to resort to asking for charity. You wouldn't have found any without a husband, alive or dead."

"But you've found each other now," Stella said. "And that's what matters."

Only she and Lyndy knew she was speaking to herself as much as to them.

"Indeed," Lyndy said, rising, pulling Stella up with him. "Shall we leave them to it then?"

"Yes, you have so much to catch up on," Stella agreed. Outside, one boisterous shout was echoed by another. Startled awake, Miss Stancliffe snorted, tipped her back, and dozed off again. Over her increasingly loud wheezing, Stella added, "Including getting to know your grandsons."

"My grandsons." Mrs. Stancliffe, practically giddy at the idea, allowed the words to slip slowly off her tongue.

The couple said their good-byes and snuggled into the saddle, Stella's arms wrapped around Lyndy's waist as they rode home together on the back of Beau.

"Yet again, you've done the impossible," Lyndy chuckled.

"What is that?"

"You made Crotchety Cole grin." His body shook with laughter. Stella held on tighter. "That's what Alice and I used to call her anyway."

"Uh-huh," was all she could offer, unable to share his mirth. Something was nagging at her.

"But alas, it seems I'm incapable of making you smile. What is it, my love? What could possibly be upsetting you?"

She set her chin on his shoulder. "I'm happy for them, but something Mrs. Cole, I mean Mrs. Stancliffe, said is bothering me. 'Helena was the keeper of secrets.' I've tried to dismiss it from my mind and can't seem to do it. What did Mrs. Stancliffe mean?"

"But we know all the secrets now, don't we? Mrs. Cole's baby, Mother's affair with Sir Edwin. What more could there be?"

"That's what's bothering me. There has to be something else."

"Why, Stella? Why must there be?"

"Because we still haven't figured out who killed Mrs. Nelson."

CHAPTER 33

Stella rested her head against the metal wall of the train carriage, the rhythmic sway and *clickity-clack* of the tracks lulling her almost to sleep. Beyond the cigar-smoke-laden velvet drapes that framed the window, pools of water dotted the soggy heathland. Each one reflected a different part of the thickly overcast sky. How odd to be taking the train to a garage that repaired automobiles. If only she hadn't crashed hers—they'd get there faster.

Sir Edwin leaned forward to peer out and admire the vanishing view. "Looks like snow. Shame. How lovely the sun has been this morning."

Learning Sir Edwin's automobile was ready to be picked up, Stella and Lyndy had decided to tag along. They'd inquire at the garage about repairs to the Daimler. Although it was drivable once Mr. Gates repaired the flat tire, it was too damaged to make the journey to Bournemouth reliably. And if they got a few answers out of Sir Edwin along the way? All the better.

With that in mind, Stella shouldn't have been surprised when Lyndy demanded, "Is it true you and my mother had an affair?"

"Lyndy!" *So much for the subtle approach the English are famous for.*

Sir Edwin sat back and coughed into his fist. "Frances told you this, did she?"

"She told my wife, to be precise, but unlike Mother, my wife and I have no secrets."

"Yes, well," Sir Edwin said. "How long have you been married? Give it time."

"I say!" Lyndy bristled at the comment. Stella couldn't blame him.

"It's true, then, that you and Lady Atherly kept each other company the night Mrs. Nelson died?" she asked.

"Yes, we sipped sherry and talked long into the night." Sir Edwin crossed his arms and legs and challenged Stella with his stare. "If that's what you're asking."

"You told the police you were with your wife."

"I did. I believed it would save us all the embarrassment."

"So you say," Lyndy said. "Neither you nor Mother fancied starting up again?"

"I would, without hesitation," Sir Edwin said as calmly as if he'd been pointing out the wet snow that now splattered against the window. "It's no secret there's no love lost between Isabella and me. But alas, your mother, to her credit, is far more loyal than I."

"Then why did she invite you to spend Christmas with us?"

"No doubt that was orchestrated by Alice and Freddy. They quite fancy each other, if I'm not mistaken." How could anyone be mistaken, the way Alice and Sir Edwin's son swooned over each other? "Does this satisfy your honor, my boy? May I be allowed to enjoy the countryside in peace?"

"I have one more question," Stella said.

Sir Edwin winked. "For you, my girl, I'll answer two."

Stella inwardly cringed and shifted closer to Lyndy, who roughly tugged at the edge of the lap rug he and Stella shared.

"What were you and Captain Stancliffe talking about right before the Point-to-Point Race?"

Was he telling you he saw you driving the auto that killed Mrs. Nelson?

Sir Edwin, brushing soot from his lapel, chuckled. Thank heaven he couldn't read her mind. "Ears ringing, were they?"

Stella stiffened in surprise. "You were talking about me?"

"Your Triple R Farm for Horses and Ponies. The captain had heard I'd visited and asked my opinion. Whether it was as worthy of a cause as it seemed. Your charity is quite original, and he didn't know what to make of it."

Did she believe him?

"I got the idea from the Home of Rest for Horses, who are doing something similar in London."

"Ah, I didn't know. But for what it's worth, my dear, I complimented you and your charity and encouraged him to donate what he could. Shame he never got the chance."

With these last words hovering over them like the dark clouds outside, they quietly rode the last few miles. Stella stared through the snow splatters, seeing only the Point-to-Point starting line, and piecing together Captain Stancliffe's final moments in yet another attempt to connect his death with Mrs. Nelson's. Neither was what they first appeared. Mrs. Nelson's death was initially chalked up to poison, yet she was killed by an automobile. Captain Stancliffe's death seemed to be an accident, yet his pony had been given something that caused it to collapse. As they rumbled over the bridge crossing the River Avon, Stella realized they'd passed through Christchurch and she hadn't noticed.

The steam whistle screeched, the train slowed, and the conductor passed, calling out the station's name. They rose to disembark.

Lyndy put an arm out to stop Sir Edwin from leaving the carriage. "I must know."

"What is it, my boy? Still stewing over the notion of your mother and me?"

Lyndy's jaw tightened, but he shook his head. "Are you my father?"

Stella held her breath. She'd suspected the same thing, but like the proverbial elephant in the room, she'd sensed it was too tricky, too tender of a subject to talk about. For Lyndy to ask showed how much it had weighed on his mind. She laid a comforting hand on his back.

"Good Lord, no," Sir Edwin roared. "Is that what you've been thinking? No wonder you've been so terse."

Stella sighed in relief, but Lyndy wouldn't let it go.

"But I'm named for you."

"Your mother's way of easing the blow, perhaps?"

"But—"

"Lyndy, my boy, trust me. It wasn't from a lack of trying." He chuckled again, patting Lyndy's shoulder. Lyndy shrugged him off and brushed his coat where Sir Edwin had touched him. "I often wondered if your mother was incapable of conceiving a child."

Is that why she was so concerned about Stella producing an heir? Because she had difficulty?

"It isn't my place to say more," Sir Edwin added as if he hadn't already said too much, "but rest assured, you were born long after all that ended."

The clank of metal on metal reverberated off the unbroken line of brick and white limestone, gabled buildings spanning block after block of city streets. Their hired cab steered the horses alongside one, a long, low building gaping with multiple wide, painted, stable-like doors. All were closed but one. From it wafted the pungent odor of gasoline, which mingled with the sea-scented air. Surprisingly, Stella didn't mind the smell. A sign running the length of the building read WILSEY & SONS

MOTOR WORK & REPAIR. A tall, thin man in grease-stained overalls greeted them at the open door.

"I'm here to fetch my Martini," Sir Edwin said without preamble. "I do believe you're finished with it?"

"We are, sir. If you'll care to follow me."

"Might we look about?" Lyndy said, with unabashed curiosity, his relief at being his father's son unquestionably augmented by the presence of so many autos.

"Be my guest."

The pair split up to admire the collection in various need of repair. While Lyndy inspected the sleek lines of a forest-green Napier, Stella was drawn to what looked like an electric dog-cart. She slipped her fist through the splintered hole in its side. Parked beside it sat a black and yellow Wolseley, which appeared in pristine condition. A youth in similar overalls sauntered by. When Stella asked what was wrong with it, he explained that they'd repaired that auto already.

"Quite the mess it was too," he said, wiping his hands with a frayed, gray rag. "Headlights smashed, fender bent. The grill was crumpled like it'd collided with a horse or a stag. Still even had hair in it." He stuffed the rag into the deep pocket of his overalls. "You'd be surprised how many we see with damage like that."

Stella casually circled the car, admiring the repair work they'd accomplished. She would've never known. Then she saw something on the floor well by the passenger's seat. It was an elaborately etched hip flask. She crouched down to retrieve it. She held it up for the young auto engineer to see.

"I suppose this doesn't help."

She'd heard of drivers having accidents after attending parties or drinking at a pub. Was there any doubt the same alcohol that slurred their words or made them stumble impaired their ability to drive?

"Couldn't say." Tight-lipped and annoyed, the youth snatched the flask from her hands. "Wouldn't want the customer thinking we nick things."

"I wasn't—"

"Look here," Sir Edwin said, marching over as the older man backed the Martini into the street. "Isn't that . . . ? Did you remove something out of my motorcar?"

What was he going to say?

"Give it here, young man."

The auto engineer placed the flask on Sir Edwin's open palm, stammering alternating apologies and denials. "We didn't take anything from your Martini, Sir Edwin. I promise you. We know nothing about this."

Sir Edwin seemed to scrutinize every detail. Glancing up, he caught Stella watching him as closely.

"Shall we, Lyndy, my boy?" Tossing the flask back onto the seat, Sir Edwin strolled toward his awaiting automobile. He climbed in and revved the engine. A flock of startled pigeons alit from a nearby roof and flapped furiously away.

"If we must." Lyndy gingerly slid his hand across the front fender of a silver Rolls-Royce, which was missing a steering wheel.

Stella took a step to join him, glancing down as the monogram etched in the middle of the flask caught the light. She hadn't noticed it before.

Oh, my God!

Stella dashed to Lyndy's side, grabbed his arm, and tugged him toward the door.

"One minute more, my love. I just want to—"

"Lyndy," she said, dropping her voice so no one else could hear, "we've got to get back to Rosehurst! I know who killed Mrs. Nelson and Captain Stancliffe."

She just didn't know why.

CHAPTER 34

They stopped, and the thunder of the motor cut off, but Stella still gripped the steering wheel. Lyndy hesitated, his foot on the running board, and followed her gaze. The farm spread out before them. The green grazing lawns sparkled as the low afternoon sun caught the melted snow still clinging to the blades of grass. More than a dozen horses and several New Forest Ponies clustered together in groups beneath the sheltering oak trees. A scattering of birds in silhouette against the sky, frightened by the motorcar's approach, flittered back to their roosts. There wasn't a person in sight. It was so peaceful.

That was about to change.

He and Stella had left Sir Edwin at Morrington Hall and headed here in the Daimler, Stella not wanting to wait for the horses to be saddled. The Daimler sputtered and complained, but as Stella had maintained, it had gotten them here quickly. Along the journey, Stella explained her suspicions. Lyndy couldn't help but be impressed with his wife's deduction.

But was she right?

"Hello!" Green called as he stepped from the nearest stable, donning his laboratory coat, his worn leather bag clutched in his fist. He smiled and waved at the sight of them. A horse's whinny echoed behind him. "Didn't expect to see you, my lady, my lord."

"I bet you didn't," Stella muttered, swatting at the motoring veil around her face. When it didn't come loose, she yanked her hat from her head. She launched out of the motorcar, leaving Lyndy scrambling to follow.

"You!" she shouted, running at the veterinarian. "You killed Mrs. Nelson and Captain Stancliffe."

Green dropped his bag. It landed with a hard thud on the ground. He slumped to a crouch, his head in his hands, and began sobbing.

Not quite what Lyndy expected.

Obviously, not what Stella had either. She stopped in her tracks, hugging herself as if not knowing what to do next, and stared down at him.

"I am so, so sorry. So, so, sorry." The vet rocked back and forth on his heels, dragging his coat through the wet grass. When he raised his head, tears streaking down his cheeks, he pressed his hand over his mouth. "It was an accident. I swear. I didn't mean to do it. I didn't even know I did." He coughed, choking on his tears.

"But your automobile?" Stella demanded. "You knew you'd hit something."

"I'd been drinking, my lady," the sniveling man explained. "I quite fancy the pub, you see. The Knightwood Oak. The regulars welcomed me right away. But I was celebrating and had too much that night; we all had. The publican had to throw me and a couple of others out. On the way home, I hit something."

"Bloody hell. How could you not suspect?" Lyndy said. "For God's sake, man, you were the one who found her."

Green violently shook his head. "I swear I thought I'd hit a deer, or worse yet, a pony. What else would do such damage to my motorcar?" He took a few quick gasping breaths, sniffled, and stood. "If anyone found out I'd hurt an animal, I'd lose this job. So, I said nothing. You've got to believe I never imagined . . ." Retrieving a handkerchief from his coat, he wiped his nose.

"It's safe to say you're going to lose your position anyway," Lyndy scoffed.

"I didn't even know you owned an automobile," Stella said. "A Wolseley, right?"

Wiping his nose again, he nodded. "Normally, I couldn't afford such a luxury, but it was both a Christmas and a congratulatory present from my uncle, an executive at Wolseley Motors. He was so proud when I accepted this position."

"That's why the police didn't know you had one either," Stella mused, speaking more to herself than anyone.

"Make it a habit of hitting things, do you?" Lyndy sneered.

Green winced. "No, my lord. That night was the first time I'd driven it."

Stella held up her hands in protest. "I can believe Mrs. Nelson's death was an accident, but what about Captain Stancliffe? His horse was given something before the race, and you, Mr. Green, were the one who did it."

The vet's shoulder slumped. He bowed his head and covered his eyes with his hand.

"I panicked. I hadn't realized what I'd done to the poor housekeeper until Captain Stancliffe confronted me that morning. He'd seen me drive by that night." The vet lowered his hand. His eyes had grown puffy and red. "I readily admitted ignorance of my crime and declared my deepest remorse. He'd seemed to believe me, accepting my self-recrimination as punishment enough. Or so he said. But then I overheard him ask to speak to Lady Lyndhurst after the race."

"And you slipped Major something, like an opium-laced sugar cube?"

Like he'd done to sedate Orson.

Mr. Green, again hiding behind his hand, nodded.

"I always have them in my bag. At best, it would buy me time to figure out how to convince the captain not to tell anyone. At worst, the pony would throw its rider, which, for such an accomplished equestrian, wouldn't amount to much. I never meant for the captain to die."

"There's no excuse, Mr. Green. Two people are dead because of you," Stella said, compassion and revulsion warring across her face.

Lyndy had no such conflict; he wanted to punch the man. Such stupidity, such a wanton waste of human life. The man deserved to be beaten. *If not that lecherous cretin, Stott, then Green will do.* But Stella, having read his intention on his face, put a calming hand on him, staying his rising fist.

"Inspector Brown needs to be told," she said.

The vet opened his eyes, glazed over and shining with tears, and stared unseeing over Lyndy's shoulder. Lyndy fought the urge to follow the man's gaze but lost.

Behind him sat the parked Daimler.

"If I could bring them back . . ." the vet said, his voice a monotone. "If I could right this wrong, I would." He abruptly threaded his hands into his hair and pulled violently. "By God, how I wish I'd stuck with the carriage and Honey and never gotten in that motorcar!"

"What now?" the vet asked, his arms limp by his sides, exhausted from his confession.

"Off to prison with you, is what," Lyndy was saying when the sun's glint off the gun's pearl handle caught Stella's eye.

She froze as Ernie Stott crept around the side of the stable, holding the derringer in front of him. Was that Uncle Jeb's gun? The one he'd stolen off Pistol Prescott, the one that got him sent to jail? When he'd been released last month, her uncle, wanting a clean slate before returning to Kentucky, had given it to Stella. How could she not have realized it was gone?

Stella held her palms up. "Mr. Stott! What are you doing here?"

"Followed you, didn't I? Good thing too. It seems you're in the company of a killer."

Having grabbed Mr. Green by the collar, Lyndy let go and stepped away from the vet. Ernie Stott raised the derringer higher, aiming not at Mr. Green but alternatingly between Stella and Lyndy, taking deliberate steps toward them. Despite the cool breeze rustling among the nearby oak trees, the workman's forehead beaded with sweat.

"Put the gun down, Ernie," Stella pleaded.

The workman continued his advance, swaggering toward them.

"You heard my wife. Put the bloody gun down," Lyndy demanded.

"We have unfinished business, you and I." He motioned with the gun between himself and Stella.

Catching the man's meaning, Lyndy snarled, "Over my dead body."

"Lyndy!" Stella warned.

Ernie Stott leveled the gun at Lyndy's head. "Now that, my lord, I can accommodate." The workman's lip curled in a sardonic smile.

As Stella lurched forward, trying to shield him, Lyndy flung his arm in front of her to stop her, giving a momentary advantage to the gunman. He'd moved in to closer range.

"Make nice, and I won't need to kill your husband."

Again, Stella froze. Her shallow, jagged breath filled her ears, spasms of panic surging through her. Her heart was ready to burst.

What did this man want from her? Did she have to ask?

"Get in the car, milady. Now!"

Stella flinched. "Okay. No need to shout."

With another blatant lie hovering on her lips, she caught a flash of motion from the corner of her eye. Instinctively, she glanced in that direction. Martin Green was disappearing behind the stable. With everyone else distracted, he'd taken the opportunity to slip away.

How disheartening!

As she faced Mr. Stott again, Stella squared her shoulders, a resigned hollow space opening in her chest. Mr. Green's escape grieved her. She'd believed the vet's remorse was sincere. She'd clung to the possibility that he'd made tragic, horrible mistakes but wasn't inherently evil. Oddly, the dispelled hope freed her from her paralysis and guilt of doing what it took to save herself and Lyndy from this imminent threat.

"I'll gladly come with you," she said, the words slick and bitter in her mouth. She pushed Lyndy's arm down and stepped away from him. He clutched the back of her duster coat, stopping her.

Lyndy choked with unconstrained concern. "Stella, what are you doing?"

She turned to regard his hold with disdain. "Let go, Lyndy." Immediately mouthing, "Trust me."

Lyndy, his lips tight and teeth clenched, reluctantly released her coat. Stella shivered at the sheer rage aimed at the workman. *If looks could kill . . .*

"Who should drive, you or me?" With fingertips tingling and going numb, she held the keys out toward him, afraid her fear and disgust would cause them to shake.

"I knew you'd have a change of heart." A smug grin slithered across Ernie Stott's face.

The workman bridged the gap between them with a giant stride, possessively grabbing the keys and her hand. His was rough as sandpaper with calluses. Stella's breath hissed through her teeth. The keys dug into her palm. He was crushing her knuckles together.

Like Daddy.

The workman spewed words about being wronged and unappreciated, about what she owed him, while waving the gun, keeping Lyndy at bay. She heard little of it, swallowing the bile in her throat as her defiance and anger brewed. When the workman, caught up in his triumph, lowered the gun, she grabbed his wrist with her free hand and kicked his shin. Too strong for her, he jerked both their hands and the weapon upward, smashing her in the cheek. Flashes of light filled her sight, but she wouldn't let go. Lyndy lunged forward.

The three tumbled together in a heap as the growing roar of an auto engine filled her ears. Daddy's Daimler was careening toward them with Mr. Green at the wheel.

"My lady, My lord! Get out of the way!" the vet shouted, frantically waving at them to move.

Startled, Ernie released his grip, and Stella yanked her hand free. Lyndy latched on to her duster coat, and together they scrambled out of the pathway of the oncoming automobile.

"Put the gun down, or I'll run you over," Mr. Green shouted.

Nonplussed, the workman trained his derringer at the driver and pulled the trigger. The sharp pop of the pistol was scarcely audible over the auto's engine mere yards away.

A plume of blood exploded from Mr. Green's shoulder. He slumped forward against the steering wheel, but the Daimler surged straight toward its original target. Realizing his danger, Ernie Stott panicked, shooting at the Daimler again and again, puncturing the radiator, fender, and headlights. At the last minute, he leaped out of its way. Poised to pounce like a wildcat, Lyndy tackled him to the ground. He smashed the man's hand several times against the ground, forcing the gun out of his hand. Stella rushed to grab it as the Daimler rolled past, smashing into a stone stable. Steam hissed violently from the engine as Mr. Green, jolted from his slumped position, slipped sideways and out of sight.

"I've slept with your wife's knickers under my pillow," the

workman taunted as Lyndy struggled to keep the more muscular man on the ground.

Heat stung Stella's ears and face. Nausea threatened to empty her stomach. Had she ever been so violated?

"You bastard!" Lyndy landed several powerful blows to the side of the man's head. Ernie Stott's body sagged beneath him. Lyndy bashed him again.

"Stop! Lyndy! You could kill him."

"Not that he doesn't deserve it," Lyndy hissed, his face red, a vein visibly pulsing in his forehead. He roughly flipped Ernie Stott onto his stomach and wrenched the wool scarf from around his neck.

She crouched next to Lyndy as he secured the man's wrists, tightening the knot so hard the unconscious man groaned. Lyndy sat back on his heels, and they watched Mr. Stott, anticipating additional resistance. Seeing none, Stella ferociously wrapped her arms around her husband, resting her unbruised cheek against his shoulder. She held him tightly until Lyndy's muscles relaxed, and their breathing, scented by the freshly trampled earth, slowed in synchrony. In one of the stables, a horse snorted. Rising to her feet, she urged Lyndy to join her. Standing over the wretched boiler man, Stella couldn't help but imagine those she'd seen dead or dying, her father forefront in her mind.

"No one deserves it."

"This one comes close." Lyndy shoved Ernie Stott's shoulder with the tip of his boot. The workman groaned again, but his body gave no resistance. Satisfied their prisoner was secured, Lyndy turned his back on him and took Stella in his arms. "You're hurt." He gently kissed her swollen cheek.

"I'm fine." Stella twisted in his embrace to glance over her shoulder at the Daimler. "But Mr. Green? I'm afraid to find out."

Stella peeled away from Lyndy's arms and hesitantly approached her father's auto, which was wrecked beyond repair.

The vet hadn't escaped but, in what she assumed was an ironic attempt to make amends, had employed the same weapon he used in taking Mrs. Nelson's life—an automobile—to save hers and Lyndy's. Despite his crimes, he didn't deserve to die like this either.

Mr. Green lay sprawled unconscious across the seat, the bloom of blood spreading across his shoulder like spilled port. Splotched and splattered, his work coat was more red than white. She leaned against the padded leather edge of the passenger seat and reached toward the vet's neck. To her relief, she found a pulse. He was still alive.

CHAPTER 35

"I can't believe you never suspected him, Inspector," Lady Isabella said, rummaging through her bag. She produced a pair of knitting needles and a length of white, knitted lace. "Even one of my daughters would've been able to spot a miscreant like that one right off."

Lyndy resisted the urge to roll his eyes.

While still at the farm, they'd sent a stable hand to fetch the inspector, who'd arrived in good time with Dr. Lipscombe and Constable Waterman in tow. It was gratifying to see that wretched Stott handcuffed and hauled into the back of the police wagon. As Brown took charge of the onerous situation, it was settled between them that Lyndy would escort Stella home, and Brown would soon follow. They'd changed and had gathered around the Christmas tree awaiting dinner when the policeman was announced.

"To be honest, Lady Isabella," the inspector said, turning his hat in his hand, "I must admit to being shortsighted in considering Martin Green a suspect, especially with Sir Edwin the more obvious one. Beg your pardon, sir."

"As luck would have it, Inspector," Sir Edwin, winking at Mother, said, "Lady Lyndhurst's insight outweighs your incompetence. So all's forgiven."

In the glow of the yule log, still burning in the hearth, Lyndy caught the unreadable glance between Stella and his mother. Was that a nod of approval, of gratitude? It was almost imperceptible, but Stella's face brightened, lighting up like the Christmas tree behind her. Could Mother be thanking Stella for her help and discretion? Could there be peace between them at last?

"From what I've heard," Stella's great-aunt Rachel said, "if it weren't for the young ones, those crooks would've gotten away like a black cat on a moonless night."

"One could say that," Brown muttered.

"But how did you know, my girl, that it was the veterinarian?" Sir Edwin asked.

"The flask in the Wolseley. The one I thought you recognized."

"It's very much like one Freddy owns." Sir Edwin indicated his son whispering something to Alice and not paying them attention. "Said he'd left it at the local pub."

He'd suspected Freddy!

"Freddy's been at a pub?" Lady Isabella hissed.

Her husband ignored her. "But how did you make the logistical leap from the hip flask to the housekeeper's death?"

"The flask had Mr. Green's initials on it. The auto must've belonged to him."

"Meaning no disrespect, my lady," Inspector Brown said, "but the number of men with the initials MG in the area is quite numerous. I can think of two off the top of my head."

"But do any of those others live along Mistletoe Lane?" Stella asked.

"Did he tell you that? He's too recent to the area to appear in any directory."

"How else could he have found Mrs. Nelson on his way from his home to Morrington Hall that morning and come across the Daimler when I wrecked it? There are only a handful of cottages in that area. It couldn't be a coincidence."

"That's still a fantastical stretch of the imagination," Lady Isabella scoffed over the clicking of her needles.

"Not if you consider Major's odd behavior during the Point-to-Point Race."

"What does that have to do with anything?"

"Everything," Lyndy said, coming to Stella's defense. "Didn't we all see Green give sugar cubes to the ponies beforehand? As a vet, he often laces them with sedatives."

"Mrs. Cole said the captain saw the driver who killed Mrs. Nelson," Stella said.

"And who else but that driver would want to silence Captain Stancliffe?" Sir Edwin said, the truth lighting up his face.

"Exactly," Stella said.

"And who else but my brilliant bride would make those connections?" Lyndy said, taking Stella's hand and kissing it.

"Well, it's inexcusable if you ask me, Inspector," Lady Isabella said, unable to let it go. "You cast aspersions on my husband, suspecting him of murdering a housekeeper, of all people. It has tarnished our family name."

Hypocritical cow!

Lyndy opened his mouth to remind the good Lady Isabella that she had caused all the fuss by refuting her husband's alibi, but with one challenging look from Stella, Lyndy stayed his tongue. If his wife wanted peace, he'd not be the one to disturb it. Instead, he yanked down on his waistcoat.

"But why was the housekeeper out on that stretch of road at night to begin with?" Papa asked, setting aside the spyglass and fossil bone he'd been inspecting.

"I think I know," Stella offered. "She was on her way to the Oakhills' cottage. She knew she'd sent the family spoiled mince pies. I think she wanted to warn them."

"But in the middle of the night?" Lady Isabella said.

"Not even a fit of delirium could counteract decades of service," Stella said. "Mrs. Nelson died as she lived, with the welfare of others her priority."

"Well, bless her heart," Great-aunt Rachel said.

"Indeed. And what of that blighter Stott? I hope you've thrown him down a hole, Inspector." Lyndy couldn't get the image of that man's hand on Stella out of his mind. How dare he!

"Have no concern on that account, my lord," Brown said as if reading Lyndy's mind, a slight satisfied smile on his lips. "That one will never bother you or Lady Lyndhurst again."

"I should hope not," Mother said. "Proves I was right to be skeptical about making improvements to the manor that allowed in all manner of ruffian."

Now there's the mother I know.

"How is Mr. Green, Inspector?" Stella asked, dodging the inevitable comments from Lady Isabella about "all manner of ruffian."

"He'll be in hospital sometime yet, but he's to fully recover," Brown said. "He gained consciousness long enough to offer his confession."

Soon after, Brown excused himself, leaving silence, interrupted only by the rhythmic scraping of Lady Isabella's knitting needles, in his wake. As Stella gazed at the Christmas tree, Lyndy contemplated the flickering, crackling flames of the fire.

"How very odd," Mother mused. "To allow a prisoner to recover, only so you can hang him properly."

"I say, Frances. How morbid of you," Papa said, glancing at his pocket watch.

"I hope his efforts in saving us from Mr. Stott will stay the executioner, at least, Lady Atherly," Stella said.

Having enough of this conversation, Lyndy rose and began pacing the length of the carpet. The whole business left a sour taste in his mouth. He fiddled with the posy hidden in his pocket, biding his time.

"Oh, Stella, do stop calling me Lady Atherly. You may call me Frances. We are family, after all."

Frances? Lyndy swiveled on his heel to regard his mother. She was smoothing her skirt and wouldn't meet his eye. It was all the proof Lyndy needed. *Christmas miracles do occur.*

"Stay the executioner, indeed!" Lady Isabella tsked. "That man who calls himself a veterinarian deserves everything that's coming to him, even if it is the noose."

"Does a man not deserve a little pity for his reckless mistakes, especially if he's willing to atone for them?" Sir Edwin asked.

"Absolutely not. I'm surprised you should have to ask," his wife said.

Was Lady Isabella making clear she knew of her husband's reckless mistakes? From his mother's rigid posture, she believed so. Lyndy despised the notion of his mother being unfaithful. But should she or Sir Edwin pay for their indiscretion for the rest of their life? They hadn't killed anyone after all.

"But what about the Christmas ideal of charity and goodwill?" Stella said, ever in search of that ideal.

"Even for murderers?" Lady Isabella scoffed.

"For anyone," Stella said. "Maids who steal mince pies. Impoverished widows with lame horses. Irritable cooks with tragic pasts."

"Mothers with ungrateful daughters," Sir Edwin muttered as Lyndy passed by.

"And yes," Stella continued, "men who tragically but accidentally kill people or mistake friendliness for affection. Don't they deserve our pity, if not our compassion?"

How his wife could find space in her generous heart for such people was beyond Lyndy. Yet wasn't that something he loved about her?

"I agree with Stella," Papa said. "It's what we all should strive for this time of the year. Now, shall we speak of something else? Alice? Don't you have something you'd like to share? I do say it will lighten the mood."

"What is it, Alice?" Mother said.

Alice looked to Papa, who nodded encouragingly. Alice lowered her eyes, her cheeks rosy as she reached for Freddy's hand across the settee. "Freddy and I are engaged."

Lyndy stepped out of the way as Stella flew from her seat to fling her arms around his sister.

"Oh, Alice! I'm so happy for you!"

"Well, ain't that finer than a frog's hair split three ways!" Great-aunt Rachel clapped her hands and cackled with joy.

Lady Isabella dropped her knitting and scowled at Mother. "How can this be?"

Mother shrugged. "I know as much about this as you do, Isabella."

"Freddy approached me this morning, and I gave my blessing," Papa said, jutting out his chin. "We hadn't the need to consult you ladies. Besides, this is what Alice wants."

"You knew about this?" Lady Isabella swiveled in her seat to address her husband.

"Why else did you think we came to Morrington Hall for Christmas?" Sir Edwin said innocently. Lady Isabella swiveled back to glare at Mother.

Lyndy shook Freddy's hand, chasing away the impeding dread that, with the marriage, Lady Isabella would become family, and then kissed his sister's cheek.

"May you be as happy as I am," he whispered in her ear. He meant it. Alice deserved as much love and affection as any man could give.

"Thank you, Lyndy." But her delighted reply was marred by a motorcar thundering up the drive.

"Who the devil could that be?" Papa said, crossing over to the French windows.

Stella and the newly engaged couple joined him. Lyndy didn't have to. He knew who it was.

"Gosh! I'd say that's the most fabulous motor I've ever seen," Freddy said. "Come look, Father."

Curious, Sir Edwin pushed out of his chair. Great-aunt Rachel held out her arms, and Sir Edwin obligingly pulled her to her feet. Mother and Lady Isabella, who'd resumed her knitting, stubbornly refused to budge.

"You're right there," Stella said. "It's even nicer than Daddy's Daimler."

"And as shiny as that tiara on your head," Great-aunt Rachel added.

Lyndy sauntered over and pushed the door open. The air was damp but warmer than it had been in days. He motioned to Stella to accompany him outside.

"Thank you, Wellston," he said to the driver. "Mrs. Downie has your dinner. Afterward, I'll see you get a ride back into town."

The chauffeur touched the brim of his cap. "Much obliged, my lord."

"Lyndy?" Stella said, watching the chap head down the path to the back of the manor. "What's this all about?"

Lyndy gestured toward the motorcar. He could smell the new leather seats from here. "Happy Christmas, my love."

"This is mine?" Stella ran her finger along the front fender. "But I crashed the Daimler only yesterday. And then, of course, at the farm—"

"I ordered it long before," Lyndy interrupted before any more talk of Green or Stott ruined the moment. "It was to arrive by Christmas, but it barely made it by year's end."

"Then it's perfectly timed," Stella said. "What better way to celebrate New Year's, to start our first whole new year together, with a clean break . . ."

"From your father's ghost."

She nodded slowly, thoughtfully. Suddenly Lyndy wondered if he'd read her wrong. Perhaps she didn't want to replace the motorcar. Perhaps she fancied the Daimler, which brought her to Morrington that fateful day in May, repaired and running again.

Without warning, she rushed at him, throwing her arms around his neck, a smile flooding her face. He caught her before she toppled them onto the gravel.

"Thank you, Lyndy. I love it!"

Ah, I do know my wife, after all. He pulled the posy of mistletoe tied with a red ribbon from his pocket and held it above their heads.

"Merry Christmas, my love. You alone made it a special one to remember."

The words had scarcely left his lips before she pressed hers against them. Could Lyndy ask for a more delightful gift?

ACKNOWLEDGMENTS

Writing about Christmas for 365 days is a challenge. But I didn't go into the endeavor without the requisite deep love of the season. I'd like to thank my mom who, without fail, turned my childhood home, year after year, into a magical Christmas wonderland, complete with edible gingerbread cookies lining the kitchen shelves, my dad who sold fresh Christmas trees and always saved the best in the lot for us, and my Aunt Sandy Lynch who gifted me a precious tree ornament every year, all of which I still have these many decades later. Without them instilling in me the joy and spirit of the season from such an early age, I have little doubt I would've been able to sustain the wonderment necessary to capture the awe of Christmas day after day throughout an entire year (sweltering July included.)

I'd also like to thank fellow author and real-life New Forest commoner, Sally Marsh, as well as veterinarian Dr. Rebecca Madison Cox, who graciously answered all my questions about horses, ponies, and miscellaneous veterinary tasks. If I failed to ask the right ones or got my facts mixed up, it's on me.

To Brian, Maya, Mom, and Jacqueline, thank you for your unwavering love and support, three hundred and sixty-five days a year.

AUTHOR'S NOTE

British Christmas traditions may feel, for the most part, quite familiar. However, the New Forest Point-to-Point Boxing Day race is an annual holiday event unlike any other. The first race of its kind is said to have occurred over 250 years ago when a neighbor challenged another to a horserace from one church steeple to another. Over time, the "steeple-to-steeple" or "point-to-point" races evolved into two types of jump racing: steeplechase and national hunt, each governed by a predetermined route or track and a standard set of rules. However, The New Forest is one of the few places in the world that maintains the historical "point-to-point" tradition. Contestants race their New Forest Ponies across open countryside from the starting point to the finishing point. Able to take any route they choose, riders often set off in different directions. To create an additional challenge, the finishing point isn't announced until two weeks prior to race day and the starting point is kept secret until the morning of it. In this way, no rider can map out a route or anticipate the obstacles and challenges they'll face beforehand. Realistically the spectators would predominately gather at the finishing line but to illustrate the sensation caused by a woman participating in the race, I brought the curious and the cynical to the starting point as well.

A more familiar tradition, mince pies are synonymous with Christmas in the UK. But unlike today, mincemeat made with raw beef, marinated and stored in brandy on a shelf for up to two weeks, was a key ingredient in Edwardian-era mince pie recipes. If not properly sealed or thoroughly cooked, the mince-meat could spoil, and eating such spoiled beef can cause violent illness and delirium. How do I know? Unfortunately, I learned this from personal experience. When I was newly married, my husband and I lived abroad. One night, we ate cooked, but unbeknownst to us, spoiled beef. It didn't have a strong odor to warn us. It tasted a little unusual, but we'd been eating so many exotic foods we barely noticed. The next day, we suffered high fevers, debilitating illness, and yes, for me, delirium. After barely being able to get out of bed or keep anything down all day, I was suddenly consumed with the notion that we had to have animal crackers to settle our stomachs. Despite my dizziness, nausea, and muscle weakness, I put on my coat and boots and trudged out into a freezing winter night (much like the unfortunate Mrs. Nelson), aiming for a grocery store more than a mile away. What was I thinking? Luckily for me, I didn't encounter any problems, and those were, to date, the best animal crackers I've ever tasted.

In searching for a charity that would capture Stella's heart, I came across the Home of Rest for Horses, a real-life model for her Triple R Farm. Started in 1886, the charity provided a place where overworked London cab horses could rest and recuperate. The Horse Trust, having been renamed in 2006, now promotes and enhances the welfare of all horses. Visit https://horsetrust.org.uk/ to learn more.